Alfred Nutt, James MacDougall

# Folk and Hero Tales

Alfred Nutt, James MacDougall.

**Folk and Hero Tales**

ISBN/EAN: 9783744768399

Printed in Europe, USA, Canada, Australia, Japan

Cover: Foto ©Andreas Hilbeck / pixelio.de

More available books at **www.hansebooks.com**

# ARGYLLSHIRE

# FOLK AND HERO TALES.

See p. 8.  Frontispiece.

THE GIANT KILLED BY AN ARROW.

# WAIFS AND STRAYS OF CELTIC TRADITION.

ARGYLLSHIRE SERIES.—No. III.

# FOLK AND HERO TALES.

Collected, Edited, Translated, and Annotated

BY

## THE REV. J. MACDOUGALL.

WITH AN INTRODUCTION BY

### ALFRED NUTT,

*AND THREE ILLUSTRATIONS BY E. GRISET.*

LONDON :
DAVID NUTT, 270-271, STRAND.

1891.

# CONTENTS.


| | PAGE |
|---|---|
| PREFACE . . . . . . . | vii |
| INTRODUCTION.—JAMES MacDougall . . . | ix |
|     „     ALFRED NUTT . . . | xiii-xxix |


Aim and objects of folk-lore study.—Necessity for scientific methods of investigation.—The nature-myth theory of interpretation; reason for the discredit into which it has fallen.—Sketch of the development of folk-lore studies.—Indication of the nature-myth theory within certain limits.—The Elysium of the Gael according to the oldest Irish texts and according to modern folk-belief.—The value of Celtic evidence for the solution of the folk-lore problem.—The value of Celtic folk-lore as a key to the Celtic temperament.


| | | PAGE |
|---|---|---|
| I. | HOW FINN KEPT HIS CHILDREN FOR THE BIG YOUNG HERO OF THE SHIP, AND HOW BRAN WAS FOUND | 1 |
| II. | FINN'S JOURNEY TO LOCHLAN, AND HOW THE GREY DOG WAS FOUND AGAIN . . . . | 17 |
| III. | THE LAD OF THE SKIN COVERINGS . . . | 27 |
| IV. | HOW FINN WAS IN THE HOUSE OF BLAR-BUIE (YELLOW-FIELD), WITHOUT THE POWER OF RISING UP OR OF LYING DOWN . . . . | 56 |
| V. | THE SMITH'S ROCK IN THE ISLE OF SKYE . | 73 |
| VI. | THE BARE-STRIPPING HANGMAN . . . | 76 |
| VII. | A TALE OF THE SON OF THE KING OF IRELAND AND THE DAUGHTER OF THE KING OF THE RED CAP . | 145 |
| VIII. | THE SON OF THE STRONG MAN OF THE WOOD, WHO WAS TWENTY-ONE YEARS ON HIS MOTHER'S BREAST . . . . . . | 187 |
| IX. | THE FARMER OF LIDDESDALE . . . | 216 |
| X. | A TALE ABOUT THE SON OF THE KNIGHT OF THE GREEN VESTURE, PERFORMING HEROIC DEEDS WHICH WERE FAMED ON EARTH SEVEN YEARS BEFORE HE WAS BORN . . . . | 222 |

# NOTES.

TALE I. . . . . . . . . 259

    At the back of the wind.—Domhan Tor, the Gaelic Elysium.

TALE II. . . . . . . . . 264

    Fionn and Bran.

TALE III. . . . . . . . 265

    Fionn's Cup.—Interpretation of the tale.

TALE IV. . . . . . . . . 270

    Variants of the tale.—Fionn's wooden crier.

TALE V. . . . . . . . . 276

TALE VI. . . . . . . . . 276

    Variant versions.—The helping animals.—Sorcerers.— Rocky Path of Ben Buie.—Nonsense endings.

TALE VII. . . . . . . . 285

    Variant versions.—Mermaid.—Swan maids.—The Farmer's Son from Rannoch.—Gonachry's ship.

TALE VIII. . . . . . . . 291

    Variant versions.—Big Lad personification of oak tree.— Big Angus of the Rocks = Echo.—Water-horse, nature-myth, personification of storm blast.—Uruisg.

TALE IX. . . . . . . . 297

    Variant versions.—Supernatural aid.—Signification of word *Mart*.

TALE X. . . . . . . . . 299

    Variant versions.—Comparison of the same with our tale.

INDEX . . . . . . . 305

# PREFACE.

IN the year 1890, my friend, the Reverend JAMES MACDOUGALL, of Duror, Ballachulish, generously made over to me his fine collection of " Folk-lore Tales", taken down by him from the lips of the narrator, whose whole stock came from what he had orally received in childhood, and from no other source.

With indefatigable patience, Mr. MACDOUGALL has rescued these Tales herein given.

They are a splendid contribution to the folk-lore of the Western Highlands, and second to none in picturesque and graphic description of events herein detailed.

ARCHIBALD CAMPBELL.

# INTRODUCTION.

THE following tales were collected in the district of Duror between the summer of 1889 and the spring of 1890. They were obtained from Alexander Cameron, a native of Ardnamurchan, who was then roadman between Duror and Ballachulish. Cameron learned them from Donald McPhie and other old men whom he had known in his boyhood, but who died many years ago.

Some of the tales could have been got from other storytellers residing not far from this neighbourhood, but too often only in an imperfect state. Fragments, or bare outlines, were all that they remembered, and these they generally related in their own words, and not in the language in which they had received them from their predecessors. But it was not so with Cameron. Gifted with a good memory, he could repeat some of the tales in this collection almost word for word as he heard them told in his native place more than forty years before. For this reason, as well as on account of the excellent Ardnamurchan Gaelic in which they are expressed, none but his versions are given in this volume.

At the same time, the names of those who either knew the tales, or who, in their youth, heard them related by others, are mentioned in the notes in the Appendix. The advantage to collector and reader of adopting this course is too obvious to require any explanation.

The tales were collected at different intervals within the period already indicated. Sometimes they were taken down at the roadside, at other times in my house. In this part of the work, particular care was taken to secure accuracy. No tale was committed to writing until it had been first rehearsed from beginning to end by the narrator. Once this had been done, the task of taking it down in pencil began. The frequent interruptions which then occurred, sometimes caused Cameron to pass over some minor incident or unusual expression, but the previous rehearsal generally enabled me to remind him of the omission. When the tale had been taken down in pencil, the work of slowly transcribing it in ink followed. This also was carefully done, the first copy being closely adhered to. The only departures from it were for the sake of clearness ; and they consisted in an occasional omission or insertion of an unimportant word or phrase. The transcript thus made was afterwards read to Cameron ; and not until it had received his final approval was it considered to be ready for the press.

The translation was intended to be literal. How far this intention has been carried out, it is for others to judge. From it, however, there are at least seeming departures. For instance, the future—a tense of frequent occurrence in Gaelic—is sometimes translated by the present indicative and at other times by the present subjunctive. But this is done only when the substitution of these tenses is allowable. Again, Gaelic idioms are generally rendered into their English equivalents. Had they been rendered word for word the translation would hardly be intelligible. For who would then imagine that "the rock of the chest" (*carraig an uchd*) was the breastbone, and "the black sole of the foot" (*bonn dubh na coise*) the part of the sole under the instep? Or who would recognise in "he lifted on him" (*thog e air*), he set out on his journey ; in "he made earth-hiding on him" (*rinn e falach-talmhainn air*), he stole towards him under cover of the ground ; and in "he gave them a turn round a bush" (*thug e car mu thom dhoibh*), he slipped away from them ?  But when there is no such danger of being misunderstood, interesting idiomatic passages are translated verbally.  Thus, "*An cadal dhuit, 'Ille Righ Eirionn*", is rendered "Is it sleep to thee, Son of the King of Ireland ?" and "*Dh' éirich inntinn cho mòr*", becomes "His mind rose so high".

There is, however, one instance of close adherence to the original to which some may object.  This is the literal rendering of *tu* or *thu* into *thou*, and not into *you.*  It is, notwithstanding, justifiable on the ground of the difference between the usage in common conversation and the dialogues of the folk- and hero-tales.  In the former, an inferior or equal in age and rank is addressed *thu* (thou), but a superior in these relations is honoured with *sibh* (you).  In the latter, however, this distinction is quite unknown, so that the very king's son is called *thu*, and that even by his own servant.  If the difference which thus exists between the two usages ought to be preserved in the translation, then *thu* must be rendered *thou*, as it is in the following tales, and in those of the late Islay.

The notes at the end of the volume were written by me while the tales were passing through the press.

Mr. Alfred Nutt has contributed an Introduction in which certain questions suggested by the notes are discussed by him.

The publication of the volume is entirely due to Lord Archibald Campbell.  Every Highlander knows his lordship's zeal for the preservation of Gaelic tales and traditions, and what he has already done in that direction.  Being anxious to assist him in his later efforts, I gathered the following tales for him, and I now take this opportunity of thanking him for giving them a place in his series of *Waifs and Strays*.

In bringing this short Introduction to a close, I must

also thank Mr. Nutt for his many useful suggestions. Nor may I forget Alexander Cameron, to whose kindness I am indebted for the tales, and whose patience I must have often sorely tried while I slowly and wearisomely wrote them down to his dictation.

JAMES MacDOUGALL.

# INTRODUCTION.

THE study of folk-lore has a twofold object—corresponding to two different views of the facts connoted by the term folk-lore. We may regard these as being especially indicative of the genius and temperament of a race, especially indicative because they are furnished by that portion of the race which is in closest contact with nature, and is most removed from the influence of that uniform system of culture which tends to equalise the educated classes of all civilised people. Again, we may feel more interest in the facts themselves than in the people by whom they are furnished; struck by their apparent evidence to a state of culture profoundly different from our own, we may essay to trace their growth, to determine their origin, and to lay bare the ideas of which they are the expression. As a rule, folk-lore students have aimed at this second object, perhaps as being more easily brought into line with the historical studies, the development of which has been such a marked feature of nineteenth-century science. As a natural consequence they have had to adopt the methods of research and criticism generally accepted among historical students, and have thereby laid themselves open to the charge of pedantry and formalism from those who maintain that the study of folk-lore should be directed solely by sympathetic comprehension of the feelings of living men. The folk-lorist, to whom peasants or savages are of more interest than the superstitions by which their life is ruled or the legends by which it is cheered, is always ready to tax his brother student of the other school with securing, it may be, the bones and husks, but with missing the living power and charm of his subject.

At a comparative early stage of the study the searcher after facts as facts came to see the importance of getting them in the most genuine form obtainable. This, too, has been set down to his innate pedantry. And yet a moment's reflection shows that, important as a rigorous and accurate method is to him, it is yet more important to the student who values folk-lore as the expression of what is most essential and intimate in the consciousness of a race. If by its means we can indeed diagnose the spiritual and intellectual temper of mankind before it has been transformed and levelled by modern culture, is it not absolutely necessary that the diagnosis should be based upon ascertained fact? Yet, strange to say, men who profess the most enthusiastic sympathy for the "folk", are content to ground their enthusiasm upon material which has as much claim to be called folk-lore as the majority of circulating-library novels. Stranger still, this particular form of cant is always sure of outside countenance, and the writers are many to bewail as dreadful or shocking the desire for accurate knowledge of folk-lore, and the refusal to indulge in pretty but un-meaning generalities.

It is time to recognise that folk-lore cannot be studied piecemeal, that any attempt at making its phenomena the basis of far-reaching ethnological or sociological hypotheses, or at utilising them for the purposes of the philosopher or the artist, must be preceded by exact knowledge of these phenomena, of their origin as far as it can be determined, of their meaning as far as it can be explained. True it is, we must never forget that they are the outcome of human thought and fancy, that we must not treat them as lifeless specimens, but must strive to keep in touch with the organism to which they owe their being.

As regards Celtic " folk-psychology", to use a convenient German term, the existing materials are many, and I am far from denying that a useful as well as a most interesting work might be written by one who combined thorough knowledge of the Celt in past and present with equally thorough knowledge of comparative folk-lore, always provided the writer was fully conscious of the necessarily provisional nature of the work. But I regard the other branch of folk-lore study as by far the more important and pressing. To accurately set forth the belief and practices of the Celtic-speaking peoples, to trace their evolution, whether of form or significance, to connect them with what we know of the historic and prehistoric past of the race, this is a task to tax the energy of many scholars, a task, too, which it will soon be too late to accomplish, as many of the traditional links necessary to enable us to reconstruct the chain of testimony will have vanished with the present holders. If I have gladly availed myself of the offer made to me by Lord Archibald Campbell, and by the editors of this series, and have become their fellow-worker in the preservation of these waifs and strays of Celtic tradition, it is in the belief and hope that I am thereby furthering the achievement of that task.

To the student and lover of folk-lore, be his interest, his aims, what they may, volumes such as these, which present absolutely trustworthy material, are the first requisite. But, indeed, their interest is not confined to the folk-lorist. I venture to think that no lover of the speech and fancy of the Gael can afford to overlook these tales.

I had occasion, in the second volume of this series, to dwell at some length upon the relations between the legendary literature of modern Gaeldom and that oldest stratum of legend which is preserved in the Irish MSS., and which may be dated back to a period ranging from the 8th to the 15th century.   I purpose adding but little upon the subject.   Rather am I tempted, in view of certain opinions expressed by Mr. MacDougall in his notes, to discuss the original significance of much of this body of legend, and the methods of interpretation which he has preconised.

In several instances (*e.g.*, Notes, page 270) Mr. Mac-Dougall applies the nature-myth theory to the Gaelic tales.   Under the special form of the solar myth this system of interpretation was the dominant and ortho-dox one until a comparatively recent period.   The great collections which form the basis of folk-lore re-search were animated by its spirit, as still is much of the doctrine which necessarily enters into these as into all historical investigations.   It is worth while reviewing the fortunes of this theory, and examining the reasons of its present discredit.

In his recent work on the Arthurian legend, Prof. Rhys pathetically laments this discredit : " The terms of the solar-myth theory are so convenient," he says, " and whatever may eventually happen to the theory, nothing has as yet been found exactly to take its place."   This is quite true.   The solar-myth theory was an organic hypothesis which explained a vast number of facts, if once its premises were admitted, and which fitted in with the dominant conceptions in ethnology and pre-historic archæology.   It has, indeed, owed its fall rather to the fact that these conceptions have varied than to its inherent weakness, or to the reaction begot by the extravagance with which its claims were urged.   But as the changes in our knowledge of the past history of mankind have mostly been effected without reference to the studies of mythology and folk-lore, their effect upon these studies has never been set forth clearly, and no homogeneous theory has taken the place of the one they dispossessed.   The consequences are doctrinal anarchy in both departments of study, and party grouping of scholars according to insignificant side-issues rather than according to well-defined general principles.

The modern study of folk-lore owes its origin to Jacob and William Grimm. Most valuable work, illustrative as well as theoretical, had indeed been done by such Frenchmen as Fontenelle, Des Brosses, and Dupuis, who so largely anticipated the methods and results of the modern anthropological school. But these were men of the eighteenth century, and they lacked that sympathy with the folk-mind, that romantic enthusiasm which enabled the Grimms to divine, to interpret, and to reveal the treasures of folk-fancy. It was, indeed, this enthusiasm which endeared the new study to the men of the Romantic revival, and it was but natural that the methods which approved themselves to the Grimms should commend themselves to their generation and to that which followed.

Briefly speaking, the Grimms may be said to have looked upon European folk-lore generally as the detritus of beliefs and imaginings common to all Aryan peoples, upon much of Teutonic folk-lore specially as the detritus of those beliefs and imaginings as they found expression in the Scandinavian mythological texts, which were held to be among the oldest and most authentic monuments of Teutonic myth and cult. In the fifty years which followed the first labours of the Grimms, the idea of the community of the Aryan peoples assumed definite shape ; it was regarded as beyond cavil that they had their origin in some district of Central Asia ; that they colonised Europe in successive swarms, the more westerly settlements representing the oldest strata of immigration ; and that in race, speech, religious belief and socia  practice, the Sanskrit-speaking peoples of India, to whom we owe the Vedic poems, represented as early a  stage in Aryan evolution as any we know of.

Naturally, the ideas revealed by an examination of these Vedic poems were used to interpret other monuments of Aryan mythic belief; naturally, the Vedic creed was treated as a standard to which other Aryan creeds were referred. That much both of Vedic and of other early forms of Aryan religion was legitimately explained by the solar-myth theory, is, I think, undoubted, and although many results were fallacious, yet, on the whole, the theory approved itself as a valuable instrument of investigation.

It will be seen that there was no necessary connection between the detritus theory of folk-lore and the solar interpretation of myths. But each was made to support the other, and a logical and coherent view of folk-lore was the result. The question of diffusion—the crux of the study at present—did not arise. The Aryans had once lived all together, and possessed a common fund of beliefs and practice; the similarity in the folk-lore of the descendants of the primitive undivided Aryan race was but what might be expected. The interpretation valid for the myths in their pristine purity, was equally valid for them in their degenerated forms. The nursery-tale or jingle of to-day was the last echo of a god-myth or a priestly incantation, so that, to take an extreme instance, the four-and-twenty blackbirds baked in a pie became representatives of the hours made vocal by the incoming dawn.

But it soon became apparent that Aryan peoples (or, rather, those peoples assumed to be Aryans) had no monopoly of similarity in folk-lore, and as the special historical conditions which had been postulated in the case of the Aryans could obviously not have existed everywhere, the necessity was felt for a theory of wider scope. On the one hand, investigations into the beliefs and practices of existing savage races revealed a vast number of primitive ideas akin to those expressed in

European folk-lore, and led to the hypothesis that the latter, so far from being the detritus of the great organised systems of antiquity, rather represented the protoplasm out of which those systems were themselves formed. On the other hand, the partisans of the diffusion theory, according to which the various manifestations—religious, social, artistic—of man's activity assume shape among a definite race, at a definite centre from which they radiate, applied this theory, with great satisfaction to themselves, to various classes of folk-lore, in particular to tales, ballads, and other examples of what may be called folk-literature. Meanwhile grave doubt had been thrown upon the Asiatic origin of the Aryans, as well as upon the existence of a pan-Aryan culture, and it was urged that in any case the Vedic poems represented a late rather than an early stage of such culture, and that the method of myth-interpretation based upon them was not valid in the case of older and less complex systems. The extreme lengths to which the nature-myth theory had been pushed likewise begot a legitimate reaction, and it was further discredited by the fact that it had been made dependent upon philological equations, of which advancing knowledge demonstrated the unsoundness in many cases. The " diffusionists" were at work here likewise. Hellenic myth was largely claimed as a loan from the older civilisations of the East ; Teutonic myth, at least as presented in the Scandinavian documents, as an artificial admixture of original paganism with classic and Christian conceptions.

Just as there was no logical connection between the nature-myth system and the detritus theory of folk-lore, yet they easily fell into their places as part of one whole, and yielded each other mutual support, so the assailing arguments and researches lent each other aid, though often based upon radically opposed principles. The coherent and shapely structure of 1815-70 had to be levelled and the ground cleared of its ruins, and this work of demolition was carried on both by those whose only quarrel was with gargoyle and weathercock, and by those who condemned the building from the ground-plan upwards. The task of reconstruction has hardly begun, nor have friends or foes fully learnt to recognise each other again.

I take it there is some truth in all these views of folk-lore, certainly far more than is supposed at present in the view which was still fashionable twenty years ago. Amongst the vast mass of facts roughly classed together under the one term folk-lore, some belong to the most primitive stage of man's intellectual and social consciousness, the stage in which men belonging to different races and inhabiting different portions of the globe are still living. In the essential manifestations of consciousness, these men show a kinship as marked as any that obtains among the folk-lore products of civilised races, and unless it be held that the doctrines conveniently (whether correctly or not, I do not prejudge) termed animism—*i.e.*, the recognition of a life common to man, animals, and what we call inanimate life—originated in a definite centre, and spread all over the world by transmission, I fail to see why the latter explanation should be postulated in the case of European folk-lore. Other items, again, of European folk-lore seem to me distinctly traceable to survivals of the ideas and practices embodied in the religious and social systems of antiquity, with this distinction, however, that the " folk", the uneducated classes in direct contact with nature, held these ideas in a much ruder and simpler form than that in which they have been preserved to us by systematising thinkers or by creative artists, and that the existing folk-beliefs go back to the folk-beliefs of 2,000 years ago, rather than to the creeds and legends which have come down to us in literature. It is also, I think, self-evident that the folk-consciousness has been enriched by many and varied elements since the establishment of Christianity, and I am quite prepared to admit that many of these elements were introduced into Christendom from the Orient. I would, however, point out that all over Europe folk-conceptions and folk-practices are still, in many instances, not only different from, but strongly opposed to, the spirit and teachings of Christianity. That this latter, surely the most tremendous and penetrating influence to which European civilisation has been subjected, has shown itself powerless against so many older conceptions, and has only been able to nominally oust others by accepting a compromise all in their favour, is a testimony, the weight of which cannot be over-estimated, to the stubborn persistency with which the folk has clung to its theory of life. One hypothesis, I confess, I cannot take seriously—that which pictures the popular mind as a *tabula rasa*, and as deriving all its ideas and fancies from the higher culture of the race, and by some mysterious process transmuting them into the likeness of beliefs and practices held all over the world by races in a primitive stage of development.

With regard to the nature-myth theory, without accepting the particular mode in which it was presented, *e.g.*, by Sir George Cox, I cannot see why the "anthropological" folk-lorist should quarrel with it. If one thing seems proved, it is the existence of nature-myths among savage races. Why should the mythopœic tendency or faculty be supposed to have died out among the folk whose conditions of life and thought are so akin to those of the savage? Nor do I see why the special favour accorded to certain types of story among the folk may not be accounted for by their mythical origin and pristine significance, by their having once formed part of the religious and philosophical equipment of the race. The fact of this special favour is beyond question, and is surely more difficult to explain if the stories be denied all connection with primitive conceptions of the universe than if the connection be admitted. I know it will be said that stories which cannot possibly claim such an origin as is here indicated, are equally widespread. But these are stories of real life, stories which as a rule appeal to the sense of humour. The nature of their appeal is intelligible, their popularity needs no sanction ; but why the universal delight in stories which cannot be true, and which are everywhere untrue in the same kind of way ?

The disfavour attaching to the nature-myth interpretation of early legends (whether related of gods or heroes) is, I think, unmerited. The particular form which it assumed in the first half of this century was faulty, but the principle itself is legitimate, and no one has a right to reject it on *a priori* grounds. But it is evident that to apply it successfully requires caution, and a most searching preliminary investigation into the history of the legend as far as it can be traced. Again, the principle may be true indirectly, but false directly. The tale of Troy divine might be, as some have claimed, the record of the sun's strife with the elements ; but if the tale were told in Scotland, or elsewhere, as a simple story concerning men and women, and lived on in tradition, suffering changes in the course of time, it would be obviously illegitimate to attribute any mythological value to those changes. All that could justly be observed was that the tale found favour because it was cast in a traditional mould, because it conformed to the conventions of folk-fancy ; it could hardly be cited as exemplifying the mythical beliefs of Scotland.

Mr. MacDougall interprets stories belonging to the Finn-cycle as nature-myths. The question at once arises, Has the cycle its roots in that dim past of the Gaelic race when the mythopœic impulse was vigorously creative instead of being the mere survival it is now? If so, and if other proof is forthcoming that the Gaels had a religion of the same kind as Greeks, Teutons, or Aryan Indians, a religion in which nature-myths certainly played some part, there is no inherent impossibility in stories having lived on from that past unto our own time, and preserved with substantial fidelity the outlines of the primitive myths. But it should at once be noted that whatever theory be accepted concerning the origin of the Finn-cycle, it is certain that many of the stories belonging to it assumed a shape, probably not very different from that under which they are still current, in a period extending from the early 11th to the 15th century, and that they were influenced by events which cannot be older than the 9th or 10th century, *i.e.* by the struggle between the Irish and the invading Norsemen. When studying the Finn or Ossianic legend in the second volume of this series I emphasised this, the secondary historical element in its development. As for the primary historical element, I assumed, in common with all previous investigation, and in accordance with the apparent meaning of the earliest Irish records, that it was furnished by the life and deeds of a third-century Irishman, Finn son of Cumhal. At the same time I expressed the opinion that the historical elements in the cycle were of little importance in comparison with the romantic ones. Since then the distinguished German scholar, Professor H. Zimmer, to whom Celtic studies owe a deep debt of gratitude for his unwearied labours, and for the acuteness and ingenuity with which he has analysed the Irish records, has propounded the theory that the historical Finn was no third-century Irishman but a ninth-century Ersified Norseman, and that the non-historical elements in the Finn-cycle are Norse rather than Celtic. I have sketched the outline of this theory in the *Academy* for Feb. 14 last.

I will here only say briefly that many of the philological
and historical arguments upon which Professor Zimmer
relies have been challenged by such eminent Celtic
scholars as Mr. Whitley Stokes, Professor Kuno Meyer,
and M. d'Arbois de Jubainville. Be the new hypothesis
well founded or not, it has comparatively little bearing
upon the question whether it is allowable to interpret
part of the Finn-cycle as nature-myths. The constitu-
tive elements of an heroic saga may easily be much
older than the personality of the chief hero, who simply
succeeds to earlier attributes and adventures. Nor
would the assumed Norse origin conflict with the possible mythic nature of the tales which crystallised round
Finn ; the ninth-century Norsemen were still heathens,
and there is no reason to doubt the existence of many
nature-myths in their heathenism.

Thus before the nature-myth system of interpretation
can be applied extensively to stories of the Finn-cycle,
the date and primitive form of these stories must be
determined as far as possible—they must be examined
to see if they belong originally to the cycle, or if they
are recent additions—their possible historic basis must
be carefully discriminated. Finally, the results must be
checked by what we know from other sources of Gaelic
religion and social organisation. In the absence of such
preliminary criticism no small degree of uncertainty
must accompany every effort to interpret Gaelic legend.
Yet every effort, if made with insight and sympathy, is
of value as deepening our knowledge of, and quickening
our interest in, the legends themselves.

In his notes (p. 261) on the supernatural realm into
which the heroes of Celtic saga penetrate in search of
adventure, and from which they return laden with magic
treasures, Mr. MacDougall touches upon and materially
advances the comprehension of some very interesting
questions. The whole series of early Gaelic conceptions

concerning the Otherworld has been studied by Professor Zimmer in his admirable discussion of the Brendan legend. His conclusions may be summarised as follows : The earliest Gaelic Elysium lies across the western main in the land of the setting sun : "fair is that land to all eternity beneath its snowfall of blossoms .... the gleaming walls are bright with many colours, the plains are vocal with joyous cries, mirth and song are at home on the plain, the silver-clouded one. No wailing there for judgment, nought but sweet song to be heard. No pain, no grief, no death, no discord. Such is the land."[1] "No death, no sin, no decay, but ever we feast, and need none to serve us, ever we love, and no strife ensues," says the fairy maiden who lures away Condla.[2] When one of the princes of Faery would win the mortal Etain to be his love, he thus pictures his land and its inhabitants: "A magic land, and full of song; primrose is the hue of the hair, snow-white the fair bodies, joy in every eye, the colour of the foxglove in every cheek."[3] Such is the account preserved to us of the happy dwelling-place of the older Gaelic gods. But when Christianity prevailed there was bound to be a change in the conception; the gods lived on, but, cast down from their Olympus, they retreated into the hollow hills, and to this very day are still believed in by the Irish peasant. The oldest texts we have, although they may date back to the seventh century, already confuse the earlier conception of the western ocean island with that of the fairy realm within the hills, but the former

---

[1] From the Voyage of Bran Mac Febail, which Professor Zimmer thinks may be ascribed to the seventh century in the form under which it has come down to us. This and other translations are from renderings of Professor Zimmer's literal German version.

[2] The Voyage of Condla Ruad is as old as that of Bran Mac Febail.

[3] The Wooing of Etain belongs to the very oldest stratum of Irish legend.

lived on nevertheless, and is still potent in texts the composition of which is probably not older than the twelfth or thirteenth centuries.

I am by no means sure that Professor Zimmer is right— I will not say in his exposition of the facts—but in his interpretation of them; by no means sure that the belief in *Elysium*, the Otherworld peopled by wiser, more powerful, and, on the whole, happier beings than men, as a land within the hollow hill is not as early as that which placed it at the westernmost verge of the ocean. Be this as it may, it is interesting to compare the growth of early Gaelic belief, as recovered by Professor Zimmer from texts which are pre-Christian in their essence, with the belief of the modern Gael after sixteen centuries of Christianity. That western paradise, which, according to the German scholar, is found degraded from its pristine state in texts which go back to the seventh century of our era,—that western paradise is still, according to Mr. MacDougall, "the world of enchantment and wonder in the eyes of the living Highlander" (see notes, p. 262). It is still regarded as an island, "the green isle at the bounds of the uttermost world," it is still a land of everlasting summer, of meadows ever green, of fruit-trees ever laden. Heroes journey to it, travel through it, return from it, in just the same way as did the warrior of pre-Christian Gaeldom. The eschatology of Christianity, that feature of the new creed which more than any other was calculated to impress the rude and simple minds of the folk, has apparently been powerless to shake the delight with which the folk have listened to tales of the Otherworld, powerless to modify the essential nature of the conceptions concerning it.

Mr. MacDougall goes on to note (p. 263) that the Otherworld is not figured as the abode of the dead; *that* is placed within the hollow hill. Have we here the mingling of two strains of belief due to two different races, the one launching its dead warriors to their resting-place upon the western sea, sending them to the gods who were pictured as dwelling in the green isle, the other burying its dead in great mounds, and associating with *these* all the ideas connected with the spirit-world? Or did the pre-Christian inhabitants of these islands distinguish between the land of the supernatural beings to whom they paid worship, and that to which mankind at large went after death? Or is Professor Zimmer right, and is the hollow hill belief a secondary one originated by the disturbing influence which Christianity exercised upon the Gaelic conception of the super-natural? It may be, we can never answer these questions satisfactorily; but if they are to be answered, note must be taken as well of the belief and fancy of the modern peasant as of the mediæval poet or chronicler.

Enough has been said, I trust, to exemplify not only the nature of the problem which the folk-lorist essays to solve, but also the special value of Gaelic testimony in his eyes. Apart from all minor and secondary points, there is but one issue involved in the study of folk-lore— are the phenomena with which it deals, in the main, phenomena of growth or phenomena of decay—are they remains of successive stages of culture through which every race and all members of the race have at one time or another passed, and in which the folk-masses have lived on—ay, and are still living, to a great extent— whereas the educated classes have long since grown out of them; or are they the remains of definite systems of cult, custom, and art special to particular races, and transmitted from them to their neighbours, systems which we mostly possess at first hand, and in a form far more perfect than that recoverable from the distorted fragments preserved by the folk? Advocates of the second view hold, for instance, that all folk-tales come from India, or all cosmogonies from Babylonia, or all municipal and manorial organisation from Rome ; that the Celt was incapable of conceiving the idea of blood-brotherhood, or the Norseman that of a future world of punishment and reward.  The mind of every race was apparently a blank before it became fertilised by contact with other races, and every considerable manifestation of human thought and practice would seem to have sprung into existence fully grown, as Athene from Zeus' head.

Celtic legend, Celtic custom, afford, perhaps, the best means obtainable for testing the worth of these rival theories.   The field of investigation is not so large that it may not be surveyed with thoroughness, and the historical factors in the problem are comparatively simple.  We can trace with approximate accuracy the story of Gaeldom, whether in Ireland or Scotland, from the fourth century onwards; and the facts that the Gaels were largely isolated from the remainder of Europe by a more powerful and a hostile race ; that for most of this period all their energies were exhausted in the struggle for simple racial existence ; that, geographically and histori-cally, Gaeldom represents a backwater, so to speak, in the main stream of European life—these facts have con-tributed to perpetuate with singular vividness the archaic ideas which underlie the civilisation of the past, the modes of expression which differentiate primitive from modern art.

So much for the import of Celtic folk-lore (using the word in its widest sense) to the student of man's past. May I claim that it is of equal import to the present-day Briton ?   However much it may be regretted in certain quarters, the Celt is an abiding element in the imperial life of the British race.  Upon hearty sympathy, upon cordial co-operation between the Celtic, the Teutonic, and what other elements there may be in the fabric of our civilisation, depends more than upon aught else the continued existence, stability, and growth of that fabric. But whereas to know other races we must chiefly turn to the higher minds of the race, to the individual thinkers and artists, to know the Celt we must familiarise ourselves with a vast body of anonymous and traditional legend which has at all times faithfully reflected folk-beliefs and folk-aspirations, and which can be neither understood nor appreciated without constant reference to a conception of life and nature, the very existence of which is unknown to most men of the educated classes.

It hardly needs to speak of the intrinsic beauty of Celtic legend, of its subtle and far-reaching influence upon our national literature and art. There are many of us who amongst the dust and press of modern life have heard the voice which Condla, son of the King of Ireland, heard two thousand years ago, the voice of the fairy maiden inviting them to the magic realm of never-ending summer, of strifeless love. Alas! less fortunate than Prince Condla, we can sojourn there but for a while. But we have at least this consolation : we can bring back tidings of the fairness of that land, we can urge upon others to journey thither likewise, sure that in this we are serving the cause alike of science and of that fellow-sympathy which should knit together all the heirs of a common imperial tradition.

ALFRED NUTT.

# TALES.

# I.

## HOW FINN KEPT HIS CHILDREN FOR THE BIG YOUNG HERO OF THE SHIP,

### AND HOW BRAN WAS FOUND.

A DAY Finn and his men were in the Hunting-hill they killed a great number of deer; and when they were wearied after the chase they sat down on a pleasant green knoll, at the back of the wind and at the face of the sun, where they could see everyone, and no one at all could see them.

While they were sitting in that place Finn lifted his eyes towards the sea, and saw a ship making straight for the haven beneath the spot on which they were sitting. When the ship came to land, a Big Young Hero leaped out of her on the shore, seized her by the bows (breast), and drew her up, her own seven lengths, on (the) green grass, where the eldest son (*Macan*), of neither land-owner, nor (of holder) of large town-land dared mock or gibe at her. Then he ascended the hill-side, leaping over the hollows and slanting the knolls, till he reached the spot on which Finn and his men were sitting.

He saluted Finn frankly, energetically, fluently; and Finn saluted him with the equivalent of the same words. Finn then asked him whence did he come, or what was he wanting? He answered Finn that he had come through night-watching and tempest of sea where he was; because he was losing his children, and it had been told him that there was not a man in the world who could keep his children for him but him, Finn, King of the Feinne. And he said to Finn, "I lay on thee, as crosses and spells and seven fairy fetters of travelling and straying to be with me before thou shalt eat food, or drink a draught, or close an eye in sleep."

Having said this, he turned away from them and descended the hillside the way he ascended it. When he reached the ship he placed his shoulder against her bow, and put her out. He then leaped into her, and departed in the direction he came until they lost sight of him.

Finn was now under great heaviness of mind, because the vows had been laid on him, and he must fulfil them or travel onwards until he would die. He knew not whither he should go, or what he should do. But he left farewell with his men, and descended the hillside to the seaside. When he reached that he could not go farther on the way in which he saw the Big Young Hero depart. He therefore began to walk along the shore, but before he had gone very far forward, he saw a company of seven men coming to meet him.

When he reached the men he asked the first of them what was he good at? The man answered that he was a good Carpenter. Finn asked him how good was he at Carpentry? The man said that, with three strokes of his axe, he could make a large, capacious, complete ship of the alder stock over yonder. "Thou art good enough," said Finn ; "thou mayest pass by."

He then asked of the second man, what was he good at? The man said that he was a good Tracker. "How good art thou?" said Finn. "I can track the wild duck over the crests of the nine waves within nine days," said the man. "Thou art good enough," said Finn ; "thou mayest pass by."

Then he said to the third man, "What art thou good at?" The man replied that he was a good Gripper.

" How good art thou ?"  " The hold I (once) get I will . not let go until my two arms come from my shoulders, or until my hold comes with me."  " Thou art good enough ; thou mayest pass by."

Then he said to the fourth man, " What art thou good at ?"  He answered that he was a good Climber.  " How good art thou ?"  " I can climb on a filament of silk to the stars, although thou wert to tie it there."  " Thou art good enough ; thou mayest pass by."

He then said to the fifth man, " What art thou good at ?"  He replied, that he was a good Thief.  " How good art thou ?"  " I can steal the egg from the heron while her two eyes are looking at me."  " Thou art good enough ; thou mayest pass by."

He asked of the sixth man, " What art thou good at ?"  He answered, that he was a good Listener.  " How good art thou ?"  He said that he could hear what people were saying at the extremity of the Uttermost World (*Domhan Tor*).  " Thou art good enough ; thou mayest pass by."

Then he said to the seventh man, " What art thou good at ?"  He replied, that he was a good Marksman.  " How good art thou ?"  " I could hit an egg as far away in the sky as bowstring could send or bow could carry (an arrow)."  " Thou art good enough ; thou mayest pass by."

All this gave Finn great encouragement.  He turned round and said to the Carpenter, " Prove thy skill."  The Carpenter went where the stock was, and struck it with his axe thrice ; and as he had said, the Ship was ready.

When Finn saw the Ship ready he ordered his men to put her out.  They did that, and went on board of her.

Finn now ordered the Tracker to go to the bow and prove himself.  At the same time he told him that yesterday a Big Young Hero left yonder haven in his ship, and that he wanted to follow the Hero to the place in which he now was.  Finn himself went to steer the Ship, and they departed.  The Tracker was telling him to keep her that way or to keep her this way.  They sailed a long time forward without seeing land, but they kept on their course until the evening was approaching.  In the gloaming they noticed that land was ahead of them, and they made straight for it.  When they reached the shore they leaped to land, and drew up the Ship.

Then they noticed a large fine house in the glen above the beach.  They took their way up to the house ; and when they were nearing it they saw the Big Young Hero coming to meet them.  He ran and placed his two arms about Finn's neck, and said, "Darling of all men in the world, hast thou come ?"  "If I had been thy darling of all the men in the world, it is not as thou didst leave me that thou wouldst have left me," said Finn.  "Oh, it was not without a way of coming I left thee," said the Big Young Hero.  "Did I not send a company of seven men to meet thee ?"            -

When they reached the house, the Big Young Hero told Finn and his men to go in.  They accepted the invitation, and found abundance of meat and drink.

After they had quenched their hunger and thirst, the Big Young Hero came in where they were, and said to Finn, "Six years from this night, my wife was in child-bed, and a child was born to me.  As soon as the child came into the world, a large Hand came in at the chimney, and took the child with it in the cap (or hollow) of the hand.  Three years from this night the same thing happened.  And to-night she is going to be in child-bed again.  It was told me that thou wert the only man in the world who could keep my children for me, and now I have courage since I have found thee."

Finn and his men were tired and sleepy.  Finn said to the men that they were to stretch themselves on the floor, and that he was going to keep watch.  They did as they were told, and he remained sitting beside the fire.  At last sleep began to come on him ; but he had a bar of iron in the fire, and as often as his eyes would begin to close with sleep, he would thrust the bar through the bone of his palm, and that was keeping him awake.  About midnight the woman was delivered ; and as soon as the child came into the world the Hand came in at the chimney.  Finn called on the Gripper to get up.

The Gripper sprang quickly on his feet, and laid hold of the Hand.  He gave a pull on the Hand, and took it in to the two eye-brows at the chimney.

The Hand gave a pull on the Gripper, and took him out to the top of his two shoulders.  The Gripper gave another pull on the Hand, and brought it in to the neck.  The Hand gave a pull on the Gripper, and brought him out to the very middle.  The Gripper gave a pull on the Hand, and took it in over the two armpits.  The Hand gave a pull on the Gripper, and took him out to the smalls of his two feet.  Then the Gripper gave a brave pull on the Hand, and it came out of the shoulder.  And when it fell on the floor the pulling of seven geldings was in it.  But the big Giant outside put in the other hand, and took the child with him in the cap of the hand.

They were all very sorry that they lost the child. But Finn said, "We will not yield to this yet.  I and my men will go away after the Hand before a sun shall rise on a dwelling to-morrow."

At break of dawn, Finn and his men turned out, and reached the beach, where they had left the Ship.

They launched the Ship, and leaped on board of her. The Tracker went to the bow, and Finn went to steer her.  They departed, and now and again the Tracker would cry to Finn to keep her in that direction, or to keep her in this direction. They sailed onward a long distance without seeing anything before them, except the great sea. At the going down of the sun, Finn noticed a black spot in the ocean ahead of them. He thought it too little for an island, and too large for a bird, but he made straight for it. In the darkening of the night they reached it; and it was a rock, and a Castle thatched with eel-skins was on its top.

They landed on the rock. They looked about the Castle, but they saw neither window nor door at which they could get in. At last they noticed that it was on the roof the door was. They did not now know how they could get up, because the thatch was so slippery. But the Climber cried, " Let me over, and I will not be long in climbing it." He sprang quickly towards the Castle, and in an instant was on its roof. He looked in at the door, and after taking particular notice of everything that he saw, he descended where the rest were waiting.

Finn asked of him what did he see ? He said that he saw a Big Giant lying on a bed, a silk covering over him and a satin covering under him, and his hand stretched out and an infant asleep in the cap of the hand ; that he saw two boys on the floor playing with shinties of gold and a ball of silver ; and that there was a very large deer-hound bitch lying beside the fire, and two pups sucking her.

Then said Finn, "I do not know how we shall get them out." The Thief answered and said, "If I get in I will not be long putting them out." The Climber said, " Come on my back, and I will take thee up to the door." The Thief did as he was told, and got into the Castle.

Instantly he began to prove his skill. The first thing he put out was the child that was in the cap of the hand. He then put out the two boys who were playing on the

THE GIANT ASLEEP.

To face p. 6.

floor. He then stole the silk covering that was over the Giant, and the satin covering that was under him, and put them out. Then he put out the shinties of gold and the ball of silver. He then stole the two pups that were sucking the bitch beside the fire. These were the most valuable things which he saw inside. He left the Giant asleep, and turned out.

They placed the things which the Thief stole in the Ship, and departed. They were but a short time sailing when the Listener stood up and said, " 'Tis I who am hearing him, 'tis I who am listening to him !" "What art thou hearing ?" said Finn. "He has just awakened," said the Listener, "and missed everything that was stolen from him. He is in great wrath, sending away the Bitch, and saying to her if she will not go that he will go himself. But it is the Bitch that is going."

In a short time they looked behind them, and saw the Bitch coming swimming. She was cleaving the sea on each side of her in red sparks of fire. They were seized with fear, and said that they did not know what they should do. But Finn considered, and then told them to throw out one of the pups ; perhaps when she would see the pup drowning she would return with it. They threw out the pup, and, as Finn said, it happened : the Bitch returned with the pup. This left them at the time pleased.

But shortly after that the Listener arose trembling, and said: " 'Tis I who am hearing him ; 'tis I who am listening to him!" "What art thou saying now?" said Finn. "He is again sending away the Bitch, and since she will not go he is coming himself."

When they heard this their eye was always behind them. At last they saw him coming, and the great sea reached not beyond his haunches. They were seized with fear and great horror, for they knew not what they should do. But Finn thought of his knowledge-set of teeth, and having put his finger under it, found out that the Giant was immortal, except in a mole which was in the hollow of his palm. The Marksman then stood up and said: "If I get one look of it I will have him."

The Giant came walking forward through the sea to the side of the Ship. Then he lifted up his hand to seize the top of the mast, in order to sink the Ship. But when the Hand was on high the Marksman noticed the mole, and he let an arrow off in its direction. The arrow struck the Giant in the death-spot, and he fell dead on the sea.

They were now very happy, for there was nothing more before them to make them afraid. They put about, and sailed back to the Castle. The Thief stole the pup again, and they took it with them along with the one they had. After that they returned to the place of the Big Young Hero. When they reached the haven they leaped on land, and drew up the Ship on dry ground.

Then Finn went away with the family of the Big Young Hero and with everything which he and his men took out of the Castle to the fine house of the Big Young Hero.

The Big Young Hero met him coming, and when he saw his children he went on his two knees to Finn, and said: "What now is thy reward?" Finn answered and said, that he was asking nothing but his choice of the two pups which they took from the Castle. The Big Young Hero said that he would get that and a great deal more if he would ask it. But Finn wanted nothing except the pup. This pup was Bran, and his brother, that the Big Young Hero got, was the Grey Dog.

The Big Young Hero took Finn and his men into his house, and made for them a great, joyous, merry feast, which was kept up for a day and year, and if the last day was not the best, it was not the worst.

That is how Finn kept his children for the Big Young Hero of the Ship, and how Bran was found.

## MAR GHLEIDH FIONN A CHUID CLOINNE DO DH' ÒGLACH MÒR NA LUINGE,

### AGUS MAR FHUARAS BRAN.

LÀ bha Fionn agus a chuid daoin' anns a' Bheinn-sheilg mharbh iad mòran fhiadh ; agus dar bha iad sgìth an déigh na faoghaide shuidh iad sìos air tulach ait, uaine, air chùl gaoith' agus air aodann gréine, fàr am faiceadh iad gach aon 'us nach faiceadh aon idir iad.

Am feadh 'bha iad 'n an suidhe 's an ionad sin thog Fionn a shùilean ris a' mhuir, agus chunnaic e long a' deanamh dìreach air a' chaladh fo 'n àit' anns an robh iad 'n an suidhe. An uair a thàinig an long chum tìre, léum òglach mòr a mach aist' air an tràigh, agus rug e air bhroilleach oirre, agus tharruinn e i, a seachd fad fhéin, an àird air féur gorm, fàr nach robh 'chridh' aig macan fear fearainn no baile mhòir a bhi ri bùirt no fochaid oirre. An sin dhìrich e 'mach am bruthach, a' léum thar nam bac agus a' fiaradh nan cnoc, gus an d' ràinig e 'n t-àite 's an robh Fionn 'us a chuid daoine 'n an suidhe.

Bheannaich e Fionn gu briosglach, brosglach, briathrach ; agus bheannaich Fionn e le comain nam briathra céudna. An sin dh' fheòraich Fionn d'e Cia as a thàinig e, no gu dé 'bha e 'g iarraidh ?  Fhreagair e Fionn gu 'n d' thàinig e tromh fhair' oidhche agus ànradh mara fàr an robh esan, a chionn gu 'n robh e 'call a chuid cloinne, agus gu 'n robh e air innseadh dha nach robh duin' air an t-saoghal a b' urrainn a chuid cloinne 'ghleidheadh dha ach esan, Fionn Righ na Féinne.  Agus thubhairt e ri Fionn, "Tha mi 'cur mar chroisean 'us mar gheasan ort, 'us mar sheachd buaraichean sìthide, siùbhla, 's seachrain gu 'm bi thu leam-sa mu 'n ith thu biadh, no mu 'n òl thu deoch, no mu 'n dùin thu sùil 'an cadal."

Air dha so a ràdh, thionndaidh e air falbh uapa, agus theirinn e 'm bruthach an rathad a dhìrich se e. An uair a ràinig e 'n long, chàirich e 'ghualainn r' a toiseach, agus chuir e mach i. Léum e 's tigh innt' an sin, agus dh' fhalbh e 'n taobh a thàinig e gus an do chaill iad sealladh air.

Bha Fionn a nis fo sprochd mòr, a chionn gu 'n robh na bòidean air an cur air, agus gu 'm féumadh e 'n coimhlionadh, air neo siubhal air aghaidh gus am faigheadh e bàs. Cha robh fhios aige ceana 'ghabhadh e, no gu dé 'dheanadh e. Ach dh' fhàg e beannachd aig a chuid daoine, agus theirinn e 'm bruthach gu ruig taobh na mara. An uair a ràinig e sin cha b' urrainn e dol ni b 'fhaide air an t-slighe air am fac' e 'n t-Òglach Mòr a' falbh. Air an aobhar sin thòisich e air imeachd ri taobh a' chladaich, ach mu 'n deachaidh e ro fhad' air aghaidh chunnaic e seachdnar dhaoine 'tighinn 'n a choinneamh.

An uair a ràinig e na daoine dh' fheòraich e de 'n chéud fhear dhiubh, Gu dé air an robh e math? Fhreagair an duine gu 'm bu Shaor math e. Dh' fheòraich Fionn d' e gu dé cho math 's a bha e air saorsainneachd? Thubhairt an duine gu 'n deanadh e long mhòr, luchdmhor, lionta le trì buillean d' a thuaigh de 'n stoc fheàrn' ud thall. "Tha thu glé mhath," arsa Fionn; "faodaidh tu gabhail seachad."

Dh' fheòraich e 'n sin de 'n dara fear, Gu dé air an robh esan math? Thubhairt e gu 'n robh e 'n a Lorgaiche math. "Gu dé cho math 's a tha thu?" arsa Fionn. "Lorgaichidh mi 'n lach thar bharraibh nan naoi tonn 'an ceann nan naoi tràth," ars' an duine. "Tha thu glé mhath," thubhairt Fionn; "faodaidh tu gabhail seachad."

An sin thubhairt e ris an treas fear, "Gu dé air am bheil thusa math?" Fhreagair e gu 'm bu Ghramaiche math e. "Gu dé cho math 's a tha thu?" "An greim a gheibh mi cha leig mi as gus am bi mo dhà laimh as mo ghuailnibh, no gu 'm bi mo ghreim agam." "Tha thu glé mhath ; faodaidh tu dol seachad."

An sin thubhairt e ris a cheathramh fear, "Gu dé air am bheil thusa math ?" Fhreagair e gu 'm bu Streapaire math e. "Gu dé cho math 's a tha thu ?" "Streapaidh mi air ròinean sìoda gus na rionnagan ged cheangladh tu 'n sin e." "Tha thu glé mhath ; faodaidh tu gabhail seachad."

Thubhairt e 'n sin ris a' choigeamh fear, "Gu dé air am bheil thusa math ?" Fhreagair e gu 'm bu Mhèirleach math e. "Gu de cho math 's a tha thu ?" "Goididh mi 'n t-ubh bho 'n chùrr, 'us a dà shùil a' coimhead orm." "Tha thu glé mhath ; faodaidh tu gabhail seachad."

Dh' fheòraich e de 'n t-sèathamh fear, "Gu dé 'air am bheil thusa math ?" Fhreagair e gu 'm bu Chlàisdeir math e. "Gu dé cho math 's a tha thu ?" Thubhairt e gu 'n cluinneadh e gu dé 'bha iad ag ràdh 'an iomall an Domhain Toir. "Tha thu glé mhath ; faodaidh tu gabhail seachad."

An sin thubhairt e ris an t-seachdamh fear, "Gu dé air am bheil thusa math ?" Fhreagair e gu 'm bu Chuspair math e. "Gu dé cho math 's a tha thu ?" "Fhad 's a chuireadh sreang i, agus a ghiùlaineadh bogha i, chuimsichinn ubh anns an athar." "Tha thu glé mhath ; faodaidh tu gabhail seachad."

Thug so uile misneach mhòr do Fhionn. Thionndaidh e mu 'n cuairt, agus thubhairt e ris an t-Saor, "Dearbh do làmh." Ghabh an Saor far an robh 'n Stoc, agus bhuail e le thuaigh e trì uairean ; 'us mar thubhairt e bha 'n Long deas.

Dar chunnaic Fionn an Long deas, thug e òrdugh d' a dhaoin' air a cur a mach. Rinn iad sin, agus chaidh iad air bòrd innte.

Dh' òrduich Fionn an Lorgaiche 'dhol do 'n toiseach a nis, agus e g' a dhearbhadh féin. Aig a' cheart àm dh' innis e dha gu 'n d' fhàg òglach mòr an caladh ud 'n a luing an dé, agus gu 'n robh 'dhìth airsan an t-òglach a leantuinn do 'n àite 's an robh e nis. Chaidh Fionn féin a stiùradh na Luinge, agus dh' fhalbh iad. Bha 'n Lorgaiche 'g iarraidh air a cumail mar sud, n' a cumail mar so. Sheòl iad air an aghaidh ùine mhòr gun fhearann fhaicinn, ach chum iad air an aghaidh gus an robh am feasgar a' tighinn. Ann an dorchadh nan tràth, thug iad an aire gu 'n robh fearann air thoiseach orra, agus rinn iad dìreach air. An uair a ràinig iad an cladach léum iad gu tìr, agus tharruinn iad an Long.

An sin thug iad an aire do thigh mòr sgiamhach anns a' ghleann os ceann a' chladaich. Ghabh iad a suas a dh' ionn- saidh an tighe; agus an uair a bha iad a' dlùthachadh ris chunnaic iad an t-Òglach Mòr a' tighinn 'n an coinneamh. Ruith e, agus chuir e 'dhà laimh mu 'n cuairt air amhaich Fhinn, agus thubhairt e, "A ghràidh a dh' fhir an t-saoghail! an d' thàinig thu?" "Na 'm bu mhi do ghràdh a dh' fhir an t-saoghail, cha-n ann mar dh' fhàg thu mi a dh' fhàgadh tu mi," arsa Fionn. "Oh, cha b' ann gun dòigh air tighinn a dh' fhàg mi thu," ars' an t-Òglach Mòr. "Nach do chuir mi seachdnar dhaoin a' d' choinneamh?"

An uair a ràinig iad an tigh dh' iarr an t-Òglach Mòr air Fionn agus air a dhaoine dol a 's tigh. Ghabh iad ris a' chuireadh, agus fhuair iad pailteas bithidh agus dibhe.

An deigh dhoibh an acras agus an tart a chasg thàinig an t-Òglach Mòr a 's tigh fàr an robh iad, agus thubhairt e ri Fionn, "Sè bliadhna bho nochd bha mo bhean-sa 'n a laidhe- shiùbhla, agus rugadh leanabh dhomh. Cho luath agus a thàinig an leanabh air an t-saoghal, thàinig Cròg Mhòr a 's tigh air an luidheir, agus thug i leatha 'n leanabh ann an currachd na Cròige. Tri bliadhna bho 'nochd thachair a leithid céudna. Agus an nochd tha i dol a bhi 'n a laidhe- shiùbhla 'rithist. Chaidh innseadh dhomh gu 'm bu tusa an aon duine air an t-saoghal a b' urrainn mo chuid cloinne a ghleidheadh dhomh, agus tha misneach agam a nis o'n fhuair mi thu."

Bha Fionn agus a chuid daoine sgìth agus cadalach. Thubh- airt Fionn ris na daoine gu 'n robh iadsan ri iad féin a shìneadh air an ùrlar, agus gu 'n robh esan' dol a dheanamh faire. Rinn iad mar dh' iarradh orra, agus dh' fhuirich e féin 'n a shuidhe taobh an teine. Mu dheireadh thòisich an cadal air tighinn air, ach bha gàt iaruinn aig' anns an teine, agus cho tric agus a thòisicheadh a shùilean air dùnadh le cadal stopadh e 'n gàt tromh chnaimh a dheàrna, agus bha sin 'g a chumail 'n a fhaireachadh. Mu mheadhon oidhche chaidh an dara taobh do' n mhnaoi, agus cho luath 's a thàinig an leanabh air an t-saoghal, thàinig a' Chròg a 's tigh air an luidheir. Ghlaodh Fionn ris a' Ghramaiche 'bhi air a chois.

Ghrad léum an Gramaiche air a chois, agus rug e air a' Chròig. Thug e tarruinn air a' Chròig, agus thug e 's tigh i gu maol an dà shùl air an luidheir. Thug a' Chròg tarruinn air a' Ghramaiche, agus thug i mach e gu maol na dà ghualainn. Thug an Gramaiche tarruinn eil' air a' Chròig, agus thug e 's tigh i gus an amhach. Thug a' Chròg tarruinn air a Ghramaiche, agus thug i 'mach e gus an teis-meadhon. Thug an Gramaiche tarruinn air a' Chròig, agus thug e 's tigh i thar an dà achlais. Thug a' Chròg tarruinn air a' Ghramaiche, agus thug i mach e gu caol na dà choise. An sin thug an Gramaiche tréun tharruinn air a' Chròig, agus thàinig i as a' ghualainn. Agus an uair a thuit i air an ùrlar, bha tarruinn sheachd ghearran innte. Ach chuir am Famhair mòr a bha mach a' chròg eile 's tigh, agus thug e leis an leanabh an currachd na cròige.

Bha iad uile ro dhuilich gu 'n do chaill iad an leanabh. Ach thubhairt Fionn, "Cha ghéill sinn da so fathast. Falbhaidh mise agus mo dhaoine 'n déigh na Cròige mu 'n éirich grian air bruth am màireach."

Aig bristeadh na fàire thionn' Fionn agus a chuid daoine mach, agus ràinig iad an cladach fàr an d' fhàg iad an Long.

Chuir iad a mach an Long, agus léum iad air bòrd innte. Chaidh an Lorgaiche do 'n toiseach, agus Fionn g' a stiùradh. Dh' fhalbh iad, agus bha an Lorgaiche an dràst agus a rithist a' glaodhaich ri Fionn a cumail mar sud no' cumail mar so. Sheòl iad air an aghaidh astar fada gun ni 'fhaicinn rompa ach a' mhuir mhòr. Aig dol fodha na gréine thug Fionn an aire do *spot* dubh anns a' chuan air thoiseach orra. Bu bheag leis mar eilean e, 's bu mhòr leis mar èun e, ach rinn e dìreach air. 'An dorchadh na h-oidhche ràinig iad e ; agus b 'e sgeir a bh' ann, agus Caisteal tubhta le craicnibh easgann air a mullach.

Chaidh iad air tìr air an sgeir. Sheall iad timchioll a' Chaisteil, ach cha-n fhac' iad uinneag no dorus air am faigheadh iad a 's tigh. Mu dheireadh thug iad an aire gu 'm b' ann

air a mhullach a bha 'n dorus.   Cha robh fhios aca 'nis ciamar
a gheibheadh iad an àird, a chionn gu 'n robh an tubha cho
sleamhainn.   Ach ghlaodh an Streapaire, "Leigibh mise null,
agus cha bhi mi fada 'g a dhìreadh."   Ghrad léum e 'dh' ionnsaidh a' Chaisteil, agus ann an tiota bha e air a mhullach.
Sheall e 's tigh air an dorus, agus an déigh dha beachd
sònraicht' a ghabhail air gach ni a chunnaic e theirinn e far an
robh càch a' feitheamh.

Dh' fheòraich Fionn d' e gu dé 'chunnaic e.   Thubhairt e
gu 'm fac' e Famhair mòr 'n a laidhe air leabaidh, brat sioda
thairis air agus brat sròil fodha, agus a' ch ròg sìnte mach agus
naoidhean 'n a chadal 'an currachd na cròige ; gu 'm fac' e dà
ghiollan a' cluich air meadhon an ùrlair le camain òir agus ball
airgid ; agus gu 'n robh galla mhòr mhòr mhial-choin 'n a laidhe
taobh an teine, agus dà chuilean 'g a deoghal.

An sin thubhairt Fionn, "Cha-n 'eil fhios cia mar a gheibh
sinn a mach iad."   Fhreagair am Mèirleach agus thubhairt e,
" Ma gheibh mise 's tigh, cha bhi mi fada 'g an cur a mach."
Thubhairt an Streapaire, "Thig air mo mhuin-sa, agus bheir
mise 'n àird gus an dorus thu."   Rinn am Mèirleach mar dh'
iarradh air, agus fhuair e 's tigh do 'n Chaisteal.

Ghrad thòisich e air a làmh a dhearbhadh.   B' e 'chéud ni
a chuir e mach an leanabh a bha 'n currachd na cròige.   Chuir
e mach an sin an dà ghiollan a bha 'cluich air an ùrlar.   Ghoid
e 'n sin am brat sìod' a bha thairis air an Fhamhair agus am
brat sròla 'bha fodha; agus chuir e mach iad.   Chuir e 'n sin a
mach na camain òir, agus am ball airgid.   Ghoid e 'n sin an
dà chuilean a bha 'deoghal na galla taobh an teine.   B' iad sin
na nithe bu luachmhoìr a chunnaic e 's tigh.   Dh' fhàg e 'm
Famhair 'n a chadal, agus thionn' e mach.

Chuir iad na nithe 'ghoid am Mèirleach anns an Luing, agus
dh' fhalbh iad.   Cha robh iad ach goirid a' seòladh an uair a
dh' éirich an Clàisteir 'n a sheasamh, agus a thubhairt e, " Is
mi 'tha 'g a chluinntinn, is mi 'tha 'g a éisdeachd !"   "Gu dé
'tha thu cluinntinn?" arsa Fionn.   "Tha e 'n déigh dùsgaidh,"
thubhairt an Clàisteir, "agus gach ni a ghoideadh uaith'
iondrainn.   Tha e, 'am feirg mhòir, a' cur air falbh na Galla,

agus ag ràdh rithe mur falbh ise gu 'm falbh e féin. Ach is i 'Ghalla 'tha falbh."

An ùine ghoirid sheall iad as an déigh, agus chunniac iad a Ghalla 'tighinn air an t-snàmh. Bha i a' sgoltadh na fairge air gach taobh dhi 'na sradagan dearga teine. Ghabh iad eagal, agus thubhairt iad nach robh fhios aca gu dé 'dheanadh iad. Ach smaointich Fionn, agus dh' iarr e orra aon de na cuilein-ean a thilgeil a mach; theagamh an uair a chitheadh i 'n cuilean 'g a bhàthadh gu 'n tilleadh i leis. Thilg iad a mach an cuilean, agus mar thubhairt Fionn b' fhìor. Thill i leis a' chuilean. Dh' fhàg so iad toilicht 'aig an àm.

Ach goirid an déigh sin dh' éirich an Clàisteir 'us e air chrith, agus thubhairt e, "Is mi 'tha 'g a chluinntinn, is mi 'tha 'g a éisdeachd !" "Gu dé 'tha thu 'g ràdh nis ?" thubhairt Fionn. "Tha e' cur air falbh na Galla rithist, agus o nach falbh ise tha e féin a' tighinn."

Dar chual iad so bha 'n sùil as an déigh daonnan. Mu dheireadh chunnaic iad e a' tighinn, agus cha ruigeadh an fhairge mhòr seach a mhàsan. Ghabh iad eagal agus uamhunn mhòr, agus cha robh fhios aca ciod a dheanadh iad. Ach chuimh-nich Fionn air a dhéud-fios, agus air dha a mhèur a chur fo dhéud fhuair e mach nach robh bàs air an Fhanihair ach 'an aon bhall-dòbhrain a bha 'n glaic a dheàrna. Dh' éirich an Cuspair an sin, agus thubhairt e, " Ma gheibh mise aon seal-ladh dh' e bithidh e agam."

Thàinig am Famhair a' coiseachd air aghaidh troimh 'n mhuir gu ruig taobh na Luinge. An sin thog e 'n àird a chròg a bhreith air mullach a' chroinn chum an Long a chur fodha. Ach an uair a bha a' chròg gu h-àrd, thug an Cuspair an aire do 'n bhall-dòbhrain, agus leig e saighead m' a thu-aiream. Bhuail an t-saighead am Famhair auns an àite-bàis, agus thuit e marbh air an loch.

Bha iad ro thoilichte 'nis, oir cha robh ni tuillidh rompa a bha 'cur eagail orra. Chuir iad mu 'n cuairt, agus sheòl iad air an ais a dh' ionnsaidh a' Chaisteil. Ghoid am Mèirleach a rithist an cuilean, agus thug iad leò e maille ris an fhear a bh' aca. An déigh sin thill iad a dh' ionnsaidh àit an Òglaich Mhòir.

An uair a ràinig iad an caladh léum iad air tìr agus tharruinn iad an Long a suas air talamh tioram.

An sin dh' fhalbh Fionn le teaghlach an Òglaich Mhòir agus leis gach ni a thug e féin agus a dhaoin' as a' Chaisteal gu tigh sgiamhach an Òglaich Mhòir.

Choinnich an t-Òglach Mòr e 'tighinn agus an uair a chunnaic e a chuid cloinne chaidh e air a dhà ghlùn do Fhionn, agus thubhairt e, " Ciod a nis do dhuais?"  Fhreagair Fionn agus thubhairt e nach robh e 'g iarraidh ach a roghainn de 'n dà chuilean a thug iad as a' Chaisteal.  Thubhairt an t-Òglach Mòr gu 'm faigheadh e sin agus mòran tuillidh na 'n iarradh e iad.  Ach cha robh ni tuillidh a dhìth air Fionn ach an Cuilean.  B' e 'n cuilean so Bran, agus b' e 'bhràthair a fhuair an t-Òglach Mòr an Cù Glas.

Thug an t-Òglach Mòr Fionn agus a dhaoine 's tigh d' a thigh, agus rinn e dhoibh cuilm mhòr, ghreadhnach, aighearach a bha là 'us bliadhn' air chumail, agus mur b' e an latha mu dheireadh a b' fhearr cha b' e' bu mhiosa.

Sin mar ghleidh Fionn a chuid cloinne do dh' Òglach Mòr na Luinge, agus mar fhuaras Bran.

# II.

## FINN'S JOURNEY TO LOCHLAN,

### AND HOW THE GREY DOG WAS FOUND AGAIN.

A DAY Finn and his men were in the Hunting-hill, they killed a good number of deer; and when they were making ready to go home, they saw a Big Lad coming to the place where they were. He went to meet Finn, and saluted him frankly, energetically, fluently; and Finn saluted him with the equivalent of the same words.

Finn asked him whence did he come, or what was he wanting? He answered Finn and said, "I am a Lad who came from east and from west, seeking a master." Finn said to him, "I want a Lad, and if we agree I will engage thee. What is thy reward at the end of a day and year?" "That is not much," said the Lad. "I only ask that at the end of the day and year thou wilt go with me by invitation to a feast and a night's entertainment to the palace of the King of Lochlan; and thou must not take with thee a dog or a man, a calf or a child, a weapon or an adversary but thyself." To shorten the tale, Finn engaged the Lad, and he was a faithful servant to the end of the day and year.

On the morning of the last day of his engagement the Big Lad asked of Finn whether he was satisfied with his service? Finn said to him that he was perfectly satisfied. "Well," said the Lad, "I hope that I shall receive my reward, and that thou wilt go with me as thou didst promise." "Thou shalt get thy reward, and I will go with thee," said Finn.

Then Finn went where his men were, and told them

C

that that was the day on which he must go to fulfil his promise to the Lad, and that he did not know when he should return. "But," said Finn, "if I shall not be back within a day and year, let the man of you who will not be whetting his sword be bending his bow for the purpose of holding one great day on the Great Strand of Lochlan, revenging my death." When he had said this to his men, he left them farewell, and went in to his dwelling.

His Fool was sitting beside the fire, and he said to him, " Poor man, art thou sorry that I am going away ?" The Fool answered weeping, and said that he was sorry because he was going in the way in which he was going, but that he would give him an advice if he would take it." "Yes, poor man," said Finn, "for often has the advice of the King been in the head of the Fool. What is thy advice ?" " It is," said the Fool, "that thou shalt take Bran's chain with thee in thy pocket ; and it is not a dog, and it is not a man, it is not a calf, and it is not a child, and it is not a weapon, and it is not an adversary to thee. But thou shalt take it at any rate." "Yes, poor man," said Finn, leaving him farewell and departing.

He found the Big Lad waiting him at the door. The Lad said to him if he was ready that they would depart. Finn said that he was ready, and told the Lad to take the lead, because he knew the way better.

The Big Lad went off, and Finn followed him. Though Finn was swift and speedy, he could not touch the Big Lad with a stick on the way. When the Big Lad would be going out of sight at one mountain-gap, Finn would be only coming in sight on the next mountain-ridge. And they kept in that position to each other until they reached the end of their journey.

They went in to the palace of the King of Lochlan, and Finn sat down weariedly, heavily, sadly. But, instead of a feast awaiting him, the chiefs and nobles of the King of Lochlan were sitting within putting their heads together to see what disgraceful death they would decree him. One would say we will hang him, another would say we will burn him, a third would say we will drown him. At last a man who was in the company stood up, and said that they would not put him to death in any of the ways that the rest mentioned. The men who first spoke turned towards him, and asked of him what way had he of putting Finn to death that was more disgraceful than any of the ways which they mentioned. He answered them and said: "We will go with him, and send him up to the Great Glen (Glen More); and he will not go far forward there when he shall be put to death by the Grey Dog. And you know, and I know, that there is not another death in the world more disgraceful in the estimation of the Féinne than that their earthly king should fall by a cur of a dog." When they heard the man's sentence, they all clapped their hands, and agreed with him in his sentence.

Without delay they went with Finn up to the Glen where the Dog was staying. They did not go very far with him into the Glen when they heard the howling of the Dog coming. They gave a look, and, when they saw him, they said that it was time for them to flee. They turned back quickly, and left Finn at the mercy of the Dog.

Now staying and running away were all one to Finn. If he ran away he would be put to death, and if he stayed he would only be put to death ; and he would as soon fall by the Dog as fall by his enemies. And so he stayed.

The Grey Dog was coming with his mouth open, and his tongue out on one side of his mouth. Every snort which he sent from his nostrils was scorching (everything) three miles before him and on each side of him.   Finn was being tormented by the heat of the Dog's breath, and he saw clearly that he could not stand it long.   He now thought if there was any use in Bran's chain, that it was time to draw it (forth).   He put his hand in his pocket, and when the Dog was in a near distance of him he took it out and shook it towards him.   The Dog instantly stood, and began to wag his tail.   He then came on where Finn was, and licked every sore which he had, from the top of his head to the sole of his foot, until he healed with his tongue what he burned with his breath. At last Finn clapped Bran's chain about the Grey Dog's neck, and descended through the Glen, having the Dog with him in a leash.

An old man and an old woman, who used to feed the Grey Dog, were staying at the lower end of the Glen. The Old Woman happened to be at the door, and when she saw Finn coming with the Dog she sprang into the house, crying and beating her hands.   The Old Man asked of her, What did she see or what did she feel?   She said that she saw a great thing, as tall and as handsome a man as she ever beheld, descending through the Glen, having the Grey Dog with him on a leash.   "Though the people of Lochlan and of Ireland were assembled", said the Old Man, "among them all there would not be a man who could do that but Finn, King of the Féinne, and Bran's chain of gold with him." "Though it were that same", replied the Old Woman, "he is coming."   "We shall soon know," said the Old Man, as he sprang out.

He went forward to meet Finn, and in a few words they saluted each other.   Finn told him, from beginning to end, the reason why he was yonder.   Then the Old Man invited him to go into the house till he would throw off his weariness, and receive meat and drink.

Finn went in.   The Old Man told the Old Woman

To face p. 20.

FINN AND THE GREY DOG.

the tale which Finn told him. And when the Old Woman heard the story, it pleased her so well that she said to Finn he was perfectly welcome to stay in her house to the end of a day and year. Finn gladly accepted the invitation, and stayed there.

At the end of a day and year the Old Woman went out, and stood on a knoll near the house. She was a while looking at everything she could see, and listening to every sound that she could hear. At last she gave a look down in the direction of the shore, and beheld an exceedingly great host standing on the Great Strand of Lochlan.

She ran quickly into the house, beating her hands and crying Alas! (her despoiling!) while her two eyes were as large as a corn-fan with fear. The Old Man sprang to his feet, and asked of her, What did she see? She said that she saw a thing the like of which she never saw before. "There is an innumerable host on the Great Strand down there; and in (the host) there is a squint-eyed, red-haired man (Oscar), and I do not think that his match in combat is this night beneath the stars."

"Oh!" said Finn, as he sprang to his feet, "there thou hast the companies of my love! Let me out to meet them!"

Finn, with the Grey Dog, went down to the Strand; and when his men saw him coming, alive and hale, they raised a great shout of rejoicing, which was heard in the four corners of Lochlan. Then they and their earthly King gave each other a friendly welcome. And if the welcome between them and Finn was friendly, not less friendly was the welcome between Bran and the Grey Dog; for this was his brother that was taken with him from the Castle.

Then they took vengeance on the men of Lochlan, because of the way they were going to treat Finn,

They began at one end of Lochlan, and they stopped
not till they went out at the other end.

After they had subdued Lochlan, they returned home,
and, when they reached the Hall of Finn, they made a
great, joyful, merry feast, which was kept up for a day
and a year.

# TURUS FHINN DO LOCHLANN,

## AGUS MAR FHUARAS A RITHIST AN CÙ GLAS.

Là bha Fionn agus a chuid daoin' anns a' Bheinn-sheilg
mharbh iad dòrlach math fhiadh ; agus dar bha iad a' deanamh
deas a dhol dhachaidh chunnaic iad Gille Mòr a' tighinn fàr an
robh iad.   Chaidh e 'n coinneamh Fhinn, agus bheannaich e
Fionn gu briosglach, brosglach, briathrach ; agus bheannaich
Fionn e le comain nam briathran ceudna.

Dh' fhèoraich Fionn d' e cia as a thàinig e, no gu dé 'bha e
g iarraidh ?   Fhreagair e Fionn agus thubhairt e, " Is Gille mi
a thàinig o 'n ear agus o 'n iar a dh' iarraidh Maistir."   Thubhairt Fionn ris, " Tha Gille 'dhìth ormsa, agus ma chòrdas sinn
cuiridh mi muinntireas ort.   Gu dé e do dhuais aig ceann là 'us
bliadhna ?"   " Cha mhòr sin," ars' an Gille.   " Cha-n iarr mi
ach gu 'n téid thusa, aig ceann an là agus na bliadhna, air
chuireadh, air chuilm, agus air chuid oidhche còmhladh riumsa
gu *pàilis* Righ Lochlainn ; agus cha-n fhaod thu cù no duine,
laogh no leanabh, arm no eascar a thabhairt leat ach thu féin."
A chur an sgeòil an giorrad chuir Fionn muinntireas air a'
Ghille, agus bha e 'n a sheirbhiseach dìleas gu ceann an là
agus na bliadhna.

Air madainn an là mu dheireadh d' a ùine, dh' fheòraich
an Gille Mòr de Fhionn an robh e toilichte le 'sheirbheis ?
Thubhairt Fionn ris gu 'n robh làn thoilichte.   " Mata," thubhairt an Gille, " tha mi 'n dòchas gu 'm faigh mise mo dhuais,

agus gu 'm falbh thu leam mar gheall thu." "Gheibh thu do dhuais, agus theid mise leat," arsa Fionn.

An sin chaidh Fionn far an robh a chuid daoine, agus dh' innis e dhoibh gu 'm b' e sin an latha air am féumadh esan falbh a choimhlionadh a gheallaidh do 'n Ghille, agus nach robh fhios aige c' uin' a thilleadh e. "Ach," arsa Fionn, "mar bi mis 'air m' ais fo cheann là agus bliadhna, am fear agaibh nach bi 'géurachadh a chlaidheimh bitheadh e 'lùbadh a' bhogha air son aon latha mòr a bhi agaibh air an Tràigh Mhòir 'an Lochlann a' dioladh mo bhàis-sa." 'Nuair thubhairt e so r' a chuid daoine dh' fhàg e beannachd aca, agus chaidh e 's tigh d' a bhruth.

Bha 'n t-Amadan aige 'n a shuidhe taobh an teine, agus thubhairt e ris, "A dhuine bhochd, am bheil thu duilich mise 'bhi falbh?" Fhreagair an t-Amadan 'us e 'caoineadh, agus thubhairt e gu 'n robh e duilich e 'bhi falbh anns an dòigh anns an robh e 'falbh, ach gu 'n tugadh esan comhairl' air na 'n gabhadh e i. "Gabhaidh, a dhuine bhochd," thubhairt Fionn, "oir is minic a bha comhairl' an righ ann an ceann an amadain. Ciod i do chomhairle?" "Tha," thubhairt an t-Amadan, "gu 'n toir thu leat slabhraidh Bhrain 'ad phòca; agus cha chù 's cha dhuin' i, cha laogh 's cha leanabh i, agus cha-n arm 'us cha-n eascar dhuit-s' i. Ach bheir thu leat i co dhiù." "Bheir, a dhuine bhochd," thubhairt Fionn, "'us e 'fàgail beannachd aige 's a falbh."

Fhuair e 'n Gille Mòr a' feitheamh air aig an dorus. Thubhairt an Gille ris ma bha e deas gu 'm bitheadh iad a' falbh. Thubhairt Fionn gu 'n robh e deas, agus dh' iarr e air a' Ghille fhéin an céum toisich a ghabhail, a chionn gu 'm b' e a b' eòlaich' air an t-slighe.

Dh' fhalbh an Gille Mòr, agus lean Fionn e. Ged bha Fionn luath astarach, cha chuireadh e maide 'm *pàirt* a' Ghille Mhòir air an rathad. Dar bhitheadh an Gille Mòr a' dol as an fhradharc air an aon bhealach cha bhitheadh Fionn ach a' tighinn 'am fradharc air an dara bearradh. Agus chum iad anns an t-suidheachadh sin d' a cheile gus an d' ràinig iad ceann an turuis.

Chaidh iad a 's tigh do phàilis Righ Lochlainn, agus shuidh

Fionn a sìos gu sgìth, trom, airsnealach. Ach 'an àite cuilm a' feitheamh air, bha maithean agus mòr uaislean Righ Lochlainn 'n an suidhe 's tigh a' cur an cinn ri 'chéile feuch gu dé 'm bàs tàmailteach a bheireadh iad da. Theireadh fear crochaidh sinn e, theireadh fear eile loisgidh sinn e, theireadh an treas fear bàthaidh sinn e. Mu dheireadh dh' éirich fear a bha 's a chuideachd 'n a sheasamh, agus thubhairt e, nach cuireadh iad gu bàs e air aon 's am bith de na dòighean a dh' ainmicheadh le càch. Thionndaidh na daoin' a labhair an toiseach ris, agus dh' fheòraich iad d' e gu dé an dòigh a bh' aige san air Fionn a chur gu bàs a bha ni 'bu tàmailtiche na aon air bith de na dòighean a dh' ainmich iadsan. Fhreagair e iad agus thubhairt e riù, " Theid sinn leis, agus cuiridh sinn 'suas e do 'n Ghleann Mhòr, agus cha téid e fad' air aghaidh an sin an uair a bhitheas e air a chur gu bàs leis a' Chù Ghlas. Agus tha fhios agaibh-se, agus tha fhios agam-sa nach 'eil bàs eil' air an t-saoghal a 's tàmailtiche leis an Fhéinn na 'n Righ saoghalt' a thuiteam le madadh coin." An uair a chual iad breith an duine bhuail iad am basan agus dh' aontaich iad leis 'n a bhreith.

Dh' fhalbh iad gu 'n dàil le Fionn a suas do 'n Ghleann far an robh an Cù Glas a' fuireachd. Cha deachaidh iad ro fhada leis anns a' Ghleann an uair a chual iad donnalaich a' choin a' tighinn. Thug iad sùil, agus dar chunnaic iad e thubhairt iad ri 'cheile gu 'n robh an t-àm aca-san a bhi 'teicheadh. Ghrad thill iad air an ais, agus dh' fhàg iad Fionn fo mheachainn a' choin.

'Nis b' e 'n aon chuid do Fhionn fuireachd agus teicheadh. Na 'n teicheadh e bhitheadh e air a chur gu bàs, agus na 'm fuiricheadh e cha bhitheadh e ach air a chur gu bàs ; agus bha cho math leis tuiteam leis a' Chù agus tuiteam le naimhdean. Agus le sin dh' fhuirich e.

Bha 'n Cù Glas a' tighinn le chraos fosgailte, agus a theanga 'mach air leth taobh a chraois. Bha gach smut a chuireadh e as a shròin a' losgadh trì mile roimhe agus air gach taobh dh' e. Bha Fionn 'g a' chràthadh le teas analach a' Choin, agus chunnaic e gu soilleir nach b' fhada 'b' urrainn e seasamh ris. Smaointich e 'n so ma bha féum 'an slabhraidh Bhrain gu 'n robh an t-àm a bhi 'g a tarrainn. Chuir e a làmh 'n a phòca ; agus an uair a bha 'n Cù 'an dlùth-astar da thug e 'mach i, agus chrath e ris i. Ghrad sheas an Cù, agus thòisich e air bogadh earbaill. Thàinig e 'n sin air aghaidh fàr an robh Fionn, agus dh' imlich e gach créuchd a bh' air, o mhullach a chinn gu bonn a choise, gus an do leigheis e le theanga na loisg e le 'anail. Mu dheireadh spàrr Fionn slabhraidh Bhrain mu amhaich a Choin Ghlais, agus theirinn e 's tigh an Gleann agus an Cù air lomhain aige.

An iochdar a' Ghlinne bha seann bhodach agus seann chailleach a' fuireachd a b' àbhaist a bhi biadhadh a' Choin Ghlais. Bha 'Chailleach aig an dorus ; agus dar chunnaic i Fionn a' tighinn leis a' Chù léum i 's tigh a' glaodhaich agus a' bualadh a bas. Dh' fheòraich am Bodach dhi gu dé 'chunnaic i, no gu dé 'dh' fhairich i? Thubhairt i gu 'm fac' i ni mòr, duine cho mòr agus cho briadh' agus a chunnaic i riamh a' téarnadh a 's tigh an Gleann 'us an Cù Glas air lomhain aige. "Ged bhith-eadh sluagh Lochlainn agus Eirionn cruinn" ars' am Bodach "cha bhitheadh duine 'n am measg uil' a b' urrainn sin a dheanamh ach Fionn, Righ na Féinne, agus slabhraidh òir Bhrain aige." "Ged b' e sin féin e," fhreagair a' Chailleach, " tha e a' tighinn." "Cha-n fhada gu uair fhios," ars' am Bodach 'us e 'leum a mach.

Ghabh e air aghaidh 'an coinneamh Fhinn, agus ann am beagan bhriathar chuir iad fàilt' air a chéile. Dh' innis Fionn da, bho thoiseach gu deireadh, an t-aobhar mu 'n robh e 'n sud. An sin dh' iarr am Bodach air dol a 's tigh gus an leigeadh e dheth a sgìos, agus gus am faigheadh e biadh agus deoch.

Chaidh e 's tigh. Dh' innis am Bodach do 'n Chaillich an sgéul a dh' innis Fionn da. Agus an uair a chual a' Chailleach an sgéul chòrd e rithe cho math agus gu 'n d' thubhairt i ri Fionn gu 'm b' e a làn-bheatha fuireachd anns an tigh aice-se gu ceann latha 's bliadhna. Ghabh Fionn ris a' chuireadh gu toileach, agus dh' fhuirich e 'n sin.

An ceann latha 's bliadhna chaidh a' Chailleach a mach, agus sheas i air cnoc laimh ris an tigh. Bha i greis a' sealltainn air gach ni a chitheadh i, agus ag eisdeach ris gach sian a chluinneadh i. Mu dheireadh thug i sùil a sios ris a chladach, agus chunnaic i sluagh anabarrach mòr 'nan seasamh air Tràigh Mhòir Lochlainn.

Ghrad ruith i 's tigh a' bualadh a bas agus ag éigheach a creach, agus a dà shùil cho mòr ri guit leis an eagal. Léum am Bodach air a chois, agus dh' fheòraich e dhi gu dé 'chunnaic i? Thubhairt i gu 'm fac' i ni nach fac' i riamh roimh' a leithid. "Tha sluagh gun àireamh air an Tràigh Mhòir sin shìos, agus tha aon fhear claon ruadh ann, agus cha-n éil mi smaointeachadh gu 'm bheil a chéile còmhraig an nochd fo na rion·nagaibh." "Oh," thubhairt Fionn 'us e 'léum air a chois, "sin agad cuideachdan mo ghràidh! Leig a mach mi 'n an coinneamh."

Dh' fhalbh Fionn leis a' Chù Ghlas a sìos a dh' ionnsaidh na 'Tràghad; agus an uair a chunnaic a chuid daoin' e 'tighinn beò slàn g' an ionnsaidh, thog iad iolach mhòr ghàirdeachais a chualas ann an ceithir cheàrnaibh Lochlainn. An sin chuir iad féin agus an Righ Saoghalta fàilte chàirdeil air a chéile. Agus ma bha 'n fhàilt eadar iadsan agus Fionn càirdeil cha bu lugha na sin a bha 'n fhàilt eadar Bran agus an Cù Glas cairdeil, oir b' e so a bhràthair a thugadh maille ris as a' Chaisteal.

An sin thug iad dioghailt air na Lochlannaich a chionn mar bha iadsan 'dol a dheanamh air Fionn. Thòisich iad ann an dara ceann Lochlainn, agus cha do stad iad gus an deachaidh iad a mach air a cheann eile.

An déigh dhoibh Lochlann a chur fo chìs thill iad dachaidh, agus an uair a ràinig iad Talla Fhinn rinn iad cuilm mhòr, ghreadhnach, aighearach a bha là 'us bliadhn' air chumail.

# III.

## THE LAD OF THE SKIN COVERINGS.

ON a certain day of old, Finn thought that he would go to hunt to the White Glen. He took with him as many of his men as were at hand at the time, and they went to the Glen.

The hunt began, and when it was over no man who was present ever saw such a sight of dead deer.

It was a custom with the Fein (Féinn), after they had gathered together the deer they killed, to sit down and take a rest. They would then divide the deer among them, each man taking with him a small or large burden as he was able. But on this day they killed many more than all that were at the hunt could take with them.

While Finn was considering what he should do with the remainder, he gave a look, and saw a Big Lad coming over the side of the mountain, and making straight for the place in which they were assembled with so great speed that never before did they see a man so fast as he. "Some one is coming towards us here," said Finn, "and 'tis before him his business is, or else I am deceived." They all stood looking at the Big Lad who was coming, but he took not a long time till he was in their very midst.

He saluted Finn frankly, energetically, fluently ; and Finn saluted him with the equivalent of the same words. Then Finn asked of him whence did he come, or whither was he going, or what was he wanting. He said that he was the Son of the Lady of Green Insh (*Innis Uaine*), and that he came from that as far as

this seeking a Master.   Finn answered, "I have need
of a servant, and I do not care although I engage thee
if we agree about the reward."   "That would not be
my advice to thee," said Conan.   "Conan, thou hadst
better keep quiet, and mind thine own business ; and I
will do my business," said the Big Lad.   Every one
present was wondering at the Big Lad's dress, for it
consisted of skin coverings.   Not less did they wonder
at the appearance of his great strength of body.   And
they were somewhat afraid that he would disgrace them
before he would part with them.   Finn then asked of
him what reward would he be asking to the end of a day
and year ?   The Big Lad said that he asked nothing but
that there should be no apartness of meat or of drink
between them at the table within, or on the plain without,
or in any place in which they should take food to the
end of the day and year.   "Thou shalt get that," said
Finn ; and they agreed.

Then they began to lift the deer with them.   One
would take with him one, and another would take with
him two, till all had their burdens except the Big Lad.
But they left many more deer than they took with them.
Finn then told the Big Lad to take with him a burden.
The Big Lad began to pull the longest and the finest
part of the heather that he could see, till he had a great
heap beside him.   Then he began to make a rope of the
heather, and to place a deer on every deer's length that
he would twine till he had every deer that was left in
one burden.

When the burden was ready he told the rest to lift it
on his back.   They came, and as many went about the
burden as could surround it ; but though as many and
as many more of the Fein would have been assembled
as were present on that day they could not put wind
between it and (the) earth.   When the Big Lad saw this
he told them to stand out of his way.   He then took

hold of the rope and put a turn of its end about his fist, he bent his back, put a balk on his foot, and threw the burden over his shoulder. Every one of the Fein looked at his neighbour, but spake not a word.

When the Big Lad got the burden steady on his back he said, "I am but a stranger in this place; let one of you therefore go before to direct me in the way." Every one looked at his neighbour to see who would go. At last Conan answered that he would go if the rest would carry his deer home. Finn said that his deer would be carried home if he would take the lead. Conan threw the deer off him, sprang before the Big Lad, and told him to follow him.

Conan went away as fast as he could, and the Big Lad went away after him. There were two big nails on the two big toes of the Big Lad, and they went but a short distance when he left not a hair's-breadth of skin on the back of Conan between the top of his two shoulders and the back of his two feet with the two big nails which were on his feet. At last Conan began to lose his distance, for he was growing weak with loss of blood; and in a short time he was under the necessity of stopping and of sitting down where he was. When the Big Lad saw that Conan yielded he went past him, and stop he made not till he let his burden go at the dwelling of Finn.

Then he sprang in, and put on a fire. He cooked food for every man who was at the hunt, and set the food of each man apart, except his own food and that of Finn. The Fein came home at last; and when they went in they wondered greatly to see the food ready before them, but they made no remark.

After the supper (was over) the Fein sent for Finn, and Conan spoke and said: "Did I not tell thee that we should get disgraced by the Lad whom thou didst engage? His match in strength is not in the Fein. Thou must put him out of our way until his time shall be out." "Well," said Finn, " I do not know what I can do with him unless I send him away to Lochlan to seek the four-sided cup, and he has there a day and a year's journey however well he may walk." They were all quite pleased with this, and told Finn to send him off as soon as he could. Finn answered and said : "Before a sun shall rise on a dwelling he will get his leave to travel on the journey."

Without delay he sent for the Lad of the Skin Coverings, and said to him that he was sorry to ask him to go on this long journey, but that he hoped he would not refuse. The Big Lad asked him on what business was he sending him, or whither had he to go? Finn said that he got word from Lochlan that he would get the four-sided cup if he would send a man for it. " I sent them word to come and meet us with it, and that we would go and meet them. I am desirous that thou wilt go to seek it to-morrow, and I know that they will meet thee coming with it." "Well, Finn," said the Big Lad, " thou knowest and art assured that they shall not meet me with it, for numerous are the heroes who have shed their blood on the field beneath the spears of Lochlan for the sake of the four-sided cup which they have had since four-and-twenty years, and which thou hast not yet got. How now dost thou think, Finn, that I can take it out (of their hands) unassisted? But since I promised to do what thou wouldst ask me, I will go seek it for thee."

On the next morning, before a sun shone, the Big Lad was ready for the journey. Then he lifted his own skin-coverings on him, and strode away ; and the swift March wind which was before him he would overtake, and the swift March wind which was behind him would not keep (pace) with him. At that rate of travelling onwards he did not slacken the speed of his chace till he struck his palm against a (door) bar at the palace of the King of Lochlan that night.

The palace of the King of Lochlan was kept by seven guards. The Big Lad knocked (at the gate of) the first guard, and the first guard asked him whence was he, or whither was he going? He replied that he was a servant who had come from Finn, King of the Fein, on a message to the King of Lochlan. Word went to the King that such a man was at the door. The King asked if any man was with him. The Lad-in-waiting said that there was not. The King then gave orders to let him in. The (gate of the) first guard was opened for him, and he got in, and in like manner every (gate with a) guard until he got through the seven guards. He was taken into the place where the King was, and the King told him to sit down. The Big Lad sat, for he was tired after the journey which he had made. He gave a look through the room, and noticed as beautiful a cup as he ever saw standing on a table. He said to the King of Lochlan, " That is a beautiful vessel which thou hast there." The King said that it was that, and also a cup of virtues. The Big Lad asked what virtues did it possess? The King answered that there was no fill that he would order to be in it which would not be in it immediately. The Big Lad, being thirsty after the journey which he had made, thought that its full of water on the table would be a good thing. Then he rose up, took hold of the cup, and drank all that was in it. He next turned his face to the door ; and if he asked for an opening in, he asked not for an opening out, for he leaped over the seven guards, having the cup with him.

Then he lifted his own skin-coverings on him, and strode away on the path on which he came ; and the swift March wind which was before him he would over-take, but the swift March wind which was behind him would not keep (pace) with him.  At that rate of travelling onwards he did not slacken the speed of his chace till he struck his palm against a (door) bar at Finn's dwelling on that night.

He went in, and handed the cup to Finn.  "Thou wert not long away," said Finn.  "Did I not tell thee before thou didst leave that they would meet thee coming with it ?"  The Big Lad answered : "Thou knowest and art assured that they did not meet me coming with it.  But I reached Lochlan, and I got the cup in the King's palace, and I made the journey forward and back again."

"Silence, babbler !" said Conan.  "There are some in the Fein who can run on ben-side or on glen-strath as well as thou canst, and they could not do the journey in double the time in which thou sayest thou didst it.  But come to cut a leap with me as far as the Green Lakelet at the foot of Ben Aidan, and I will know if thou hast made the journey."  "O, Conan ! I am more needful of food and a little wink of sleep than of going to cut leaps with thee."  "If thou wilt not go, we will not believe that thou hast made the journey," said Conan.

The Big Lad rose and went with him ;  and they reached the Green Lakelet.  Conan asked the Big Lad to cut a leap across the Lakelet.  "It is thou that brought me here, and I am tired," said the Big Lad ; "therefore cut the first leap thyself."  Conan took a race and cut a leap, but sank to the balls of his two hips in the leafy marsh on the other side of the Lakelet.  The Big Lad cut his leap without any race, and went over Conan's head on the hard ground on the other side of the Lakelet.  He then leaped it back back-foremost, and forward front-foremost, before Conan got his haunches out of the bog.

When Conan got his feet on the hard ground he said

that the roots gave way under his feet, and that he sank! "But come and race with me to the top of Ben Aidan, and I will know if thou hast made the journey." "Conan, I am more needful of a little wink of sleep than of going to race with thee to the top of Ben Aidan." However, he went. At a stride or two the Big Lad went past Conan, and gave not another look after him till he was on the top of the Ben. He then stretched himself on a green hillock and slept.

He knew not how long he slept, but it was the panting of Conan climbing the Ben which wakened him. He sprang quickly to his feet, and said, "Did I make the journey now, Conan?" "Come, wrestle with me, and I will know if thou hast made the journey," said Conan. They embraced each other. Conan told the Big Lad to put his turn. "Put thou thy turn first, Conan, for it is thou who wanted to begin." Conan tried to put his turn, but he did not move the Big Lad.

The Big Lad then bent over Conan, and with his weight threw him, and bound his three smalls with his leather garter.

The Big Lad now took it as an insult that the most contemptible man in the Fein was despising and bullying him; and he gave a vow that he would not return to Finn any more. He went away, and left Conan bound on the top of the Ben.

The night was coming, and Finn was wondering that the two men who went away were not returning. At last fear struck him that the Big Lad had killed Conan, and therefore he told his men that they must go seek them. Before the sun rose on the next morning he divided his men in companies, and sent a company to each corner of the Ben, and told them to travel on till they should all meet on the top of the Ben. About the evening of the day they met, and found Conan bound by his three smalls in one thong.

Finn told one of his men to go over, and unbind Conan. Oscar went, and took a long time trying to do that, but for every knot which he would untie seven other knots would go on the thong. At last he said to Finn, " I cannot loose this thong !" Then Goll sprang over, thinking that he could do better. He began to untie the thong ; but, as happened to Oscar, it beat him. If it was not tighter when he ceased, it was not a bit looser. At last he lifted up his head in wrath, and said, " There is not a man in the Fein who can unbind Conan !"

Finn now got afraid that Conan would be dead before they could get him released. But he remembered his knowledge set of teeth ; and having put his finger under it he discovered that there was 'not a man in the world who could unbind him but the Smith of the White Glen, or else the man who bound him.

He then sent away Goll and Oscar to tell the Smith what befell Conan. They reached the Smith, and told him the business on which they were. The Smith told them to gather together every four-footed beast which was between the back of Ben Aidan and the top of the White Glen, and send them past the door of his smithy. " And," said he, " if I then come out in peace good is my peace, but if I come out in wrath evil is my wrath."

Oscar and Goll then returned to Finn, and told him what the Smith said to them. Finn said that the hunt must be started. The hunt was started, and that was the Great Hunt of the White Glen. Since the first hunt was started never was there so great a number of four-footed beasts assembled as were (together) on that day. Then they sent them past the door of the smithy. The Smith came out and asked what was yonder ? They answered, " All the four-footed beasts between the top of Ben Aidan and the head of the White Glen, as he wanted."

The Smith said, "You have done well enough, but turn back every one of those creatures to the place from which you have taken them, and I will then go to unbind Conan." They did that, and the Smith went to the top of Ben Aidan, and released Conan.

When Conan got released he was so ashamed on account of what befell him that he drew away down the Ben as fast as he could, and that he cast not a look behind him till he went out to the neck in the sea. Out of that, he would not come for Finn or for a man in the Fein. But the tide was rising at the time, and when the water began to enter his mouth he thought that it was better for him to go ashore, and return home after the rest.

On a certain evening after that, when Finn and his men were coming home from the Hunting-ben they beheld a Lad coming to meet them. He took his way where Finn was, and said to him that he was sent from the Queen of Roy (*Ruaidh*) to Finn, King of the Fein, and that he was laying on him as crosses, and as spells, and as seven fairy fetters of travelling and straying, that he would neither stop nor take rest until he would reach the Queen of Roy's (*Ruaidh*) place. Having said this he turned towards them the back of his head, and departed ; and they had not a second look of him.

The Fein looked at each other, for they thought that some evil was to happen to Finn, because no man was asked to go but himself. They said to him that they were sorry because he was going alone, and because they knew not when he would come, or where they would go to seek him. But Finn said to them that they were not to be anxious about his coming to the end of a day and year.

Out of that standing he departed with his arms on him. He travelled onward far long and full long over bens, and glens, and heights, and a stop went not on his foot till he came in sight of Green Insh (*Innis Uaine*). There he beheld a man going to lift a burden of rushes on his back.   When he saw the man throwing the burden over his shoulder he thought that he was the Lad of the Skin Coverings.   He began to approach him under cover (make earth-hiding on him) till he got near him. Then he showed himself, and when the man who was there looked at him in the face he knew that he was the Lad of the Skin Coverings.   He sprang with a hasty step where he was, seized him in his two arms, and said, " Darling of all men in the world ! is it thou ?" The Big Lad answered and said, " If I were thy darling of all the men in the world, the most insignificant man whom thou hadst in the Fein would not have been bully-ing me, and making me the subject of mocking witti-cisms."   " Well," said Finn, " I was sorry enough, but I could not help it.   I was afraid that the men would rise up against me, and become unruly ; I therefore left Conan in his opinion.   But I knew thou didst make the journey, and we will be as good friends to each other as we ever were.   Wilt thou go with me once more on this little journey ?"   " Well," said the Big Lad, " I do not know.   Look down in yonder hollow under us, and thou shalt see my mother on her knees cutting rushes, and a turn of her right breast over her left shoulder.   If thou shalt get a hold of the end of the breast do not let it go till thou shalt get thy first request from her."

Finn went away a while on his hands and feet, and another while dragging himself (along) on his belly, till he got within a distance to take a spring.   Then he gave a spring, and got a hold of the end of the breast.   The Lady of Green Insh cried who was there ?   He replied, that Finn, King of the Fein, was there, asking his first boon of her.   She said what boon would he ask that he would not get ?   He said, " Let thy son go with me once more on this little journey."   The Lady said, " If I had known that it was that which thou wouldst ask, thou wouldst not have got it though thou shouldst take the breast from my chest, but since I promised it thou shalt get it. But I will have one promise from thee before thou goest, and that is that thou shalt take home to me himself and all that shall fall with him." "I hope that the matter will not end in that way, and that he will return home whole." "If he will, good shall not befall thee, Finn. However, be off on your journey."

Then Finn and the Big Lad went away on their journey, ascending hills and descending hollows, travelling over bens and glens and knolls till the gloaming of night was coming on them. They were growing weary, and were wishing to reach some place where they would get permission to take rest. They were but a short time travelling after that, when they beheld an exceedingly fine place before them, with fine large houses built on large green fields. Finn said to the Big Lad, "Let us take courage, for we are not far from houses." Shortly after that they reached the place.

Finn saw a man coming to meet them, and he knew that he was the very Lad who came with the message to him.

He asked of him what need had he of him now? The Lad answered and said that there were two big houses opposite him, one with door-posts of gold and doors of gold, and the other with door-posts of silver and doors of silver, that he was to take his choice of them to stay in, and that he would see when he would enter what he had to do there. The Lad having said this turned away from them, and left them where they were standing.

Finn looked in the face of the Big Lad, and said to him, "Which one of these houses shall we take to stay in?" The Big Lad said, "We will have the more honourable one ; we will take the one with the doors of gold."

They took their way over to the door. The Big Lad

laid hold of the bar, and opened the door.   Then they went in.   When they looked there was a great sight before them, but the Big Lad thought nothing of it. There were eighteen score and eight Avasks (*Amhaisg*) standing on the floor.   When they got Finn and the Big Lad inside the door they sprang towards it, and shut it; and put on it eighteen score and eight bars, The Big Lad went and put on it one great bar, and so firmly did he put the bar on that every bar they put on fell off.   Then the Avasks made eighteen score and eight laughs; but the Big Lad made one great guffaw of a laugh and deafened all that they made.   Then the Avasks said, "What is the cause of thy laugh, little man?" The Big Lad said, "What is the cause of your own laughter, big men all?"   They said, "The cause of our laughter is that it is a pretty, clustering, yellow head of hair which thou hast on thee to be used as a football out on yonder strand to-morrow."   "Well," said the Big Lad, "the cause of my laugh is that I will seize the man of you with the biggest head and smallest legs, and that I will brain all the rest of you with him."   He then saw a man with a big head; and having laid hold of him by the smalls of his two feet he began braining them in one end of the band and stopped not till he went out at the other end.   When he was done he had only as much of the feet as he held in his fists.

He and Finn put the dead bodies out, and made three heaps of them at the door.   They shut the door then, and made food ready, for there was abundance of it in the house.

After they had taken the food the Big Lad asked of Finn, "Whether wilt thou sleep or watch the door?" Finn answered, "Sleep thou, and I will watch the door." And so they did.   But before the Big Lad slept Finn asked of him, "With what shall I waken thee if distress shall come upon me at the door?"   "Strike the pillar (or block) of stone, which is behind the hearth, on me in the breast-bone, or else take with thy dirk the breadth of thy thumb from the top of my head." "Quite right," said Finn, " sleep on."

Finn was watching the door, but for a long time he was feeling nothing coming. At break of dawn he noticed the conversation of ten hundred coming to the door. He lifted the block of stone, and struck the Big Lad with it in the chest. The Big Lad sprang quickly to his feet, and asked Finn what he felt? "The conversation of ten hundred is at the door," said Finn. "That is right yet," said the Big Lad, " let me out."

The Big Lad went out to meet them. He began in one end of them, attacked them violently below and above them, and left none of them alive to tell the evil tale, but one man with one eye, one ear, one hand, and one foot, and he let him go. Then he and Finn collected the dead bodies, and put them in the three heaps with the rest. They afterwards went in, and waited till the next night came.

After supper the Big Lad asked of Finn, "Whether wilt thou sleep or watch to-night?" Finn said, "Sleep thou, and I will watch." The Big Lad went to sleep, and Finn was watching the door. A short time before sunrise, Finn heard the conversation of two thousand coming, or the Son of the King of Light alone. He sprang up, and with his dirk took the breadth of the face of his thumb from the top of the Big Lad's head. Instantly the Big Lad sprang to his feet, and asked of Finn what did he feel? Finn answered, "The conversation of two thousand, or the Son of the King of Light alone is at the door." "Oh, then, I dare say that thou must be as good as thy promise to my mother," said the Big Lad, "but let thou me out." Finn opened the door, the Big Lad went out, and it was the Son of the King of Light who was before him.

Then the two champions embraced each other, and wrestled from sunrise to sunset, but the one threw not the other, and the one spake not to the other during the whole time. They let each other go, and each one of them went his own way. Early next morning, before sunrise, the Big Lad went out, and his companion met him. They wrestled from sunrise to sunset, but the one threw not the other, and the one spake not to the other. They let each other go, and each one of them went his own way. The third day the heroes met, and embraced each other. They fought all day long till twilight, and the two fell side by side cold and dead on the ground.

Finn was dreadfully sorry for the Big Lad. But he remembered his promise to the Lad's mother, and said to himself that it must be fulfilled. He took out the silk covering which was over them where they slept, wrapped it about the two bodies, and took them with him on his back. He drew away with a hard step over bens and glens and hillocks, ascending hills and descending hollows, and stop or rest he made not till he reached the house of Green Insh (*Innis Uaine*).

The mother of the Big Lad met him at the door, and said to him, "Hast thou come?" Finn answered that he had come, but not as he would wish. She said to him, "Didst thou do as I told thee?" Finn said, "Yes, but I am sorry indeed that I had to do it." She said, "Everything is right. Come in." Finn went in, and laid the burden on the floor. He unloosed the covering, and the two lads were locked in each other's arms as they fell.

When the Lady of Green Insh saw the two lads she smiled and said, "Finn, my Darling, well is it for me that thou didst go on this journey." She then went over into a closet, and having lifted a flag which was on the floor, took out a little vessel of balsam which she had there. She then placed the two lads mouth to mouth, face to face, knee to knee, thumb to thumb, and rubbed the balsam to the soles of their feet, to the crowns of their heads, and to all parts of their skins which touched each other. The two lads stood up on the floor kissing one another.

" Now, Finn," said she, " there thou hast my two sons. This one was stolen from me in his infancy, and I was without him till now. But since thou has done as I told thee, thou art welcome to stay here as long as thou desirest."

They were so merry in the house of Green Insh that the time went past unknown to them. On a certain night the Lady of Green Insh said to Finn, " To-morrow there will be a day and a year since thou didst leave the Fein, and they have given up hope of thee. The man of them who is not whetting his sword is pointing his spear to-night for the purpose of going away to seek thee. Make ready to depart to-morrow, and I will let my son go with thee. For if thou shalt arrive alone they will give thee such a tumultuous welcome that they will smother and kill thee. But when you will arrive my son will enter before thee, and say to them, if they will promise him that they will rise up one after another to give thee a quiet, sensible welcome, that he will bring their earthly king home whole and sound to them."

Finn agreed to this with all his heart, and he and the Big Lad went away on their journey homewards on the morning of the next day. They had a long distance to go, but they took not long accomplishing it.

When they reached Finn's Hall (*Talla*) the Big Lad went in first, and what his mother said proved true. Every man was getting ready his sword and spear. The Big Lad asked of them what were they doing? They told him that. Then the Big Lad said to them what his mother told him to say.  They willingly consented to do that.  He then called on Finn to come in.  Finn came, and one rose after another as they promised. They got their earthly king back once more.  The Big Lad returned home, and if he has not died since he is alive still.

## GILLE NAN COCHLA-CRAICINN.

LÀ àraidh bho shean, smaointich Fionn gu 'n rachadh e 'sheilg do 'n Ghleann Gheal.  Thug e leis a' mheud d' a dhaoin' agus a bha aig laimh 's an àm, agus ràinig iad an Gleann.

Thòisich an fhaoghaid, agus dar bha i seachad cha-n fhaca duin' a bha làthair a leithid de shealladh air féidh mharbh riamh roimhe.

Bha e 'n a chleachdainn aig an Fhéinn, an déigh dhoibh na féidh a mharbh iad a thrusadh còmhla, suidhe sios agus an anail a leigeil.  Rinneadh iad an sin na féidh 'n a measg, gach aon a toirt leis eallach bheag no mhòr mar b' urrainn e. Ach air an latha so mharbh iad tuillidh mòr na 'b' urrainn na bh' aig an t-seilg a thabhairt leò.

Am feadh a bha Fionn a' smaointeachadh gu dé 'dheanadh e ris a chòr, thug e sùil, agus chunnaic e Gille Mòr a' tighinn thar leacainn a' mhonaidh agus a' deanamh dìreach air an àit' anns an robh iad cruinn, le luathas cho mòr agus nach fac' e riamh roimhe duine cho luath ris.  "Tha cuid-éiginn a' tighinn oirnn an so," arsa Fionn, "agus is ann roimhe 'tha 'ghnothuch, air neò tha mi air mo mhealladh."  Sheas iad uil' ag amharc air a' Ghille Mhòr a bha 'tighinn, ach cha b' fhada gus an robh e 'n an teis-meadhoin.

Chuir e fàilt air Fionn gu briosglach, brosglach, briathrach ; agus chuir Fionn fàilt air le comain nam briathra céudna. An sin dh' fhaighnichd Fionn d' e cia as a thàinig e, no c' àit' an robh e 'dol, no gu dé 'bha e 'g iarraidh? Thubhairt e gu 'm b' esan Mac Mnà Innse Uaine, agus gu 'n d' thàinig e bho sin gu ruig so, ag iarraidh Maistir. Fhreagair Fionn, "Tha Gille 'dhìth orm-sa, agus tha mi coma ged chuireas mi muinntireas ort ma chordas sinn mu 'n duais." "Cha b' e sin mo chomhairle dhuit," arsa Conan. "Is fearr dhuit-sa, a Chonain, fuireachd sàmhach, agus an aire 'thabhairt air do ghnothuch féin; agus ni mise mo ghnothuch féin," thubhairt an Gille Mòr. Bha gach duin' a làthair a' gabhail ioghnaidh de dh' éideadh a' Ghille Mhòir, oir b' e cochuill-chraicinn a bh' ann. Cha bu lugha 'n t-ionganntas a ghabh iad de choltas mòr-spionnaidh a bhodhaige. Agus bha sgàth orra gu 'n cuireadh e tàmailt orra mu 'n dealaicheadh e riutha. An sin dh' fheòraich Fionn d' e gu dé 'n duais a bhitheadh e 'g iarraidh gu ceann là 's bliadhna. Thubhairt an Gille Mòr nach robh e 'g iarraidh ach nach bitheadh leth-oireachas bithidh no dibhe eatarra aig a' bhòrd a 's tigh, no air an raon a mach, no ann an àit' air bith anns an gabhadh iad biadh gu ceann là 's bhadhna. "Gheibh thu sin," thubhairt Fionn; agus chòrd iad.

An sin thòisich iad air togail leò nam fiadh. Bha fear a bheireadh aon leis, agus bha fear a bheireadh dithis leis gus an robh 'n eallchan ac' uile ach aig a' Ghille Mhòr. Ach dh' fhàg iad mòran tuillidh fhiadh n' a thug iad leò. An sin dh' iarr Fionn air a' Ghille Mhòr eallach a thabhairt leis. Thòisich an Gille Mòr air spìonadh a chuid a b' fhaide 's a bu mhìn' a chitheadh e de 'n fhraoch gus an robh dùn mòr aige laimh ris. An sin thòisich e air sìoman a dheanamh de 'n fhraoch, agus air fiadh a chur air gach fad féidh a shniamhadh e gus an robh a h-uile fiadh a dh' fhàgadh aig' anns an aon eallaich.

An uair a bha 'n eallach deas dh' iarr e air càch a togail air a mhuin. Thàinig iad, agus chaidh uibhir agus a b' urrainn iathadh mu 'n cuairt do 'n eallaich m' a timchioll; ach ged bhitheadh urad agus urad eile de 'n Fhéinn cruinn agus a bh' ann air an là sin, cha chuireadh iad gaoth eadar i agus talamh. An uair a chunnaic an Gille Mòr so, dh' iarr e orra seasamh as an rathad air. Rug e 'n sin air an t-sloman agus chuir e car d' a cheann m' a dhòrn, lùb e 'dhruim, chuir e bailc air a

chois, agus thilg e 'n eallach thar a ghualainn.  Choimhead
gach aon de 'n Fhéinn air a chéile, ach cha d' thubhairt iad
facal.

An uair a fhuair an Gille Mòr an eallach socrach air a
mhuin thubhairt e, "Cha-n 'eil annam-sa ach coigreach anns
an àite so ; uime sin rachadh fear agaibh fhéin air thoiseach a
dheanamh an rathaid domh."  Choimhead gach aon air a
chéile feuch cò rachadh ann.  Mu dheireadh fhreagair Conan
gu 'n rachadh esan ann, na 'n giùlaineadh càch na féidh aige
dhachaidh.  Thubhairt Fionn gu 'n rachadh na féidh aig' a
ghiùlan dachaidh na 'n gabhadh esan an céum toisich.  Thilg
Conan dheth na féidh, agus léum e air thoiseach air a' Ghille
Mhòr, agus dh' iarr e air esan a leantainn.

Dh' fhalbh Conan cho luath agus a b' urrainn e, agus dh'
fhalbh an Gille Mòr as a dhéigh.  Bha dà ionga mhòr air dà
òrdaig mhòir a' Ghille Mhòir, agus cha deachaidh iad ach
goirid gus nach d' fhàg e rioba craicinn air cùlaobh Chonain,
eadar mullach an dà shlinnein agus cùl an dà chois, leis an
dà ionga mhòir a bh' air a chasaibh.  Mu dheireadh thòisich
Conan air call astair, oir bha e fàs lag le call fala ; agus an
ùine ghoirid b' eiginn da stad agus suidhe far an robh e.  An
uair a chunnaic an Gille Mòr gu 'n do ghéill Conan chaidh e
seachad air, agus stad cha d' rinn e gus an do leig e as an
eallach aig bruth Fhinn.

An sin léum e 's tigh agus chuir e air teine.  Bhruich e
biadh do gach duin' a bh' aig an t-seilg, agus chuir e biadh
gach duin' air leth ach a bhiadh féin agus biadh Fhinn.
Thàinig an Fhéinn dachaidh mu dheireadh, agus an uair a
chaidh iad a 's tigh ghabh iad ioghnadh mòr am biadh fhaicinn
deas rompa.  Ach cha do ghabh iad dad orra.

An déigh na suipeireach chuir an Fhéinn fios air Fionn,
agus labhair Conan agus thubhairt e, " Nach d' innis mise dhuit
gu 'm faigheadh mid ar tàmailteachadh leis a' Ghille air an do
chuir thu muinntireas ?  Cha-n 'eil a choimeas an neart anns
an Fhéinn.  Féumaidh tu a chur as an rathad oirnne gus am bi
'n ùin' aige mach."  " Mata," thubhairt Fionn, " cha-n 'eil fhios
agam-sa gu dé 'ni mi ris mur cuir mi air falbh e do Lochlann
a dh' iarraidh a' Chupain Chéathraraich, agus tha astar latha 's

bliadhn' aig' an sin air fheothas 'g an coisich e." Bha iad uile làn thoilichte le so, agus thubhairt iad ris a chur air falbh cho luath 's a b' urrainn e. Fhreagair Fionn agus thubhairt e, " Mu 'n éirich grian air bruth gheibh e cead siubhal air an astar."

Chuir e fios gun dàil air Gille nan Cochla-Craicinn, agus thubhairt e ris gu 'n robh e duilich leis iarraidh air dol air an turus fhada so, ach gu 'n robh e 'n dòchas nach diùltadh e falbh. Dh' fheòraich an Gille Mòr ciod an t-saothair air an robh e 'g a chur, no ceana bh' aige ri dol? Thubhairt Fionn gu 'n d' fhuair e fios a Lochlann gu 'm faigheadh e 'n Cupan Ceathraraich na 'n cuireadh e duin' air a shon. " Chuir mise fios g' an ionnsaidh iad a thighinn 'n ar coinneamh leis, agus gu 'n rachadh sinne 'n an coinneamh-san. Tha mi toileach gu 'm falbh thusa g' a iarraidh am màireach, agus tha fhios agam gu 'n tachair iad ort a' tighinn leis." " Mata, Fhinn," ars' an Gille Mòr, " tha fhios agus cinnt agad nach tachair iad orm leis, oir is lìonmhor laoch a dhòirt fhuil air an raon fo shleaghaibh Lochlainn air tàilleabh a' Chupain Cheathraraich a th' aca bho cheann ceithir bliadhna fichead, agus nach d' fhuair thu fhathast. Cia mar a nis, a tha thu 'smaointeachadh, Fhinn, gu 'n tabhair mise mach leam féin e? Ach o 'n gheall mi gu 'n deanainn an rud a dh' iarradh tu orm falbhaidh mi g' a shireadh dhuit."

Mu 'n do shoillsich grian air an ath mhadainn bha 'n Gille Mòr deas airson an astair. An sin thog e 'chochaill-chraicinn féin air agus shìn e air falbh ; agus gaoth luath a' Mhàirt a bh' air thoiseach air bheireadh e oirre, agus gaoth luath a' Mhàirt a bh' air dheireadh air cha chumadh i ris. Aig an t-siubhal sin air aghaidh dha cha do leig e'n spéid a fhaoghaid gus an do bhuail e 'bhas ri crann aig pàilis Righ Lochlainn an oidhche sin.

Bha pàilis Righ Lochlainn air a gleidheadh le seachd gèairrd. Bhuail an Gille Mòr aig a' chéud ghèarrd, agus dh' fheòraich a' cheud ghèarrd d' e Cia as a bha e, no ceana 'bha e dol? Fhreagair e gu 'm bu ghill' e a thàinig o Fhionn, Righ na' Féinne, air ghnothùch gu Righ Lochlainn. Chaidh fios a dh' ionnsaidh an Righ gu 'n robh a' leithid do dhuin' aig an dorus.

Dh' fheòraich an Righ an robh duine leis ach e féin.  Thubhairt an Gille-freasdail nach robh.   An sin dh' iarr an Righ a leigeil a 's tigh.   Chaidh a' chéud ghèarrd fhosgladh dha agus fhuair e s' tigh, agus mar sin gach gèarrd gus an d' fhuair e tromh na seachd gèairrd.

Chaidh a thabhairt a 's tigh do 'n àite far an robh an Righ, agus dh' iarr an Righ air suidh' a dheanamh.   Rinn an Gille Mòr suidhe, oir bha e sgìth an déigh an astair a rinn e.   Thug e sùil air feadh an t-seòmair, agus thug e 'n aire do chupa cho briadh' agus a chunnaic e riamh 'n a sheasamh air bòrd.  Thubhairt e ri Righ Lochlainn, " Is briadh' an soitheach a th' agad an sin."   Thubhairt an Righ gu 'm b' e sin a bh' ann, agus cupa buadhach cuideachd.   Dh' fheòraich an Gille Mòr gu dé na buadhan a bh' air ?   Fhreagair an Righ nach robh làn a dh' òrduicheadh e 'bhi ann nach bitheadh ann air ball.  Smaointich an Gille Mòr agus e pàiteach an déigh an astair a rinn e gu 'm bu mhath a làn de dh' uisg' air a' bhòrd.   An sin dh' éirich e agus rug e air a' chupa, agus dh' òl e na bh' ann.  Thug e 'n sin 'aghaidh air an dorus ; agus ma dh' iarr e fosgladh a 's tigh cha d' iarr e fosgladh a mach, oir léum e thar nan seachd gèairrd agus an cup' aige leis.

An sin thog e 'chochaill-chraicinn féin air, agus shìn e as air an t-sligh' air an d' thàinig e ; agus gaoth luath a' Mhàirt a bh' air thoiseach air bheireadh e oirre, agus gaoth luath a' Mhàirt a bh' air dheireadh air cha chumadh i ris.   Air an t-siubhal sin air aghaidh dha cha do leig e spéid a fhaoghaid gus an do bhuail e 'bhas ri crann aig bruth Fhinn air an oidhche sin.

Chaidh e 's tigh agus shìn e 'n cupa do Fhionn.   " Cha robh thu fada," thubhairt Fionn.   " Nach d' innis mise dhuit mu 'n d' fhalbh thu gu 'n tachradh iad ort a' tighinn leis ?" Fhreagair an Gille Mòr, " Tha fhios agus cinnt agad, Fhinn, nach do thachair iad orm a' tighinn leis.   Ach ràinig mise Lochlann, agus fhuair mi 'n cupa 'm pàilis an Righ, agus rinn mi 'n t-astar air ais agus air aghaidh."

" Uist ! a ghlagaire," thubhairt Conan 'us e 'freagairt.   " Tha feadhainn anns an Fhéinn a ruitheas cho math riut-sa air sliabh beinne no air srath glinne, agus cha deanadh iad an t-astar 'an dùbladh na h-ùin' a tha thusa 'g ràdh anns an d' rinn thu e.

Ach thig a ghearradh léum còmhla rium-sa gu ruig an Lochan Uain' aig bun Beinn Éudain, agus aithnichidh mis' an d' rinn thu 'n t-astar." "Ù! 'Chonain, is féumaiche mis' air biadh agus lochdan cadail fhaotainn na falbh a ghearradh léum còmhla riut-sa." "Mur téid thu ann cha chreid sinn gu 'n d' rinn thu 'n t-astar," arsa Conan.

Dh' éirich an Gille Mòr agus dh' fhalbh e leis, agus ràinig iad an Lochan Uaine. Dh' iarr Conan air a' Ghille Mhòr léum a ghearradh thar an Lochain. "Is tusa 'thug mise an so agus tha mise sgìth,"ars' an Gille Mòr; "uime sin gearr féin a' chéud léum." Ghabh Conan roid, agus ghearr e léum, ach chaidh e fodha gu ruig ubhal na dà chruachain anns a' bhoga duillich air taobh eile 'n Lochain. Ghearr an Gille Mòr a léum gun roid idir, agus chaidh e thar ceann Chonain air a' chruaidh air taobh eil' an Lochain. Léum e 'n sin air ais e 'n comhair a chùil agus air aghaidh an comhair a bheòil mu 'n d' fhuair Conan a leth deiridh as an dìg.

Dar fhuair Conan a chasan air a chruaidh thubhairt e gu 'n d' fhàilnich am freumh fo 'bhuinn; agus gu 'n deach e fodha! "Ach falbh a chuir réis comhla rium-sa gu mullach Beinn Éudain, agus aithnichidh mise ma rinn thu 'n t-astar." "A Chonain, is féumaiche mis' air lochdan cadail na air dol a chur réis còmhla riut-sa gu mullach Beinn Éudain." Ach co dhiù dh' fhalbh e. Air sith no dhà chaidh an Gille Mòr seachad air Conan, agus cha tug e sùil tuillidh as a dhéigh gus an robh e air mullach na Beinne. Shìn e 'n sin e féin air toman gorm, agus chaidil e.

Cha robh fhios aige gu dé cho fada 'sa chaidil e, ach b' e àinich Chonain a' dìreadh na Beinne 'dhùisg e. Ghrad léum e air a bhuinn agus thubhairt e, "An d' rinn mi 'n t-astar a nis, a Chonain?" "Thig a ghleachd còmhla riumsa, agus aithnichidh mis' an d' rinn thu an t-astar." Chaidh iad 'an dromannan a chéile. Dh' iarr Conan air a' Ghille Mhòr a char a chur. "Cuir thusa do char an toiseach, a Chonain; oir is tu 'dh' iarr tòiseachadh." Dh' fheuch Conan a char a chur, ach cha d' thug e glidneachadh air a' Ghille Mhòr. An sin lùb an Gille Mòr e féin thairis, agus le chudrom leag e Conan, agus cheangail e a thrì caoil còmhla le éill ioscaide.

An so ghabh an Gille Mòr e 'na thàmailt gu 'n robh an aon duine 'bu leibidich' a bh' anns an Fhéinn ri tàir agus ri munganachd air, agus thug e bòid nach tilleadh e ri Fionn tuillidh.  Dh' fhalbh e, agus dh' fhàg e Conan ceangailt' air mullach na Beinne.

Bha 'n oidhch' a' tighinn, agus bha Fionn a' gabhail ioghnaidh nach robh 'n dithis a dh' fhalbh a' tighinn.  Mu dheireadh bhuail an t-eagal e gu 'n do mharbh an Gille Mòr Conan, agus uime sin thubhairt e r' a dhaoine gu 'm féumadh iad falbh g' an iarraidh.  Mu 'n d' éirich grian air an ath mhadainn rinn e 'dhaoine 'n am buidhnibh, agus chuir e buidheann do gach oisinn de 'n Bheinn, agus dh' iarr e orra siubhal gus an coinnicheadh iad uil' air mullach na Beinne.  Mu fheasgar an latha choinnich iad a chéile, agus fhuair iad Conan ceangailt' air a thrì chaoil ann an aon éill.

Dh' iarr Fionn air aon d' a dhaoine dol a null agus Conan fhuasgladh.  Dh' fhalbh Oscar, agus thug e ùine mhòr a' feuchainn ri sin a dheanamh, ach an àite gach snaim a dh' fhosgladh e rachadh seachd snaimean eil' air an éill.  Mu dheireadh thubhairt e ri Fionn, "Cha-n urrainn mis' an iall so fhosgladh !"  An sin léum Goll a null, agus e 'smaointeachadh gu 'n deanadh esan ni' b' fhearr.  Thòisich e air fosgladh na h-éille, ach mar thachair do dh' Oscar dh' fhairslich i air.  Mur robh i ni' bu teinne dar sguir e dh' i cha robh i dad ni 'bu laise.  Mu dheireadh thog e a cheann le féirg agus thubhairt e, "Cha-n 'eil duine 's an Fhéinn a 's urrainn Conan fhuasgladh."

Ghabh Fionn a nis eagal gu 'm bitheadh Conan marbh mu 'm faigheadh iad fhuasgladh.  Ach chuimhnich e air a dhéud-fios, agus air dha a mhèur a chur fodha fhuair e mach nach robh duin' air an t-saoghal a b' urrainn Conan fhuasgladh ach Gobhainn a' Ghlinne Ghil air neò am fear a cheangail e.  An sin chuir e Goll agus Oscar air falbh a dh' innseadh do 'n Ghobhainn mar thachair do Chonan.

Ràinig iad an Gobhainn agus dh' innis iad da 'n t-saothair air an robh iad.  Thubhairt an Gobhainn riù iad a chruinn-neachadh a h-uile ceithir-chasach a bha eadar cùl Beinn Éudainn agus bràigh a' Ghlinne Ghil, agus an cur seachad air dorus na ceàrdaich aige-san.  "Agus" (ars' e) "ma thig mis' an sin a mach le sìth is math mo shìth, ach ma thig mi mach le feirg is olc m' fhearg."

An sin thill Oscar agus Goll air an ais a dh' ionnsaidh Fhinn, agus dh' innis iad da ciod a thubhairt an Gobhainn riù. Thubhairt Fionn gu 'm féumadh an fhaoghaid a bhi air a gluasad. Chaidh an fhaoghaid a ghluasad, agus b' i sin Faoghaid Mhòr a' Ghlinne Ghil. O'n ghluaiseadh a' chéud fhaoghaid cha robh riamh roimh' a leithid do bheathaichean ceithir-chasach cruinn agus a bh' ann air an là sin. An sin chuir iad seachad iad air dorus na ceàrdaich. Thàinig an Gobhainn a mach agus dh' fheòraich e dhiù gu dé 'bha sud ? Fhreagair iad gu 'n robh a h-uile ceithir-chasach eadar cùl Beinn Éudainn, agus bràigh a' Ghlinne Ghil mar dh' iarr e. Thubhairt an Gobhainn, "Rinn sibh glé mhath, ach tilleadh gach créutair dhiù sin air an ais do 'n àit' as an d' thug sibh iad, agus falbhaidh mis' an sin a dh' fhuasgladh Chonain." Rinn iad sin, agus dh' fhalbh an Gobhainn gu mullach Beinn Éudainn, agus dh' fhuasgail e Conan.

An uair a fhuair Conan fuasgailte bha tàmailt cho mòr air airson mar dh' éirich dha, agus gu 'n do tharrainn e leis a' Bheinn cho luath agus a b' urrainn e, agus nach d' thug e sùil as a dhéigh gus an deachaidh e mach air an loch gu ruig an amhaich. As a sin cha d' thigeadh e airson Fhinn no airson duin' a bh' anns an Fhéinn. Ach bha 'n làn a' dìreadh aig an àm, agus an uair a thòisich an t-uisg' air dol 'n a bhéul smaointich e gu 'm b' fhearr dha dol air tìr, agus falbh dhachaidh an déigh chàich.

Air feasgar àraidh an déigh sin, an uair a bha Fionn agus a dhaoin' a' tighinn dachaidh as a' Bheinn-Sheilg chunnaic iad Gille 'tighinn 'n an coinneamh. Ghabh e fàr an robh Fionn, agus thubhairt e ris gu 'n robh esan air a chur o Bhanrigh na Ruaidh gu Fionn, Righ na Féinne, agus gu 'n robh e 'cur mar chroisean agus mar gheasan agus mar sheachd buaraichean sìthde siùbhle 's seacharain air nach stadadh e agus nach gabhadh e fois gus an ruigeadh e 'n t-àit' aig Ban righ na Ruaidh. Air dha so a ràdh thionndaigh e cùl a chinn riù, agus dh' fhalbh e, agus cha robh an ath shealladh aca dh' e.

Sheall an Fhéinn air a chéile, oir smaointich iad gu 'n robh

droch rud ri éirigh do Fhionn, a chionn nach d' iarradh air
duine falbh ach air féin. Thubhairt iad ris gu 'n robh iad
duilich gu 'n robh e falbh 'n a ònar agus gun fhios aca c' uin'
a thigeadh e no c' àit' an rachadh iad g' a iarraidh. Ach
thubhairt Fionn riù gun iad a bhi 'n iomagain m' a thighinn gu
ceann là agus bliadhna.

As an t-seasamh sin dh' fhalbh e le chuid 'armachd air.
Shiubhail e air aghaidh cian fhada agus làn fhada thar bheann 'us
ghleann 'us mhullaichean, agus stad cha deachaidh air a chois gus
an d' thàinig e 'm fradhare Innse Uaine. An sin chunnaic e
duine agus e 'dol a thogail eallach luachrach air a mhuin. 'N uair
'chunnaic e 'n duin' a tilgeil na h-eallaich thar a ghualainn smaointich e gu'm b'e Gille nan Cochla-Craicinn a bh'ann. Thòisich
e air falach-talmhainn a dheanamh air gus an d'fhuair e dlùth dha.
An sin leig e ris e féin da, agus an uair a choimhead am fear
a bh' ann air anns an aodann dh' aithnich e gu 'm b' e Gille
nan Cochla-Craicinn a bh' aige. Léum e le sùrdaig chabhaig
fàr an robh e, agus rug e air eadar a dhà laimh, agus thubhairt
e, "A ghràidh a dh' fhir an t-saoghail! an tu 'th' ann?" Fhreagair an Gille Mòr agus thubhairt e, "Na 'm bu mhi do ghràdh
a dh' fhir an t-saoghail cha bhitheadh an aon duine cho leibid-
each agus a bh' agad anns an Fhéinn ri munganachd agus ri
bùirt mhagaidh orm." "Mata," thubhairt Fionn, "bha mise
glé dhuilich, ach cha robh comas agam air. Bha eagal orm gu
'n éireadh na daoin' ann am aghaidh, agus gu 'n rachadh iad
air aimhreith; uime sin leig mi le Conan a bhi na bheachd
féin. Ach bha fhios agam-sa gu 'n d' rinn thu 'n t-astar, agus
bithidh sinn 'n ar càirdean d' a chéile cho math 's a bha sinn
roimhe. An téid thu air an turus bheag so fathast leam?"
"Mata," thubhairt an Gille Mòr, "cha-n 'eil fhios agam-sa.
Seall a sios anns a' ghlaic ud fodhainn, agus chi thu mo
mhàthair air a dà ghlùn a' buain luachrach agus car d' a cìch
dheis thar a gualainn chèarr. Ma gheibh thu greim air ceann
na cìche na leig as e gus am faigh thu 'chéud achain uaipe."

Dh' fhalbh Fionn greis air a mhàgan agus greis eile 'g a
shlaodadh féin air a bhroinn gus an d' fhuair e 'n astar léum
a thabhairt. An sin thug e léum, agus fhuair e greim air ceann
na cìche. Ghlaodh Bean Innse Uaine cò bha 'n sin? Fhreag-

air esan gu 'n robh Fionn, Righ na Féinne 'g iarraidh a' chéud
achain oirre. Thubhairt ise gu dé 'n achain a shireadh e nach
faigheadh e. Thubhairt esan, "Leig le d' mhac dol air an
aon turus bheag so fathast leam." Thubhairt a' Bhean, "Nan
robh fhios agam-sa gu 'm b' e sin a bha thu 'g iarraidh cha-n
fhaigheadh tu e ged bheireadh tu 'chìoch o 'n bhroilleach agam,
ach o 'n thubhairt mi e gheibh thu e. Ach bithidh aon
ghealladh agam uait mu 'm falbh thu, agus is e sin gu 'n toir
thu dhachaidh do m' ionnsaidh e féin agus na thuiteas cuide
ris." "Tha mi 'n dòchas nach bi a 'chùis mar sin, agus gu 'n
tig e dhachaidh slàn." "Ma thig cha mhath a dh' éireas
dhuit-sa, Fhinn. Ach cò dhiù bitheadh a falbh air ar turus."

An sin dh' fhalbh Fionn agus an Gille Mòr air an turus, a'
dìreadh chnoc 'us a' tearnadh ghlac, a' siubhal thar bheann 'us
ghleann 'us thulaichean, gus an robh glòmain na h-oidhch' a
tighinn orra. Bha iad a' fàs sgìth agus bha toil aca àit-éiginn a
ruigheachd far am faigheadh iad fois a ghabhail. Cha robh
iad ach goirid a' siubhal an déigh sin 'n uair a chunnaic iad
àit anabarrach briadh' air thoiseach orra le tighean mòra
briadha air an togail air dailtean mòra gorma. Thubhairt
Fionn ris a' Ghille Mhòr, "Gabhadh mid misneach, oir cha-n
'eil sinn fada bho thighean." Goirid an déigh sin ràinig iad an
t-àit e.

Chunnaic Fionn duin' a' tighinn 'n an coinneamh, agus dh'
aithnich e gu 'm b' e a' cheart Ghille 'thàinig leis an fhios g' a
ionnsaidh a bh' ann. Dh' fheòraich e dh' e gu dé 'm féum a
bh' aig' air a nis? Fhreagair an Gille agus thubhairt e gu 'n
robh dà thigh mhòr m' a choinneamh, aon diù le ursannan òir
agus dorsan òir air, agus an aon eile le ursannan airgid agus
dorsan airgid air, gu 'n robh e ri 'roghainn diù a ghabhail gu
fuireachd ann, agus an uair a rachadh e 's tigh gu 'm faiceadh
e gu dé 'bh' aige ri 'dheanamh ann. Air do 'n Ghille so a ràdh
thionndaidh e air falbh uapa agus dh' fhàg e iad far an robh iad
'n an seasamh.

Choimhead Fionn 'an aodann a' Ghille Mhòir, agus thubhairt
e ris, "Cia am fear de na tighean so a ghabhas sinn gu fuireachd ann?" Thubhairt an Gille Mòr, "Bithidh am fear a
's urramaich' againn : gabhaidh sinn fear nan dorsan òir."

Ghabh iad a null a dh' ionnsaidh an doruis.   Rug an Gille
Mòr air a' chrann, agus dh' fhosgail e 'n dorus.   An sin chaidh
iad a 's tigh.   'N uair a choimhead iad bha seallamh mòr air
thoiseach orra, ach cha do smaointich an Gille Mòr dad d' e.
Bha ochd agus ochd fichead déug amhasg 'n an seasamh air an
ùrlar.   'N uair a fhuair iad Fionn agus an Gille Mòr air taobh a
's tigh an doruis léum iad, agus dhùin iad e ; agus chuir iad ochd
agus ochd fichead déug crann air.   Dh' fhalbh an Gille Mòr
agus chuir e aon chrann mòr air, agus leis cho teann agus a
chuir e 'n crann air thuit a h-uile crann a chuir iadsan air dheth.
An sin rinn na h-Amhaisg ochd agus ochd fichead déug gàire,
agus rinn an Gille Mòr aon ghlag mòr gàire, agus bhodhair e na
rinn iadsan uile.   An sin thubhairt na h-Amhaisg, " Gu dé e fàth
do ghàire, 'fhir bhig ?"   Dh' fheòraich an Gille Mòr, " Gu dé e
fàth bhur gàire féin, a dhaoine mòra gu léir ?"   Thubhairt
iadsan, " Is e fàth ar gàire-ne gur bòidheach an ceann gaganach
buidh' a th' ort gu bhi 'n a bhall iomaineach air an tràigh ud a
mach am màireach."   " Mata," thubhairt an Gille Mòr, " is e
fàth mo ghàire-sa gu 'in beir mi air an fhear a 's mò ceann
agus a 's caoile casan agaibh, agus gu 'n spad mi càch uile
leis."   An sin chunnaic e fear agus ceann mòr air, agus rug e
air chaol dà chois' air, agus thòisich e anns an dara ceann 'g an
spadadh, agus cha do stad e gus an deachaidh e mach aig
a' cheann eile dhiù.   'N uair 'bha e deas cha robh aig' ach
na bha 'n a dhà dhòrn de na casaibh.

Chuir e féin agus Fionn a mach na cuirp agus rinn iad trì
dùin diù aig an dorus.   Dhùin iad a' sin an dorus, agus rinn
iad deas biadh, oir bha pailteas dh' e 's tigh.

An déigh dhoibh am biadh a ghabhail dh' fheòraich an
Gille Mòr de Fhionn, " Cia dhiù a chaidleas tu no 'dh' fhaireas
tu 'n dorus ?"   Fhreagair Fionn, " Caidil thusa agus fairidh
mis' an dorus."   Agus mar sin rinn iad.   Ach mu 'n do
chaidil an Gille Mòr dh' fheòraich Fionn d' e, " Ciod leis an
dùisg mi thu ma thig éiginn orm anns an dorus ?"   " Buail an
carragh cloiche 'tha cùl an téin' orm ann an carraig an uchd,
air neò thoir lùd d' òrdaig' a mullach mo chinn leis a' bhiodaig."   " Ro cheart," thubhairt Fionn, " caidil air d' aghaidh."

Bha Fionn a' faireadh an doruis, ach ré ùin' fhada cha robh

e 'faireachadh dad a' tighinn. Mu bhristeadh na fàire dh'
fhairich e còmhradh dheich céud a' tighinn chum an doruis.
Thog e 'n carragh cloiche, agus bhuail e 'n Gille Mòr leis
anns an uchd. Ghrad léum an Gille Mòr air a chois, agus dh'
fheòraich e de Fhionn gu dé a dh' fhairich e ? "Tha còmhradh
dheich céud anns an dorus," thubhairt Fionn. "Tha sin
ceart fathast," ars' an Gille Mòr, "leig thusa 'mach mise."

Chaidh an Gille Mòr a mach 'n an coinneamh, thòisich e 's
an dara ceann diù, thug e ruathar fòpa 's tharta, agus cha d' fhàg
e duin' a dh' innseadh an tuairisgéil beò dhiù ach aon fhear
air leth-shùil, air leth chluais, air leth laimh 'us air leth chois,
agus leig e 'shiubhal dha. An sin thrus e féin agus Fionn na
cuirp, agus chuir iad anns na trì dùin iad còmhla ri càch. An
sin chaidh iad a 's tigh, agus dh' fheith iad gus an d' thàinig
an ath oidhche.

An déigh na suipearach dh' fheòraich an Gille Mòr de
Fhionn, "Co ac' a chaidleas tu, n' a dh' fhaireas tu 'nochd ?"
Thubhairt Fionn, "Caidil thusa agus fairidh mise." Chaidh an
Gille Mòr a chadal, agus bha Fionn a' faireadh an doruis.
Tacan romh éiridh na gréine dh' fhairich Fionn còmhradh dhà
mhile 'tighinn, airneò Mac Righ an t-Soluis 'n a ònar. Léum
e, agus thug e lèud aghaidh òrdaig' a mullach cinn a' Ghille
Mhòir leis a' bhiodaig. Ghrad léum an Gille Mòr air a
bhuinn, agus dh' fheòraich e de Fhionn gu dé a dh' fhairich
e? Fhreagair Fionn, "Tha còmhradh dhà mhile 's an dorus,
airneò Mac Righ an t-Soluis 'n a Ònar." "Ù! mata, tha
mise creidsinn gu 'm féum thusa 'bhi cho math 's do ghealladh do m' mhàthair," ars' an Gille Mòr. "Ach leig thusa
mach mise." Dh' fhosgail Fionn an dorus, chaidh an Gille
Mòr a mach, agus b' e Mac Righ an t-Soluis a bha roimhe.

An sin chaidh an dà churaidh 'an dromannan a chéile, agus
ghleachd iad o éirigh gu ruig laidhe gréine, ach cha do leag an
dara fear am fear eile, agus cha do labhair an dara fear ris an
fhear eile ré na h-ùine. Leig iad as a chéile, agus ghabh gach
fear dhiù a rathad féin. Moch air an ath mhadainn, romh
éirigh na gréine, chaidh an Gille Mòr a mach, agus choinnich
a chompanach e. Ghleac iad o éirigh gu laidhe gréine, ach
cha do leag an dara fear am fear eile, agus cha do labhair an

dara fear ris an fhear eile.  Leig iad as a chéile, agus ghabh gach aon diù a rathad féin.  An treas là choinnich na laoich, agus chaidh iad 'an dromannan a chéile.  Ghleac iad ré 'n là gu dorchadh nan tràth, agus thuit an dithis taobh ri taobh fuar marbh air a bhlàr.

Bha Fionn fuathasach duilich airson a' Ghille Mhòir.  Ach chuimhnich e air a ghealladh da mhàthair agus thubhairt e ris féin gu 'm féumadh e 'bhi air a choimh-ghealladh.  Thug e mach am brat sìod' a bha thairis orra fàr an robh iad 'n an cadal, rol e mu 'n cuairt air an dà chorp e, agus thug e leis air a mhuin iad.  Tharrainn e le céum cruaidh thar bheann 'us ghleann 'us thulaichean, a' dìreadh chnoc 'us a' tèarnadh ghlac, agus stad no tàmh cha d' rinn e gus an d' ràinig e tigh Innse Uaine.

Choinnich Màthair a' Ghille Mhòir e aig an dorus, agus thubhairt i ris, "An d' thàinig thu?"  Fhreagair Fionn gu 'n d' thàinig ach nach b' ann mar bu mhath leis.  Thubhairt ise ris, "An d' rinn thu mar dh' iarr mis' ort?"  Thubhairt Fionn, "Rinn, ach is duilich leam gu 'n robh e agam r' a dheanamh."  Thubhairt ise, "Tha na h-uile ni ceart.  Thig a 's tigh."  Chaidh Fionn a 's tigh, agus leig e 'n eallach air an ùrlar.  Dh' fhuasgail e 'm brat, agus bha 'n dà ghille mar thuit iad glaist' 'an làmhan a chéile.

An uair a chunnaic Bean Innse Uaine an dà ghile rinn i fèith-ghàire, agus thubhairt i, "A ghràidh Fhinn, is math dhomh-sa gu 'n deachaidh tu air an turus so."  Dh' fhalbh i null do chùil, agus thog i leac a bh' air an ùrlar agus thug i mach soitheach beag iocshlaint a bh' aice 'n sin.  Chuir i 'n dà ghille béul ri béul, aghaidh ri aghaidh, glùn ri glùn, òrdag ri ordaig, agus shuaith i 'n iocshlaint ri bonnaibh an cas, ri mullach an cinn, agus ri h-uile crioman a bha beanachd r' a chéile d' an craicionn.  Dh' éirich an dà ghill' air an ùrlar a' pògadh a chéile.

"'Nis, Fhinn," thubhairt i, "sin agad mo dhà mhac-sa.  Chaidh am fear so 'ghoid uam 'n a naoidhean, agus bha e 'g am dhìth gus a so.  Ach o 'n rinn thusa mar dh' iarr mis' ort, is e do bheatha fuireachd an so cho fad' agus a thogras thu."

Bha iad cho sunntach' an tigh Innse Uaine, 'us gu 'n deachaidh an ùine seachad gun fhios doibh.  Air oidhch' àraidh thubhairt Bean Innse Uaine ri Fionn, " Bithidh là 's bliadhn' am màireach o 'n dh' fhàg thusa 'n Fhéinn, agus tha iad an déigh dùil a thabhairt dìot.    Am fear aca nach' eil a' géurachadh a chlaidheimh tha e a rinneadh a shleagha 'nochd airson falbh g' ad iarraidh.   Dean deas airson falbh am màireach, agus leigidh mise mo mhac leat.   Oir ma ruigeas tu leat fhéin, ni iad a' leithid de dh' othail riut 'us gu 'm mùch agus gu 'm marbh iad thu.   Ach an uair a ruigeas sibh theid mo mhac-sa 's tigh air thoiseach ort, agus their e riutha ma gheallas iad dhasan gu 'n éirich fear an déigh fir aca a chur fàilte shocrach, chiallach ort, gu 'n d' thoir esan thu slàn fallainn dhachaidh g' an ionnsaidh."

Dh' aontaich Fionn ri so le uile chridhe, agus dh' fhalbh e féin agus an Gille Mòr air an turus dhachaidh air madainn an ath latha.   Bha astar mòr aca ri 'dhol, ach cha robh iad fada 'g a dheanamh.

An uair a ràinig iad Talla Fhinn chaidh an Gille Mòr a 's tigh air thoiseach, agus mar thubhairt a mhàthair b' fhìor. Bha gach fear a' cur an òrdugh a chlaidheimh agus a shleagha. Dh' fheòraich an Gille Mòr dhiù gu dé a bha iad a' deanamh ? Dh' innis iad sin da, 'am briathran goirid.   An sin thubhairt an Gille Mòr riù a' ni a dh' iarr a mhàthair air a ràdh.   Dh' aontaich iad gu toileach sin a dheanamh.   Ghlaoth e' n sin air Fionn tighinn a 's tigh.   Thàinig Fionn, agus dh' éirich fear an déigh fir mar gheall iad.   Fhuair iad an Righ saoghalt' air ais aon uair eile.   Thill an Gille Mòr dhachaidh, agus mar do chaochail e bho sin tha e beò fhathast.

---

# IV.

## HOW FINN WAS IN THE HOUSE OF BLAR-BUIE (YELLOW-FIELD),

### WITHOUT THE POWER OF RISING UP OR OF LYING DOWN.

A DAY Finn and his men were in the Hunting-hill they had done a great deal of travelling before they fell in with the deer, but before the close of the day had arrived they killed a good number of them. They then sat down to rest themselves, and consult each other to see what direction they should take next day.

While they were conversing, Finn gave a look down into the glen which was beneath them, and saw the appearance of a strong hero making straight towards them. He said, "The appearance of a stranger is coming towards us here." Conan replied, "If he is coming without business, he will not leave without business." But before they had much more conversation about him the young hero was standing before them.

He gave Finn the salutation of the day, and Finn saluted him courteously.

Finn then asked of him whence he came, or what business had he yonder. He said, "I am a servant who has travelled far long and full long seeking a master, and I will not go further until you refuse me." "Well," said Finn, "I want a servant, and if we agree about the reward I do not care though I engage thee." "That would not be my advice to thee," said Conan. "I thought thou didst get enough of those wandering lads already."  " Silence, rascal !" said the Lad ; "often has thy loquacity put thy head in trouble, and I am deceived if thou shalt not experience some trouble on account of the talk of this day."  " Never mind," said Finn, "for thy appearance will answer for thee, at any rate.  What is thy reward to the end of a day and year?"  "That you and your men will go on invitation with me to a feast and night's entertainment when my time will be out," said the Lad.  When Finn heard that his men were to go with him he took courage that no evil thing could befall them being together ; and therefore he said to the Lad that he would get his reward.

When the time had passed, Finn and his men were in a house of conference considering which of them should go after the Lad, for he had a very swift appearance. Finn said, "We will let Caoilte (Slender) after him, and I do not believe but that he will keep sight of him.  Cuchulin will go after Caoilte, and we will follow them."  And so they did.

The Big Lad set off bare-headed, bare-footed, without strength for battle or for sane action, from gap to height, and from height to glen, and through glen to strath.  Caoilte (Slender) went after him, and when the Big Lad would be going out of sight on the first gap Caoilte would be coming in sight on the next ridge.  Cuchulin was in the same distance to Caoilte, and all the men to Cuchulin.  They kept in that order till they reached Blar-buie (or Yellow-field).

The Big Lad then stood till the last man of the Fein came on.  Then he took his way over to a large, fine house, which stood opposite him.  He opened the door of the house, and invited them to go in and be seated.

Finn went in first, and his men followed him.  All of them got seats against the walls except Conan.  He was behind, and because all the seats were full before he arrived he had no choice but to drop down and stretch himself on the hearthstone. They were so tired after the journey which they had made that they were at first contented with the seats alone. But when they had a rest they began to grow impatient, because the feast was not coming. Finn at last told one of his men to go out and try if he could see any person coming with food to them. One or two attempted to rise from their seats, but could not. Their haunches stuck to the seats, the soles of their feet to the floor, and their backs to the walls. Each one of them then looked at his neighbour. Conan cried from the hearth-stone to which his back and hair were clinging, "Did I not tell thee in good time what would happen to thee with thy wandering lads?" Finn spake not a word, because he was in great anxiety about the death-strait in which they were. But he remembered his knowledge set of teeth, and having put his finger under it, discovered that there was nothing that would release them from the place in which they were but the blood of the three sons of the King of Insh Tilly filtered through silver rings into cups of gold.

He did not know who would get the blood for him, but he remembered that Lohary (*Laoghaire*), Son of the King of Hunts (*Righ nan Sealg*), and Oscar were that day absent from the company. He had the Wooden Crier (or whistle), which he never blew except when he happened to be in some death-strait or other. But when he would play on it, its sound would pass through the seven borders of the world, and to the extremity of the Uttermost World. And he knew that when Lohary and Oscar would hear the sound they would come from any quarter in which they would be.

He blew the Wooden Crier (whistle) three times, and before the sun rose next day Oscar was crying outside the wall, "Art thou here, Finn?" "Who is there?" said Finn, inside the house. "Thou art changed indeed when thou wouldst not know my voice while there is only the breadth of a house wall between us.   I, Oscar, am here, and Lohary is with me.   What have we now to do?"

Finn told them the situation and peril in which they were, and that nothing could release them from it but the blood of the three Sons of the King of Insh Tilly filtered through rings of silver into cups of gold. " Where shall we watch for the purpose of finding them?" said Oscar.   Finn said, " Thou shalt watch well the ford-mouth of the river over yonder, at the going down of the sun.   But it is yet early in the day.   See if you can find food for us, for we are hungry.   But, Oscar, remember to take thy Gaper (dart) with thee."

Oscar and Lohary set their faces in the direction of the Big House which was over against them.   When they arrived at the house the people residing there were making ready the dinner.   Lohary said to Oscar, " Take thou the lead."   Oscar took the lead, and was keeping his eye in every corner to see what he might behold.   When he reached the cooking-place he looked in, and saw the appearance of a fierce hero lifting a quarter of a deer out of a caldron.   He said to Lohary, " Follow me, and take the food with thee, and I will face the man."   He went in, but no man was now to be seen. But a look he gave he saw a large buzzard with out-spread wings ready to pounce down on his head.   He drew his Gaper, and darted it at the buzzard.   He broke its wing off, and the buzzard itself fell on the floor, and he saw not another sight of it.   He and Lohary now made the house their own, and took with them every bit of food of which they got hold.

They reached the house where Finn and his men were. They made a hole on the wall of the house, and threw in piece after piece for every man till all the men who were there got something, but Conan.   He lay on his back on the hearth-stone, having his hands and feet together with his back bound to the flag-stone, so that they could not give him a bit except what they let down through the roof of the house, and which he then seized with his mouth.   In this way he got a morsel or two.

Oscar then asked of Finn what had they to watch at the ford-mouth of the river besides the three Sons of the King of Insh Tilly.   "A great host will accompany them," said Finn.   "And how shall we know the three Sons of the King of Insh Tilly from any other three men of the host ?"   "They will walk apart from the host on the right hand, and have on them green apparel."   "We will know them now," said Oscar.

Then Oscar and Lohary went away to find the rings and cups for filtering and holding the blood.   After they had found them they went to watch at the ford-mouth.   At the going down of the sun they heard a loud sound coming.   Oscar looked in the direction whence he heard the sound, and saw a great host coming in sight.   He now called on Lohary to be ready.   Lohary said, "We will go ashore out of the water, and meet them on dry land."   And so they did.

When the great host came near they cried, "Who are the two tall, uncomely Lubbers who are standing there at mouth of ford and beginning of night ?   Whoever they are it is time for them to be getting afraid."   Oscar cried, " A third of your fear be on yourselves, and a small third of it be on us."   "You will then wait to your hurt," said the great host.   Then they went to meet each other, but Oscar and Lohary assailed them violently under them and over them till they left not a man of them alive to tell the tale.

They turned back.   Next morning they told Finn what befell them, but that they saw not the King's Sons.   "Where shall we watch next night?" said Oscar.   " Watch well the ford-mouth of the river to-night yet," said Finn.   "But meantime get us food, for we are hungry. And remember to take with thee thy three-edged blade and thy shield to-day."

The two heroes reached the Big House. Oscar was more guarded this day, because he knew not what might meet him. When he got a look of the Cooking-house he saw inside a dreadfully big man, having four hands, lifting the flesh out of the caldron. He went in, but no man was now to be seen. He looked about the place, and saw a large eagle going to throw at him an egg which she held in her talon. He lifted his shield between him and the egg, but the blow sent him on one knee beside the caldron. He saw that he could not be ready with his blade before the eagle would be at him ; he therefore lifted the caldron of soup which was on the floor, and poured it on her head. She gave a terrible shriek and went through the wall, and he had not a second look of her.

Then he and Lohary went away with the food, and succeeded in giving a share to every man as on the day before. But poor Conan's share was smaller.

When the time came they went away to the ford-mouth, and advanced further on the other side of the river than they went on the previous night. Shortly after they arrived they saw a very large host coming towards them. When they came near they cried, "Who were the two tall, uncomely Lubbers who were standing yonder above the ford-mouth of the river in the evening ? Whoever they are, it is . time for them to be getting afraid." "Two-thirds of your fear be on yourselves, and a little third of it be on us," said Oscar. Then they assailed them on each side until they went out on the opposite side, and left not a man of them alive to tell the tale.

They turned back and told Finn that the King's children did not come that night yet. Finn told them that they were to get them food that day again. "But,

Oscar, remember thy spear and shield, and if thy spear will taste the blood of the Winged Dragon of Sheil, the King of Insh Tilly shall be without a son to-night."

They went away, and turned their faces towards the Big House. Oscar took the lead, as he was accustomed to do. He was keeping his eye pretty sharply before him to see who would be in the Cooking-house this day. When he got a look of it he beheld a handsome, strong man with two heads and four hands lifting the flesh out of the caldron. He said to himself that it was time for him to be ready. When he entered no man was to be seen ; but a large Winged Dragon, having two serpent heads on her, was standing on the floor. Oscar whispered to Lohary, " Make thou for the food, and I will make for the Dragon." He then lifted his shield and drew his spear, and with one thrust he sent the spear through one head, and a bit of it through the other head of the Dragon. The Dragon fought terribly, but she was at last growing weak with the loss of blood. Then Oscar drew back the spear for the purpose of thrusting it again into the monster, but as soon as the spear came out of her flesh she went out of his sight, and he had not the next sight of her.

They got the food, and went away with it to their friends. When they arrived, Finn asked Oscar, " Did thy spear taste blood ?" " A cubit length and hand-breadth of it drank greedily," said Oscar. Then they managed to give a share of the food to every man as on the previous days. But Conan's share was (still) smaller.

As soon as the greying of the evening came, Finn said to Oscar, " Let thy rings and cups be with thee to-night."

Then the two heroes went away to the ford-mouth of the river. This evening they advanced farther on the other side of the river than they had yet gone. They were but a short time waiting when they beheld an exceedingly great host coming towards them, and on the right hand the three Sons of the King of Insh Tilly wearing green garments. Oscar asked Lohary, "Whether wilt thou face the three Sons of the King of Insh Tilly or the great host?" Lohary said, "I will face the three Sons of the King of Insh Tilly, and thou shalt face the great host." When they approached each other the great host cried, "Who were the two tall, uncomely Lubbers who were standing above the ford-mouth of the river in the evening? Whoever they are it is time for them to flee to-night." "Three-thirds of your fear be on yourselves, and none at all of it on us," said Oscar.

Then Oscar advanced to meet the great host, and Lohary faced the three Sons of the King. There was a hard fight between Oscar and the host ; but he prevailed over them at last, and left not a man of them alive. Then he went in haste where Lohary was. Lohary had the three Sons of the King on their two knees, and they had Lohary on one knee. When Oscar saw that Lohary had the upper hand, it was not on helping him he directed his attention, but on the blood, for it was pouring out rapidly on the meadow. He began to filter it through the silver rings into the cups of gold, but before all the cups were full the bodies grew so stiff that out of them more would not flow.

The two heroes went away with what they had to the house in which Finn and his men were. When they reached it, Oscar cried that they had come, having the blood with them. "Well," said Finn, "rub it to every bit of you which may touch the house, from the top of your heads to the soles of your feet." They did that, and went in. They began to release the men by rubbing the blood to every bit of them which stuck to the seats, or the wall, or the floor. In that manner they released every man in the house but Conan.  For him they left only the stain which remained on the cups, but that same sufficed to release every bit of him but the back of his head.  The hair and skin stuck to the hearth-stone, and they had no alternative but to leave him bound as he was.

Finn and his men then went home, very happy that they escaped the great peril in which they were.  They had not gone very far when they looked behind them, and saw Conan coming.  They at once stood where they were until he came forward.  There he was without a fibre of hair, or a strip of skin between the top of his head and the back of his neck.  For when he perceived that the rest had gone away and left him behind, he gave his head a great pull and left his skin and hair bound to the hearth-stone.  From that day forth people called him " Bald Conan without hair".

Finn and his men reached their home, and he gave word and oath that he would never again engage wandering lads.

---

## MAR BHA FIONN 'AN TIGH A' BHLÀIR-BHUIDHE

### GUN CHOMAS ÉIRIDH NO LUIDHE.

---

LÀ bha Fionn agus a dhaoin' anns a' Bheinn-Sheilg rinn iad mòran siubhail mu 'n d' amais iad air na féidh, ach mu 'n d' thàinig deireadh an là mharbh iad dòrlach math dhiù. Shuidh iad an sin a sìos a chur seachad an sgìos, agus a chur an comhairle r' a chéile féuch gu dé 'n taobh a ghabhadh iad air an ath latha.

Am feadh a bha iad a' còmhradh, thug Fionn sùil a sìos an gleann a bha fòpa, agus chunnaic e coltas laoich neartmhoir a' deanamh dìreach orra. Thubhairt e, "Tha coltas coigrich a' tighinn oirnn an so." Fhreagair Conan, "Ma tha e 'tighinn gun ghnothuch, cha-n fhalbh e gun ghnothuch." Ach mu 'n d' fhuair iad mòran tuillidh còmhraidh a dheanamh m' a thimchioll, bha 'n laoch òg 'n a sheasamh m' an coinneamh.

Chuir e fàilt an latha air Fionn, agus chuir Fionn fàilt air gu h-aoidheil.

An sin dh' fheòraich Fionn d' e, Cia as a bha e, no gu dé 'n gnothuch a bh' aige 'n sud? Fhreagair e, "Is Gille mi a shiubhail cian fhada 's làn fhada 'g iarraidh maistir, agus cha téid mi ni' s faide gus an diùlt thusa mi." "Mata," arsa Fionn, "tha Gille 'dhìth orm-sa, agus ma chòrdas sinn mu 'n duais tha mi coma ged chuireas mi muinntireas ort." "Cha b' e sin mo chomhairle dhuit," arsa Conan. "Shaoil mi gu 'n d' fhuair thu do leòir de na gillean fuadain sin cheana." "Cuist, a ghàrlaich!" ars' an Gille, "is minic a chuir do luathaire-theanga do cheann ann an dragh, agus tha mise air mo mhealladh mur fairich thu cuid di air tàileas bruidhne 'n latha diugh." "Coma leat," arsa Fionn; "oir ni do choltas an gnothuch dhuit co dhiù. Gu dé e do dhuais gu ceann là 's bliadhna?" "Gun téid thu féin agus a h-uile duin' a th' agad air chuireadh, air chuilm, agus air chuid oidhche còmhla rium-sa 'n uair a bhitheas m' ùine 'mach," ars' an Gille. An uair a chuala Fionn gu 'n robh a chuid daoine ri dol leis, ghabh e misneach nach b' urrainn droch rud éiridh dhoibh, 'us iad còmhla; agus uime sin thubhairt e ris a' Ghille gu 'm faigheadh e a dhuais.

An uair a chaidh an ùine seachad, bha Fionn agus a dhaoine 'n tigh comh-agail cò aca 'rachadh as déigh a' Ghille, oir bha coltas ro astarach air. Thubhairt Fionn, "Leigidh sinn Caoilt' 'as a dhéigh, agus cha chreid mise nach cum e sealladh air. Theid Cuchuilinn an déigh Chaoilte, agus leanaidh sinne iadsan." Agus mar sin rinn iad.

Thionn an Gille Mòr air falbh 'us e ceann-rùisgte, cas-rùisgte, gun spionadh catha no céille, o bhealach gu mullach, agus o mhullach gu gleann, agus o ghleann gu srath. Dh fhalbh Caoilt' as a dhéigh, agus an uair a bhitheadh an Gille Mòr a' dol as an fhradharc air a' chéud bhealach bhitheadh

Caoilte 'tighinn anns an fhradharc air an ath bhearradh.   Bha
Cuchuilinn mar sin do Chaoilte, agus na daoin' uile mar sin
do Chuchuilinn.   Chum iad anns an ordugh sin gus an
d' ràinig iad am Blàr-buidhe.

Sheas an Gille Mòr a' sin gus an d' thàinig an duine mu
dheireadh de 'n Fhéinn air aghaidh.   An sin ghabh e null gu
tigh mòr briadha a bha m' a choinneamh.   Dh' fhosgail e dorus
an tighe, agus dh' iarr e orra 'gabhail a 's tigh agus suidhe
'dheanamh.

Chaidh Fionn a 's tigh an toiseach, agus lean a chuid daoin' e.
Fhuair iad uile àiteachan suidhe ri taobhan a' bhalla, ach Conan.
Bha esan air dheireadh, agus a chionn gu 'n robh a' h-uile
àite-suidhe làn mu 'n d' ràinig e, cha robh aige ach e féin a
leigeil sìos agus a shìneadh air lic-an-teinntein.   Bha iad cho
sgìth, an déigh an astair a rinn iad, 'us gu 'n robh iad toilichte,
'n toiseach, leis na h-àiteachan suidhe amhain.   Ach an uair a
fhuair iad an anail, thòisich iad air fadal a ghabhail nach robh
a' chuilm a' tighinn.   Mu dheireadh, dh' iarr Fionn air aon d' a
dhaoine dol a mach féuch am faiceadh e duin' air bith a'
tighinn le biadh g' an ionnsaidh.   Thug fear no dhà oidheirp
air éirigh bho 'n àiteachan suidhe, ach cha b' urrainn iad. Lean
am màsan ris na h-àitean-suidhe, buinn an cas ris an ùrlar, agus
an dromannan ris na ballachan.   Choimhead gach aon diù 'n
sin air a' cheile.   Ghlaodh Conan bharr lic-an-teinntein, agus
a dhruim agus 'fhalt air leantainn rithe, " Nach d' innis mise
tràth mar dh' éireadh dhuit le d' ghillean fuadain?"   Cha d'
thubhairt Fionn guth, a chionn gu 'n robh e 'n iomagain mhòir
mu 'n teinn-bàis anns an robh iad.   Ach chuimhnich e air a
dhéud-fios, agus chuir e a mhèur fodha, agus fhuair e 'mach
nach robh ni air bith a dh' fhuasgladh iad as an àit' anns an
robh iad ach fuil triùir chloinne Righ Innse Tille air a sìoladh
tromh amalan airgid ann an cupachan òir.

Cha robh fhios aige cò a gheibheadh an fhuil dha, ach
chuimhnich e gu 'n robh Laoghaire, Mac Righ nan Sealg, agus
Oscar a dhìth air as a' chuideachd an là so.   Bha 'n Gurra-
fiodha aige, nach do shéid e riamh ach an uair a bhitheadh e
'n teinn bàis air chor-eiginn.   Ach an uair a sheinneadh e i
rachadh a fuaim troimh sheachd iomaill an domhain, agus gu

iomall an Domhain Toir. Agus bha fhios aige, 'n uair a chluinneadh Laoghaire agus Oscar an fhuaim, gu 'n tigeadh iad a ceàrn
air bith anns am bitheadh iad.

Shéid e 'n Gurra-fiodha trì uairean, agus mu 'n d' éirich grian
air an ath mhadainn bha Oscar a' glaodhaich air taobh a mach
a bhalla, "Am bheil thu so, Fhinn?" "Cò 'tha sin?" thubhairt
Fionn o 'n taobh a 's tigh. "Is e 'n dà latha e 'nuair nach
aithnicheadh tu mo ghuth-sa agus nach 'eil ach lèud balla tighe
eadarainn. Tha mise, Oscar, an so, agus Laoghaire còmhla
rium. Gu dé a th' againn r' a dheanamh a nis?"

Dh' innis Fionn doibh an suidheachadh agus an cruaidh-
chàs anns an robh iad, agus nach robh ni air bith a dh'
fhuasgladh iad as ach fuil trì Mic Righ Innse Tille air a sìoladh
ann an cupaichean òir troimh amalan airgid. "C' àit' am fair
sinn airson am faotainn?" thubhairt Oscar. Thubhairt Fionn,
" Bheir thu aire mhath do bhéul-àtha na h-amhann 'ud thall mu
dhol fodha gréine. Ach cha-n 'eil e fathast ach tràth anns an
latha. Féuch am faigh sibh biadh dhuinn-ne, oir tha sinn air
acras. Ach, Oscair, cuimhnich do Chraosnach a thabhairt
leat."

Thug Oscar agus Laoghaire an aghaidh air an Tigh Mhòr a
bha thall m' an coinneamh. An uair a ràinig iad an tigh, bha
iad a' deasachadh na dinnearach. Thubhairt Laoghaire ri
Oscar, " Gabh thusa 'n toiseach." Ghabh Oscar an toiseach,
agus bha e cumail a shùil anns gach oisinn féuch gu dé
'chitheadh e. An uair a ràinig e àite na còcaireachd thug e
sùil a 's tigh, agus chunnaic e coltas ceatharnaich fhiadhaich a'
togail ceithreimh féidh a coire. Thubhairt e ri Laoghaire,
" Lean mise, agus thoir leat am biadh, agus bheir mise 'n aghaidh
air an duine." Chaidh e 's tigh, ach cha robh duine nis ri
fhaicinn. Ach sùil g' an tug e, chunnaic e clamhan mòr le
sgiathan sgaoilte deas gu léum a nuas air a cheann. Tharrainn
e 'Chraosnach, agus thilg e air a' chlamhan i. Bhrist e sgiath
dheth, agus thuit an clamhan féin air an ùrlar, agus cha-n fhac
e an ath shealladh dh 'e. Rinn e féin agus Laoghaire an so
an tigh dhoibh fhéin, agus thug iad leò gach nìr bithidh air an
d' fhuair iad greim.

Ràinig iad an tigh anns an robh Fionn agus a dhaoine.

Thug iad toll air balla 'n tighe, agus thilg iad a 's tigh pìos an déigh piosa do gach duine gus an d' fhuair a' h-uile duine 'bh' ann ni-éiginn ach Conan. Bha esan air a dhruim air lic-an-teinntein, le lamhan agus le chasan maille r' a dhruim ceangailte ris an lic, air chor agùs nach b' urrainn iad mìr a thoirt da ach na leigeadh iad a sìos tromh mhullach an tighe, agus a ghlacadh e féin an sin le 'bhéul. Mar so fhuair e greim n' a dhà.

An sin dh' fheòraich Oscar de Fhionn gu dé 'bha aca ri fhaireadh aig béul-àth na h-amhann a thuillidh air triùir Mhac Righ Innse Tille. "Bithidh sluagh mòr còmhla riù," arsa Fionn. "Agus cia mar dh' aithnicheas sinn triùir Mhac Righ Innse Tille seach triùir air bith eile de 'n t-sluagh?" "Bithidh iad a' coiseachd air leth air an t-sluagh air an laimh dheis, agus deiseachan uain' orra." "Aithnichidh sinn a nis iad," thubhairt Oscar.

An sin dh' fhalbh Oscar agus Laoghaire a dh' fhaotainn nan amalann agus nan cupachan airson na fala a shìoladh agus a ghleidheadh. An déigh dhoibh am faighinn dh' fhalbh iad leò a dh' fhaireadh a bheòil-àtha. Aig dol fodha gréine dh' fhairich iad fuaim mhòr a' tighinn. Thug Oscar sùil an rathad o 'n d' fhairich e 'n fhuaim, agus chunnaic e sluagh mòr a' tighinn anns an fhradharc. Ghlaodh e 'n so air Laoghaire bhi deas. Thubhairt Laoghaire, "Theid sinn air tìr as an uisge, agus coinnichidh sinn iad air talamh tioram." Agus mar sin rinn iad.

An uair a thàinig an sluagh mòr dlùth dhoibh ghlaodh iad, "Cò iad an dà Luidealach Mhòr mhi-sgiamhach a tha 'n sin 'n an seasamh aig béul àtha 'us anmoich? Cò air bith iad tha 'n t-àm ac' a bhi 'gabhail an eagail?" Ghlaodh Oscar riù, "Trian d' ar n' eagal oirbh fhéin agus trian bheag dh' e oirnn-ne." "Feithidh sibh mata ri bhur n' aimhleas," ars' an sluagh mòr. An sin chaidh iad 'an coinneamh a chéile, ach thug Oscar agus Laoghaire ruathar fòp' agus tharta gus nach d' fhàg iad duine 'dh' innseadh an tuairisgeil beò dhiù.

Thill iad air an ais. Air an ath mhadainn dh' innis iad do Fhionn mar dh' éirich dhoibh, ach nach fhac' iad Clann an Righ. "C' àit 'an dean sinn faire an ath oidhche?" thuirt Oscar. "Fair gu math béul-àtha na amhann a' nochd fhathast," arsa Fionn. "Ach faidh dhuinn biadh an dràst, oir tha sinn air acras. Agus cuimhnich gu 'n toir thu leat do lann trì fhaobharach agus do sgiath an diugh."

Ràinig an dà laoch an Tigh Mòr. Bha Oscar ni 'b' fhaicil-iche 'n là so, a chionn nach robh fhios aige gu dé 'thachradh air. 'N uair a fhuair e sealladh air tigh na còcaireachd, chunnaic e duine fuathasach mòr agus ceithir lamhan air a 's tigh, a' togail na feòla as a' choire. Chaidh e 's tigh, ach cha robh duine 'nis ri fhaicinn. Thug e sùil mu 'n cuairt air an àit', agus chunnaic e fir-eun mòr a' dol a thilgeil air ubh a bh' aige 'n a spùl. Thog e 'a sgiath eadar e agus an t-ubh, ach chuir am buile air a leth-ghlùn e laimh ris a' choire. Chunnaic e nach b' urrainn e bhi deas le 'lann mu 'm bitheadh am fìr-eun aige; uime sin thog e 'n coir' èanraich a bh' air an ùrlar, agus thaom e air mullach a chinn e. Thug e sgriach fhuathasach as, agus chaidh e troimh 'n bhalla, agus cha robh 'n ath shealladh aige dh' e.

An sin dh' fhalbh e féin agus Laoghaire leis a' bhiadh', agus fhuair iad roinn a thabhairt do gach duine mar air an latha roimhe. Ach bha roinn Chonain bhochd ni 'bu lugha.

An uair a thàinig an t-àm dh' fhalbh iad a dh' ionnsaidh a' bhéul-àtha, agus chaidh iad ni 'b' fhaid' air an aghaidh, air taobh eile na h-amhann, no chaidh iad air an fheasgar roimhe. Goirid an déigh 'dhoibh ruigheachd, chunnaic iad sluagh ro mhòr a' tighinn orra. An uair a thàinig iad am fagus ghlaodh iad, "Cò an dà Luidealach mhòr mhi-sgiamhach a bha 'n sud 'n an seasamh os ceann béul-àtha na h-amhann anns an anmoch? Cò air bith iad tha n' t-àm dhoibh a bhi 'gabhail an eagail." "Dà thrian d' 'ur n' eagal a bhi oirbh fhéin, ach trian bheag dh' e 'bhi oirnn," thuirt Oscar. An sin bhuail iad orra as gach taobh gus an deachaidh iad a mach air an taobh eile dhiù, agus nach d' fhàg iad duin' a dh' innseadh an tuairisgeil beò dhiù.

Thill iad air an ais, agus dh' innis iad do Fhionn nach d thàinig Clann an Righ air an oidhche sin fathast. Thubhairt Fionn riù iad a dh' fhaotainn bithidh dhoibh-san an là sin a rithist. "Ach, Oscair, cuimhnich do shleagh agus do sgiath, agus ma bhlaiseas i fuil Beithir Sgiathach na Seile bithidh Righ Innse Tille 'nochd gun Mhac."

Dh' fhalbh iad, agus thug iad an aghaidh air an tigh mhòr. Ghabh Oscar air thoiseach mar b' àbhaist da. Bha e 'gleidh-eadh a shùil gu math biorach fèuch cò bhitheadh an tigh na còcaireachd an là so. 'Nuair 'fhuair e sealladh air chunnaic e duin' eireachdail, calma, air an robh dà cheann agus ceithir lamhan, a' togail na feòla as a' choire. Thubhairt e ris fhéin gu 'n robh an t-àm aige-san a bhi deas. 'Nuair a chaidh e 's tigh cha robh duine ri' fhaicinn, ach bha Beithir Mhòr Sgiathach, agus dà cheann nathrach oirre, 'n a seasamh air an ùrlar. Chagair Oscar ri Laoghaire, " Dean thus' air a' bhiadh, agus ni mis' air a' Bheithir." Thog e 'sgiath, agus tharrainn e a shleagh ; agus le aon sàthadh chuir e 'n t-sleagh troimh aon cheann, agus pìos di tromh 'n cheann eil' aig a' Bheithir. Ghleachd a' Bheithir gu fuathasach, ach mu dheireadh bha i a' lagachadh le call fala. An sin tharrainn Oscar an t-sleagh air a h-ais los a sàthadh anns a' Bhéist a rithist, ach cho luath agus a thàinig an t-sleagh as a feòil chaidh i as an fhradharc air, agus cha robh an ath shealladh aige dhi.

Fhuair iad am biadh, agus dh' fhalbh iad leis a dh' ionnsaidh an cairdean. An uair a ràinig iad, dh' fheòraich Fionn de dh' Oscar, "An do bhlais do shleagh air fuil ?" "Fad laimh·choille dhi agus dòrn dh' òl gu titheach," ars' Oscar. An sin fhuair iad roinn de 'n bhiadh a thabhairt do gach duine mar air na làithean roimhe. Ach bha cuid Chonain ni' bu lugha.

Cho luath agus a thàinig ciaradh an fheasgair, thubhairt Fionn ri Oscar, "Bitheadh d' amalan agus do chupaichean leat an nochd."

An sin dh' fhalbh an dà laoch gu béul-àtha na h-amhann. Air an fheasgar so chaidh iad ni 'b' fhaid' air an aghaidh thar na h-aimhne na chaidh iad fathast. Cha robh iad ach goirid a' feitheamh an uair a chunnaic iad sluagh mòr mòr a' tighinn orra, agus triùir Chloinne Righ Innse Tille air an laimh dheis, agus deiseachan uain' orra. Dh' fheòraich Oscar de Laoghaire, "Cò dhiù a bheir thus' an aghaidh air trì Mic Righ Innse Tille, no air an t-Sluagh Mhòr ?" Thubhairt Laoghaire, "Bheir mise 'n aghaidh air trì Mic Righ Innse Tille, agus bheir thu féin an aghaidh air an t-Sluagh Mhòr." 'Nuair 'dhlùthaich iad air a chéile ghlaodh an Sluagh Mòr, "Cò iad an dà Luidealach Mhòr mhi-sgiamhach a bha 'n an seasamh os ceann béul-àtha na h-amhann anns an anmoch? Cò air bith iad tha 'n t-àm dhoibh a bhi teicheadh an nochd." " Tri trian d' 'ur n' eagal a bhi oirbh fhéin, agus gun dad idir d' e oirnn-ne," ars' Oscar.

An sin chaidh Oscar an coinneamh an t-sluaigh mhòir, agus thug Laoghaire 'n aghaidh air triùir Mhac an Righ. Bha cruaidh chath eadar Oscar agus an Sluagh, ach bhuadhaich e orra mu dheireadh agus cha d' fhàg e duine beò dhiù. An sin chaidh e le cabhaig fàr an robh Laoghaire. Bha triùir Mhac an Righ air an dà ghlùn aig Laoghaire, agus Laoghaire air a leth-ghlùn aca-san. An uair a 'chunnaic Oscar gu 'm b' ann aig Laoghaire 'bha 'n làmh an uachdair, cha b' ann air a chuideachadh a thug e ionnsaidh ach air an fhuil, oir bha i a' taomadh gu bras air an lòn. Thòisich e air a sìoladh tromh na h-amalan airgid anns na cupaichean òir, ach mu 'n robh na cupaichean uile làn dh' fhàs na cuirp cho rag agus nach sileadh tuillidh asda.

Dh' fhalbh an dà laoch leis na bh' aca 'dh' ionnsaidh an tighe 's an robh Fionn agus a dhaoine. An uair a ràinig iad e ghlaodh Oscar gu 'n robh iad air tighinn agus an fhuil aca. " Mata," thubhairt Fionn, " suathaibh i ris a h-uile mìr dhibh a bheanas do 'n tigh, o mhullach 'ur cinn gu bonnaibh 'ur cas." Rinn iad sin, agus chaidh iad a 's tigh. Thòisich iad air na daoine fhuasgladh leis an fhuil a rubadh ris gach mìr dhiù 'bha leantainn ris na h-àiteachan-suidhe, no ris a' bhalla, no ris an ùrlar. Dh' fhuasgail iad mar sin gach duin' a bha 's tigh ach Conan. Cha d' fhàg iad air a shon-san ach am blàth a dh' fhuirich air na cupaichean, ach dh' fhoghainn sin féin a dh' fhuasgladh gach mìr dh' e, ach cùl a chinn. Lean am falt agus an craicionn ri lic-an-teinntein agus cha robh dòigh ac' ach fhàgail ceangailte mar bha e.

An sin dh' fhalbh Fionn agus a dhaoine dhachaidh ro thoilichte gu 'n d' fhuair iad as a ghàbhadh mhòr anns an robh iad. Cha deachaidh iad ro fhada 'n uair a sheall iad 'n an déigh, agus a chunnaic iad Conan a' tighinn. Sheas iad gun dàil fàr an robh iad gus an d' thàinig e air aghaidh. Bha e 'n sin gun ròineag fuilt no ribe craicinn, eadar mullach a chinn agus cùl amhaich. Oir an uair a dh' fhairich e gu 'n

d' fhalbh càch agus gu 'n d' fhàg iad esan 'n an déigh, thug e
slaodadh mòr air a cheann, agus dh' fhàg e 'fhalt agus a
chraicionn ceangailte ri lic-an-teinntein.  O 'n là sin a mach
b' e 'theireadh daoine ris, " Conan Maol gun fhalt."

Ràinig Fionn agus a dhaoine 'n dachaidh, agus thug e
bòid agus briathar nach cuireadh e muinntireas air gillean
fuadain tuillidh.

## V.

## THE SMITH'S ROCK IN THE ISLE OF SKYE.

THERE was a report that the Fians (Fingalians) were asleep in this Rock, and that if anyone would enter it and blow the Wooden-Crier (Whistle), which lay beside Finn, three times, they would rise up alive and well as they formerly were.

A Smith who lived in the island heard the report, and resolved that he would attempt to enter the Rock. He reached the place where it was ; and, having formed a good idea of the key-hole, he returned to the smithy, and made a key which fitted the hole. He then went back to the Rock, and, as soon as he turned the key in the hole, the door opened, and he saw a very great and wide place before him, and exceedingly big men lying on the floor. One man, bigger than the rest, was lying in their midst, having a large hollow baton of wood lying beside him.

He thought that this was the Wooden-Crier (Whistle). But it was so large that he was afraid that he could not lift it, much less blow it. He stood for a time looking at it, but he at last said to himself that, as he came so far, he would try at any rate. He laid hold of the Wooden-Crier, and with difficulty raised its end up to his mouth. He blew it with all his might, and so loud was the sound it produced that he thought the Rock and all that was over it came down on the top of him. The huge unwieldy men who lay on the floor shook from the tops of their heads to the soles of their feet.

He gave another blast on the Wooden-Crier, and
with one spring they turned on their elbows. Their
fingers were like the prongs of wooden grapes, and
their arms like beams of bog-oak. Their size and the
terrible appearance they had put him in such fear that
he threw the Wooden-Crier from him, and sprang out.
They were then crying after him, " Worse have you
left us than as you found us, worse have you left us
than as you found us." But he looked not behind him
until he got outside and shut the door. He then drew
the key out of the hole, and threw it out into the lake
which is near the Rock, and which is called to this day
the Lake of the Smith's Rock.

## CREAG A' GHOBHA 'S AN EILEAN SGITHE-ANACH.

BHA iomradh gu 'n robh **na** Fianntan 'n an cadal anns a'
Chreig so, agus na '**n** rachadh duine 's am bith a 's tigh
innte, agus an Gurra-fiodha 'bha 'n a laidhe ri taobh Fhinn a
shéideadh trì uairean, gu 'n éireadh iad a suas beò, slàn mar
bha iad roimhe.

Chuala Gobha 'bha 's an eilean an t-iomradh, agus chuir e
roimhe gu 'm feuchadh e ri dol a 's tigh do 'n Chreig. Ràinig
e 'n t-àite 's an robh i; agus an déigh dha beachd math a
ghabhail air toll na h-iuchrach, thill e do 'n cheàrdaich, agus
rinn e iuchair a fhreagair do 'n toll. Chaidh e 'n sin air ais a
dh' ionnsaidh na Creige, agus cho luath agus a chuir e car 's
an iuchair anns an toll dh' fhosgail an dorus, agus chunnaic
e àite ro mhòr agus ro fharsainn air thoiseach air, agus
daoine anabarrach mòr 'n an laidhe air an ùrlar. Bha aon
fhear 'bu mhò na càch 'n a laidhe 'n am meadhon, agus
cleith mhòr de mhaide agus e fosgailte troimhe 'n a laidhe
laimh ris.

Smaointich e gu 'm b' e so an Gurra-fiodha. Ach bha e cho mòr agus gu 'n robh eagal air nach b' urrainn e a thogail, no idir a shéideadh. Sheas e 'g amharc air car ùine, ach mu dheireadh thubhairt e ris fhéin gu 'm feuchadh e co dhiù bho 'n thàinig e cho fada. Rug e air a' Ghurra-fiodha, agus thog e air éiginn a cheann an àird r' a bhéul. Shéid e le uile neart e ; agus, leis an fhuaim a rinn e, shaoil e gu 'n do thuit a' Chreag agus na bha os a ceann a nuas air a mhuin. Chrith na slaoid mhòra 'bh' air an ùrlar o mhullach an cinn gu bonnaibh an cas. Thug e 'n ath shéideag air a' Ghurra-fiodha, agus a dh' aon léum thionndaidh iad air an uilnibh. Bha 'm meòir mar mheòir gobhlaige, agus an gàirdeinnean mar shailean daragan-daraich. Chuir am mèud agus an coltas uamhasach a bh' orra a leithid do dh' eagal air 'us gu 'n do thilg e uaith' an Gurra-fiodha, agus gu 'n do léum e 'mach. Bha iad an sin a' glaodhaich as a dhéigh, " Is miosa dh' fhàg no mar fhuair, is miosa dh' fhàg no mar fhuair." Ach cha d' thug esan sùil 'n a dhéigh gus an d' fhuair e mach, agus an do dhruit e 'n dorus. Shlaod e 'n sin an iuchair as an toll, agus thilg e 'mach i anns an lochan a tha laimh ris a' Chreig, agus ris an abrar gus an latha 'n diugh Lochan Chreag a' Ghobha.

## VI.

### THE BARE-STRIPPING HANGMAN.

BEFORE now there was a King in Ireland who was twice married, and who had a son by each of his wives. The name of the first wife's son was Cormac, and the name of the second wife's son was Alastir (Alexander). His father was very proud of Cormac, and was always accustomed to take him with him to the Hunting-hill.

The King had a Hen-wife, who, with a sad and sorrowful countenance, went, on a certain day, in to the place where the Queen was. The Queen asked what was troubling her? "Great is that and not little, Queen of misery!" said the Hen-wife. "What does that mean?" "That the King is so fond of Cormac, the son of the first wife, that he will leave the kingdom to him, and that your son will be penniless." "If that is the King's pleasure, it cannot be helped." "Oh! nevertheless, the case need not so happen. If thou wilt give me what I shall ask of thee I will make thy son King." "What then is the reward which thou wilt ask for doing that?" "That is not much: as much meal as will thicken the little black jar and as much butter as will make it thin, the full of my two (outer) ear-holes of wool, and the breadth of one of my haunches of flesh." "How much meal will thicken the little black jar?" "Fourteen chalders." "How much butter will make it thin?" "As much as thy seven cow-houses will produce to the end of seven years." "What now is the full of thy two ear-holes of wool?" "As much as thy seven sheep-houses will produce in seven years." "And what now is the breadth of one of thy haunches of flesh?" "As much as thy seven ox-houses will produce to the end of seven years." "That is a great deal, woman." "Yes, but it is little in comparison with the third of Ireland." "It is," said the Queen, "and thou shalt get it. But what plan wilt thou take for making my son King?" "Cormac was yesterday complaining that he was not well. When the hunters will come home thou shalt say to the King that Cormac must stay at home to-morrow, and that Alastir must go in his stead to the Hunting-hill. I will make a drink for Cormac, and thou shalt give it to him after the rest have gone away, and he shall never again trouble thy son from being King." This pleased the Queen well, and she promised that she would do as the Hen-wife told her.

The women were thinking that no one was hearing them while they were devising mischief; but all the time Alastir was eavesdropping behind the door, and was very much displeased, because he and Cormac were as fond of each other as two brothers ever were. He considered what he should do, and resolved to tell the women's intention to Cormac as soon as he would come home.

Cormac came home about evening. He was pretty tired, and was not feeling better than he was in the morning. Alastir went where he was, and told him everything that happened between his mother and the Hen-wife. Poor Cormac got afraid, and said to Alastir what should he do? Alastir replied, "Have courage, and I will devise a scheme by which we shall get out of their way, and we shall not trouble them any more. To-morrow I shall go with my father to the Hunting-hill, but I shall not proceed far on the way when I shall say that I will return home because I do not like going to the hill.  Before I arrive my mother will go in with the drink to thee.  Thou shalt take hold of the cup out of her hand, but for man or thing that thou hast ever seen, taste not out of it, and put it not near thy mouth.  Thou shalt lift thy hand as if thou wert going to drink ; and then thou shalt spring out, holding it in thy hand.  I will have the two fleetest horses in the stable waiting for thee, and we will go away."  And so they did.

Next day he went but a short distance with his father, when he refused to go farther, and returned home.  He knew the time when Cormac would get the drink, and resolved that the horses should be ready as he promised.  But scarcely had he them saddled, when Cormac came out in haste, having the cup with him in his hand.  Alastir cried to him, " Leap into thy saddle quickly, and stick to what thou hast."

He did that, and they both went off as fast as the horses' feet would carry them.  They kept going forward without stop or rest until their horses were giving up.  Then they dismounted and sat down in the place where they were.

Alastir said to Cormac, " Show me the cup now." He took hold of the cup from his brother's hand, and having got a little stick, said, " We shall now see what stuff is in the cup."  He dipped the stick in the stuff, and put a drop of it in an ear of each one of the horses.  " What art thou doing in that manner ? " said Cormac.  " Wait a little, and thou shalt see," said Alastir.  In a short time the horses began to go round in a state of dizziness, and before long they fell cold and dead on the earth.  " Think you, Cormac, what would have happened to you if you had drunk the potion ? "  " What, but that I should have been dead now," said Cormac.

While they were conversing four ravens came, and

settled on the carcases of the horses. They began to peck the eyes out of the horses, and when they ate the eyes they flew away in the air. But they went only a short distance, when they uttered piercing screams and fell dead on the earth. "What now is thy opinion of the drink, Cormac?" "What, but if I had drunk of it that I would not have been here at present," said Cormac.

Alastir rose up, and having taken the four ravens with him in a napkin, he and his brother went away again on their journey. Alastir was keeping a step in advance, because he had virtues about him by which he knew what was to meet them. They kept going forward till they came to a small town.

Alastir went in to a Cooking-house in the town, and told the Cook to dress the ravens as well as he ever dressed birds, but not to put finger or hand near his mouth till he had them dressed, and till he had washed his hands well, and very well. "What does that mean?" said the Cook. "I never before dressed food which I might not taste." "Taste not and eat not a bit of these, otherwise thou shalt not get them at all." The Cook promised to do as he was told.

After the Cook had dressed the ravens, and received payment for his labour, Alastir tied them in his napkin, and he and Cormac departed again on their journey. On the way, Alastir said, "There is a large wood before us in which are staying four-and-twenty robbers who never allowed a man to pass them without killing him, and who will not let us pass if they can prevent us." "What shall we do?" said Cormac. "Leave that to me," replied Alastir.

When they were going through the wood they noticed a pretty little plain above the road on which they were walking, and the robbers lying on their backs basking themselves in the sun at the upper end of the plain. They kept going forward, but when they were just passing beneath the place in which the robbers were, two of them cried, "Who are the two impertinent fellows who would dare pass by on this way without asking us?" They all took their way down where the two strangers were, and said to them that they were going to strike their heads off them. "Oh, then," said Alastir, "there is no help for it. We are tired and hungry, and if you would allow us to eat a bite of food before you would put us to death, we would be obliged to you." "If you have food, take it quickly," said the robbers. "We have food," said Alastir, "and you too will get some of it if you like."

Then he opened the napkin, and divided the ravens into twenty-six pieces, a piece for every man in the company. "Now," said he, "you shall wait until you are all served, and you shall begin to eat together, for if some of you eat their own share first they will fight the rest for their share, and you will wound and kill each other." Hereupon the robbers made a loud, mocking laugh, but they said that they would do as they were told. When they were all served, Alastir lifted up his hand, and cried, "Eat now." They did so, and praised the food. But it was not long till one after another of them began to sit, and every one that sat fell asleep, and out of that sleep he was waking no more. At last they were all in the sleep of death.

"Now," said Alastir, "that is over, and the way is clear before us as far as the Castle of the King of Riddles. Thou shalt travel as the King of Ireland, and I will travel as thy Servant. If thou art told to do anything thou shalt say that it is the Servant who does that in the country out of which thou hast come. When thou shalt reach the Castle of the King of Riddles thou must put a Riddle or solve a Riddle, and if thou do not that thy head shall be placed on a stake in the wall, which is before the door. Many of our sort reached the Castle before us, and as they could not put a riddle or solve a riddle, their heads were placed on the stakes of the wall. There is one stake still empty, and thy head shall be placed on it if neither thou, nor I for thee, will put or solve a riddle to-night."

They reached the Castle. The King of Riddles gave them a great welcome, for he thought that it was to ask his daughter they came, like those who preceded them. They were but a short time in when food was placed before them, but ere they began to take it the King of Riddles said, " King of Ireland, put a riddle or solve a riddle." The King of Ireland answered, and said, " It is the Servant who does that in the country from which I came." " Get thy Servant down, then," said the King of Riddles. The Servant came. " Servant of the King of Ireland, put a riddle or solve a riddle," said Riddle King. The Servant answered, " One killed two, two killed four, four killed twenty-four, and two escaped." The King of Riddles thought, but he could not solve the riddle. At last he said to the Servant, " Go away just now, and thou shalt get the solution of the riddle to-morrow." After the dinner was over they spent the rest of the night telling interesting tales until bedtime came.

Then the King of Riddles sent word for his daughter and her twelve maidens in attendance. He said to the maidens that whoever of them would find the solution of the riddle from the beginning from the Servant of the King of Ireland would get his son in marriage and half the kingdom. They said that they would try. He then turned to his daughter, and promised her her choice of a sweetheart and half the kingdom, if she could find the solution of the riddle from the beginning.

The maidens were awhile considering in what manner they could find out the solution of the riddle.  At last they agreed to put the Servant in the very coldest and worst room which was in the Castle, where there were holes on the walls, and the windows were broken, and wind and rain (were) coming in at them ; that they would put his Master in the best room which was in the house; and that they would say to the Servant that he would get as good a bed and room as his Master had if he would tell the solution of the riddle from the beginning.  And they did so.

The Servant was not very long in bed when he felt the door opening.  He turned on his pillow, and beheld a young, comely maiden standing on the floor.  He understood very well what was on her mind.  The maiden said, "Is it sleep to thee, Servant of the King of Ireland ?"  "It is not sleep to me ; for it is no sleeping quarters I have got, wind and cold under me, and wind and rain over me.  Far will I carry the name of this house when I shall go away."  "Thou shalt get as good a bed as thy Master has, if thou tell me the solution of the riddle from the beginning."  But he did not tell her that, and he allowed her to go back to the rest without it.  They then came one after another, but it befell them as it befell her.

As soon as the last of them went out, the Servant went to his Master's room, and the Master went to the Servant's room.  He was but a short time there when the King's daughter went in.  She said, as the maidens before her said : "Is it sleep to thee, Servant of the King of Ireland ?"  "It is not sleep to me ; for it is no sleeping quarters I have got, with wind and cold under me, and wind and rain above me.  Far will I carry the name of this house when I shall go away."  "Well, thou shalt get as good a bed as thy Master has if thou wilt tell me the solution of the riddle from the beginning." But he did not tell her that, and she went away.

Next morning the King of Riddles asked the maidens if they had got the solution of the riddle? They said that they had not. He then asked of his daughter if she got it, and she said that she had not.

When they sat down at their breakfast the King of Riddles said : "King of Ireland, put a riddle or solve a riddle." "As I told thee last night, it is my Servant who is accustomed to put a riddle or answer a riddle for me." "Get thy servant down, then." The Servant came. "Servant of the King of Ireland, put a riddle or solve a riddle," said the King of Riddles. "I did not get the solution of the first riddle yet," said the Servant. "Thou insolent fellow, is it keeping up chat with me thou art? Put a riddle or solve a riddle, otherwise thy head shall be struck off thee at breakfast time, and placed on a pale in the wall." "I will put a riddle, then," said the Servant. "Let me hear it," said the King of Riddles.

[The Servant put a riddle which he composed on the things which befell himself and his Master on the night before. The King of Riddles solved that riddle, but the first one beat him. To shorten this part of the tale, the King of Riddles gave his daughter to the King of Ireland.]

Alastir remained many days with them, passing the time hunting and fishing. On a certain day, while he was fishing on a rock near the sea, and thinking what he should do—go away or stay with Cormac—he heard a loud splash in the sea at the foot of the rock. Before he got time to look one way or another, a large Dog-Otter sprang out of the water, seized him by the two ankles, and went out with him on the sea. He saw not again a blink of earth or of sky until he was left above the reach of the tide in the very prettiest bay he ever saw, with smooth, white sand from the margin of the wave to the green grass.   He was now in Lochlan.

In a short time the Dog-Otter returned, having a fresh-water salmon with him in his mouth.   He left the salmon at Alastir's feet, and said to him : "When thou art going on any long journey, or when any hardship is coming upon thee, take a bite of this fish beforehand. Here thou shalt make a bothy, and shalt stay in it till thou shalt see more than me, and till thou shalt get more than my advice."

He put up the bothy that same night.   He then boiled a piece of the salmon, and after eating it he felt stronger than he ever was.

On the next morning he rose up, and went out before breakfast to the end of his bothy.   He stood, and saw the Great White-buttocked Deer coming straight towards the place in which he was standing, and the White Red-eared Hound after him, chasing him keenly.   When the Deer was nearing him, the Hound had hold after hold of the Deer ; and in going past, the Hound gave forth a bark, and sprang at the neck of the Deer, and left him dead at Alastir's feet.

"Now," said the Hound to Alastir, " thou wert faithful to thy brother, and thou shalt receive thy reward. When thou art going on any long journey, or when any hardship is coming upon thee, thou shalt eat beforehand a bite of the fresh-water salmon, and a bite of this deer, and from anything which thou shalt (afterwards) see or hear no further injury shall befall thee. And before that will fail thee thou shalt be told what thou art to do."   Then the White Red-eared Hound wished him good success, and departed.

Alastir took the deer in to his bothy, and left it beside the salmon.   He made ready his breakfast, and ate a piece of the salmon and a piece of the deer.   He then went out, and having given a look away from him, he saw coming a large-sized man having the appearance of a King, and twelve Champions with him. They came straight to the place in which he was.

The King said to him : "How hadst thou the courage or the boldness of coming to kill my large White-buttocked deer ?" "Thy deer came of its own accord my way, I had need of food, and I killed thy deer," said Alastir. "Well," said the King, "since thou didst kill my deer, thou must fight with my Champions until thou shalt fall or until they shall." "I am alone, King," said Alastir, "you are many, along with that I am without a sword." "Thou shalt not be without a sword," said the King ; "thou shalt get my sword, and if thou take thy life out of peril with it, it shall be thine own." "I will try, at any rate," said Alastir. "But I ask of thee as a favour that thou wilt let me eat a bite of food before I shall begin." "Thou shalt get that," said the King, while he was reaching him his sword.

He went into his bothy, and ate a bite of the fish and a bite of the deer. When he was done he thrust the King's sword into the carcass of the deer, and it went as easily through it as though it were water. "The success of this thrust be with each stroke," said Alastir. He felt that he himself was in great courage and in full strength, and turned out to the fight.

The King said that he would get the advantage of the Fein—man after man. One of the Champions was sent out opposite him. But they were not long at sword-play when the Champion of the King fell, heavily wounded, on the ground. Alastir shouted to the next man to come on. He came ; but in a short time he fell wounded on the ground like the first man. A like thing befell the third man.

When the King saw his three Champions dropping blood and dying, he said to the Stranger, "Whatever place is thy native country, thou art a Champion at any rate." Alastir then called to the rest to come on quickly if he had to go through them all. But the King put a stop to the contest. He turned to Alastir, and said to him, "Thou hast won thy sword with victory, and thou shalt get it. Go with me and I will make thee better off than thou art here." Then Alastir asked of him as a kindness to leave the bothy standing as it was, since he did not know but that he must return to it yet. He got his request, and went away with the King.

On the way, the King was under a heavy stupor for the loss of his three Champions. But at last he said to himself, that the one he had found was as good as the three he had lost. They kept going forward through wood, over heath, and over moss, until they arrived at a fine large Castle the like of which Alastir never saw before. The King told him to go in along with him. The Champions took their own way, and Alastir entered with the King.

Food and drink were put before Alastir, and the King told him to eat and drink. He replied that he would not eat a bite of his food, and that he would not drink a drop of his drink until he would tell him the reason why he brought him yonder. The King understood that he had a Champion, and said that he would tell him that.

"I had four daughters. Three of them were taken from me by the Big Giant who is staying in the Black Corrie of *Ben Breck* (or the Speckled Mountain). He came at first at the time of the going down of the Sun, and took away the first of them in my own presence and in the presence of my Champions, and I saw her no more. I sent my Champions after him, and they followed him to his Castle. But when they reached it, as a sudden blast of east wind would strip bracken in winter, he swept the heads off them. Only one escaped to tell me the tale of distress. At the end of seven years he came again, and as it happened at first it happened that time. At the end of another seven years he came, and took the third one with him. My Champions resolved that they would have revenge on him, and that they would bring my daughter home to me. They went away under full armour to watch the Castle of the Black Corrie of the *Ben Breck*. After they had watched it during three rounds of the Sun they got no opportunity of the Giant. At last they were growing heavy for want of sleep and weak for want of food, and therefore resolved that they would go to the Castle and see what was within. They found the way to the Den of the Giant, and saw that he was in a heavy sleep. They said to each other that that was the time for them to have revenge for the King's daughter, and to take the head off the Giant. They sprang towards him, and struck off his head with their swords. No sooner had they done that than a large golden eagle sprang down, and struck the first Champion on the face, and knocked him down. The golden eagle did the same thing on the next man. When the rest saw that, they fled. But scarcely had they got outside through the gate of the Castle than they saw the Giant coming after them, and his head on him as it was before. When they saw him, they stretched away, and those of them who escaped made no stay until they arrived here. But those of them that fell into his hands, he bared to the skin, and hanged up on hooks against the turrets of the Castle. Now, the fourth one of my daughters is about a day and year of the age of the rest when they were stolen from me. But to any one who will bring home to me the Black Brood-mare which is on the Ben, and on which a halter never went, belong my daughter and as far as the half of my kingdom."

" Good is thine offer, King," said Alastir. " He is a

sorry fellow that would not make his utmost endeavour to earn it." "I knew that thou wert a Champion," said the King, "and if thou wilt do it thou shalt get thy promised reward, and much more. On the morning of next day thou shalt reach my Stable, and wilt get thy choice of a bridle."

On the next morning, Alastir reached the Stable, and found many men and Champions before him who were going to try and catch the Black Brood-mare, as he himself was, for the sake of getting the King's daughter as a reward. The Stable was opened, and each one selected a bridle for himself.

They then went away to the mountain to catch the Black Brood-mare. They were travelling through glens, over bens, and through hollows until they got a sight of her. Alastir tried to get before her, but as soon as she saw him she ascended the face of the Ben, sending water out of the stones, and fire out of the streams, fleeing from him. They followed after her until the darkening of night came on them, and then they turned home without her.

When they reached the Castle they told the King how it befell them. He said to them that another day was coming, and that another sun was to go round, and that to the man who would bring home to him the Black Brood-mare at the end of a tether would belong his daughter, and as far as the half of his kingdom. When they heard this, every man and every Champion made ready to go to the Ben before sunrise on the following day.

When the next morning came each one of them turned away in the full belief that it was with himself the victory would be when returning. They reached the Ben. Some of them were going on their bellies through hollows, some creeping along the beds of streams, others were peeping over ridges, and taking advantage of every gap to see if they could get a sight of the Black

Brood-mare. At last they saw her on the sunny side of the Glen-of-the-Sun (*Gleann-na-gréine*). Each man made ready as well as he could, to catch her. But no better befell them that day than on the day before, for she was sending water out of the stones and fire out of the streams fleeing before them. At the going down of the sun, they were further from her than they were in the morning. Then they returned home weariedly, sadly, hungrily.

When they reached the Castle the King sent out his Gillie-in-attendance, to ask with whom the victory was. The Gillie brought word back to him that they had seen her, but that they got not within catching distance of her, or even within a stone-cast of her. Then the King sent word to them that the morrow was the third day of their trial, and that he would be as good as his promise to any one of them who would bring home to him at end of rein, the Black Brood-mare. When they heard this, each running Champion and each fighting Champion was under heavy anxiety, for they could not do more than they had already done. But they resolved that they would once more try to catch her.

After the supper was over, Alastir, as he was going through the Castle, met the Sorceress (*Iorasglach-ùrlair*) of the King. "Son of the King of Ireland," said she, "thou art wearied, sad, and under a heavy stupor." Alastir answered that he was. "Thou didst not take the advice of thy friends. To-night thou shalt go back to thine own bothy, and thou shalt take a bite of the fish and a bite of the deer. But before thou go away thou shalt turn back where the King is, and thou shalt say to him that to-morrow is the last day which you have for catching the Black Brood-mare, and that thou shalt not go after her unless thou shalt get thy choice of a bridle before thou wilt depart. He will then go with thee, and when you reach the Stable thou wilt see a door on thy right hand, and thou shalt tell him to open the door in order that thou shalt take thy choice of a bridle out of that place. He will open the door for thee, and thou see hanging from the wall an old bridle which was not in the head of horse or mare for twenty-seven years, and thou shalt take it with thee. When thou wilt reach the mountain thou shalt give the rest the slip (or turn about a bush), and go before the Black Brood-mare. As soon as thou wilt come in sight of her thou shalt shake the bridle towards her; and she will come with a neigh and put her head in the bridle. Thou shalt then leap on her back, and ride her home to the King."

Alastir went away from the Sorceress as well pleased as he was since the day the Dog Otter left him ashore in the land of Lochlan.

On the third day the Champions got ready, and went away to the Mountain to catch the Black Brood-mare. When they reached they took advantage of every cover till they thought that they were as near her as they could get. But Alastir gave them the slip, and left them. He did not stop until he got ahead of the Black Brood-mare. She was coming, bearing a terrible appearance, driving water out of the stones and fire out of the streams with the speed of her running. Then Alastir lifted up the bridle and shook it towards her. As soon as the Brood-mare heard the jingling of the bridle she stood, and made a hard neigh, which Mac-talla of the rocks (echo) answered four miles round. She laid down her two ears along the back of her head, she came at the gallop, and thrust her head into the bridle. Then Alastir leaped on her back, and rode her home to the King. When the other Champions saw the stranger riding away with the Black Brood-mare, all their *sud* and their *sad* (*cheerfulness* and *hope*) forsook them, and they returned home.

On this night the King came out to meet them. When he saw that it was the Stranger who had the victory he took his way over where he was, went on his two knees to do him honour, and said, " I thought that thou wert a Champion indeed, and thou hast proved it at last. Now, ask any cattle or person, jewel or value, which is in my kingdom, and thou shalt get it along with the reward which I promised for this deed."

The King made a great feast on that night. But before the feast was over word came to the King from the Big Giant of the Black Castle in the Ben Breck (Speckled Mountain) that he would come for the fourth daughter at the end of a day and year from that night. This message put the King in ill humour and in anxiety. He turned to the Champions, and said to them that he was sorry because he could not fulfil what he had promised unless they themselves would find out the place in which the soul of the Bare-Stripping Hangman was hid, and kill him. " My Champions struck his head off already, but he put it on him again, and he was as alive as he ever was. He defied them, and said that in spite of them he would take all my daughters with him. Now, he is coming at the end of a day and year from this night, and to the man of you who will put him out of life shall belong my daughter and all my kingdom."

All the Champions were under anxiety because they did not know how they could kill the Bare-Stripping Hangman. But when they separated, the Sorceress (*Iorasglach-ùrlair*) met Alastir, and said to him, " Son of the King of Ireland, I hope that thou hast received thy reward to-night." He told her everything that happened, and how the condition on which the King's daughter would be found was harder now than it was before. She was lying on the floor, and she rose up quickly in a sitting posture. She took hold of her hair in her hand, and made a loud laugh, and said, "Son of the King of Ireland, success was always with thee and shall be with thee still if thou wilt take my advice."   "If I can I will do anything that thou wilt ask of me, for I have found thee true thus far, and I have full confidence in thee now," said Alastir. "Well, said the Sorceress (*Iorasglach*), " from the spot on which thou art standing thou shalt go away under full armour, and remember that thou shalt not part with the King's sword until thou get a better.   Thou shalt go first to thy bothy and eat a bite of the deer and a bite of the fish.   Thou shalt then come out to the door of thy bothy, and thou shalt set thy face towards the Rocky Path of the Yellow Mountain (Ben Buie), and thou shalt not look behind thee, and thou shalt not turn a step back for any difficulty or hardship which may meet thee until thou reach the Great Castle which is at the end of the Mountain Path.   There thou shalt see a woman looking out at the high window of the Castle."   The Sorceress now took a writing out of her bosom, and said, "When thou shalt see the woman thou shalt know her, and say to her that thou hast a writing for her.   She will then come and open the door to thee, and tell thee what thou hast to do after that.   Thou mayest now set off on thy journey.   The blessing of the King is in thy company, the blessing of his daughter is with thee, and thou hast my blessing.   Now, whatsoever thing the woman will ask thee to say or to do, be sure that thou fulfil it."

Alastir took courage, and went away straight to his bothy, and on the next morning, before sunrise, he departed on his journey through the Rocky Mountain Path of Ben Buie (Yellow Mountain).   He kept going forward far long and full long until the Path grew so full of fissures and sharp-pointed rocks that he was under the necessity of hanging on his belly to go over them. At last even the jagged rocks failed, and there was nothing before him but a great chasm between lofty precipices which were as deep under him as they were high over his head. He gave a look on each side of him, and saw the Path running in to the side of one of the precipices in so narrow a ledge that there was not the breadth of a footsole in it. Then he got afraid that he was astray, and he was going to return. But a large buzzard came flying across over his head, and cried to him, "Son of the King of Ireland, remember the advice of the Sorceress (*Iorasglach-ùrlair*)." At once he remembered his promise to the Sorceress, and said to himself that he would go forward as long as the breath would be in him. He was then hanging from cliff to cliff and leaping from ledge to ledge, until the path began to grow better. At last he got on the smooth way. He then went as fast as he could go over the rocks, for the evening was coming and a sight of the Castle was not to be seen. The ascent was so steep that he could make no great speed. But he won the top at last. He said to himself that he would not take long now, and he ran as fast as he could down the hill-side. He was thinking that when he got to the foot of the brae every hardship would be over, but when he reached it they were, to all appearance, only beginning. Instead of the Castle, he saw a large Red Lake before him. He gave a look on each side of him to see if he could behold a way in which he could get over the Lake, but he saw only rocky precipices, and it was enough for a bird on the wing to go over them. He was in a dilemma (house of conference) whether he should return or go forward, when he heard the buzzard crying over his head, "Son of the King of Ireland, take neither fright nor apprehension in presence of any difficulty or hardship which will meet thee." When he heard this he took courage, and kept going forward on the Path into the Lake. At first he wondered that he was not sinking in the Lake, but in a short time he saw that the road on which he was walking was scarcely covered with water. He kept straight on the path until he arrived at the other side of the Lake. As soon as he got his feet on dry land he lifted up his head, and saw a beautiful green field before him, and a large Castle at the end of the field. Twilight had come, and therefore he hastened forward to the Castle.

When he reached the Castle, he saw a woman looking out at one of the windows. He cried that he had a letter for her. She descended quickly, and opened the door to him. He handed her the letter. She caught it out of his hand, and told him to wait until she would see what was in it. As soon as she read the letter she bounded towards him and seized his hand in both her hands, and kissed it. She took him in, and asked of him what way did he come? He said that he came through the Rocky Path of Ben Buie (Yellow Mountain). "If so," said she, "thou hast need of meat and of drink." She set meat and drink before him, and told him to be quick, because he had a great deal to do.

As soon as he was done she took him in to the armoury, and told him to try whether he could lift the sword which was over against the wall. He tried that, but he could not put wind between it and the earth. She opened a press which was on a side of the house, and took out of it a little bottle of balsam. She drew a cup of gold, and put a little drop out of the little bottle into it, and said to him, "Drink of it." He did that. He again seized the sword, and he could lift it with both hands. She gave him another little drop, and then he could lift the sword with one hand. She gave him the third drop, and no sooner did he drink it than he felt stronger than he ever was. He seized the sword, and he could work with it as lightly and airily as he could work with the King's sword.

" Now," she said to him, " there is a big Giant having two heads on him, staying in this Castle, and he is coming home in a short time. Come with me, and I will set thee standing on the *ùdabac* (or porch), where thou shalt get an opportunity of striking him when he stoops to come in under the lintel. Be sure that thou strike him well, and send the two heads off him : for if thou send but one head off him, he will take hold of that one, and kill thee with it, as he did many others before thee."

He went away without delay, and stood on the porch (*ùdabac*) as she told him. He was not long there when he saw the Giant coming with a fairy motion.

When he reached the door he bent his heads, and gave a grunt. Alastir took the advantage of him, and struck him with all his might. With the stroke he threw one of the heads off him, and half of the other head. Then the Giant gave dreadful leaps and screams, but before he found time to turn round, Alastir struck the other half of the second head off him, and he fell a dead carcass on the earth.

The woman came out, and said to him, " Well done, Son of the King of Ireland. Success is with thee, for my father's blessing is with thee." He then asked of her who she was. She replied that she was the oldest daughter the King of Ben Buie had. " Thou art going away," she said, " to seek the soul of the Bare-Stripping Hangman, in order that thou mayest save my youngest sister from him. Come in and I will let thee away on thy journey before a sun will rise to-morrow."

He went in, she washed his feet, and he went to bed.

Before the red-cock (heath-cock) crowed, and before a sun rose on dwelling or on mountain, she was on foot, and had breakfast waiting him. After he had risen and got his breakfast, she took a letter out of her bosom, and handed it to him, saying, "Thou shalt keep this carefully until thou reach the Great Castle of the eight turrets, and thou shalt give it to the woman whom thou shalt see looking out at one of the roof windows of the Castle. She gave a pull on her own little bottle of balsam, and on her cup of gold, and gave him a drink. She then put him on the head of the way, she wished a blessing to accompany him, and said that she would remain yonder until he would return. He left the King's sword in the Castle, and went away with the sword of the Giant. The path on which he was walking was smoother than the one on which he travelled the day before. He got on well, but the distance was so long that the night began to come upon him before he came in sight of the Castle. About the greying of the evening he saw the turrets of the Castle far from him. He took courage and hardened his step, and though it was a long distance from him, he took not long to reach it.

There were such high walls about the Castle that he was not seeing by what way he could get in. But he gave his head a lift, and saw a woman looking out at a window, and cried that he had a letter for her. She came down and opened a large iron door which was on the wall. After she had read the letter, she took hold of him by the hand and brought him in.

She then looked at the sword which he had, and asked him where did he find it?   He told her that he got it from the woman who was in the Castle in which he was the night before.   There was another large sword standing beside the wall, and she told him to try if he could lift it.   With difficulty he put wind between it and the earth.   " None that came before thee did even that much," said the woman.   She gave him a drink out of her little bottle of balsam in a cup of gold, and then he could play the sword with both hands.   She gave him the next drink, and he could play the Giant's sword as nimbly as he could play the sword of the King.

" Now," said she, " thou hast no time to lose.   The Great Giant of the three heads, three humps, and three knobs is staying here, and he will come home in a moment.   Come with me and I will put thee in a place where thou shalt get an opportunity of striking him."   He went with her, and she set him standing on a bank which was on the opening side of the great iron door on the wall.   Then she said, " When the Giant stoops to come under the lintel, be sure to strike him before he can get his heads lifted, and to send the three off him with the first stroke, for if he get time to rise he will take thee asunder in bits, as he did those that came before thee."

The Giant came, and stooped beneath the lintel, but before he got through the door, Alastir struck him with all his might, and sent two of his heads off and half the third.   The Giant gave a leap, and one of the humps struck the lintel and put it out (of its place).   Then he fell, and before he got time to rise and give the next leap, Alastir struck him the second time, and sent the other half of the third head off him.   With a great, melancholy groan the Giant fell a dead carcass on the ground.

H

The woman came out then and said, " Well done, Son of the King of Ireland.   The blessing of my father and of my sister is with thee, and thou shalt have my blessing now."   Then he asked of her who she was ?   She answered that she was the second daughter of the King of Ben Buic.   " Thou art going away to seek the soul of the Bare-Stripping Hangman, in order that thou mayest save my youngest sister from him, and if thou come alive out of the next Castle which thou shalt reach, thou needst not be afraid of either thing or person that may meet thee any more, for everything shall succeed with thee to the end of thy journey.   But thou hast no time to lose."   She took him in, served him with meat and drink, and put him to bed.

After he had got his breakfast next morning she gave him a drink out of her little bottle of balsam in a cup of gold.   She then put her hand in her bosom, and took out of it a letter, and said to him, " Thou shalt give this to the woman whom thou shalt see standing in the door of the Castle to which thou shalt come."

He now went away, having with him the great sword with which he struck the heads off the Giant.   He got on smoothly until he arrived at the next Castle, a great shapeless mass of a place without window or turret on it.   He saw the woman standing in the door, and cried to her that he had a letter for her.   She seized the letter, and after she had read it, she laid hold of him by the hand, and took him in.

She washed his hands and feet with a mixture of water and milk.   She then looked at his sword, and said to him, where did he find yon blade?   He replied that he found it in the Castle in which he was last night.   "Since thou hast got thus far, thy sword will serve thee, and thou shalt not part with it as long as the breath is in thee till thou reach the end of thy journey.   The Great Fiery Dragon of the Seven Serpent Heads and of the Venomous Sting is staying in this Castle. *She* will come at sunrise to-morrow, and thou must meet her outside, for if she get inside, neither thou nor I will be seen alive any more." She then sent him to sleep in a warm, comfortable bed.

She herself remained awake, and when the time for him to rise came, she wakened him. She gave him his breakfast, and after his breakfast a drink out of her little bottle of balsam in her cup of gold. He then grasped his sword, and turned out.

Scarcely had he got over the threshold of the door when he felt the Dragon coming. He made ready for her, and as soon as she came a hard contest began between them. He was defending himself from the heads, while she was wounding him with a large sting which she had in the end of her tail. They carried on the fight to the time of the going down of the sun. Then she said to him, "Thy bed is thine to-night yet, but meet me before sunrise to-morrow." The Dragon went her own way, and he returned in to the Castle.

The woman washed his sores, put balsam to every wound which was on his body, and sent him to bed.

When he awoke next morning he felt that he was as whole and sound as he ever was. After he had risen, and had got his breakfast and a drink of the balsam, he took with him his sword and went to meet the Dragon. They fought from morning to evening, he defending himself from the heads, and she wounding him with the sting of her tail. At going down of sun they stopped. She went her own way, and he returned to the Castle.

The woman served him this night as she did on the night before. When he awoke on the third morning he was as whole of his sores as he ever was. After he had got his breakfast and a drink of the balsam, he grasped his sword, and went to meet the Dragon.

On this morning he heard her coming with horrible screaming. But he thought that since he stood the two days before, he would try her this day yet. The Monster came, and they went at each other. She was shooting stings out of each mouth at him, and he was defending himself from her with his sword. About the greying of the evening he was growing weak, but if he was, he understood that she also was losing her strength. This gave him courage, and he closed boldly with her. At the going down of the sun she gave up, and stretched herself on the ground.

" Now," said she, " thou hast vanquished me, but the advantage was with thee. At night thou wert getting thy sores washed and healed, and thou wert warm and comfortable at the fireside in my Castle. But if I had got half an hour's time of the warmth of the fire, thou hadst returned no more than those who came before thee." Alastir now drew his sword, and with seven strokes sent the seven heads off the Dragon. But at the seventh stroke she gave her tail a lift, and struck him in the side. He fell as if he were dead, and he neither saw nor felt anything further until he awoke about midnight.

The woman was then washing and healing his sores. When she was done of that she put him to bed. On the next morning she went where he was, and asked of him how he felt. He answered that he felt strong (and) sound. " That is good," said she ; " the greater part of thy trials are now past."

When he arose and got his breakfast, she said to him, " Thou hast killed the Great Giant of the Two Heads in the Castle at the end of the Rocky Path of Ben Buie, thou hast killed the Great Giant of the Three Heads, Three Humps, and Three Knobs in the Great Castle of the Seven Turrets, and thou hast killed the Fiery Dragon of the Seven Serpent Heads and of the Venomous Sting in this Gloomy Castle. Only one of those who came before thee on the journey on which thou art going got thus far. He came over the Rocky Path of the Yellow Mountain (Ben Buie), and over the Path of the Red Lake almost drowned. He got through broken ground past the first two Castles, but he could not go past this Castle without going through it. The Fiery Dragon met him at the door, and killed him. But thou hast come on the right path, and success was with thee thus far. I will not keep thee longer, for thou hast many things yet to do. Thou hast got but a day and year for killing the Bare-Stripping Hangman, and if thou hast not thy work finished before then, he will take away with him my fourth sister as he took us. I will go with thee, and put thee on the head of the way. Thou shalt neither stop nor rest until thou reach the Great Barn of the Seven Stoops (*Criúb*), of the Seven Bends (*Lúb*), and of the Seven Couples. Thou shalt see under the Barn on the Yellow Knoll of the Sun, a really old Man cutting divot with a turf-spade. Thou shalt tell him the business on which thou art, and he will tell thee what thou must say and do after that. Thou shalt take advice from every one that will give it to thee faithfully. The blessing of the King is with thee, the blessing of the Sorceress is with thee, the blessing of Sunbeam, my sister, is with thee, the blessing of Light-of-Shade is with thee, and thou hast also my blessing. Be going on thy journey, and everything will be right when thou returnest."

Then he went away. He was travelling onwards far long and full long. When he began to grow wearied he remembered his achievements and his victory. This lightened his mind, and he got on his way well. In the very midst of his thoughts he came in at the head of the very prettiest Glen he ever beheld. He said to himself, "It must be that I am not now far from the Great Barn of the Seven Couples." Before he let the word out of his mouth, he beheld the Barn a little before him, and the very prettiest Knoll that he ever saw, shining like gold in the sun, in the bottom of the Glen, and the very Man of the oldest appearance whom he ever beheld, cutting divot with a turf-spade on one side of the Knoll.

He took his way where the Man was, and gave him the salutation of the day. The man answered him briskly and vigorously, much younger in his talk than he was in his appearance, and asked him where was he from? " I came from the Castle of the King of Lochlan, through the Rocky Path of the Ben Buie, through the Castle at the end of the Path where I killed the Great Giant of the Two Heads, through the Great Castle of the Eight Turrets where I killed the Great Giant of the Three Heads, Three Humps, and Three Knobs, through the Gloomy Castle of the Fiery Dragon of the Seven Serpent Heads and of the Venomous Sting, and from that as far as this, to see if thou wouldst tell me where I can find the Soul of the Bare-Stripping Hangman?" The Old Man gave him a look in the face, and said, " Let me see thy sword, Hero." Alastir drew his sword out of the scabbard, and handed it to him. The Old Man took hold of the sword between his two fingers, and put it between him and the light. He then handed it back and said, " Let me see thee flourishing thy sword, Hero." Alastir seized the sword, and gave a back sweep and a front sweep with it as lightly as though it were the deer-knife that would be in his fist. The Old Man bounded towards him and took him by the hand and said, " Hero, thou hast come the way thou hast mentioned. I cannot tell thee where the Soul of the Bare-

Stripping Hangman is now, for it fled out of the place where it was four days ago.  But it may be that my father will tell thee."  "Oh, is thy father alive, or can I see him?"  "He is alive.  Yonder he is carrying the divot on his back.  Go where he is and ask him."

Alastir reached the Man carrying the divot, and asked of him if he knew where the Soul of the Bare-Stripping Hangman was hidden.  The Old Man answered, " No, it fled out of the place where it was three days ago. But it may be that my father will tell thee."  "Oh, is thy father alive, or may I see him?"  "Oh, he is alive, and thou canst also see him.  Yonder he is, over there casting the divot."  Alastir reached the man who was casting the divot, and said to him, could he tell where the Soul of the Bare-Stripping Hangman was hidden? He answered, " I cannot, for it fled out of the place where it was two days since.  But it may be that my father will tell thee."  "Oov, Oov, sir, can I see thy father, or is he able to speak to me, for he must be very old ?"  " Oh, thou canst see him, and he can speak to thee.  Yonder he is laying the divot."  Alastir reached the man who was laying the divot, and asked of him, could he tell where the Soul of the Bare-Stripping Hangman was hidden ?  He answered, " I cannot, for it fled out of the place where it was yesterday. But reach my father, and he will tell thee where thou canst find it."  " What sort of man is thy father? Can I see him, or can he speak to me ?"  " Thou shalt see him, and he will speak to thee, and tell thee what thou hast to do after this."  " But where shall I see him ?"  " He is in a little bunch (*sopan*) of moss behind the crooked stick (*maide-cròm*).  But I myself must go with thee.  When thou art speaking to him thou shalt take extreme care that thou go not within hands' length of him, for if he get a hold of a bit of thy body, he will bruise thee like a grain of barley under a quern-stone.

Before you part he will ask a hold of thy hand, and if thou give it to him he will bruise it until it shall be as small as the pin of a black pudding. But here is a wedge of oak," handing him a stout piece off the head of a caber, "and thou shalt give it to him when he asks thy hand."

They went in to the house where the Old Man was. The divot-layer took down a large armful of moss from behind the crooked stick (*maide-cròm*), and laid it on the hearth-stone. "The little bunch (*sopan*) is great, sir," said the Son of the King of Ireland. "Greater than that is my father within it," said the divot-layer. He took his father out of the little bunch (bunchie), and placed him on the flag-stone. "What is thy need of me now, son," said the father. "It is a long time since thou didst seek me." The son answered, "There is a Young Champion here who is seeking to know where the Soul of the Bare-Stripping Hangman is hidden." "Son of King Cormac in Ireland, which way hast thou come thus far?" inquired the Man of the Little-bunch of Moss. Alastir told him every step he took from the day he left his father's house, and everything that befell him up to that day. "Truthfully thou hast told me everything, Son of the King of Ireland. Thy father has burnt the Hen-wife, and thy mother is under sorrow for thee. Her prayer and her blessing follow thee, the blessing of the Young King of Riddles follows thee, the blessing of the Young Queen of Riddles follows thee, the blessing of the King of Lochlan follows thee, the blessing and victory of the Sorceress follow thee, and my blessing will follow thee. Thou wert faithful to thy brother, and every man and beast that shall meet thee will be faithful to thee. And, brave Hero, give me a shake of thy hand, and I will tell thee where thou shalt find the Soul of the Bare-Stripping Hangman." The Old Man stretched out his hand, and Alastir stretched out the wedge of oak to him. He seized the wedge, gave it a bruising and a shaking, and made pulp (*cothan*) of it. When he let it go he said, "Son of the King of Ireland, hard is thy hand, and it would need be thus far. Thou art tired, thirsty and hungry, thou art worthy of meat and drink, and thou shalt get both. After thy supper thon shalt go to bed, and at sunrise to-morrow thou shalt be ready for thy journey. Thou shalt keep going forward without turning, without stopping, without looking behind thee till thou reach the Thick-foliaged Grove of the Trees (*Doire Dlùth-dhuilleach nan Craobh*). Thou shalt see there the Swift-footed Hind of the Cliffs, near which neither dog nor man ever got. Thou shalt catch her, open her, and find a Salmon in her stomach. Thou shalt open the Salmon, and in its belly thou shalt find the Green Duck of the Smooth Feathers. In the belly of the Duck thou shalt find an Egg, and thou shalt catch the Egg and break it before it touch the ground. For if it touch the ground thou shalt never after that see king, or man, or men. But though thy hand is hard it will not break the Egg without my help." He felt beside him in the moss, and took out of it a little jar. He handed the jar to Alastir, and said, "There is ointment for thee. As soon as thou shalt reach the Thick-foliaged Grove of the Trees thou shalt pour the ointment on thy hands, and rub with them every bit of thy skin which happens to be naked, or which thou mayest think that the blood of Hind, or scale of Salmon, or feather of Duck, or shell of Egg will touch. Thou shalt accept hospitality from every man or beast that gives it thee without asking. And thou thyself shalt know what thou hast to do after that. Catch this ointment now, and take it with thee, and be ready for thy journey as I told thee." Alastir knew that it was not safe for him to stretch out his hand for the little jar. So he stretched out his sword, and said, " Put the little jar on the point of my finger." The Old Man did that, and grasped the sword in his hand, and bruised it till it was as round as a bit of stick. Then he said, " Thou shalt accomplish thy task. Thou shalt then return on the way on which thou hast come. Thou shalt take the King of Lochlan's daughters out of the Castles in which they are, (and bring them) with thee. Thou shalt then take thy way to the Castle of the Speckled Mountain (Ben Breck), where thou shalt find the Great Giant stretched, dead on the floor. Thou shalt cut off him the head and the feet as far as the knees, and shalt take them with thee to the Castle of the King of Lochlan. When thou shalt arrive at the Castle thou shalt put on a great fire, and when it is in the heat of its burning thou shalt throw them on the top of the fire. As soon as they shall get a singeing in the flame they shall become as handsome a young man as man ever saw. He is a brother of the King of Lochlan, who was stolen from his mother, when he was a child, by the Fiery Dragon. She was keeping him yonder under spells, doing every mischief he could on the King until thou didst come. Now, do as I told thee, and my blessing will accompany thee."

On the next day Alastir went away on his journey. He kept going forward far long and full long. The evening was coming on him, the calm, still clouds of day were departing, and the dark, gloomy clouds of night were approaching, the little nestling, folding, yellow-tipped birds were taking to rest at the roots of the bushes, and in the tops of the tree tufts, and in the snuggest, pretty, sheltered little holms they could choose for themselves. At last he was growing tired, and weak with hunger. He gave a look before him, and whom did he see but the Dog of the Great Headland? When they met each other, the kind Dog gave him a salutation and welcome heartily. He asked of him whither was he going? Alastir told him that he was going to seek the Soul of the Bare-Stripping Hangman. The Dog said to him, "The night is coming, and thou art wearied; come with me, and I will give thee the best hospitality I can to-night." He went with the Dog willingly. They reached the Lair of the Dog, and that was the dry, comfortable place, with abundance of fire, venison of deer, and of hinds and roes. He got enough to eat, and a warm, comfortable bed, with the skins of stags under him, and the skins of hinds and roes over him.

Next morning he got his breakfast of the same kind of food as he had at his supper. When he was going away the kind Dog said to him, "Any time a strong tooth that will not yield its hold, or a fast strong foot that will travel on the rocky top (*creachann*) of mountain, or run on the floor of glen, will do thee service, think of me, and I will be at thy side." He gave the kind Dog great thanks, and departed on his journey.

He kept going forward far long and full long, until he was growing tired and evening was coming on. He gave a look before him, and whom did he see coming to meet him but the Brown Otter of the Stream of Guidance. When they met, the Otter gave him a cheery salutation, and asked of him where was he going? Alastir told him that. "The night is coming and thou art wearied; come with me to-night, and thou shalt get the best hospitality I can give." He went with the Otter to his Cairn. That was the warm, comfortable place, with abundance of fire and enough of the fish of salmon and grilse. He got his supper well and very well, and as easy a bed as he ever slept on of the smooth bent of the fresh-water Lakes. Next morning he got his breakfast of the same sort as he had for his supper on the night before. When he was going away, the Otter said to him, "Any time a strong tail to swim under water, or to stem each current and rapid, will be of service to thee, think of me, and I will be at thy side." Alastir gave thanks to the kindly Otter, and departed.

He travelled on far long and full long, until he was growing tired and night was coming. He gave a look before him, and whom did he see squatting on a stone, but the Great Falcon of the Rock of Cliffs? When they met, the Falcon asked of him where was he going? and Alastir told him the journey on which he was. "The night is coming, and thou art wearied and hungry," said the Falcon; "thou hadst better stay with me to-night, and I will give thee the best hospitality I can." He went with the Falcon to his own sheltered cliff. That was the dry, comfortable place, where he got abundance of the flesh of every kind of birds, and a bed of feathers as easy as he ever lay on. Next morning, after he had got his breakfast, the Falcon said to him, "Any time a strong, supple wing which can travel through air or over mountain, will be of service to thee, think of me, and I will be at thy side."

He did not go far forward, when he came in sight of the Thick-foliaged Grove of the Trees. He reached the Grove, and scarcely had he got in when the Swift-footed Hind of the Cliffs sprang out and ascended the mountain. He stretched away after her, but the faster he went the farther she would be from him. When he exhausted himself pursuing her, he thought of the Dog, and said, "Would not the Dog of the Great Headland be useful here now?" No sooner did the word go out of his mouth than the Dog was at his side. He told the Dog that he was exhausted following the Hind, and that he was then farther from her than he was when he began to pursue her.

The Dog went after her, and he went after the Dog till they reached the side of the Green Lakelet. Then the

Dog caught the Hind, and left her at Alastir's feet. It was then that Alastir remembered the ointment. He poured it quickly on his hands, and rubbed it to every bit of his skin that the Hind's blood might touch. He then tackled the Hind, and opened her. But if he did open her it was not without a fight, for her hoofs were so sharp and her feet so strong that if it were not for the ointment she would take him asunder in bits. When he opened the stomach the Salmon leaped out of it into the Green Lakelet.

He went after the Salmon round the Lakelet; but when he would be at one bank, the Salmon would be under another bank. At last he remembered the Brown Otter of the Stream of Guidance, and on the spot he was at his side. He told the Otter that the Salmon was in the Lakelet, and that he could not get a hold of it. The Otter sprang out quickly into the water, and in a short time came back with the Salmon, and laid it at Alastir's feet. Alastir seized the Salmon, but as soon as he made a hole on its belly, the Duck of the Smooth Feather and Green Back sprang out, and flew to the other side of the Lakelet, and lay down there. He went after her; but when he reached that side on which she was, she rose and went back to the side which he had left. When he saw that he could not catch her, he remembered the Great Falcon of the Rock of the Cliffs, and in an instant he was at his side. He told him how the Duck got away, and that he could not catch her. The Falcon sprang quickly after her, and in an instant came with her and left her at Alastir's feet.

Alastir remembered that if the egg should touch the ground everything was lost. He therefore opened the Duck cautiously, and as soon as the Egg came in sight he seized it quickly in his hand, but the Egg gave a bounce out of his fist, and sprang the three heights of a man in the air. But before it struck the earth, Alastir got a hold of it, and gave it a hard bruising between his two hands and two knees, and crushed it in fragments.

He had now finished everything which he had got to do. He therefore returned the way he came. He found the path as smooth and safe as it formerly was full of obstacles and dangers. In a short time he reached the Gloomy Castle of the Fiery Serpent. The woman met him at the door, and cried, " Darling of the Men of the World ! thou hast conquered, and thou shalt receive thy reward." She went away with him, and in a short time they reached the Great Castle of the Eight Turrets. Light-of-Shade met them at the door, and went away with them. Then they reached the Great Castle at the end of the Rocky Path, and found Sunbeam waiting them. She went away with them, and they reached the Castle of the Great Giant of Ben Breck, and found him stretched dead on the floor. Alastir seized his own Great Sword, and took the head and feet as far as the knees off him. He tied them up and took them with him.

" Now," said Sunbeam, " to-night is the night in which the Great Giant was to come for my youngest sister, and my father is in heavy sorrow, because he is sure that thou hast been killed, since thou didst not return before now. He has all his men assembled to meet the Giant when he will arrive. But his sorrow will be turned to cheerfulness, and his sadness to laughter. When he comes to meet us, thou shalt tell him how it befell thee since the day in which thou didst depart to this night."

When they were nearing the Castle, they saw a great host awaiting the coming of the Giant. The King and all in the Castle were sad and sorrowful for the maiden who was to be taken from them. But in the midst of their grief, the King gave a look out of the window, and saw Alastir coming with three women in his company, and the head and feet of the Giant over his shoulder. He sprang out to meet him, seized him between his two arms, and kissed him. "Darling of the Men of the World! I knew that victory would be with thee, and I will be as good as my promise to thee. But since thou hast brought home all my daughters, thou shalt get thy choice of them, from the oldest one to the youngest." "Well," said Alastir, "she whom I went to save from the Bare-Stripping Hangman is my choice." When each of the rest heard this she was sorry that he did not choose herself. But since he won the victory, and did so much for them, they all consented that he should get the one he chose.

The King then asked Alastir what was he going to do with the head and feet of the Giant. "Before I eat food or take a drink thou shalt see that," said Alastir. He then got fuel, and made a large fire, and when the fire was in the heat of its burning, he threw the head and feet in the midst of the flame. As soon as the hair of the head was singed and the skin of the feet burnt, the very handsomest young man they ever beheld sprang out of the fire. "Oh, the son of my father and mother who was stolen in his childhood!" said the King, springing over and embracing him in his arms. When they saluted each other, they all went in to the Castle.

The King resolved that Alastir and his daughter should be married that very night. But when Alastir heard this, he said, "King of Lochlan, thine offer is good enough. But I will not marry thy daughter, nor will I enter into possession of a bit of thy kingdom, until thou shalt send for the Young King of Riddles and the Young Queen of Riddles to the wedding." The King now fell into great anxiety, because he did not know in what direction he should send for them. In the midst of his thoughts he remembered the Sorceress. He went where she was, and told her Alastir's request. Get thou everything else ready, and I will have them here before sunrise to-morrow," said the Sorceress. And what she said proved true. The first look the King gave next morning in the direction of the sea, he saw two coracles (*curachs*) coming to the shore. Out of one of them came Cormac and his wife, and out of the other came the Sorceress.

Alastir sprang out to meet them, and that was the affectionate welcome they gave each other! The King came to meet them, and he gave them a cordial salutation. They went to the Castle, and the marriage was consummated. After the marriage was over, they made a great feast which lasted a day and year. At the end of that time Cormac and his wife returned to their own place, and Alastir and his wife went with them. Cormac remained in the Castle of the King of Riddles, but Alastir went back to his father's place. When his mother saw him she gave him a great welcome, and his father rejoiced greatly when he heard that Cormac was the Young King of Riddles. The King now made another great feast for Alastir and his wife and for all who were about him.

And I got nothing but butter on a live coal, porridge in a basket, (and) paper shoes. They sent me (for water) to the stream, and they (the paper shoes) came to an end.

---

## AN CROCHAIRE LOM-RUSGACH.

---

Bha Righ roimhe so 'an Éirinn a bha pòsda dà uair, agus aig an robh mac ris gach té d' a mhnaibh. B' e ainm mac na céud mhnà Cormac, agus ainm mac na dara mnà Alastair. Bha athair ro mhòr mu Chormac, agus bhitheadh e daonnan 'g a thabhairt leis do 'n Bheinn-sheilg.

Bha Cailleach-chearc aig an Righ, agus air là àraid chaidh i 's tigh fàr an robh a' Bhan-righ, agus coltas tùrsach, brònach oirre. Dh' fheòraich a' Bhan-righ dhi gu dé 'bha cur oirre? "Is mòr sin agus cha bheag, a Bhan-righ na truaighe!" "Gu dé 's ciall d' a sin?" "Gu 'm bheil an Righ cho gaolach air Cormac, mac na céud mhnà, agus gur ann aige 'dh' fhàgas e 'n righeachd 'us gu 'm bi do mhac-sa falamh." "Cha-n 'eil comas air sin ma 's e toil an Righ e." "Ù, ged tha, cha ruig a' chùis leas a bhi mar sin. Ma bheir thu dhomhs' an rud a dh' iarras mi ort ni mi do mhac 'n a righ." "Gu dé, mata, an duais a bhitheas tu 'g iarraidh airson sin a dheanamh?" "Cha mhòr sin: na ni tiugh an crogan dubh de mhin, agus na ni tana de dh' ìm e, làn ailleagan mo dhà chluais de chlòimh, agus lèud mo dhara màis de fheòil." "Gu dé na ni tiugh an crogan dubh de mhin?" "Ceithir salldraichean déug." "Gu dé 'nis a ni tana de dh' ìm e?" "Na bhitheas air do sheachd tighean cruidh gu ceann sheachd bliadhna." "Gu dé 'nis làn ailleagan do dhà chluais de chlòimh?" "Na bhitheas air do sheachd tighean chaorach gu ceann sheachd bliadhna." "Agus gu dé 'nis lèud do dhara màis de fheòil?" "Na bhitheas air do sheachd tighean dhamh gu ceann sheachd bliadhna." "Tha sin mòr, a bhean." "Tha, ach is beag e seach trian de dh' Eirinn." "Is beag," thubhairt a' Bhan-righ, "agus gheibh thu e. Ach gu dé 'n seòl a ghabhas tu air mo Mhac-sa 'dheanamh 'n a righ?" "Bha Cormac a' gearan an dé nach robh e gu math. 'Nuair a thig an luchd-seilg dhachaidh their thu ris an Righ gu 'm féum Cormac fuireachd aig an tigh am màireach, agus do dh' Alastair dol do 'n Bheinn-sheilg 'n a àite. Ni mise deoch do Chormac, agus bheir thusa dha i an déigh do chàch falbh, agus cha chuir e dragh tuillidh air do mhac-s' o bhi 'na righ." Chòrd so gu math ris a Bhan-righ, agus gheall i gu 'n deanamh i mar dh' iarr a' Chailleach-chearc oirre.

Bha na mnathan a' smaointeachadh nach robh duine 'g an cluinntinn am feadh a bha iad a' dealbhadh an uilc, ach ré na h-ùine bha Alastair ri farchluais aig cùl an doruis. Bha e ro dhiombach mu 'n ni a bha iad a' dol a dheanamh, a chionn gu 'n robh e féin agus Cormac cho gaolach air a chéile 's a bha dà

I

bhràthair riamh.   Smaointich e gu dé 'dheanadh e, agus chuir
e roimhe beachd nam ban innseadh do Chormac cho luath
agus a thigeadh e dhachaidh.

Thàinig Cormac dhachaidh mu fheasgar.   Bha e gu math
sgìth, agus cha robh e 'g a fhaireachdainn féin n' a b' fhearr na
bha e anns a' mhadainn.   'Chaidh Alastair fàr an robh e, agus
dh' innis e dha gach nì a thachair eadar a mhàthair agus a'
Chailleach-chearc.   Ghabh Cormac bochd an t-eagal, agus
thubhairt e ri Alastair gu dé 'dheanadh e ?   Fhreagair Alastair,
" Bitheadh misneach agad, agus ni mise dòigh air am faigh
sinn air falbh as an carabh, agus cha chuir sinn dragh tuillidh
orra.   Falbhaidh mise 'm maireach le m' athair do 'n Bheinn-
sheilg, ach cha téid mi fad' air an t-slighe 'n uair a their mi ris
gu 'n till mi dhachaidh a chionn nach tagh leam dol do 'n
Bheinn.   Mu 'n ruig mise, theid mo mhàthair a 's tigh leis an
deoch gu d' ionnsaidh.   Beiridh tu air a' chòrn as a laimh,
ach air son ni no neach a chunnaic thu riamh na blais as, agus
na cuir a chòir do bheòil e.   Togaidh tu do làmh mar gu 'm
bitheadh tu dol a dh' òl, agus an sin léumaidh tu 'mach leis ann
ad laimh.   Bithidh an dà each 'is luaith 'a th' anns an stàbul
agams' a' feitheamh ort, agus falbhaidh sinn."   Agus mar sin
rinn iad.

Air an ath latha cha deachaidh Alastair ach goirid le athair
an uair a dhiùlt e dol ni 'b' fhaide, agus a thill e dhachaidh.
Bha fhios aig' air an àm anns am faigheadh Cormac an deoch,
agus chuir e roimhe gu 'm bitheadh na h-eich deas aige mar
gheall e.   Ach mu 'n gann a bha iad aige fo 'n dìollaidibh,
thàinig Cormac a mach le cabhaig, agus an còrn aige 'n a
laimh.   Ghlaodh Alastair ris, " Léum gu grad a' d' dhìollaid,
agus lean ris na th' agad."

Rinn e sin, agus dh' fhalbh iad le cheile cho luath 's a
bheireadh casan nan each iad.   Chum iad air an aghaidh gun
stad gun tàmh gus an robh na h-eich a' tabhairt thairis orra.
An sin theirinn iad, agus shuidh iad sìos anns an àite 's an
robh iad.

Thubhairt Alastair ri Cormac, " Leig fhaicinn domh an còrn
a nis ?"   Rug e air a' chòrn a laimh a bhràthar, fhuair e
bioran, agus thubhairt e, " Chi sinn a nis gu dé 'n stuth a th'

anns a' chòrn." Thum e 'm bioran anns an stuth, agus chuir e boinne dh' e 'an cluais gach aon de na h-eich. "Gu dé 'tha thu deanamh mar sin ?" arsa Cormac. "Feith beagan, agus chi thu," thubhairt Alastair. An ùine ghoirid thòisich na h-eich air dol mu 'n cuairt anns an tuainealaich, agus cha b' fhada gus an do thuit iad fuar marbh air an talamh. "Saoil, a Chormaic, na 'n d' òl thu 'n deoch gu dé 'thachradh dhuit?" ars' Alastair. "Gu dé ach gu 'm bithinn marbh roimhe so," thubhairt Cormac.

Am feadh a bha iad a' còmhradh, thàinig ceithir fithich, agus laidh iad air carcaisibh nan each. Thòisich iad air piocadh nan sùl as na h-eich, agus an uair a dh' ith iad na sùilean dh' itealaich iad air falbh anns an athar. Ach cha deachaidh iad ach goirid an uair a thug iad sgriachan goint' asda, agus a thuit iad marbh air an talamh. "Gu dé do bharail a nis air an deoch, a Chormaic ?" thubhairt Alastair. "Gu dé ach na 'n d' òl mi dhi, nach robh mi 'so an dràsd'," arsa Cormac.

Dh' éirich Alastair, agus thug e leis na ceithir fithich ann an neapacain, agus dh' fhalbh e féin agus a bhràthair a rìs air an turus. Bha Alastair a' gleidheadh a' chéum thoisich, a chionn gu 'n robh buaidhean air leis an robh fhios aige gu dé bha ri tachairt orra. Chum iad air an aghaidh gus an d' thàinig iad gu baile beag.

Chaidh Alastair a 's tigh do thigh-còcaireachd anns a' bhaile, agus dh' iarr e air a' Chòcaire na fithich a ghréidheadh cho math 's a ghréidh e eòin riamh, ach gun e chur mèur no làmh a chòir a bheòil gus am bitheadh iad gréidht' aige, agus gus an glanadh e a lamhan gu math agus gu ro mhath. "Gu dé is ciall d' a sin ?" thubhairt an Còcaire. "Cha do ghréidh mise biadh riamh roimhe nach fhaotainn a bhlàsad." "Na blais agus na h-ith mìr dhiù so, air neo cha-n fhaigh thu idir iad." Gheall an Còcaire gu 'n deanadh e mar dh' iarradh air.

An déigh do 'n Chòcaire na fithich a ghréidheadh, agus paidheadh fhaotainn airson a shaothair, cheangail Alastair iad 'n a neapaicin, agus dh' fhalbh e féin agus Cormac a rìs air an turus. Air an rathad thubhairt Alastair, "Tha coille mhòr romhainn anns am bheil ceithir robairean fichead a' fuireachd nach do leig duine riamh seachad orra gun a mharbhadh, agus nach leig sinne seachad ma 's urrainn iad ar bacadh." "Gu dé ni sinn," thubhairt Cormac. "Fàg sin agamsa," fhreagair Alastair.

An uair a bha iad a' dol troimh 'n choille thug iad an aire do lianaig bhòidhich os ceann an rathaid air an robh iad ag iomachd, agus do na robairean 'g am blìonadh féin ris a ghréin aig bràigh na lianaige. Chum iad air an aghaidh, ach an uair a bha iad dìreach a' dol seachad fo 'n àit' anns an robh na robairean, ghlaodh dithis dhiù, "Cò an dà bheadagan bhalaich aig am bitheadh a chridhe dol seachad air an t-slighe so gun sinne fheòraich?" Ghabh iad uile 'nuas far an robh an dà choigreach, agus thubhairt iad riù gu 'n robh iad a' dol a chur nan ceann diù. "Oh! mata," ars' Alastair, "cha-n 'eil comas air. Tha sinne sgìth agus acrach, agus na 'n leigibh sibh leinn greim bithidh itheadh mu 'n cuireadh sibh gu bàs sinn bhitheadh sinn 'n ar comain." "Ma tha biadh agaibh, gabhadh e gu h-ealamh," thubhairt na robairean. "Tha biadh againn," thubhairt Alastair, "agus gheibh sibhse cuid d' e ma thoilicheas sibh."

An sin dh' fhosgail e a neapaicin, agus rinn e na fithich 'n an sia pìosan fichead, pìos airson gach fear a bh' anns a' chuideachd. "A nis," thubhairt e, "feithidh sibh gus am bi sibh uile riaraichte, agus tòisichidh sibh air itheadh còmhla, oir ma dh' itheas cuid agaibh an earrann féin an toiseach léumaidh iad air càch airson an earrann-san, agus millidh agus marbhaidh sibh a chéile." A' so rinn na robairean gàire mòr fanaid, ach thubhairt iad gu 'n deanadh iad mar dh' iarradh orra. An uair a bha iad uile riaraichte thog Alastair a suas a làmh, agus ghlaodh e, "Itheadh a nis." Rinn iad sin, agus nìhol iad am biadh. Ach cha b' fhada gus an do thòisich fear an déigh fir dhiù ri suidhe 'dheanamh, agus a h-uile fear a shuidheadh thuiteadh e 'n a chadal, agus as a' chadal sin cha robh e dùsgadh tuillidh. Mu dheireadh bha iad uile 'n cadal a' bhàis.

"A nis," thubhairt Alastair, "tha sud seachad, agus tha 'n rathad réidh romhainn gu ruig Caisteal Righ Ceist. Falbhaidh tusa a' d' Righ Eirionn, agus falbhaidh mise 'am ghille agad. Ma dh' iarrar ort ni air bith a dheanamh their thu gur e 'n

gille 'bhitheas a' deanamh sin anns an dùthaich as an d' thàinig
thusa. An uair a ruigeas tu Caisteal Righ Ceist, féumaidh tu
Ceist a chur no Ceist fhuasgladh, agus mur dean thu sin théid
do cheann a chur air stob anns a' ghàradh a tha mu choinneamh
an doruis. Ràinig mòran d' ar seòrsa-ne an Caisteal romhainn,
agus a chionn nach b' urrainn iad ceist a chur no ceist
fhuasgladh chaidh an cinn a chur air stuib a' ghàraidh. Tha
aon stob falamh ann fathast, agus théid do cheann-sa 'chur air
mur cuir, no mar fuasgail thusa, no mis' air do shon, Ceist
a nochd."

Ràinig iad an Caisteal. Chuir Righ Ceist fàilte mhòr orra,
oir shaoil e gu 'm b' ann a dh' iarraidh a nighinn a thàinig iad,
mar na feadhainn a thàinig rompa. Cha robh iad ach goirid a
's tigh an uair a chaidh biadh a chur mu 'n coinneamh, ach mu
'n do thòisich iad air a ghabhail thubhairt Righ Ceist, "A
Righ Eirionn, cuir ceist no fuasgail ceist." Fhreagair Righ
Eirionn, agus thubhairt e, "Is e 'n gille 'bhitheas a deanamh sin
anns an dùthaich as an d' thàinig mise." "Faigh a nuas do
ghille, mata," arsa Righ Ceist. Thàinig an gille. "'Ille Righ
Eirionn, cuir ceist no fuasgail ceist," thubhairt Righ Ceist.
Fhreagair an Gille, "Mharbh a h-aon a dhà, mharbh a dhà
ceithir, mharbh ceithir ceithir thar fhichead, agus thàrr dithis
as." Smaointich Righ Ceist, ach cha b' urrainn e a' cheist
fhuasgladh. Mu dheireadh thubhairt e ris a' Ghille, "Bi falbh
an dràsd, agus gheibh thu fuasgladh na ceist am màireach." An
déigh na dinnearach chaith iad an còr de 'n oidhche 'g
innseadh sgeòil thaitneach gus an d' thàinig àm dol a laidhe.

An sin chuir Righ Ceist fios air a nighinn agus air a dà
mhaighdein coimhideachd dhéug. Thubhairt e ris na maighdeannan, có air bith aca a gheibheadh fuasgladh na ceist' o thùs
bho Ghille Righ Eirionn, gu 'm faigheadh i 'mhac-san r' a
phòsadh agus leth na rìgheachd. Thubhairt iad gu 'm
feuchaidh iad ris. Thionndaidh e 'n sin r' a nighinn, agus
gheall e dhi a roghainn leannain, agus leth na righeachd na 'm
faigheadh ise fuasgladh na ceist' o thùs.

Bha na maighdeannan greis a' meòrachadh gu dé 'n dòigh
air am faigheadh iad a mach fuasgladh na ceiste. Mu dheireadh
chòrd iad an Gille 'chur anns an aon seòmar a b' fhuaire 's bu

mhiosa 'bha 's a Chaisteal, fàr an robh tuill air na ballachan, agus a bha na h-uinneagan briste, agus gaoth 'us uisge 'tighinn a 's tigh orra ; gu 'n cuireadh iad a Mhaistir anns an t-seòmar a b' fhearr a bha 's tigh ; agus gu 'n abradh iad ris a' Ghille, gu 'm faigheadh e leaba agus seòmar cho math 's a bh' aig a' Mhaistir na 'n innseadh e fuasgladh na ceist o thùs.  Agus mar sin rinn iad.

Cha robh 'n Gille ro fhada 'n a laidhe an uair a dh' fhairich e 'n dorus 'g a fhosgladh.   Thionndaidh e air a chluasaig, agus chunnaic e maighdean òg dhreachmhor 'n a seasamh air an ùrlar.   Thuig e gu ro mhath gu dé 'bh' air a h-aire.   Thubhairt a' mhaighdean ris, " An cadal dhuit, 'Ille Righ Eirionn ?"  " Cha chadal ; oir cha-n fhàrdach chadail a fhuair mi, gaoth 'us fuachd fodham, agus gaoth 'us uisg' os mo cheann.   Is fad' a bheir mi ainm an tighe so 'n uair a dh' fhalbhas mi."  " Gheibh thu leaba cho math agus a th' aig do Mhaistir ma dh' innseas tu dhomhsa fuasgladh na ceist' o thùs."   Ach cha d' innis e sin di, agus leig e leatha falbh as eugmhais a dh' ionnsaidh chàich.   Thàinig iadsan an sin aon an deigh aoin, ach dh' eirich dhoibh mar dh' eirich dhise.

Cho luath 's a chaidh an té mu dheireadh dhiù a mach, dh' fhalbh an Gille do sheòmar a Mhaistir, agus chaidh a Mhaistir do sheòmar a' Ghille.   Cha robh e ach goirid an sin an uair a thàinig nighean an Righ a 's tigh.   Thubhairt i mar thubhairt na maighdeannan roimpe, " An cadal dhuit, 'Ille Righ Eirionn ?" " Cha chadal ; oir cha-n fhàrdach chadail a fhuair mi, gaoth 'us fuachd fodham, agus gaoth 'us uisg' os mo cheann.   Is fada 'bheir mi ainm an tighe so 'n uair a dh' fhalbhas mi."   " Mata, gheibh thu leaba cho math 's a th' aig do Mhaistir ma dh' innseas tu dhomhsa fuasgladh na ceist' o thùs."   Ach cha d' innis e sin di, agus dh' fhalbh i.

Air an ath mhadainn dh' fheòraich Righ Ceist de na maighdeannan an d' fhuair iad fuasgladh na ceiste ?   Thubhairt iad nach d' fhuair.   Dh' fheòraich e 'n sin d' a nighinn an d' fhuair ise i ?   Agus thubhairt i nach d' fhuair.

An uair a shuidh iad sios aig am braiceas thubhairt Righ Ceist, " A Righ Eirionn, cuir ceist no fuasgail ceist."   " Mar dh' innis mi dhuit an raoir is e mo Ghille 'bhitheas a' cur ceist

no fuasgladh ceist air mo shon." " Faigh a nuas do Ghille,
mata." Thàinig an Gille. " 'Ille Righ Eirionn, cuir ceist no
fuasgail ceist," arsa Righ Ceist. " Cha d' fhuair mi fuasgladh
na céud cheist fhathast," ars' an Gille. " A bheadagain
bhalaich, an ann a' cumail bruidhne riumsa 'tha thu ? Cuir
ceist no fuasgail ceist, airneo bithidh do cheann air a chur
dhìot air a' chéud-lomaidh, agus air a chur air an stob anns a'
ghàradh." " Cuiridh mi ceist mata," ars' an Gille. " Cluinneam
i, mata," fhreagair Righ Ceist.

[Chuir an Gille ceist a rinn e air na nithibh a thachair dha
fhéin agus d' a Mhaistir air an oidhche roimhe. Dh' fhuasgail
Righ Ceist a' cheist sin, ach dh' fhairslich a chéud té air. A
ghiorrachadh a' chuid so de'n sgéul, thug Righ Ceist a nigheann
do Righ Eirionn, agus chaidh am pòsadh gu 'n dàil, agus banais
mhòr a dheanamh air an son.]

Dh' fhuirich Alastair leò mòran làithean, a' cur seachad na h-
ùine ri seilg agus ri iasgach. Air là àraid, agus e 'g iasgach air
creig laimh ris a' mhuir, agus a' smaointeachadh gu dé 'dheanadh
e, falbh no fuireachd le Cormac, chual e plub mòr anns an
loch aig bun na creige. Mu 'n d' fhuair e sealltainn a null no
'nall, léum Dobhar-chù Mòr as an uisge, rug e air dhà chaol-cois-
se air, agus dh' fhalbh e 'mach leis air a' mhuir. Cha-n fhac e
tuillidh lèus talaimh no athair gus an d' fhàgadh e os ceann an
làin anns an aon òb a bu bhòidhche a chunnaic e riamh le
gainmheich mhìn, gheal o bhéul na tuinne gu féur gorm. Bha
e 'nis ann an Lochlann.

An ùine ghoirid thill an Dobhar-chù air ais agus bradan fior-
uisg' aige 'n a bhéul. Dh' fhàg e 'm bradan aig casan Alastair
agus thubhairt e ris, " Turus fada 's am bith air am bi thu dol,
no cruaidh-chàs 's am bith a bitheas a' 'tighinn ort, gabh greim
de 'n iasg so romh laimh. Ni thu bothan a' so agus fanaidh tu
ann gus am faic thu tuillidh na mise, agus am faigh thu tuillidh
na mo chomhairle-sa."

Chuir e 'suas am bothan an oidhche sin féin. Bhruich e 'n
sin pìos de 'n bhradan, agus an déigh dha itheadh dh' e dh'
fhairich e ni 'bu treise na bha e riamh.

Air an ath mhadainn dh' éirich e, agus chaidh e 'mach romh
chéud-lomaidh gu ceann a' bhothain. Sheas e, agus chunnaic

e 'm Fiadh Mòr Céir-gheal a' tighinn dìreach air an àite 's an robh e 'n a sheasamh, agus an Gaothar Geal, Cluas-dhearg a bha as a dhéigh 'g a ruith gu dian. An uair a bha 'm Fiadh a' dlùthachadh air, bha breth air bhreth aig a Ghaothar air an Fhiadh ; agus anns an dol seachad thug an Gaothar tathunn as, agus léum e 'n amhaich an Fhéidh, agus dh' fhàg e marbh e aig casan Alastair.

"Nis," ars' an Gaothar ri Alastair, "bha thusa dìleas do d' bhràthair, agus gheibh thu do dhuais. Turus fada 's am bith air am bi thu 'dol, no cruaidh-chàs 's am bith a bhitheas a' tighinn ort, ithidh tu romh laimh greim de 'n bhradan fhìor-uisge agus greim de 'n fhiadh so ; agus o aon ni a chi no 'chluinneas tu, cha-n éirich béud dhuit tuillidh. Agus mu 'n teirig sin duit gheibh thu fios gu dé ni thu." An sin ghuidh an Gaothar Geal, Cluas-dhearg soirbheachadh math leis, agus dh' fhalbh e.

Thug Alastair am fiadh a 's tigh d' a bhothan, agus dh' fhàg e laimh ris a' bhradan e. Rinn e a bhraiceas, agus dh' ith e pìos de 'n bhradan agus pìos de 'n fhiadh. Chaidh e 'sin a mach, agus air dha sùil a thabhairt uaithe, chunnaic e duine mòr a' tighinn 'us coltas righ air, agus dà churaidh dhéug còmhla ris. Thàinig iad dìreach a dh' ionnsaidh an aite 's an robh e.

Thubhairt an Righ ris, "Ciamar a bha 'chridhe no 'dhànachd agad tighinn a mharbhadh an Fhéidh Mhòir Chéirghil agamsa ?" "Thàinig d' fhiadh leis féin ann am rathad, bha féum agam air biadh, agus mharbh mi e," ars' Alastair. "Mata," ars' an Righ, "o 'n mharbh thu 'm fiadh féumaidh tu cath ri m' chuid curaidhean-sa gus an tuit thusa no iadsan," "Tha mise 'm aonar, a Righ," ars' Alastair, "tha sibh-se 'n ur mòran, còmhla ri sin tha mi gun lann agam." "Cha bhi thu gun lann," thubhairt an Righ. "Gheibh thu mo lann-sa, agus ma bheir thu do bheatha as leis, is leat fhéin e." "Feuchaidh mi co dhiù," thubhairt Alastair. "Ach tha mi 'g iarraidh mar fhàbhar gu 'n leig thu leam gréim bithidh itheadh mu 'n tòisich mi." "Gheibh thu sin," thubhairt an Righ, 'us e a sìneadh a chlaidheimh dha.

Chaidh Alastair a 's tigh d' a bhothan, agus dh' ith e greim de 'n iasg agus greim de 'n fhiadh. An uair a bha e réidh shàth e claidheamh an Righ ann an carcais an fhéidh, agus chaidh e cho furasda troimhe agus ged' b' uisg' e. "Buaidh an t-sàthaidh so a bhi leis gach buille," ars' Alastair. Dh' fhairich e gu 'n robh e féin ann am mòr-mhisnich agus an làn neart, agus thionn e 'mach a dh' ionnsaidh a' chatha.

Thubhairt an Righ ris gu 'm faigheadh e cothrom na Féinne, fear an déigh fir. Chaidh aon de na curaidhnean a chur a mach m' a choinneamh. Ach cha b' fhada 'bha iad ag iomairt lann an uair a thuit curaidh an Righ tròm-leònt' air a' bhlàr. Ghlaodh Alastair ris an ath fhear tighinn air aghaidh. Thàinig e, ach an ùine ghoirid thuit e leònt' air a bhlàr mar thuit a chéud fhear. Dh' éirich a leithid eile do 'n treas fhear.

An uair a chunnaic an Righ a thriùir churaidh a' sileadh fala agus a' bàsachadh thubhairt e ris a' choigreach, "Ge b' e àit' a 's dùthaich dhuit is curaidh thu co dhiù." Ghlaodh Alastair an sin ri càch tighinn air an aghaidh gu grad ma bha aige-san ri dol trompa uile. Ach chuir an Righ stad air an iomairt. Thionndaidh e ri Alastair, agus thubhairt e ris, " Choisinn thu do chlaidheamh le buaidh, agus gheibh thu e. Falbh leamsa agus ni mis' thu ni 's fearr na tha thu 'n so." An sin dh' iarr Alastair air mar chaoimhneas am bothan fhàgail 'n a sheasamh mar bha e gun fhios nach féumadh e tilleadh ann fathast. Fhuair e iarrtas, agus dh' fhalbh e leis an Righ.

Air an rathad bha 'n Righ fo thròm-cheal airson call a thri churaidhnean. Ach, mu dheireadh, thubhairt e ris féin gu 'n robh an t-aon a fhuair e cho math ris an triùir a chaill e. Chum iad air an aghaidh tromh choille, thar monaidh, agus thar mòintich gus an d' ràinig iad Caisteal mòr, briadha nach fhac Alastair riamh roimhe a leithid. Dh' iarr an Righ air dol a 's tigh còmhla ris. Ghabh na curaidhnean an rathad féin, agus chaidh Alastair a 's tigh leis an Righ.

Chaidh biadh agus deoch a chur mu choinneamh Alastair, agus dh' iarr an Righ air òl agus itheadh. Fhreagair e nach itheadh e greim d' a bhiadh agus nach òladh e boinne d' a dheoch gus an innseadh e dha an t-aobhar airson an d' thug e 'n sud e. Dh' aithnich an Righ gu 'm b' e curaidh a bh' aige, agus thubhairt e gu 'n innseadh e sin da.

"Bha ceathrar nighean agam.    Chaidh triùir dhiù 'thabhairt
uam le Famhair Mòr a tha 'fuireachd 'an Coire Dubh na
Beinne Brice.    Thàinig e 'n toiseach an àm dol fodha na
gréine, agus thug e leis a' chéud té dhiù 'am làthair fhéin
agus 'an làthair mo chuid churaidh, agus cha-n fhaca mi
tuillidh i.    Chuir mi mo churaidhnean 'n a dhéigh, agus lean
iad e a dh' ionnsaidh a' Chaisteil aige.    Ach an uair a ràinig
iad e, mar sgathadh piorradh de ghaoith near rainneach anns
a' gheamhradh chuir e na cinn diù, agus cha d' fhuair ach aon
as a dh' innseadh sgeòil a chruadail dhomh.    An ceann sheachd
bliadhna thàinig e rithist, agus mar thachair air tùs thachair air
an uair sin.    An ceann sheachd bliadhn' eile, thàinig e agus thug
e leis an treas té.    Chuir mo chuid churaidhnean rompa gu 'm
bitheadh dìoghailt ac' air, agus gu 'n d' thugadh iad mo nighean
dachaidh g' am ionnsaidh.    Dh' fhalbh iad fo 'n làn armachd
a dh' fhaireadh Caisteal Coire Dubh na Beinne Brice.    An
déigh dhoibh fhaireadh ré thri chuairt gréine cha d' fhuair iad
cothrom air an Fhamhair.    Mu dheireadh bha iad a' fàs tròm
a dhìth cadail, agus lag a dhìth bithidh ; agus chuir iad rompa
gu 'n rachadh iad a dh' ionnsaidh a' Chaisteil agus gu 'm
faiceadh iad dé 'bha 's tigh.    Fhuair iad a dh' ionnsaidh Ùig
an Fhamhair, agus chunnaic iad gu 'n robh e 'n tròm chadal.
Thubhairt iad r' a cheile gu 'm b' e sin an t-àm dhoibh nighean
an Righ a dhìoghailt, agus an ceann a thabhairt de 'n Fhamhair.
Léum iad g' a ionnsaidh, agus bhuail iad an ceann deth le
'n claidhibh.    Cha bu luaith' a rinn iad sin na léum fìr-eun
mòr a nuas, agus a bhuail e 'chéud churaidh anns an aodann,
agus a leag se e.    Rinn e a ni céudn' air an ath fhear.    Agus
an uair a chunnaic an còrr sin theich iad.    Ach mu 'n gann a
fhuair iad a mach tromh gheat' a' Chaisteil chunnaic iad am
Famhair a' tighinn 'n an déigh, agus a cheann air mar bha e
roimhe.    An uair a chunnaic iad e shìn iad as, agus stad cha
d' rinn na fhuair dhiù as gus an d' ràinig iad so.    Ach a chuid
dhiù a thuit 'na lamhan, rùisg e gus an craicionn, agus chroch
e suas air cromagaibh ri turaidibh a' Chaisteil.    'Nis tha
cheathramh té do 'm nigheanaibh mar là 'us bliadhna do dh'
aois chàich an uair a chaidh an goid uam.    Ach aon 's am
bith a bheir dhachaidh g' am ionnsaidhsa an Àlaire Dhubh a

tha anns a' Bheinn, agus air nach deachaidh taod riamh is leis mo nighean agus gu leth mo rìgheachd."

"Is math do thairgse, a Righ," ars' Alastair. "Is mairg nach deanadh a dhìchioll g' a cosnadh." "Dh' aithnich mi gu 'm bu churaidh thu," ars' an Righ; "agus ma ni thu e gheibh thu do dhuais agus mòran tuillidh. Air madainn an ath latha ruigidh tu an stàbul agamsa, agus gheibh thu do roghainn sréine."

Ràinig Alastair an Stàbul air an ath mhadainn, agus fhuair e mòran dhaoine agus churaidhnean air thoiseach air a bha 'dol a dh' fhéuchainn an Alaire Dhubh a ghlacadh, mar bha e féin, airson nighean an Righ fhaotainn mar dhuais. Chaidh an Stàbul fhosgladh, agus thagh gach aon srian air a shon fhéin.

Dh' fhalbh iad an sin do 'n Bheinn a bhreith air an Àlaire Dhuibh. Bha iad a' siubhal troimh ghleanntaibh, thar bheanntaibh, agus tromh ghlacaibh gus an d' fhuair iad sealladh oirre. Dh' fhéuch Alastair ri faotainn air thoiseach oirre; ach cho luath 's a chunnaic i e thog i ri aghaidh na Beinne, a' cur uisg' as na clachan agus tein' as na h-alltan, a' teicheadh roimhe. Lean iad as a déigh gus an d' thàinig dorchadh na h-oidhch' orra, agus an sin thill iad dachaidh as a h-eugmhais.

An uair a ràinig iad an Caisteal dh' innis iad do 'n Righ mar dh' éirich dhoibh. Thubhairt e riù gu 'n robh là eile 'tighinn agus grian eile ri dol mu 'n cuairt, agus am fear a bheireadh dhachaidh an Àlaire Dhubh air cheann taoid dhasan gu 'm bu leis a nighean agus gu ruig leth na rìgheachd. An uair a chual iad so, rinn gach duine agus gach curaidh deas airson falbh do 'n Bheinn romh éiridh gréine air an ath là.

An uair a thàinig an ath mhadainn thionn gach aon diù air falbh 'an làn bheachd gu 'm b' ann aige féin a bhitheadh a' bhuaidh a' tilleadh. Ràinig iad a' Bheinn. Bha cuid dhiù 'dol air am broinn tromh thuill, cuid a' crùban tromh na h-uillt, cuid eile a' fàireinneachd agus a' gabhail fàth air gach bealach feuch am faigheadh iad sealladh air an Àlaire Dhuibh. Mu dheireadh chunnaic iad i air taobh deisear Ghlinn-na-gréine. Chaidh gach fear an òrdugh cho math 's a b' urrainn e gu greim a dheanamh oirre. Ach cha d' éirich ni 'b' fhearr dhoibh air an là sin na air an là roimhe, oir bha i 'cur uisg' as na clachan

agus teine as na h-alltaibh a' teicheadh rompa.   Aig dol fodha
na gréine bha iad ni 'b' fhaide uaipe na bha iad anns a'
mhadainn.   Thill iad an sin dachaidh gu sgìth, airsnealach,
acrach.

An uair a ràinig iad an Caisteal chuir an Righ a mach a'
Ghille freasdail a dh' fheòraich co aige 'bha bhuaidh.   Thug
an Gille fios air ais g' a ionnsaidh gu 'm fac iad i, ach nach d'
fhuair iad 'an astar glacaidh oirre, no eadhon an urchair cloiche
'n a dàil.   An sin chuir an Righ fios g' an ionnsaidh gu 'm b' e
'm màireach an treas là d' an deuchainn, agus do aon air bith aca
'bheireadh dhachaidh dha san an Àlaire Dhubh air cheann
taoid gu 'm bitheadh esan cho math 's a ghealladh.   An uair a
chual iad so, bha gach curaidh ruith agus gach curaidh stréipe
fo thròm iomagainn, oir cha b' urrainn iad tuillidh a dheanamh
na rinn iad cheana.   Ach chuir iad rompa gu 'm feuchadh iad
aon uair eile an Àlaire Dhubh a ghlacadh.

An déigh do 'n t-suipeir a bhi seachad choinnich Alastair, 'us
e 'dol tromh 'n Chaisteal, an Iorasglach-ùrlair aig an Righ.   "A
Mhic Righ Eirionn," thubhairt i, "tha thu sgìth, airsnealach,
agus fo thròm cheal."   Fhreagair Alastair gu 'n robh.   "Cha
do ghabh thusa comhairle do chàirdean.   Théid thu 'nochd air
d' ais gu d' bhothan féin, agus gabhaidh tu greim de 'n iasg
agus greim de 'n fhiadh.   Ach mu 'm falbh thu tillidh tu air d'
ais far am bheil an Righ, agus their thu ris gur e 'm màireach
an là mu dheireadh a th' agaibh airson an Àlaire Dhubh a
ghlacadh, agus nach teid thusa 'n a déigh mur faigh thu do
roghainn sréine mu 'm falbh thu.   Their e riut gu 'm faigh thu
sin.   Falbhaidh e 'n sin leat, agus dar ruigeas sibh an stàbul
chi thu dorus air do laimh dheis, agus their thu ris an dorus
fhosgladh chum gu 'n tabhair thu do roghainn sréin' as an àite
sin.   Fosglaidh e 'n dorus dhuit, agus chi thu crocht' air a'
bhalla seann srian nach robh 'an ceann eich no capaill o
cheann sheachd bliadhna fichead, agus bheir thu leat i.   An
uair a ruigeas tu a' Bheinn bheir thu car mu thòm do chàch,
agus gabhaidh tu air thoiseach air an Àlaire Dhuibh.   Cho
luath 's a thig thu 'm fradharc dhi crathaidh tu an t-srian rithe,
agus thig i le sitir, agus cuiridh i a ceann 's an t-sréin.

Léumaidh tu 'n sin air a drùim, agus marcaichidh tu dhachaidh i dh' ionnsaidh an Righ."

Dh' fhalbh Alastair o 'n Iorasglaich cho toilichte 's a bha e bho 'n là a dh' fhàg an Dobhar-chù e air tìr 'am fearann Lochlainn.

Air an treas là chuir na curaidhnean an òrdugh, agus dh' fhalbh iad do 'n Bheinn a bhreith air an Àlaire Dhuibh. An uair a ràinig iad, bha iad a' gabhail fàth air gach sgàth gus an robh iad a' smaointeachadh gu 'n robh iad cho dlùth oirre 's a b' urrainn iad faotainn. Ach thug Alastair car mu thòm dhoibh, agus dh' fhàg e iad. Cha do stad e ach gus an d' fhuair e air thoiseach air an Àlaire Dhuibh. Bha i 'tighinn, agus coltas uamhasach oirre, a' spoltadh uisg' as na clachaibh agus tein' as na h-alltaibh le luathas a ruith. An sin thog Alastair suas an t-srian, agus chrath e rithe i. Cho luath 's a chual an Àlaire slinnrich na sréine sheas i, agus rinn i cruaidh shitir a fhreagair Mac-talla nan Creag ceithir mìle mu 'n cuairt. Leag i dà chluais a sìos ri cùl a cinn, thàinig i 'n a cruaidh ruith, agus spàrr i a ceann anns an t-sréin. An sin léum Alastair air a druim, agus mharcaich e dhachaidh i 'dh' ionnsaidh an Righ. An uair a chunnaic na curaidhnean eile 'n coigreach a' marcachd air falbh leis an Àlaire Dhuibh, thuit an *sud* agus an *sad* uile uapa, agus thill iad dachaidh.

Air an oidhche so thàinig an Righ a mach 'n an coinneamh. An uair a chunnaic e gu 'm b' e 'n Coigreach aig an robh a' bhuaidh ghabh e null fàr an robh e, chaidh e aìr a dhà ghlùn da, agus thubhairt e ris, "Bha mi a' smaointeachadh gu 'm bu churaidh thu a rìreadh, agus dhearbh thu mu dheireadh e. 'Nis, ni no neach, séud no luach a th' anns an righeachd agam- sa iarr, agus gheibh thu e maille ris an duais a gheall mi airson a ghniomh so."

Rinn an Righ cuilm mhòr air an oidhche sin. Ach mu 'n robh a' chuilm seachad thàinig fios a dh' ionnsaidh an Righ o Fhamhair mòr a' Chaisteil Dhuibh anns a' Bheinn Bhric gu 'n tigeadh e airson na ceathramh h-ighinn an ceann là agus bliadhn' o 'n oidhche sin. Chuir an teachdaireachd so an Righ fo mhì-ghean agus fo thròm iomagainn. Thionndaidh e ris na curaidhnibh, agus thubhairt e riù gu 'n robh e duilich

nach b' urrainn e an ni a gheall e a chomh-ghealladh mur
faigheadh iad féin a mach an t-àit' anns an robh anam a'
Chrochaire Lom-rusgaich 'am falach, agus mur cuireadh iad as
da. "Chuir na curaidhnean agamsa 'n ceann d' e cheana,
ach chuir e air e rithist, agus bha e cho beò 's a bha e riamh.
Dhùlanaich e iad, agus thubhairt e gu 'n tugadh e leis mo
nigheannan uile ge b' oil leò. A nis tha e 'tighinn an ceann
là agus bliadhn' o nochd, agus am fear agaibhs' a chuireas as
da is leis mo nighean agus mo righeachd uile."

Bha na curaidhnean uile fo iomagainn a chionn nach robh
fhios aca cia mar chuireadh iad as do 'n Chrochaire Lom-
rusgach. Ach an uair a sgaoil iad o chéile choinnich an
Iorasglach-ùrlair Alastair, agus thubhairt i ris, "A Mhic Righ
Eirionn, tha mi 'n dòchas gu 'n d' fhuair thu do dhuais a
nochd." Dh' innis e dhi gach ni a thachair, agus mar bha 'n
cùmhnant air am faighteadh nighean an Righ ni 'bu duiliche
nis na bha e roimhe. Bha i 'n a sìneadh air an ùrlar, agus
ghrad dh' éirich i 'n a suidhe. Rug i air a falt 'n a laimh, agus
rinn i glag mòr gàire, agus thubhairt i, "A Mhic Righ Eirionn,
bha buaidh leat riamh, agus bithidh i leat fathast ma ghabhas tu
mo chomhairle-sa." "Ni air bith," ars' Alastair, "a dh' iarras
tu orm ni mise nia 's urrainn mi, oir fhuair mi fìor thu gu ruig
so agus tha làn earbs' agam asad a nis." "Mata," thuirt an
Iorasglach, "as an àit anns am bheil thu a' d' sheasamh
falbhaidh tu fo d' làn armachd, agus cuimhnichidh tu nach
dealaich thu ri claidheamh an Righ gus am faigh thu ni 's
fearr. Théid thu 'n toiseach gu ruig do bhothan féin, agus
ithidh tu greim de 'n fhiadh agus greim de 'n iasg. Thig thu
'n sin a mach gu dorus do bhothain, agus cuiridh tu d' aghaidh
air Aisridh Chreagach na Beinne Buidhe, agus cha sheall thu
as do dhéigh, agus cha thill thu céum air d' ais airson càis no
cruadail a choinnicheas tu gus an ruig thu Caisteal Mòr a th'
aig ceann na h-Aisridh. Chi thu 'sin boirionnach ag amharc a
mach air uinneig àird a' Chaisteil." An so thug an Iorasglach
a mach sgrìobhadh as a broilleach, agus thubhairt i, "An uair a
chi thu 'm boirionnach aithnichidh tu i, agus their thu rithe gu
'm bheil sgrìobhadh agad dhi. Thig i 'n sin, agus fosglaidh i
'n dorus dhuit, agus innsidh i gu dé 'bhitheas agad r' a dheanamh

an déigh sin. Faotaidh tu 'nis siubhal air do thurus. Tha
beannachd an Righ a' d' chuideachd, tha beannachd a nighinn
leat, agus tha mo bheannachd-s' agad. 'Nis ge b' e ni a dh'
iarras am boirionnach ort a ràdh no 'dheanamh bi cinnteach gu
'n coimh-gheall thu e."

Ghabh Alastair misneach, agus dh' fhalbh e dìreach a dh'
ionnsaidh a bhothain, agus romh éiridh gréin' air an ath
mhadainn dh' imich e air a thurus troimh Aisridh Chreagach na
Beinne Buidhe. Chum e air aghaidh cian fhada agus làn
fhada gus an d' fhàs an Aisridh cho sgorach, bhiorach agus gu
'n robh e 'm féum crochadh air a bhroinn a dhol thairis oirre.
Mu dheireadh theirig na sgoran féin, agus cha robh roimhe ach
glomhas mòr eadar stallan chreag a bha cho domhainn fodha
's a bha iad àrd os a cheann. Thug e sealladh air gach taobh
dh' e, agus chunnaic e 'n Aisridh a ruith a 's tigh ri taobh aon
de na stallan 'n a bac cho caol, agus nach robh lèud bonn cois'
innte. An sin ghabh e 'n t-eagal gu 'n robh e air sheachran
agus bha e 'dol a thilleadh. Ach thàinig clamhan mòr ag
itealaich tarsainn os a cheann, agus ghlaodh e ris, "A Mhic
Righ Eirionn, cuimhnich comhairle na h-Iorasglach ùrlair."
Anns a' mhionaid chuimhnich e 'ghealladh do 'n Iorasglaich,
agus thubhairt e ris féin gu 'n cumadh e air aghaidh cho fad 's a
bhitheadh an deò ann. Bha e 'n sin a' crochadh o sgor gu sgor
'us a' léum o bhac gu bac gus an do thòisich an Aisridh air fàs
ni 'b' fhearr. Mu dheireadh fhuair e air an rathad réidh. Dh'
fhalbh e 'n sin cho luath 's a b' urrainn e dol thar nan Creag,
oir bha 'm feasgar a' tighinn, agus cha robh sealladh do 'n
Chaisteal ri fhaicinn. Bha 'n uchdach cho cas agus nach b'
urrainn e cabhag mhòr a dheanamh. Ach mu dheireadh
bhuanaich e 'm mullach. Thubhairt e ris féin nach bitheadh e
fada tuillidh, agus ruith e cho luath 's a b' urrainn e leis a
bhruthach. Bha e 'smaointeachadh an uair a gheibheadh e aig
bun na h-uchdaich gu 'm bitheadh na h-uile cruadal seachad,
ach an uair a ràinig e sin cha robh iad a réir coltais ach a' tois-
eachadh. An àit' a' Chaisteil 's ann a chunnaic e Loch mòr
dearg air thoiseach air. Thug e sùil air gach taobh fèuch am
faiceadh e rathad air am faigheadh e thar an Loch, ach cha-n
fhac e ach stallachan chreag, agus bu leòir do dh' èun air iteig

dol thairis orra. Bha e ann an tigh-comhagail co dhiù 'thilleadh e no rachadh e air aghaidh an uair a chual e 'n clamhan a' glaodhaich os a cheann, " A Mhic Righ Eirionn, na gabh eagal no sgàth romh chàs no romh chruadail air bith a thachras ort." An uair a chual e so ghabh e misneach, agus chum e air aghaidh air an Aisridh a 's tigh do 'n Loch. An toiseach bha iongantas air nach robh e 'dol fodha 's an Loch, ach an ùine ghoirid chunnaic e gu 'n robh an t-slighe air an robh e 'g imeachd air éiginn còmhdaichte le uisge. Chum e dìreach air an t-slighe gus an d' ràinig e taobh eil' an Loch. Cho luath 's a fhuair e 'chasan air talamh tioram thog e 'cheann, agus chunnaic e dail bhòidheach, ghorm air thoiseach air, agus Caisteal Mòr aig ceann na dalach. Bha dorchadh nan tràth air tighinn, agus uime sin ghreas e air aghaidh a dh' ionnsaidh a' Chaisteil.

An uair a ràinig e 'n Caisteal chunnaic e boirionnach ag amharc a mach air aon de na h-uinneagaibh. Ghlaodh e gu 'n robh litir aige dhi. Ghrad theirinn i, agus dh' fhosgail i 'n dorus dha. Shìn e dhi an litir. Rug i oirre as a laimh, agus dh' iarr i air feitheamh gus am faiceadh i gu dé 'bh' innte. Cho luath agus a léugh i 'n litir léum i agus rug i air a laimh 'n a dà laimh, agus phòg i i. Thug i 's tigh e, agus dh' fheòraich i dh' e gu dé 'n rathad a thàinig e? Thubhairt e gu 'n d' thàinig e troimh Aisridh Chreagach na Beinne Buidhe. " Ma 's ann," ars' i, "tha féum agad air biadh agus air deoch." Chuir i biadh agus deoch m' a choinneamh, agus dh' iarr i air a bhi ealamh a chionn gu 'n robh mòran aige r' a dheanamh.

Cho luath 's a bha e deas thug i 's tigh e do sheòmar nan arm, agus dh' iarr i air e dh' fhéuchainn am b' urrainn e 'n claidheamh a bha thall ri taobh a' bhalla 'thogail. Dh' fhéuch e ris, ach cha chuireadh e gaoth eadar e agus an talamh. Dh' fhosgail i preas a bha air taobh an tighe, agus thug i 'mach as botulan locshlaint. Tharrainn i 'cuach òir, agus chuir i déuran innt' as a bhotulan, agus thubhairt i ris òl dh' e. Rinn e sin. Rug e rìs air a' chlaidheamh, agus thogadh e le 'dhà laimh e. Thug i dha déuran eile, agus an sin thogadh e 'n claidheamh le aon laimh. Thug i dha an treas déur, agus cha bu luaith' a dh' òl se e na dh' fhairich e ni 'bu neartmhoire na bha e riamh. Rug e air a chlaidheamh, agus dh' oibricheadh e leis cho aotrom uallach agus a dh' oibricheadh e le claidheamh an Rìgh.

"Nis," thubhairt i ris, "tha Famhair Mòr agus dà cheann air, a' fuireachd anns a' Chaisteal so, agus tha e tighinn dachaidh an ùine ghoirid. Thig thusa leamsa, agus cuiridh mi a' d' sheasamh thu air an Ùdabac, far am faigh thu cothrom air a bhualadh an uair a chromas e 'thighinn a 's tigh fo 'n àrd-dorus. Bi cinnteach gu 'm buail thu gu math e, agus gu 'n cuir thu 'n dà cheann d' e; oir mur cuir thu dh' e ach aon beiridh e air an aon sin, agus cuiridh e as duit leis mar rinn e air mòran air thoiseach ort."

Dh' fhalbh e gun dàil, agus sheas e air an Ùdabac mar dh' iarr i air. Cha robh e fada 'n sin an uair a chunnaic e 'm Famhair a' tighinn agus siubhal sìth aige.

An uair a ràinig e 'n dorus chròm e 'chinn, agus thug e roc as. Ghabh Alastair an cothrom air, agus bhuail e le uile neart e. Leis a' bhuille thilg e fear de na cinn dh' e, agus leth a' chinn eile. An sin thug am Famhair léumannan agus sgriachan fuathasach as, ach mu 'n d' fhuair e tionndadh chuir Alastair leth eile an dara cinn d' e, agus thuit e 'n a chlosaich mhairbh air an talamh.

Thàinig am boirionnach a mach, agus thubhairt i ris, "Is math a fhuaras thu, a Mhic Righ Eirionn. Tha soirbheachadh leat, oir tha beannachd m' athar a' d' chois." Dh' fheòraich e 'n sin di cò i? Fhreagair i gu 'm b' ise 'n nighean 'bu shine 'bh' aig Righ na Beinne Buidhe. "Tha thusa 'falbh," thùbhairt i, "a dh' iarraidh anam a' Chrochaire Lom-rusgaich chum gu 'n tèarainn thu mo phiuthar a 's òige bhuaith. Thig a 's tigh, agus leigidh mis' air falbh thu air do thurus mu 'n éirich grian am màireach."

Chaidh e 's tigh, ghlan i chasan, agus chaidh e laidhe.

Mu 'n do ghoir an coileach-ruadh, agus mu 'n d' éirich grian air bruth no air beinn, bha i air a cois, agus a' bhraiceas aice 'feitheamh air. An déigh dha éiridh agus a bhraiceas fhaotainn, thug i litir as a broilleach, agus shìn i dha i, ag ràdh, "Gleidhidh tu so gu cùramach gus an ruig thu Caisteal Mòr nan Ochd Turaitean, agus bheir thu i do 'n bhoirionnach a chi thu 'g amharc a mach air aon de dh' uinneagaibh mullaich a' Chaisteil."

Thug i tarrainn air a botulan iocshlaint féin, agus air a cuaich
òir, agus thug i dha deoch. Chuir i 'n sin e air ceann na
slighe, ghuidh i beannachd a bhi 'n a chuideachd, agus
thubhairt i gu 'm fanadh ise 'n sud gus an tilleadh e. Dh'
fhàg e claidheamh an Righ anns a' Chaisteal, agus dh'
fhalbh e le claidheamh an Fhamhair. Bha 'n t-slighe air an
robh e 'g imeachd ni 'bu réidhe na 'n té air an do shiubhail e
'n là roimhe. Fhuair e air aghaidh gu math, ach bha 'n t-astar
cho fada 's gu 'n do thòisich an oidhch' air tighinn mu 'n d'
thàinig e 'n sealladh a' Chaisteil. Mu chiaradh an fheasgair
chunnaic e turaitean a' Chaisteil fada bhuaithe. Ghabh e
misneach agus chruadhaich e 'chéum, agus ged b' fhada
bhuaithe cha b' fhada 'g a ruigheachd.

Bha ballachan cho àrd mu 'n cuairt do 'n Chaisteal 'us
nach robh e faicinn gu dé 'n dòigh air am faigheadh e 's tigh.
Ach thug e togail d' a cheann, agus chunnaic e boirionnach ag
amharc a mach air uinneig, agus ghlaodh e gu 'n robh litir aige
dhi. Thàinig i 'nuas agus dh' fhosgail i dorus mòr iaruinn a
bh' air a' bhalla. An déigh dhi 'n litir a léughadh rug i air
laimh air, agus thug i 's tigh e.

Choimhead i 'n sin air a' chlaidheamh a bh' aige, agus dh'
fheòraich i dh' e c'àit' an d' fhuair se e ? Dh' innis e dhi gu 'n
d' fhuair o 'n bhoirionnach a bh' anns a' Chaisteal anns an robh
e 'n oidhche roimhe sin. Bha claidheamh mòr eile 'n a
sheasamh ri taobh a' bhalla, agus thubhairt i ris e dh'
fhéuchainn am b' urrainn e 'thogail. Chuir e gaoth air
éiginn eadar e agus talamh. "Cha d' rinn gin a thàinig
romhad an uibhir sin féin," ars' am boirionnach. Thug i dha
deoch as a botulan iocshlainte féin ann an cuaich òir, agus an
sin chluicheadh e 'n claidheamh le dhà laimh. Thug i dha an
ath dheoch, agus chluicheadh e claidheamh an Fhamhair cho
fileanta 's a chluicheadh e claidheamh an Righ.

"Nis," thubhairt i, "cha-n 'eil ùin' agad ri chur seachad.
Tha Famhair mòr nan trì cheann, nan trì meall, agus nan trì
chnap a' fuireachd a so, agus thig e dhachaidh a thiota.
Fhalbh thusa leamsa, agus cuiridh mi thu 'n àite fàr am faigh
thu cothrom air a bhualadh." Chaidh e leatha, agus chuir i e
'n a sheasamh air bac a bh' air taobh an fhosglaidh do 'n dorus

mhòr iaruinn a bh' air a' bhalla. An sin thubhairt i, " 'N uair
a chromas am Famhair a thighinn fo 'n àrd-dorus bi cinnteach
gu 'm buail thu e mu 'm faigh e 'chinn a thogail, agus gu 'n cuir
thu dh' e 'n trì leis a' chéud bhuile, oir ma gheibh e éiridh bheir
e as a' chéil' a' d' mhìrean thu mar rinn e orra-san a thàinig air
thoiseach ort."

Thàinig am Famhair, agus chròm e fo 'n àrd-dhorus, ach mu
'n d' fhuair e tromh 'n dorus bhuail Alastair e le uile neart,
agus chuir e dithis de na cinn d' e, agus leth an treas fir.
Thug am Famhair léum as, agus bhuail fear de na mill an
t-àrd-dhorus, agus chuir e mach e. An sin thuit e, agus mu 'n
d' fhuair e éiridh, agus an ath léum a thabhairt bhuail Alastair
e 'n dara h-uair, agus chuir e 'n leth eile de 'n treas ceann d' e.
Le ròmhan mòr tiamhaidh thuit am Famhair 'n a chlosaich
mhairbh air a' bhlàr.

Thàinig am boirionnach a mach an sin, agus thubhairt i, " Is
math a fhuaras thu, a Mhic Righ Éirionn. Tha beannachd m'
athar agus mo pheathar a' d' chois, agus bithidh mo bheannachd-s' agad a nis." An sin dh' fheòraich e dhi cò i ?
Fhreagair i gu 'm b' ise dara nighean Righ na Beinne Buidhe.
" Tha thusa 'falbh a dh' iarraidh anam a' Chrochaire Lom-
rusgaich chum gu 'n tèaruinn thu mo phiuthar a 's òige
bhuaithe, agus ma thig thu beò as an ath Chaisteal a ruigeas tu
cha ruig thu leas eagal a ghabhail roimh ni no neach a thachras
ort tuillidh, oir soirbhichidh leat gu ceann do thuruis. Ach
cha-n 'eil tìm agad ri chall." Thug i 's tigh e, ghabh i aige gu
math le biadh agus le deoch, agus chuir i laidhe e.

An déigh dha 'bhraiceas fhaotainn air an ath mhadainn thug
i dha deoch as a botulan ìocshlaint 'n a cuaich òir. Chuir i
'sin a làmh 'n a broilleach, agus thug i mach as litir, agus
thubhairt i ris, " Bheir thu so do 'n bhoirionnach a chi thu 'n a
seasamh 'an dorus an ath Chaisteil gus an tig thu."

An so dh' fhalbh e agus an claidheamh mòr aige leis an do
chuir e na cinn de 'n Fhamhair. Fhuair e air aghaidh gu réidh
gus an d' ràinig e 'n ath Chaisteal, Ùsp Mhòr de dh' àite gun
uinneag, gun turait air. Chunnaic e 'm boirionnach 'n a
seasamh 's an dorus, agus ghlaodh e rithe gu 'n robh litir aige

dhi.    Ghlac i 'n litir, agus an déigh dhi a léughadh rug i air laimh air, agus thug i 's tigh e.

Ghlan i a lamhan agus a chasan le anaghlais uisge agus bhainne.    Choimhead i 'n sin air a' chlaidheamh, agus thubhairt i ris c' àit' an d' fhuair e 'n lann ud.    Fhreagair e gu 'n d' fhuair anns a' Chaisteal anns an robh e 'n raoir.    "O 'n fhuair thu gu ruig so ni do chlaidheamh an gnothuch dhuit, agus cha dealaich thu ris am fad 's a bhitheas an deò annad gus an ruig thu ceann do thuruis.    Tha Beithir Mhòr Theinnteach nan Seachd Cinn Nathrach 's a Ghath-Nimhe 'fuireachd anns a' Chaisteal so.    Thig i aig éiridh gréine 'm màireach, agus féumaidh tu a coinneachadh a mach, oir ma gheibh i 's tigh cha-n fhaicear thusa no mise beò tuillidh."    Chuir i 'n sin a laidh e ann an leaba bhlàth, sheasgair.

Dh' fhuirich i féin 'n a faireachadh, agus an uair a thàinig an t-àm dhasan éiridh dhùisg i e.    Thug i dha a bhraiceas, agus an déigh a bhraiceis deoch as a botulan ìocshlaint 'n a cuaich òir.    Ghlac e 'n sin a chlaidheamh, agus thionn e 'mach.

Mu 'n gann a fhuair e thar stairsnich an doruis dh' fhairich e a' Bheithir a' tighinn.    Rinn e deas air a son, agus cho luath 's a thàinig i thòisich còmhrag chruaidh eatorra.    Bha esan 'g a dhìon féin o na cinn, agus ise 'g a lot le gath mòr a bh' aice 'am barr a h-earbaill.    Chum iad air a' chath gu àm dol fodha na gréine.    An sin thubhairt i ris, " Is leat do leaba 'nochd fhathast, ach coinnich mise romh éiridh gréine 'm màireach."    Chaidh a' Bheithir a rathad féin, agus thill esan a 's tigh do 'n Chaisteal.

Ghlan am boirionnach a chréuchdan, chuir i ìochslaint ris gach lot a bh' air a chorp, agus chuir i laidhe e.

An uair a dhùisg e air an ath mhadainn dh' fhairich e gu 'n robh e cho slàn fhallain agus a bha e riamh.    An déigh dha éiridh, agus a bhraiceas agus deoch de 'n ìocshlaint fhaotainn thog e leis a chla dheamh, agus chaidh e 'n coinneamh na Beathrach.    Ghleachd iad o mhadainn gu feasgar, esan 'g a dhìon féin o na cinn, agus ise 'g a lot le gath a h-earbaill.    Aig dol fodha gréine stad iad.    Chaidh ise a rathad féin, agus thill esan do 'n Chaistea .

Ghabh am boirionnach aig' air an oidhche so mar rinn i air

an oidhche roimhe. An uair a dhùisg e air an treas madainn bha e cho slàn o chréuchdan 's a bha e riamh. An déigh dha 'bhraiceas agus deoch de 'n locshlaint fhaotainn ghlac e chlaidh- eamh, agus chaidh e 'n coinneamh na Beathrach.

Air a mhadainn so chual e i 'tighinn agus sgriachail oillteil aice. Ach smaointich e bho 'n sheas e 'n dà là roimhe, gu 'm féuchadh e i an latha so fathast. Thàinig a' Bhéist, agus chaidh iad 'n a chéile. Bha ise 'tilgeil ghath as gach béul air, agus bha esan 'g a dhìon féin uapa le 'chlaidheamh. Mu chiaradh an fheasgair bha e 'fàs lag, ach ma bha dh' aithnich e gu 'n robh ise cuideachd a' call a neart. Thug so misneach dha, agus dhlùthaich e rithe gu cruaidh. Aig dol fodha gréine thug i thairis, agus shìn si i féin air a' bhlàr.

"Nis," thubhairt i, "rinn thu 'n gnothuch orm, ach bha 'n cothrom agad. Anns an oidhche bha thu faotainn do chréuchdan a ghlanadh agus a shlànachadh, agus bha thu gu blàth seasgair ri taobh an teine anns a' Chaisteal agamsa. Ach na 'n d' fhuair mise leth uair a thìm de bhlàthas an teine cha do thill thusa ni 's mò na 'n fheadhainn a thàinig air thoiseach ort." Tharrainn Alastair a chlaidheamh an so, agus le seachd buillibh chuir e na seachd cinn de 'n Bheithir. Ach air an t-seachdamh buille thug i togail air a h-earball, agus bhuail i anns an taobh e. Thuit e mar gu 'm bitheadh e marbh, agus cha-n fhac agus cha d' fhairich e dad tuillidh gus an do dhùisg e mu mheadhon oidhche.

Bha 'm boirionnach a' sin a' glanadh agus a' slànachadh a chréuchdan. An uair a bha i deas de sin chuir i laidhe e. Air an ath mhadainn chaidh i far an robh e, agus dh' fheòraich i dh' e cia mar bha e 'g a fhaireachdainn féin? Fhreagair e gu 'n robh gu làidir fallainn. "Is math sin," thubhairt i. "Tha chuid a 's mò a d' dhéuchainnibh seachad a nis."

An uair a dh' éirich e agus a fhuair e 'bhraiceas, thubhairt i ris, "Mharbh thu Famhair Mòr nan Dà Cheann 'an Caisteal ceann Aisridh Chreagach na Beinne Buidhe, mharbh thu Famhair Mòr nan Trì Cheann, nan Trì Meall, agus nan Trì Chnap 'an Caisteal Mòr nan Ochd Turaitean, agus mharbh thu Beithir Theinnteach nan Seachd Cinn Nathrach agus a' Ghath nimhe anns a' Chaisteal Ùdlaidh so. Cha d' fhuair ach

aon dhiubhsan a thàinig romhad air an turus air am bheil
thusa dol tighinn gu ruig so.  Thàinig esan thar Aisridh
Chreagach na Beinne Buidhe, agus thar Aisridh an Loch
Dheirg air iom-bàthadh.  Fhuair e tromh thalamh-toll
seachad air a' chéud dà Chaisteal, ach cha b' urrainn e dol
seachad air a' Chaisteal so gun dol troimhe.  Choinnich a'
Bheithir Theinnteach e aig an dorus, agus chuir i as da.  Ach
thàinig thus' air an t-slighe cheart, agus bha buaidh leat gu
ruig so.  Cha bhi mise 'g 'ad ghleidheadh ni 's faide, oir tha
mòran agad r' a dheanamh fhathast.  Cha d' fhuair thu ach
latha 's bliadhna airson cur as do 'n Chrochaire Lom-rusgach,
agus mar bi d' obair deas agad roimhe sin bheir e leis mo
cheathramh piuthar mar thug e leis sinne.  Falbhaidh mise
leat, agus cuiridh mi air ceann na slighe thu.  Cha stad agus
cha tàmh thu gus an ruig thu Sabhal Mòr nan Seachd Crùb,
nan Seachd Lùb, agus nan Seachd Suidheachan.  Chi thu fo
'n t-Sabhal air Cnoc Buidhe na Gréine fior sheann duine a'
gearradh sgroth le Làir-chaibe.  Innsidh tu dha an t-saoir air
am bheil thu, agus innsidh esan duitsa gu dé a their agus a ni
thu 'n a dhéigh sin.  Gabhaidh tu comhairle bho gach aon a
bheir dhuit i gu dìleas.  Tha beannachd an Righ a' d' chois,
tha beannachd na h-Iorasglaich a' d' chois, tha beannachd
Gath-gréine, mo phiuthar, a' d' chois, tha beannachd Soillse-
dubhair a' d' chois, agus tha mo bheannachd-s' agad mar
an céudna.  Bi siubhal air do thurus, agus dean mar dh'
iarr mis' ort, agus bithidh gach ni ceart an uair a thilleas
thu."

An sin dh' fhalbh e.  Bha e 'siubhul air aghaidh cian
fhada agus làn fhada.  An uair a thòisich e air fàs sgìth
chuimhnich e air éuchd agus air a bhuaidh.  Thug so aotrom-
achadh air 'inntinn, agus fhuair e air aghaidh gu math air a
shlighe.  An teis-meadhoin a smaointean thàinig e 's tigh air
ceann an aon Ghlinne 'bu bhoidhche 'chunnaic e riamh.
Thubhairt e ris féin, " Féumaidh nach 'eil mi fada bho Shabhal
Mòr nan Seachd Suidheachan a nis."  Mu 'n do leig e 'm facal
as a bhéul chunnaic e 'n Sabhal beagan air thoiseach air,
agus an aon Chnoc 'bu bhòidhche a chunnaic e riamh a'
soillseachadh mar òr ri gréin 'an iochdar a' Ghlinne, agus an

aon duine 'bu shine coltas a chunnaic e riamh a' gearradh sgroth le làir-chaibe air leth taobh a' chnuic.

Ghabh e far an robh an Duine, agus chuir e fàilt an là air. Fhreagair an Duin' e gu brosglach, sgairteil, fada ni 'b' òige 'na chainnt na bha e 'n a choltas, agus dh' fheòraich e dh' e cia as a thàinig e? Fhreagair Alastair, "Thàinig mi bho Chaisteal Righ Lochlainn, tromh Aisridh Chreagach na Beinne Buidhe, tromh Chaisteal ceann na h-Aisridh far an do mharbh mi Famhair Mòr nan Dà Cheann, tromh Chaisteal Mòr nan Ochd Turaitean far an do mharbh mi Famhair Mòr nan Trì Cheann, nan Trì Meall, agus nan Trì Chnap, tromh Chaisteal Ùdlaidh na Beithir Theinntich nan Seachd Cinn Nathrach agus a' Ghath-nimhe, agus as a' sin gu ruig so féuch an innseadh tusa dhomh c' àit am faighinn anam a' Chrochaire Lom rusgaich?" Thug an Seann Duine sùil air anns an aodann, agus thubhairt e, "Leig fhaicinn domh do chlaidheamh, a Laoich." Tharrainn Alastair a chlaidheamh as an truaill, agus shìn e dha e. Rug an Seann Duin' air a' chlaidheamh eadar a dhà mhèur, agus chuir e eadar e agus lèus e. Shìn e 'n sin air ais e, agus thubhairt e, " Faiceam thu a' fleadhadh do chlaidheamh, a Laoich." Rug Alastair air a' chlaidheamh, agus thug e cuairt chùil agus cuairt bheòil leis cho aotrom, agus ged b' e sgian an fhéidh a bhitheadh 'n a dhòrn. Léum an Seann Duine, agus rug e air laimh air, agus thubhairt e, " A Laoich, thàinig thu an rathad a thubhairt thu. Cha-n urrainn mise innseadh dhuit c' àit' am bheil anam a' Chrochaire Lom-rusgaich a nis, oir theich e as an àit anns an robh e bho cheann cheithir làithean. Ach faodaidh gu 'n innis m' athair dhuit e." "Oh, am bheil d' athair beò, no 'n urrainn mise fhaicinn?" "Tha e beò. Sud e 'giùlan nan sgroth air a mhuin. Rach far am bheil e, agus feòraich dh' e."

Ràinig Alastair Fear-ghiùlan nan-sgroth, agus dh' fheòraich e dh' e, an robh fhios aige c' àit' an robh anam a' Chrochaire Lom-rusgaich 'am falach? Fhreagair an Seann Duine, "Cha-n' eil ; theich e as an àit' anns an robh e bho cheann trì làithean. Ach faodaidh gu 'n innis m' athair dhuit." "Oh, am bheil d' athair beò, no 'm faod mise fhaicinn?" "Oh, tha e beò, agus is urrainn thu fhaicinn cuideachd. Sud e thall a' tilgeil

nan sgroth.  Rach agus feòraich dh' e." Ràinig Alastair am fear
a bha 'tilgeil nan sgroth, agus thubhairt e ris am b' urrainn e innseadh c'àit an robh anam a' Chrochaire Lom-rusgaich am falach?
Fhreagair e, "Cha-n urrainn, oir theich e as an àit' anns an
robh e bho cheann dà latha.  Ach faodaidh gu 'n innis m'
athair dhuit."  "Ùbh! ùbh! a Dhuine, an urrainn mise d'
athair fhaicinn no 'm bheil e 'n comas bruidhinn rium?  Oir
féumaidh gu 'm bheil e ro shean."  "Ù, is urrainn thu fhaicinn,
agus is urrainn esan bruidhinn riut.  Sud e 'cur nan sgroth."
Ràinig Alastair am fear a bha 'cur nan sgroth, agus dh' fheòraich e dh' e am b' urrainn e innseadh c' àit' an robh anam
a' Chrochaire Lom-rusgaich am falach?  Fhreagair e cha-n
urrainn, oir theich e as an àit anns an robh e 'n dé.  "Ach
ruig m' athair, agus innsidh esan duit c' àit' am faigh thu e."
"Gu dé 'n seòrsa duine 'th' ann a' d' athair?  An urrainn mise
fhaicinn, no 'n urrainn esan bruidhinn rium?"  "Chi thu e,
agus bruidhnidh e riut, agus innsidh e dhuit gu dé 'th' agadsa
r' a dheanamh 'n a dhéigh so."  "Ach c'àit 'am faic mi e?"
"Tha e ann an sopan còinnich cùl a' Mhaide-chrùim.  Ach
féumaidh mi féin dol leat.  An uair a bhitheas tu 'bruidhinn
ris, bheir thu ro-aire nach teid thu 'm fad laimh dha, oir ma
gheibh e greim air mìr de d' cholainn bruthaidh e thu mar
spiligein eòrna fo lic brathann.  Mu 'n dealaich sibh iarraidh
e do làmh ort, agus ma bheir thu dha i bruthaidh e i gus am
bi i cho caol ri deilg maraige.  Ach so dhuit geinn daraich
(agus e 'sìneadh dha durc de cheann cabair), agus bheir thu
dha e 'n uair a dh' iarras e do làmh."

Chaidh iad a 's tigh do 'n tigh fàr an robh an Seann Duine.
Thug Fear-chur-nan-sgroth ultach mòr còinnich a nuas o chùl
a' mhaide-chrùim, agus chuir e air lic-an-teinntein e.  "Tha an
Sopan Mòr, a Dhuine," thubhairt Mac Righ Eirionn.  "Is mò
na sin m' athair 'n a bhroínn," arsa Fear-chur-nan-sgroth.
Thug e mach athair as an t-sopan, agus chuir e air an lic e.
"Gu dé d' fhéum orm a nis, a Mhic," ars' an t-athair.  "Is
fada bho nach d' iarr thu roimhe mi."  Fhreagair am Mac,
"Tha Curaidh Òg a' so a tha 'g iarraidh fios c' àit am bheil
anam a' Chrochaire Lom-rusgaich am falach."  "A Mhic
Righ Cormaic an Éirinn, gu dé 'n rathad a thàinig thu gu ruig

so ?" dh' fheòraich Fear-an-t-Sopain-Choinnich. Dh' innis
Alastair dha gach céum a thug e bho 'n latha 'dh' fhàg e tigh
athar, agus gach ni a thachair dha gus an là ud. " Is firin-
neach a dh' innis thu dhomh, a Mhic Righ Eirionn. Loisg
d' athair a' Chailleach-chearc, agus tha do mhàthair fo bhròn
air do shon. Tha 'guidhe 's a beannachd a' d' dhéigh, tha
beannachd Righ Òg Ceist a' d' dhéigh, tha beannachd Ban-
righ Òg Ceist a' d' dhéigh, tha beannachd Righ Lochlainn a'
d' dhéigh, tha beannachd agus buaidh na h-Iorasglaich a' d'
dhéigh, agus bithidh mo bheannachd-s' a' d' dhéigh. Bha
thusa dìleas do d' bhràthair, agus bithidh gach beathach agus
gach duin' a choinnicheas thu dìleas dhuitsa. Agus, a Thréun-
laoich, thoir dhomh crathadh de d' laimh, agus innsidh mise
dhuit c' àit am faigh thu anam a' Chrochaire Lom-rusgaich."
Shìn an Seann Duine 'mach a làmh, agus shìn Alastair an geinn
daraich dha. Rug e air a' gheinn, thug e bruthadh agus
crathadh air, agus rinn e cothan d' e. An uair a leig e as e
thubhairt e, " A Mhic Righ Eirionn, is cruaidh do làmh,
agus dh' fhéumadh i gu ruig so. Tha thu sgìth, air phathadh
agus air acras, is airidh thu air biadh agus air deoch, agus
gheibh thu sin. An déigh do shuipeir theid thu laidhe,
agus aig éiridh gréine 'm 'màireach bithidh tu deas airson du
thuruis. Cumaidh tu air d' agaidh gun tilleadh, gun stad,
gun sealltainn as do dhéigh gus an ruig thu Doire Dlùth-
dhuilleach nan Craobh. Chi thu 'n sin Eilid Luath-chasach
nan Stùchd nach d' fhuair cù no duine riamh 'n a còir.
Beiridh tu oirre, fosglaidh tu i, agus gheibh thu bradan anns a
mhaodal aice. Fosglaidh tu 'm bradan, agus ann am broinn
a' bhradain gheibh thu Lach uaine na h-ite réidh. Ann am
broinn an Lach gheibh thu Ubh, agus beiridh tu air an Ubh
eadar do dhà laimh, agus brisidh tu e mu 'm bean e do 'n
bhlàr. Oir ma bheanas e do 'n bhlàr cha-n fhaic thu Righ,
no duine no daoine gu bràth as a dhéigh sin. Ach ged tha do
làmh cruaidh cha bhrist i 'n t-Ubh gun mo chuideachadh-sa."
Dh' fhéuch e laimh ris anns a' chòinnich, agus thug e mach
crogan. Shìn e 'n crogan do dh' Alastair, agus thubhairt e,
" Sin agad ola. Cho luath 's a ruigeas tu Doire Dlùth-
dhuilleach nan Craobh dòirtidh tu an ola air do làmhaibh, agus

rubaidh tu leò a h-uile mìr do d' chraicionn a bhitheas rùisgte, no ris an saoil thu gu 'm bean fuil Éilde, no lann Bradain, no ite Lach, no plaosg Uibhe.   Gabhaidh tu aoidheachd o bheathach no bho 'dhuin' a bheir dhuit i gun iarraidh.   Agus bithidh fios agad féin gu dé 'bhitheas agad r' a dheanamh 'n a dhéigh sin.   Beir air an ola so 'nis, agus thoir leat i, agus bi deas airson do thuruis mar dh' iarr mis' ort."   Bha fhios aig Alastair nach robh math dha a làmh a shìneadh airson a' Chrogain.   Le sin shìn e a chlaidheamh, agus thubhairt e, " Cuir an Crogan air barr mo mheòir."   Rinn an Seann Duine sin, agus rug e air a' chlaidheamh 'n a dhòrn, agus bhrùth se e gus an robh e cho cruinn ri bioran maide.   An sin thuhhairt e, " Ni thu 'n gnothuch.   An uair a bhristeas tu an t-Ubh bithidh an Crochaire Lom-rusgach marbh.   Tillidh tu 'n sin air d' ais an rathad a thàinig thu.   Bheir thu leat nigheannan Righ Lochlainn as na Caistealaibh anns am bheil iad.   Gabhaidh tu 'n sin gu Caisteal na Beinne Brice fàr am faigh thu 'm Famhair Mòr 'n a shìneadh marbh air an ùrlar.   Gearraidh tu dheth an ceann agus na casan gu ruig na glùinean, agus bheir thu leat iad gu Caisteal Righ Lochlainn.   An uair a ruigeas tu an Caisteal cuiridh tu teine mòr air, agus an uair a bhitheas e an teas a ghabhalach tilgidh tu iad 'n drùim an teine.   Cho luath 's a gheibh iad dathadh anns an lasair fàsaidh iad 'n an òganach cho dreachmhor agus a chunnaic duine riamh.   Is bràthair e do Righ Lochlainn a chaidh a ghoid o mhàthair leis a' Bheithir Theinntich an uair a bha e 'n a leanabh.   Bha i 'g a chumail an sud fo gheisibh a' deanamh gach cron a b' urrainn e air an Righ gus an d'. thàinig thusa.   Nis, dean mar dh' iarr mis' ort, agus bithidh mo bheannachd-s' a' d' chois."

Air an ath mhadainn dh' fhalbh Alastair air a thurus.   Chum e air aghaidh cian fhada agus làn fhada.   Bha 'm feasgar a' tighinn air, neòil shìobhalta, shàmhach an là a falbh, agus neòil dhubha, dhorcha na h-oidhche 'teachd, na h-eòin bheaga, bhuchallach, bhachlach, bharra-bhuidh a' gabhail mu thàmh 'am bunaibh nam preas, agus 'am barraibh nan dos, agus anns na h-innseagaibh fasgach, bòidheach, a bu laghaiche a thaghadh jad dhoibh féin.   Mu dheireadh bha e fàs sgìth, agus fann le acras. Thug e sùil air thoiseach air, agus cò 'chunnaic e ach Madadh-na-Maoile Mòire. An uair a choinnich iad a chéile chuir am Madadh còir fàilt agus furan air gu cridheil. Dh' fheòraich e dh' e cean' a bha e dol? Dh' innis Alastair dha gu 'n robh e 'dol a dh' iarraidh anam a' Chrochaire Lom-rusgaich. Thubhairt am Madadh ris, "Tha 'n oidhch' a' tighinn, agus tha thu sgìth; thig còmhla riumsa, agus bheir mi dhuit an aoidheachd a 's fearr a 's urrainn mi 'nochd." Dh' fhalbh e leis a' Mhadadh gu toileach. Ràinig iad fail a' Mhadaidh, agus b' e sin an t-àite tioram, seasgair le pailteas teine, sithionn fhiadh, 'us eildean 'us earbaichean. Fhuair e gu leòir ri' itheadh, agus leaba bhlàth shocrach le béin fhiadh fodha, agus béin éildean agus earbaichean thairis air.

Air an ath mhadainn fhuair e 'bhraiceas de 'n cheart seòrsa bithidh a bh' aig' air a shuipeir. An uair a bha e falbh thubhairt am Madadh còir ris, "Uair air bith a ni fiacail làidir nach géill 'n a greim no cas luath lùghmhor a shiùblas creachann beinne no ruitheas air ùrlar glinne féum dhuit cuimhnich ormsa, agus bithidh mise ri d' thaobh." Thug e buidheachas mòr do 'n Mhadadh chòir, agus dh' fhalbh e air a thurus.

Chum e air aghaidh cian fhada agus làn fhada gus an robh e fàs sgìth, agus dorchadh na n tràtha' tighinn. Thug e sùil air thoiseach air, agus cò 'chunnaic e 'tighinn 'n a choinneamh ach Dóbhran Donn Shruth an Iùil. An uair a choinnich iad chuir an Dóbhran fàilte shunntach air, agus dh' fheòraich e dh' e c' àit' an robh e dol? Dh' innis Alastair sin da, "Tha 'n oidhche 'tighinn, agus tha thu sgìth; thig leamsa 'nochd, agus gheibh thu 'n aoidheachd a 's fearr a 's urrainn mis' a thabhairt duit." Chaidh e leis an Dóbhran a dh' ionnsaidh a' Chùirn aige. B' e sin an t-àite blàth, seasgair le pailteas teine, agus gu leòir de dh' iasg bradain agus bànaig. Fhuair e 'shuipeir gu math agus gu ro mhath, agus leaba cho socrach 'us air an do laidh e riamh de riasg réidh nan Lochan-uisge. Air an ath mhadainn fhuair e 'bhraiceas de 'n cheart seòrsa a bh' aig' air a shuipeir an oidhche roimhe. An uair a bha e falbh thubhairt an Dóbhran ris, " Uair air bith a ni earball làidir a shuàmh fo 'n loch no 'chur gach sruth agus gach caisil féum dhuit, cuimh-nich orm-sa, agus bithidh mise ri d' thaobh." Thug Alastair buidheachas do 'n Dóbhran laghach, agus dh' fhalbh e.

Shiubhail e air aghaidh cian fhada agus làn fhada gus an robh e fàs sgìth, agus an oidhch' a' tighinn. Thug e sùil air thoiseach air, agus cò 'chunnaic e 'n a ghurach air cloich ach Seabhag Mòr Chreag nan Sgeilp. An uair a choinnich iad dh' fheòraich an Seabhag dh' e c' àit' an robh e 'dol, agus dh' innis Alastair dha an turus air an robh e. "Tha 'n oidhch' a' tighinn, agus tha thu sgìth agus acrach," ars' an Seabhag; "is fearr dhuit fuireachd leamsa 'nochd, agus bheir mi dhuit an aoidheachd a 's fearr' a 's urrainn mi." Dh' fhalbh e leis an Seabhag g' a Sgeilp fhasgaich féin. B' e sin an t-àite tioram, seasgair far an d' fhuair e pailteas de shithinn gach seòrs' èun, agus leaba de dh' iteagaibh cho socrach agus air an do laidh e riamh. Air an ath mhadainn, an déigh dha 'bhraiceas fhaotainn, thubhairt an Seabhag ris, "Uair air bith a ni sgiath lùghmhor, làidir a shiùbhlas tromh athar no thar bheann agus thar loch féum dhuit cuimhnich ormsa, agus bithidh mise ri d' thaobh."

Cha deachaidh e ro fhad' air aghaidh an uair a thàinig e 'm fradharc Doire Dlùth-dhuilleach nan Craobh. Ràinig e 'n Doire, agus mu 'n gann a fhuair e 's tigh, léum Eilid Luath-chasach nan Stùchd a mach, agus thog i ris a' Bheinn. Shìn e as a déigh, ach mar bu luaith' a dh' fhalbhadh esan b' ann a b' fhaide 'bhitheadh ise bhuaithe. An uair a chlaoidh se e féin 'g a leantainn chuimhnich e air a' Mhadadh agus thubhairt e, "Nach bu mhath Madadh na Maoile Mòire 'so a nis?" Cha luaith' a chaidh am facal as a bhéul na bha 'm Madadh r' a thaobh. Dh' innis e do 'n Mhadadh gu 'n robh e air a chlaoidh-eadh as déigh na h-Éilde, agus gu 'n robh e ni 'b' fhaide uaipe 'n sin na bha e 'n uair a thòisich e air a leantainn.

Dh' fhalbh am Madadh 'na déigh, agus dh' fhalbh esan an déigh a' Mhadaidh gus an d' ràinig iad taobh an Lochain Uaine. An sin rug am Madadh air an Eilid, agus dh' fhàg e i aig casaibh Alastair. B' ann a' sin a chuimhnich Alastair air an ola. Ghrad thaom e i air a lamhaibh, agus *rub* e i ris gach mìr d' a chraicionn ris am faodadh fuil na h-Éilde beantainn. Chaidh e 'n sin an carabh na h-Éilde, agus dh' fhosgail e i. Ach ma dh' fhosgail cha b' ann gun chath, oir bha crodhain cho biorach agus a casan cho làidir, agus mur bhi an ola gu 'n tug i as a chéile 'n a mhìribh e. An uair a dh' fhosgail e 'mhaodal léum am Bradan a mach aiste do 'n Lochan Uaine.

Chaidh e 'n déigh a' Bhradain mu 'n cuairt air bruachaibh an Lochain, ach an uair a bhitheadh esan aig aon bhruaich bhith- eadh am Bradan fo bhruaich eile. Mu dheireadh chuimhnich e air Dóbhran Donn Shruth an Iùil, agus air ball bha e ri 'thaobh. Dh' innis e do 'n Dóbhran gu 'n robh 'm Bradan anns an Lochan, agus nach b' urrainn e greim fhaotainn air. Ghrad léum an Dóbhran a mach do 'n uisge, agus an ùine ghoirid thàinig e air ais leis a' Bhradan, agus dh' fhàg e aig casaibh Alastair e. Rug Alastair air a' Bhradan, ach cho luath 's a thug e toll air a bhroinn léum Lach na h-ite réidh agus an drùim uaine mach, agus dh' itealaich i gu taobh thall an Lochain, agus laidh i 'n sin. Dh' fhalbh e 'n a déigh, ach an uair a ràinig e 'n taobh air an robh i dh' éirich i agus chaidh i air a h-ais gus an taobh a dh' fhàg e. 'Nuair a chunnaic e nach b' urrainn e breith oirre chuimhnich e air Seabhag Mòr Chreag nan Sgeilp, agus ann an tiota bha e ri 'thaobh. Dh' innis e dha mar fhuair an Lach as, agus nach b' urrainn esan breith oirre. Ghrad léum an Seabhag as déigh na Lach, agus ann an tiota thàinig e leatha agus dh' fhàg e i aig casaibh Alastair.

Chuimhnich Alastair na 'm beanadh an t-Ubh do 'n bhlàr gu 'n robh na h-uile ni caillte. Uime sin dh' fhosgail e 'n Lach gu faicilleach, agus cho luath 's a thàinig an t-Ubh anns an t- sealladh ghrad rug e air 'n a laimh. Ach thug an t-Ubh breab as a dhòrn, agus léum e trì àirde duine anns an athar. Ach mu 'n do bhuail e 'n talamh fhuair Alastair greim air, agus thug e cruaidh bhruthadh air eadar a dhà laimh agus a dhà ghlùn, agus chuir e 'n a bhruanaibh e.

Bha gach ni a fhuair e ri 'dheanamh criochnaicht' aige nis. Thill e uime sin air ais an taobh a thàinig e. Fhuair e 'n t- slighe cho réidh thèarainte 's a bha i roimhe làn chunnart agus chnap-starraidh. An ùine ghoirid ràinig e Caisteal Ùdlaidh na Beithir Theinntich. Choinnich am boirionnach e aig an dorus,

agus ghlaodh i, " A ghràidh a dh' fhir an t-Saoghail ! thug thu
buaidh, agus gheibh thu do dhuais !"    Dh' fhalbh i leis, agus
an uine ghoirid ràinig iad Caisteal Mòr nan Ochd Turaitean.
Choinnich Soills' an Dubhair iad anns an dorus, agus dh' fhalbh
i leò.   Ràinig iad an sin Caisteal Mòr ceann na h-Aisridh
Chreagach, agus fhuair iad Gath-gréine 'g am feitheamh.   Dh'
fhalbh i leò, agus ràinig iad Caisteal Famhair Mòr na Beinne
Brice, agus fhuair iad e 'n a shìneadh marbh air an ùrlar. Rug
Alastair air a chlaidheamh mhòr fhéin, agus thug e 'n ceann
agus na casan fo na glùinibh dheth.   Cheangail e suas iad, agus
thug e leis iad.

"Nis," thubhairt Gath-gréine, " is e 'nochd an oidhche' anns
an robh am Famhair Mòr ri tighinn airson mo pheathar a 's
òige, agus tha m' athair 'an tròm bhròn a chionn gu 'm bheil e
cinnteach gu 'n deachaidh thusa 'mharbhadh o nach do thill thu
roimhe so.   Tha dhaoine uile cruinn aige 'thabhairt coinneamh
do 'n Fhamhair an uair a ruigeas e.   Ach thig a bhròn gu gean,
agus a thùrsadh gu gàire.   An uair a thig e 'n ar coinneamh
innsidh tu dha mar dh' éirich dhuit o 'n là anns an d' fhalbh
thu gus an oidhche nochd."

An uair a bha iad a' dlùthachadh ris a' Chaisteal chunnaic
iad feachd mòr a' feitheamh ri teachd an Fhamhair.  Bha 'n
Righ agus na bha 's a' Chaisteal gu tùrsach, brònach airson na
h-ighinn a bha gu bhi air a toirt uapa.  Ach am meadhon a
bhròin thug an Righ sùil a mach air uinneig, agus chunnaic e
Alastair a' tighinn le triùir bhoirionnach 'n a chuideachd, agus
ceann 'us casan an Fhamhair aige thar a ghualain.  Léum e
mach 'n a choinneamh, agus rug e air eadar a dhà laimh, agus
phòg se e.  "A ghràidh a dh' fhir an t-Saoghail ! bha fhios agam
gu 'm bitheadh buaidh leat, agus bithidh mise cho math 'us
mo ghealladh dhuitsa.   Ach o 'n thug thu féin dachaidh mo
chuid nighean uile gheibh thu do roghainn diù o 'n té 's sine
gus an té 's òige."   "Mata," thubhairt Alastair, " an té 'chaidh
mise a thèarnadh o 'n Chrochaire Lom-rusgach is i sin mo
roghainn."   An uair a chuala gach té do chàch so bha iad ro
dhubhach nach do roghnaich e iad féin.  Ach o 'n thug e
mach a bhuaidh, agus a rinn e na h-uibhir air an son dh'
aontaich iad uile gu 'm faigheadh e 'n té a roghnaich e.

An sin dh' fheòraich an Righ do dh' Alastair gu dé 'bha e 'dol a dheanamh ri ceann agus ri casan an Fhamhair. "Mu 'n ith mi biadh agus mu 'n òl mi deoch chi thu sin," ars' Alastair. Fhuair e 'n sin connadh agus rinn e teine mòr, agus an uair a bha 'n teine 'an teas a ghabhalach thilg e 'n ceann agus na casan ann am meadhon na lasrach. Cho luath 's a dhathadh falt a' chinn, agus a loisgeadh craicionn nan cas léum an t-aon Òganach a bu dreachmhoir' a chunnaic iad riamh a mach as an teine. "O, mac mo mhàthar agus m' athar a chaidh a ghoid 'n a leanabh!" ars' an Righ, agus e 'léum a null agus a' breith air eadar a dhà làimh. An uair a dh' fhàiltich iad a chéile chaidh iad uile 's tigh do 'n Chaisteal.

Chuir an Righ roimhe gu 'm bitheadh Alastair agus a nighean air am pòsadh an oidhche sin féin. Ach an uair a chual Alastair so thubhairt e, "A Righ Lochlainn, tha do thairgse glé mhath. Ach cha phòs mise do nighean, agus cha chuir mi seilbh ann am mìr de d' rìgheachd gus an cuir thu fios air Righ Òg Ceist agus air Ban-righ Òg Ceist a dh' ionnsaidh na bainnse." Chaidh an Righ an iomagain mhòir, a chionn nach robh fios aige gu dé 'n taobh a chuireadh e fios orra. Ann am meadhon a smaointean chuimhnich e air an Iorasglach-ùrlair. Chaidh e fàr an robh i, agus dh' innis e dhi iarrtàs Alastair. "Faigh thusa gach ni eile deas, agus bithidh iad agamsa 'n so romh éiridh gréine 'm màireach," ars' an Iorasglach. Agus mar thubhairt b' fhìor. A chéud sùil a thug an Righ ris a' mhuir air an ath mhadainn chunnaic e dà churach a' tighinn gu tràigh. A mach a té dhiù thàinig Cormac agus a bhean, agus as an té eile thàinig an Iorasglach-ùrlair.

Léum Alastair a mach nan coinneamh, agus b' i sin an fhàilte chàirdeil a chuir iad air a cheile! Thàinig an Righ nan coinneamh, agus chuir e fàilte chridheil orra. Chaidh iad a dh' ionnsaidh a' Chaisteil agus bha 'm pòsadh air a dheanamh. An déigh do 'n phòsadh a bhi seachad rinn iad cuilm mhòr a mhair là agus bliadhna. An ceann na h-ùine sin thill Cormac agus a bhean d' an àite féin, agus chaidh Alastair agus a bhean leò. Dh' fhuirich Cormac 'an Caisteal Righ Ceist, ach chaidh Alastair air ais gu àit' athar. An uair a chunnaic a mhàthair e chuir i fàilte mhòr air, agus rinn athair toileachadh mòr an

uair a chual e gu 'n robh Cormac 'n a Righ Òg Ceist.   Rinn
an Righ an so cuilm mhòr eile do dh' Alastair agus d' a bhean,
agus do na h-uile 'bha mu 'n cuairt air.

Agus cha d' fhuair mise ach ìm air éileig, brochan 'an
craidhleig, brògan paipeir.   Chuir iad an allt mi, 's theirig
iad.

# VII.

## A TALE OF THE SON OF THE KING OF IRELAND AND THE DAUGHTER OF THE KING OF THE RED CAP.

THERE was before now a King in Ireland who was twice married, and who had a son by each one of his wives. The second wife was very bad to the son of the first wife, and very devoted to her own son. She made the King buy for her son a shinty of gold and a ball of silver. The son of the first wife had only a wooden shinty and a wooden ball, but with the shinty he had he would beat his brother.

On a certain day he won many goals from his brother. His brother took this ill, and cast up to him that he had but a wooden shinty. He said, " I am preferred by my father, and as a sign of that he gave me a shinty of gold." This hurt the son of the first wife greatly. He went home, and reached the castle crying. His father came out to meet him, and said, "Poor fellow, what is the matter with thee?" " My brother has cast up to me that he was preferred by you, and that you gave him a shinty of gold while I had but a shinty of wood." Well," said his father, " he shall not have that to cast up to thee any more ; I will give thee a shinty of gold and a ball of silver."

The boy got the shinty and ball, and when his step-mother saw them with him she was greatly displeased, and told him that he was not to dare play with her son any more. He was now more wretched than he ever was, because he had not a creature that would play with him, but a deer-hound bitch which was in the castle.

He and the deer-hound bitch grew so attached to each other that there was no separation between them day or night.

A good time passed in that way, but on a certain day he went away from the castle, and reached the sea-side. He was travelling against the face of the wave, when he beheld a mermaid putting off her husk. She hid the husk in the cleft of a rock, and then she was as handsome a woman as he ever beheld. He kept his eye sharply on her to see what she was going to do. At last she leaped out in the loch and began to wash herself. He now thought that he would steal her husk.

He crawled on his knees and belly till he got a hold of the husk. He then went away, and hid himself in a place where he could see what the mermaid would do when she would miss it.

She came in, and when she did not find her husk where she had put it, she gave a look all round, and went away to the place in which the Son of the King of Ireland was hiding. She said to him, "Son of the King of Ireland, give me my husk." "I will not; thou shalt not get it without a condition." "What condition dost thou ask?" "That thou leave thy husk off thee, and that thou marry me." "I will not do that, for another man has a promise of marriage from me. A long time shall elapse before he will come for me, but I am going to wait for him. But, Son of the King of Ireland, take my advice, and deserve my blessing. Give me my husk, and I will promise to be a faithful friend to thee after this. And in any strait or hardship which may come upon thee, and in which I can give thee help, I will give it. Thou hast many trials to go through of which thou hast no knowledge, but if thou take my advice and be faithful, thou shalt get out of every strait and every hardship which shall come upon thee." When he heard this he gave her the husk. The Mermaid said, "My blessing be with thee now. Every day thou risest, come here to the sea-side, and if thou hast need of me thou shalt see me."

He went home cheerfully. Next day he reached the sea-side, and was walking against the face of the wave, as he was doing on the day before, but saw nothing. Next day he came again, but saw nothing that time also. The third day he came, and kept his eye in every bend and bay and creek to see if he could behold the Mermaid. But a look he gave at last, what did he see but three swans swimming. One of them was the White Swan of the Smooth Neck, whose brightness was like sunshine after a shower in a spring morning. He stood looking at her, and then gave his word and oath to himself that he would neither stop nor take rest on sea or on land till he should see a woman who was as handsome as the swan. The swans then swam away, and went out of sight in the ocean.

Having turned round, he beheld the Mermaid in a bay beside him. "Son of the King of Ireland," said she, "thou hast fallen in love with the White Swan of the Smooth Neck. Go home, and tell thy father to get thee a boat ; thou shalt go away in her, and set thy course in the very direction which the Swans have taken. Having said this, she went under the water, and he got not a second look of her.

He went home. He reached his father, and said to him that he was going away on a sea-voyage, and that he must get him a boat. "Thou shalt get that and a crew," said his father. "To-morrow go down to the shore, and a boat and crew shall be waiting there for thee. Gonachry (the Heart-wounder) is the name of the boat, and the crew shall be obedient to thee in everything which thou mayest ask them to do."

He reached the shore, and the boat was waiting him as his father said. He went on board of her, and set her course in the very direction which the Swans took. They were a long time sailing on the ocean without seeing land. At last land came in sight, and they made straight for it. When they reached the shore the Son of the King of Ireland told the crew to take care of the boat, and that he would go ashore. He went ashore. He noticed a large, fine house far away from him at the lower end of a great wood, and made straight for it. This was the Castle of the Big Island of the Whales (or Sea-hogs). Before he arrived at the Castle he beheld an Old Man coming to meet him. When they came within speaking distance of each other, the Old Man said, "Son of the King of Ireland, thy business is difficult for thee to get, but *they* are in existence and can be found. Thou shalt not be the worse of my advice and help, and thou shalt get them. Thou shalt stay with me to-night, and I will go with thee to-morrow."

They reached the Castle and went in. The Old Man said, "Thou hast fallen in love with the White Swan of the Smooth Neck, the young daughter of the King of the Red Cap, who is staying in the Big Island of the Spirit of the Mist. Many champions came before thee to seek Sunshine, the Young Daughter of the King of the Red Cap, but they did not return, and no more shalt thou return unless thou be hardy and faithful, and take advice. Here is for thee a needle, and a bow and an arrow, and thou shalt keep the needle till thou shalt have need of it. To-morrow morning thou shalt go away with Gonachry, thy boat, and when thou gettest her under sail thou shalt put the needle in the point of the arrow, and shalt hold it straight up in the air, and shalt set thy course in the direction in which it points when it falls in the boat.

And I will go with thee, for thou shalt not be the worse of my assistance before thou return. There is a brother of mine staying in the Beautiful Isle of the Shadow of the Stars, and we shall be in his house next night. He will tell thee what thou art to do after that, and will give thee something else which shall be useful to thee. But before I depart I must have it as a condition from thee that thou shalt put me on land here when thou returnest." "I promise that to thee," said the son of the King of Ireland.

Next morning, when the Son of the King of Ireland and the Old Man reached the shore, they found Gonachry under sail waiting them. As soon as they went on board, the Son of the King of Ireland set the needle in the point of the arrow, let the arrow off straight up in the air, and set the ship's course in the direction in which the arrow pointed when it fell. They sailed onwards the day long. At the declining of the sun they beheld land ahead of them, and made straight for it. When they reached the shore the Old Man told the Son of the King of Ireland to go ashore and proceed to the Castle.

He went ashore, and made for the Castle. As he was advancing, everything he saw was causing him great wonder. There was not a stone nor a rock that met him in which he was not beholding his own image shining. At last he came in sight of the Castle, and saw the Old Man coming to meet him.

When they met, the Old Man said, "Son of the King of Ireland, great is thy news if thou thyself knew of it. But *they* are in existence, and they can be found. Thou hast to go through many trials, but thou shalt get out of them all if thou be hardy and faithful, and take my advice. But come in, and thou shalt stay with me to-night, and I will tell thee a thing which shall be useful to thee." He followed the Old Man into the Great Castle of the Island of the Shadow of the Stars.

"Now," said the Old Man, "thou art on a journey which it is not easy for thee to accomplish. Thou hast vowed that thou wouldst not marry until thou shouldst see a woman as beautiful as the White Swan of the Smooth Neck. That is the Young Daughter of the King of the Red Cap, who is staying in the Big Isle of the Spirit of the Mist. A brother of mine is staying there, and we shall be with him next night, and he will tell thee what thou hast to do after that. When thou goest on board of Gonachry thou shalt put the thimble on the point of the arrow, and shalt let it go straight up in the air, and shalt set the course of the boat in the direction in which the thimble points when it falls. I will go with thee, for thou shalt not be the worse of my help. But before I go away I will have this condition from thee, that thou shalt put me ashore here when thou returnest."

Early next morning they went on board of Gonachry. The Son of the King of Ireland put the thimble on the point of the arrow, let the arrow go off in the air, and set the ship's course in the direction in which the thimble was pointing when it fell. They sailed onward the day long on the ocean. At the declining of the sun they saw land before them, and made straight for it. When they reached the shore the first Old Man said to the Son of the King of Ireland, " Hast thou thy needle?" He replied that he had. "Keep it carefully, for it is the first proof of thy trials." The second Old Man said, "Hast thou thy thimble?" "Yes," said the Son of the King of Ireland. "Keep it carefully, for it is the second proof of thy trials. Thou shalt now go ashore, and keep straight onward until thou shalt reach a Big

Castle. If my brother meet thee before thou shalt be at the Castle, have good courage ; but if he do not meet thee, it will be a bad sign of thy prospering after that. We will stay here till thou returnest."

The Son of the King of Ireland sprang ashore, and went away on his journey to the Castle. He knew that the Castle was in some place or other in the island, but he was not seeing it. He was keeping his eye sharply before him to see if he could behold the Old Man coming. But instead of a Castle or a man he saw a little tuft of druidic mist before him. He did not go very far forward when the little tuft of magic mist spread, and hid both earth and sky from him. He now said to himself that it was all up with him, because he could not see the Castle, and no man in the Castle could see him through the mist. In that fear he stood where he was. In a short time there came off the sea a faint breath of wind which swept away the mist, and when the mist passed away he saw the Castle before him. He kept straight towards it, but not a man was to be seen in front of him. When he came under the shadow of the walls of the Castle he noticed an Old Man coming out at the door and advancing to meet him. The Old Man said, " Son of the King of Ireland, thou didst take fright, but do not lose thy courage. Thou hast yet to go through many trials before thou shalt get Sunshine. But come in, and I will tell thee something which shall be useful to thee."

He went in. " Now," said the Old Man, " here are scissors for thee, and here are a bow and an arrow. To-morrow in the morning thou shalt stand on the Great Rock behind the Castle, and put thy scissors on the point of thine arrow, and thou shalt let it off straight up in the air. The way the scissors will be pointing when they fall, that is the way thou must set thy face. The three Swans which thou didst see are the three daughters of the King of the Red Cap, who is staying far away in this island. He is keeping them under spells until a Champion such as thou art happens to come to seek them. He then lifts the spells off them, and they become three handsome maidens. Many heroes came for them before thee, but the trials which were laid on them were so hard that not one of them won one of the maidens. But since thou hast got thus far forward I will help thee in anything which I can do for thee. The three Swans are at this very hour swimming on the Tranquil Lakelet of the Great Garden of the Trees of the Golden Apples in the Green Isle at the extremity of the Uttermost World. When thou dost reach the Lakelet thou shalt creep towards them with thine arrow, put thy needle in its point, and aim it at the one on whom thine affection is placed. As soon as the needle touches her the three will fly away from the Lake, and will not stop until they reach the Big Castle of the King of the Red Cap, their father."

Next morning he went out, and reached the top of the Great Rock behind the Castle. He put the scissors on the point of the arrow and let it off straight up in the air, and when it fell the scissors were pointing to the sea beneath the place in which he was standing. Then he went away in the direction in which the scissors pointed, until he arrived at the sea-side. But further than that he could not go. He now said to himself that he would return, and take with him Gonachry. But before he went away he gave a look, and saw the Mermaid at the margin of the wave before him.

"Son of the King of Ireland," said she, "thou art thinking of returning and taking Gonachry with thee to the Green Isle, but she will not serve thy purpose. For as soon as thou wouldst go away with her a magic mist would rise off the island, which would send you so far astray that you would never reach land. But the day thou gavest me my husk I promised to be a good friend to thee, and assist thee in the time of thy difficulty. And now I will help thee out of the strait in which thou art. Come and sit on my tail, and the magic mist of the Big Island of the Spirit of the Mist shall not put me astray until I land thee safely in the Green Isle at the extremity of the Uttermost World. But though I put thee there I shall not take thee thence. The Old Man, with whom thou wert last night, will go on board of Gonachry with the rest, and they will reach thee in the time of thy need. But, Son of the King of Ireland, see that thou lose not thy courage till they come."

Then he sat on the tail of the Mermaid. She set her face to the ocean, and swam away with great speed. They did not proceed very far when he noticed a little tuft of mist rising off the Island. The mist was coming after them, and gaining fast on them. In a short time it overtook them, and covered themselves and the sea. And it was so thick that he could not see the Mermaid's head from her tail. Then she said, " Son of the King of Ireland, what would thou and thy Gonachry do now ? " " Oh, what but that I should lose my course, and that I would not know where I was going," said he. The mist now grew very thick and dark, and the Mermaid said to him, " What thing soever thou shalt happen to see or hear, see that thou move not thy head one way or another, and that thou answer not a word which may be said to thee until I speak. It is all one with me to go on the surface of the sea or under it. I am now going to put my head under water, and then the mist of the Island of the Mist shall not put me out of my course."

Having said this, she took her head under the water, and went away with great speed. The Son of the King of Ireland was now seeing himself alone, and fear struck him that he might fall off the tail of the Mermaid. But he remembered her advice, and did as she told him. They did not proceed very far when he heard a plunge beside him. He gave a side look over his shoulder, and thought that he saw a woman in the water. Then he saw a hand in the water, and heard a voice saying, " Son of the King of Ireland, give me thy hand, for I am drowning." At the time he forgot his promise, and was going to lay hold of her by the hand, when the Mermaid put her head above water, and cried to him, " Son of the King of Ireland, take care of thyself, and remember whither thou art going. Thou thyself art in far greater danger than yon lady. Sea or air is all one to her. See that thou be on thy guard lest she come on thee in another way."

Having said this, she took her head under water again, and went away with surpassing speed, until the mist cleared off. She then took her head above water, and went away on the surface of the sea until they came in sight of land. As soon as the Son of the King of Ireland saw the land ahead of him his mind rose so greatly that he lost recollection of every fear and distress through which he had come. When they were nearing land, a gull came flying over his head, and said to him, " Son of the King of Ireland, here is a writing for thee; rise and catch it from me." But he remembered his promise, and did not answer her. " Son of the King of Ireland," said she again, " take the writing from me, and it will tell thee something of which thou hast no knowledge." But he remembered his promise the second time, and did not answer her. When they were near the shore, the loveliness of the land and beauty of the trees under fruit took his attention utterly off everything which he was told, and which he promised to do. In that state of bewilderment the gull descended the third time, and said, "Son of the King of Ireland, take hold of this writing, for it is from thy stepmother, inviting thee to thy brother's wedding." As soon as he heard his brother's name being mentioned he gave himself a lift and stretched out his hand to catch the writing. He felt himself leaning over, and going to fall in the water. He knew that if he fell in the water he should be lost. But the Mermaid noticed what was going to happen, and cried to him again, "Son of the King of Ireland, wilt thou not remember thy promise?" But he had leaned over so far that it was in the water he would be were it not that he was so near shore, and that she threw him with a jerk of her tail on dry land.

"Now," said she, "thou art on land. See that thou be faithful, and that thou forget not anything that I said to thee. Lose not thy courage, for Gonachry shall come to seek thee. Thou shalt go back with her to the Big Island of the Spirit of the Mist. When thou arrivest at that Island, the King of the Red Cap, with his three daughters, will meet thee on the shore, and he will say to thee, 'What art thou wanting, and what hast thou to give away?' Thou shalt say to him that if he and his daughters come on board thou wilt show them what thou hast; and the third Old Man will tell thee what thou shouldst do after that. Put thy bow and arrow in order, and travel onward to the Tranquil Lakelet of the Great Garden of the Golden Apples, and see that thy aim be good. One other advice : see that thou forget not thy promise in any peril or difficulty in which thou happenest to be on sea or on land. My blessing be with thee. Thou hast no further need of me."

He then went away to the Lake. As he was advancing everything was growing more beautiful, until at last the loveliness of the trees and the beauty of the land were driving out of his thoughts the business which was before him.   But he instantly remembered the advice of the Mermaid to be on his guard reaching the Lake.   A look he gave before him he beheld the Lake, and the three Swans swimming on the surface. He instantly let himself down on his knees, and went away creeping on all fours, and keeping every tree and knoll which met him between him and them until he got in the distance of a bow-shot of them. He then placed the arrow across the bow, drew the string, and with as good an aim as he could take, let off the arrow.   The arrow ran through the back plumage of the White Swan of the Smooth Neck, and, with a shriek of sudden pain, she sprang up in the air and flew away, while the other two followed her.

He kept his eye in the direction they took until they had gone so far from him that he lost sight of them.  He had then no alternative but to go away in the direction they had taken, and he travelled onward until he came to the sea-side.   Further than that he could not go.

He was walking backwards and forwards, keeping his eye in every nook, to see if he could behold the Mermaid, till he recollected that she had said to him that he would see her no more.   Then he gave a lifting on his eye towards the sea, and saw Gonachry coming.   His courage rose, he went straight to meet her, and the first persons he saw on board of her were the three Old Brothers.

As soon as Gonachry reached the shore, he went on board, and told the crew to put her about.   They did that.   He himself then sat at the helm, and set the ship's course as straight as he could in the direction the Swans took.   He kept her going until he saw, far away, land coming in sight ; but if it was far from him he took not long in reaching it.

When they were near land, the third Old Man said,

" Son of the King of Ireland, as soon as we arrive at the shore we shall see the King of the Red Cap and his three daughters waiting us. The first thing he will ask thee is, ' What art thou seeking, or what hast thou to give away?' Thou shalt take care that thou do not land, but thou shalt say to him that if he and his daughters come on board thou wilt show them some of the things which thou hast to give away. They will come on board, and thou shalt then hand the King the needle first, the thimble next, and the scissors last. Then he will hand them one after another to each in succession of his daughters, from the oldest to the youngest. And if thy favourite keep them, have good courage."

They reached land, and found the King of the Red Cap and his three daughters waiting them as the Old Man told. The Son of the King of Ireland gave them a look, and when he saw the Young Daughter of the King of the Red Cap he said, " There is my favourite, for she is as handsome in my sight as the White Swan of the Smooth Neck."

Then the King of the Red Cap cried, " Son of the King of Ireland, what art thou seeking, or what hast thou to give away ?" The Son of the King of Ireland said, " I am seeking and I will give away. If thou and thy daughters come on board, thou wilt see some of the things which I have for giving away."

They came on board. The Son of the King of Ireland handed his needle to the King of the Red Cap. The King looked at it, and handed it to his Big Daughter. The Big Daughter gave it but little attention, and handed it to the Middle Daughter. The Middle Daughter gave it no more attention than the Big one, and handed it to the Young Daughter. This one took a great liking for it, and she left neither eye nor point unexamined. When the time came for handing it back, she appeared as if she were sorry to part with it. The Son of the King of Ireland noticed this, and said to her that if she had any liking for the needle she might keep it. He now handed the thimble to the King, the King handed it to his Big Daughter, and the daughters handed it to each other until it was left with the Young Daughter, as the needle was. Then he handed the scissors to the King, and it remained, with the other things, in the possession of the Young Daughter.

"Now," said the King of the Red Cap, "Son of the King of Ireland, thou didst fall in love with the White Swan of the Smooth Neck, and thou didst vow in Ireland that thou wouldst neither stop nor take rest until thou shouldst see a woman as handsome in thy sight as the Swan. Thou hast seen her now, and that is Sunshine, my Young Daughter, and she has chosen thee with thy needle, with thy thimble, and with thy scissors. But many a one came to seek her who neither returned nor got her, and thou shalt not get her until thou win her by harder trials than this yet. Come on land, and go away with me to my Castle, and if thou win her in every trial that I will lay on thee, thou shalt get her."

The Son of the King of Ireland turned to his crew and said, "I do not know when I shall return, but have you Gonachry ready to go away. I will not return without having Sunshine with me."

He then sprang on land, having the third Old Man with him. They kept on till they arrived at the Castle of the King of the Red Cap. The King took them in to a fine room, drew out a table on the middle of the floor, and got his dice (*dìsnean*). "Now," said he, "Son of the King of Ireland, thou shalt come and play with me, and if thou win Sunshine from me thy first trial will be over, but if thou lose, thou shalt lose thy life." The play began, and the Son of the King of Ireland won three times in succession from the King of the Red Cap. "Well," said the King of the Red Cap, "thou hast won with the game of dice, but thou shalt not get her for that yet. Thou must stand another trial, and unless thou win three times in succession, thou shalt lose thy life over it."

He then drew a curtain between the two sides of the room, and put his three daughters on one side of the curtain, while he himself remained with the Son of the King of Ireland on the other side. "Now," said he to the Son of the King of Ireland, "my daughters will thrust the needle through the curtain three times, and if thou catch it except when it happens to be with my Young Daughter, thou shalt lose thy life." But Sunshine knew the trial beforehand, and whispered beforehand in the ear of the Son of the King of Ireland that it was the eye-end of the needle she would hold to him. The King of the Red Cap went in under the curtain, and gave the thimble to one of his daughters. He then returned out, and said to the Son of the King of Ireland, "Take hold of the needle." "I will not take hold of it from that one yet." The King went in a second time, and gave the scissors to another one. He then came out, and said to the Son of the King of Ireland, "Take hold of the needle." The Son of the King of Ireland again answered, "I will not take hold of it from that one yet." The King went in the third time, and gave the needle to his Young Daughter. He came out, and told the Son of the King of Ireland to take hold of it. The Son of the King of Ireland went over, and, when he saw the eye-end of the needle through the curtain, he took hold of it.

"Thou hast won" (or hast done the business), said the King of the Red Cap, "and thou shalt get her." The marriage was consummated without delay; and after it was over, the King of the Red Cap said, "If thou attempt to run away out of the Island, thine own life and that of thy wife shall be forfeited."

The Son of the King of Ireland passed a good time in the Island, but the crew were keeping Gonachry always ready for going away.  On a certain night, after the King of the Red Cap had fallen asleep, Sunshine said to her husband, "Now is thy time and thy opportunity, and if thou do not take advantage of them, thou shalt never get them again."  "We will get ready and depart then," said he.

They went away, and reached the shore.  They went then on board of Gonachry.  But as soon as the foot of Sunshine touched her, the King of the Red Cap cried in his bed, "Gonachry has gone away, and the Son of the King of Ireland has fled with my daughter.  But his Big Daughter went in and said to him, "No, it is only the sound of the wind passing through the trees of the garden thou art hearing."  As soon as Gonachry set sail he cried again, "Gonachry is off, and the Son of the King of Ireland has fled with my Young Daughter. But I will make him not go far until that shall be dear to him."

He sprang out, and went after them.  Sunshine perceived that he was coming, and said to her husband, "My father is coming, and if thou be not courageous he will sink the boat and drown us all, because his death is nowhere in the world but in a mole that he had in the very middle of the sole of his foot."

They saw him coming swimming, and sending the sea in sparks of fire before him.  The Son of the King of Ireland could not get an aim at the sole of his foot so long as he was after him.  But when he was coming alongside of the boat, Sunshine sprang to her husband, and pulled the bow and arrow out of his hands.  She then pointed the arrow to the sole of her father's foot, and, when he was passing her, sent it into the mole. He turned himself over in the sea, and was dead. Sunshine then turned to her husband, and said, " Son of the King of Ireland, be faithful to me after this, for I have killed my father for thy sake."

They kept sailing onwards to the Big Island of the Shadow of the Stars, and they landed the Second Old Man. As soon as his feet touched the shore he turned round and said, "Son of the King of Ireland, since thou wert as good as thy promise to me, thou shalt stay with me to-night." The Son of the King of Ireland went away with the Old Man, and they reached his Castle. That, indeed, was the splendid Big-House, the like of which he never saw. There was abundance of every kind of food and drink that was better than another to be found within, and the shadow of the stars was to be seen in it without. At supper the Old Man said, " Son of the King of Ireland, were it not for my brother and the virtue of his scissors thou hadst not found Sunshine."

Next morning they left farewell with the Old Man, and went away with Gonachry. They kept sailing onwards until they arrived at the Big Island of the Whales. They landed the First Old Man, and as soon as his soles struck the shore he turned round and said, " Son of the King of Ireland, thou hast got Sunshine with thee, but were it not for my second brother and the virtue of his thimble thou hadst not found her. And were it not for myself and my needle thou hadst never found out the place in which she was. But this is my dearly beloved island. I have not got a full meal since I left it." Then he reached out his arm, and took down from a cleft of a rock a great fishing-rod, with line and hook, and with a bait (*clib*) on the hook. He gave a great cast with it out on the sea, and fished a whale, and ate it. He then took cast after cast, and before

Gonachry went out of sight of the island he fished and ate seven whales!

The Son of the King of Ireland sailed back to the very haven in Ireland whence he departed. When he was landing, Sunshine said to him, "Thou art now going to thy father's house, where thy brother's wedding is to be held to-night. As soon as the greyhound bitch sees thee coming she will run to meet thee, but thou shalt take heed that she touch not a bit of thy face or of thy skin, for if she does thou shalt have no recollection of having ever seen me." "Sunshine," said he, " there is nothing in the world that can put thee out of my memory." " Remember, then, what I said to thee, and good success to thee."

He went away, and when he was nearing his father's Castle the greyhound bitch came to meet him, and before he got his arm lifted up, she sprang and struck him with her muzzle in the mouth. Immediately he forgot that he ever saw Sunshine.

He struck into the company, and his father made a great stir on his account, and his stepmother showed him more kindness than she ever did.

Sunshine said to Gonachry's crew, "Yon man has gone away, the greyhound bitch has kissed him, and he has forgotten that he ever saw me. He will not return here until I go after him and bring him back. But you will stay on board of Gonachry until I come."

She then went on land, and reached the house of an old smith the king once had. She asked leave to stay in the house, but at first he refused her that, because he had not a suitable place for such a lady. She said that she herself would put the house in order if he would let her stay. He then told her to go in, and said if she would get his wife's permission that he would not be against her. She went in, and when the Smith's wife saw the comeliness of the woman, she said that she might stay if she could make herself contented in such a place.

She put the Smith's house in exceedingly fine order with furniture and everything else that was needful in a house.

There was a large spring near the palace, and it was out of it the water was drawn for the use of the King. Sunshine was in the habit of taking a walk every evening the way of the spring, in the hope that she might see her husband ; but she did not get a look of him.

On a certain day she told the Smith to make a cock and a hen of gold for her. The Smith said that he had not enough of gold to make a cock and a hen with. She said to him that she would give him as much as would suffice. The Smith got the gold, and began to make the cock, but it beat him to make him. Then she asked the hammer from the Smith, and in a short time she had the cock ready, and made the hen afterwards. The Smith burnished them for her, and after that she took them in with her.

Next night she went to the spring. After she had reached it the head butler of the King came for water to wash the King's feet. As soon as he bent over the spring he saw the shadow of Sunshine in the water. On the spot he fell in love with her, and nothing would do but that he should get her in marriage. She asked him who he was. He answered that he was the King's chief butler. She said that she would marry him on a certain condition. "What condition wouldst thou ask that thou wouldst not get ?" said he. "Well, the condition I will have from thee is that I get beforehand a hundred pieces of gold and a bottle of the King's wine, and that thou watch at my bedside till morning. If thou do that I will marry thee to-morrow." He promised her everything that she asked of him.

He came that night to watch, and gave her a hundred pieces of gold and a bottle of wine. She said to him that it was a custom with her to have a while of play before going to bed. She then got the cock and the hen, and put them on the table. The cock sprang and pecked the hen. "Oh," said the hen, "that was not what thou owedst me, seeing that I held the eye-end of the needle to thee." The cock gave the hen another peck. "Oh," said the hen, "that was not thy due to me, seeing that I put thee on thy guard against the greyhound bitch." The sight pleased the butler greatly, for never before had he seen the like of it.

After she had gone to bed she told the butler to give her a drink of the wine. He went over to the table that was on the other side of the room, and took hold of the bottle. He tried to lift it, but it would not come away with him. His hand stuck to the bottle, the bottle to the table, and the table to the floor, and in that position he was the night long. Next morning the woman said to him, "What wert thou doing there all night ? Is that the way thou art watching my bedside ? Thou hast broken the bargain, and forfeited the gold and me." "Oh," said the butler, "the night was so frosty that my hand stuck to the bottle, the bottle to the table, and the table to the floor, and out of this I could not get. It is time for me to be at home, for if the King gets up before I arrive I shall lose my place."

The woman called for the Smith, and he came. He took hold of the butler, and gave him a terrible pulling, but he would not come with him. The Smith's wife got hot water, and poured it about the legs of the table, and they loosened from the floor. She then poured the water on the bottom of the bottle, and the bottle came away from the table, but, though she scalded the butler's hands, they would not come from the bottle. "Oh," cried the butler, "the time is up, and I must go. What shall I do?" "Oh, go as thou art," said the woman. "Oh, if the King sees the bottle I will lose my place over it." "Thou must come to the Smithy then." He went with her to the Smithy. She made the Smith hold the butler's hands in the fire, and she herself went to blow the bellows. The butler soon cried to let him go, because he could stand the pain no longer. When the time was nearly up, the woman said, " I will try one other way with thee yet." She then took hold of the bottom of the bottle, and spilt the wine on his hands, and they came away from the bottle. "Well, since I have got off, I will not return any more," said the butler, and he went away.

Next evening she met the head cook of the King at the spring, and promised to marry him if she would get one hundred pieces of gold and a pot of the King's broth, and if he would watch at her bedside till morning. He agreed to do all this, and everything happened to him as it happened to the butler, except that his hand stuck to the lid of the pot, the lid to the pot, and the pot to the floor.

On the third evening she met the head coachman of the King, and agreed to marry him if he would give her a hundred pieces of gold and watch at her bedside till morning.

He came to the Smith's house at night. At bed-time the woman placed the cock and the hen on the table. "Oh, how beautiful they are," said he. "Can they speak?" "Yes," said the woman. Then the hen sprang and pecked the cock. "Oh," said the cock, "thou didst give the old Smith's situation under the King to another smith." "Is that right?" said Sunshine to the coachman.  "Yes," said he.  "Well, thou shalt give it back to him before I marry thee."  He said nothing to this. Then the cock sprang and pecked the hen.  "Oh, that was not thy due to me, seeing that I held the eye-end of the needle towards thee," said the hen. After the woman had gone to bed, she said that she forgot to shut the door.  "I'll shut it," said the coachman.  He rose and shut the door, but his hand stuck to the bar, the bar to the door, and the door to the hinges, and out of that he did not get the night long.  Next morning she said to him what she said to the rest, and he answered as the rest did.

The Smith and his wife came, and tried to draw him from the door, but they could not.  Then they tried to pull the door off the hinges, but that beat them.  When the time had nearly run out, and he had got fully as much pain as the rest, the woman rubbed balsam to his hands, and let him go.

Next night her husband was going to marry a lady of high rank.  Every person about the Castle got an invitation to the wedding.  When they met there was something wanting, and that was some person who would amuse the company with games.  The butler said that there was a woman in the old Smith's house who could perform the most wonderful feats he ever saw.  "Oh, yes, for I saw her," said the cook.  "Oh, yes, and I also saw her," said the head coachman.  "She has a cock and hen, and they can speak.  They told me everything I ever did."  "Get her here," said the King.

Sunshine came, but her husband did not know that he had ever seen her.  She put the cock and hen on the table.  The cock sprang, and pecked the hen.  "Oh, that was not thy due to me, seeing that I held the eye-end of the needle towards thee," said the hen. The hen then sprang, and pecked the cock.  "Oh, it

was not thy due to me, seeing that I won thee thrice
with my needle, thimble, and scissors," said the cock.
The cock again sprang, and pecked the hen.  "Oh,
it was not thy due to me, seeing that I killed my father
on thy account," said the hen.  The King's Son now
began to cock his ears.  The cock sprang, and pecked
the hen the third time.  "Don't, for I put thee on thy
guard against the kiss of the greyhound bitch," said the
hen.

"Sunshine, my love of all the women in the world !"
said the Son of the King, while he sprang towards her,
put his arm about her neck, and kissed her.  He then
told the company that Sunshine was his wife, and the
daughter of the King of the Red Cap.  The bride got
leave to depart, and they kept up the feast for a day
and a year, and, if they have not left the Castle since,
they are there still.

---

# SGEULACHD AIR MAC RIGH ÉIRIONN

## AGUS NIGHEAN RIGH A' CHURRAICHD RUAIDH.

---

BHA Righ roimhe so 'an Éirinn a bha pòsda dà uair, agus aig
an robh mac ris gach té d' a mhnathaibh.  Bha 'n dara bean
ro dhona do mhac na céud mhnà, agus ro mhùirneach mu
thimchioll a mic féin.  Thug i air an Righ caman òir agus
ball airgid a cheannach d' a mac-sa.  Cha robh aig mac na
céud mhnà ach caman fiodha agus ball fiodha, ach chuireadh
e air a bhràthair leis a' chaman a bh' aige.

Air là àraidh chuir e mòran thaobhuill air a bhràthair.
Ghabh a bhràthair so gu dona, agus thilg e air nach
robh aigesan ach caman fiodha.  Thubhairt e, "Is mise
's docha le m' athair, agus mar chomhar air sin thug

e dhomh caman òir." Ràinig so mac na céud mhnà gu mòr. Dh' fhalbh e dhachaidh, agus ràinig e 'n Caisteal a' caoineadh. Thàinig 'athair a mach 'n a choinneamh, agus thubhairt e ris, "A dhuine bhochd gu dé 'tha 'cur ort ?" "Thilg mo bhràthair orm gu 'm b' e 'bu docha leibhsa, agus gu 'n tug sibh dha caman òir, agus nach robh agamsa ach caman maide." "Mata," ars' athair, "cha bhi sin aige ri thilgeil ort tuillidh; bheir mise dhuit caman òir agus ball airgid."

Fhuair am balach an caman agus am ball, agus an uair a chunnaic a mhuime iad aige, ghabh i mìthlachd mòr; agus thubhairt i ris gun a chridhe 'bhi aige cluich le mac-sa tuillidh. Bha e 'nis ni 'bu bhrònaiche na bha e riamh, a chionn nach robh créutair aige a rachadh a chluich leis, ach galla mhial-choin a bha 's a Chaisteal. Dh' fhàs e féin agus a' ghalla mhial-choin cho mùirneach m' a chéil' 'us nach robh deal-achadh eatarra a là no 'dh' oidhche.

Chaidh ùine mhath seachad mar sin, ach air aon là àraidh dh' fhalbh e o 'n Chaisteal, agus ràinig e taobh na mara. Bha e 'siubhal ri aghaidh na tuinne 'n uair a chunnaic e maighdean-mhara, agus i a' cur dhi a cochuill. Chuir i 'n cochull 'am falach 'an sgor creige, agus bha i 'n sin 'n a boirionnach cho briadha 's a chunnaic e riamh. Chum e 'shùil gu géur oirre feuch gu dé 'bha i 'dol a dheanamh. Léum i mu dheireadh a mach air an loch, agus thòisich i air i féin a ghlanadh. An so smaointich e gu 'n goideadh e 'n cochull aice.

Dh' èalaidh e air a ghlùnaibh agus air a bhroinn gus an d' fhuair e greim air a' chochull. Dh' fhalbh e 'n sin, agus chaidh e 'm falach ann an àite fàr am faiceadh e gu dé 'dhean-adh a' mhaighdean-mhara 'n uair a dh' ionndraineadh i e.

Thill i 's tigh, agus an uair nach d' fhuair i 'n cochull fàr an do chuir i e, thug i sùil ceithir thimchioll oirre, agus dh' fhalbh i dìreach a dh' ionnsaidh an àit anns an robh Mac Righ Éirionn 'am falach. Thubhairt i ris, "A Mhic Righ Éirionn, thoir dhòmhsa mo chochull." "Cha tabhair; cha-n fhaigh thu e gun chùmhnant." "Gu dé 'n cùmhnant a tha thu 'g iarraidh ?" "Gu 'm fàg thu dhìot do chochull, agus gu 'm pòs thu mise." "Cha dèan mi sin, oir tha gealladh pòsaidh aig fear eil' orm

Bithidh ùine mhòr mu 'n tig e air mo shon, ach tha mi 'dol a dh' fheitheamh ris. Ach, a Mhic Righ Éirionn, gabh mo chomhairle-sa, agus toill mo bheannachd. Thoir dhomh mo chochull, agus geallaidh mise gu 'm bi mi 'm bhan-charaid dhìleas dhuit as a dhéigh so. Agus càs no cruadal a thig ort, agus anns an urrainn mise cuideachadh a dheanamh dhuit ni mi e. Tha mòran agad ri 'dhol troimhe air nach 'eil fhios agadsa, ach ma ghabhas tu comhairle agus ma bhitheas tu dìleas gheibh thu as gach càs agus as gach cruadail a thig ort." An uair a chual e so thug e dhi an cochull. Thubhairt a' Mhaighdean-mhara, " Mo bheannachd agad a nis. A h-uile là a dh' éireas tu, thig thu so gu taobh na mara, agus ma bhitheas féum agad orm chi thu mis' ann."

Dh' fhalbh e dhachaidh gu sunndach. Air an ath latha ràinig e taobh na mara, agus bha e coiseachd ri aghaidh na tuinne mar bha e air an là roimhe, ach cha-n fhac e ni air bith. Air an dara là thàinig e rithist, ach cha-n fhac e dad air an uair sin cuideachd. Air an treas là thàinig e, agus chum e 'shùil anns gach luib, agus ób, agus camus feuch am faiceadh e 'm haigh-dean-mhara. Ach sùil 'g an tug e mu dheireadh gu dé 'chunnaic e ach tri ealachan air an t-shnàmh. B' i té dhiù eala bhàn a' mhuineil réidh, agus a soillse mar dhearrsadh gréine air cùl froise ann am madainn earraich. Sheas e 'coimhead oirre, agus thug e bóid agus briathar ris féin an sin, nach stadadh e, agus nach gabhadh e fois air muir no air tìr gus am faiceadh e bean a bha cho briadha ris an eala. An sin shnàmh na h-ealachan air falbh, agus chaidh iad as an t-shealladh anns a' chuan.

Air tionndadh dha mu 'n cuairt chunnaic e a' Mhaighdean-mhara ann an ób laimh ris. "A Mhic Righ Éirionn," thubhairt i, "ghabh thu gaol air Eala Bhàn a' mhuineil réidh. Falbh dhachaidh, agus iarr air d' athair bàta fhaotainn duit, agus falbhaidh tu innte, agus leagaidh tu do chùrsa 'cheart taobh a ghabh na h-ealachan." Air dhi so a ràdh chaidh i fodha anns an uisge, agus cha d' fhuair e 'n ath shealladh dhi.

Chaidh e dhachaidh. Ràinig e 'athair, agus thubhairt e ris gu 'n robh e 'falbh air turus cuain, agus gu ' m féumadh esan bàta fhaotainn da. "Gheibh thu sin, agus sgioba," thubhairt athair. "Am màireach rach sìos a dh' ionnsaidh a' chladaich, agus bithidh bàt' agus Sgioba 'feitheamh ort ann. Is e Gona-chridh a's ainm do 'n bhàta, agus bithidh an Sgioba ùmhal dhuit anns gach ni a dh' iarras tu orra 'dheanamh."

Ràinig e 'n cladach, agus bha 'm bàta 'feitheamh air mar thubhairt athair. Chaidh e air bòrd, agus leag e a cùrsa a' cheart taobh a ghabh na h-ealachan. Bha iad a' seòladh ré ùine mhòir air a' chuan gun fhearann fhaicinn. Mu dheireadh thàinig fearann 's an t-shealladh, agus rinn iad dìreach air. An uair a ràinig iad an cladach dh' iarr Mac Righ Éirionn air an Sgioba an aire 'thabhairt do 'n bhàta, agus gu 'n rachadh esan air tìr.

Chaidh e air tìr. Thug e 'n aire do thigh mòr, sgiamhach fada bhuaithe aig bun coille mhòir, agus rinn e dìreach air. B' e so Caisteal Eilean Mòr nam Muca-mara. Mu 'n d' ràinig e 'n Caisteal chunnaic e Seann duine 'tighinn 'n a choinneamh. An uair a thàinig iad an astar bruidhinn d' a chéile thubhairt an Seann duine, "A Mhic Righ Éirionn, tha do ghnothuch duilich dhuit fhaotainn, ach tha iad ann, agus gabhaidh iad faotainn. Cha mhisd thu mo chomhairle agus mo chuid-eachadh-sa, agus gheibh thu iad. Fanaidh tu leamsa 'nochd, agus falbhaidh mise leat am màireach."

Ràinig iad an Caisteal agus chaidh iad a 's tigh. Thubhairt an Seann duine, "Ghabh thu gaol air Eala Bhàn a' Mhuineil réidh, Nighean Òg Righ a' Churraichd Ruaidh a tha fuireachd ann an Éilean Mòr Spiorad a Cheò. Thàinig mòran chur-aidhnean air thoiseach ortsa 'dh' iarraidh Deàrsadh-gréine, Nighean Òg Righ a' Churraichd Ruaidh, agus cha do thill iad, agus cha till thusa ni 's mò mur bi thu cruadalach, dìleas, agus mur gabh thu comhairle. So dhuit snàthad, agus bogha agus saighead, agus gleidhidh tu 'n t-snàthad gus an tig féum agad oirre. Anns a' mhadainn am màireach falbhaidh tu le Gonachridh, do bhàta, agus an uair a gheibh thu i fo siùil cuiridh tu 'n t-snàthad ann am barr na saighde, agus cumaidh tu dìreach anns an athar i, agus an rathad a bhitheas an t-snàthad ag amharc an uair a thuiteas i ánns a' bhàta leagaidh tu do chùrsa. Agus falbhaidh mise leat, oir cha mhisd thu mo chuideachadh mu 'n till thu. Tha bràthair dhomhsa 'fuireachd ann an Éilean Bòidheach Faileas nan Réul, agus bithidh sinn 'n a thigh-san an ath oidhche. Innsidh esan gu dé 'ni thu as a' dhéigh sin, agus bheir e dhuit ni éiginn eile 'bhitheas a chum d' fhéum. Ach bithidh e mar chùmhnant agam ort mu 'm falbh mi gu 'n cuir thu air tìr mi 'n so 'n uair a thilleas tu." "Tha mi gealltainn sin duit," arsa Mac Righ Éirionn.

Air an ath mhadainn an uair a ràinig Mac Righ Éirionn agus an Seann duin' an cladach fhuair iad Gonachridh fo' siùil a' feitheamh orra. Cho luath 's a chaidh iad air bòrd chuir Mac Righ Éirionn an t-snàthad 'am barr na saighde, leig e an t-saighead as dìreach anns an athar, agus an rathad a bha 'n t-snàthad ag amharc an uair a thuit i leag e cùrsa na luinge. Sheòl iad air an aghaidh fad' an là. Mu chromadh na gréine chunnaic iad fearann air thoiseach orra, agus rinn iad dìreach air. An uair a ràinig iad an cladach dh' iarr an Seann duine air Mac Righ Éirionn dol air tìr agus falbh a dh' ionnsaidh a' Chaisteil.

Chaidh e air tìr, agus rinn e air a' Chaisteal. Mar bha e 'dol air aghaidh bha gach ni a chunnaic e 'cur ioghnaidh mhòir air. Cha robh clach no creag a thachradh air anns nach robh e 'faicinn 'fhaileas fhéin a' deàrsadh. Mu dheireadh thàinig e 'm fradharc a' Chaisteil agus chunnaic e Seann duine 'tighinn 'n a choinneamh. An uair a thachair iad thubhairt an Seann duine, "A Mhic Righ Éirionn, is mòr do naigheachd na 'n robh fhios agad fhéin oirre. Ach tha iad ann, agus gabhaidh iad faotainn. Tha mòran chruadal agad ri dhol troimhe, ach gheibh thu asta gu léir ma bhitheas tu cruadalach, dìleas, agus ma ghabhas tu mo chomhairle-sa. Ach thig a 's tigh, agus fanaidh tu maille riumsa 'nochd, agus innsidh mise dhuit rud a bhitheas a chum d' fhéum." Lean e 'n Seann duine 's tigh do Chaisteal Mòr Eilean Faileas nan Réul.

"Nis," ars' an Seann duine, "tha thu air turus nach 'eil furasta dhuit a dheanamh. Bhòidich thu nach pòsadh tu gus am faiceadh tu bean a bhitheadh cho bòidheach ri Eala Bhàn a' Mhuineil Réidh. Is i sin Nighean Òg Righ a' Churraichd Ruaidh a tha fuireachd 'an Eilean Mòr Spiorad a' Cheò. Tha bràthair dhomhsa 'fuireachd an sin, agus bithidh sinn aige 'n

ath oidhche, agus innsidh esan duit gu dé 'bhitheas agad r' a
dheanamh 'n a dhéigh sin.    An uair a théid thu air bòrd
Gonachridhe cuiridh tu 'm mèuran so air barr na saighde, agus
leigidh tu as e dìreach anns an athar, agus an rathad a bhitheas
am mèuran a' coimhead an uair a thuiteas e leagaidh tu cùrsa a'
bhàta.    Falbhaidh mise leat, oir cha mhisd' thu mo chuideachadh.    Ach bithidh an cùmhnant so agam ort mu 'm
falbh mi, gu 'n cuir thu air tìr mi 'n so 'n uair a thilleas tu."

Moch air an ath mhadainn chaidh iad air bòrd Gonachridhe.
Chuir Mac Righ Éirionn am mèuran 'am barr na saighde, leig
e 'n t-saighead as dìreach anns an athar, agus an rathad a bha
'm 'mèuran a' coimhead an uair a thuit e leag e cùrsa na luinge.
Sheòl iad air an aghaidh fad an là air a' chuan.    Aig cromadh
na gréine chunnaic iad fearann air thoiseach orra, agus rinn
iad dìreach air.    An uair a ràinig iad an cladach thubhairt a'
chéud Sheann duine ri Mac Righ Éirionn, "Am bheil do
shnàthad agad?"    Fhreagair e gu 'n robh.    "Gleidh gu cùramach i, oir is i céud dhearbhadh do dheuchainnean."    Thubhairt an dara Seann duine, "Am bheil do mhèuran agad?"
"Tha," arsa Mac Righ Éirionn.    "Gleidh gu cùramach e, oir
is e dara dearbhadh do dheuchainnean.    Theid thu nis air
tìr, agus cumaidh tu dìreach air d' aghaidh gus an ruig thu
caisteal mòr.    Ma choinnicheas mo bhràthair thu mu 'm bi
thu aig a' Chaisteal bitheadh deagh mhisneach agad, ach mur
coinnich is droch comhar e air do shoirbheachadh 'na dhéigh
sin.    Fanaidh sinne 'n so gus an till thu."

Léum Mac Righ Éirionn air tìr, agus dh' fhalbh e air a
thurus a dh' ionnsaidh a' Chaisteil.    Bha fhios aige gu 'n robh
an Caisteal an àit' éiginn 's an Eilean, ach cha robh e 'g a
fhaicinn.    Bha e' cumail a shùla gu géur roimhe féuch am
faiceadh e 'n duine 'tighinn.    Ach an àite Caisteil no duine 's
ann a chunnaic e badan do cheò druidheachd air thoiseach air.
Cha deachaidh e ro fhad' air aghaidh 'n uair a sgaoil am badan
ceò, agus a dh' fholuich e bhuaith' an dà chuid talamh agus
athar.    Thubhairt e 'n so ris féin gu 'n robh e deas, a chionn
nach b' urrainn e 'n Caisteal fhaicinn, agus nach b' urrainn
duin' anns a' Chaisteal esan fhaicinn tromh 'n cheò.    Anns an
eagal sin sheas e fàr an robh e.    'An ùine ghoirid thàinig oiteag

fhann ghaoith bharr na mara a sguab air falbh an ceò, agus an uair a chaidh an ceò seachad chunnaic e 'n Caisteal air thoiseach air. Chum e dìreach g' a ionnsaidh, ach cha robh duine ri fhaicinn roimhe. An uair a thàinig e fo dhubhar bhallachan a' Chaisteil thug e 'n aire do Sheann duine 'tighinn a mach air an dorus, agus a' gabhail 'n a choinneamh. Thubhairt an Seann duine, " A Mhic Righ Éirionn, ghabh thu 'n t-eagal, ach na caill do mhisneach. Tha mòran agad ri dhol troimhe fhathast, mu 'm faigh thu Deàrsadh-gréine. Ach thig a 's tigh, agus innsidh mise dhuit ni éiginn a bhitheas a chum d' fhéum."

Chaidh e 's tigh. "Nis," ars' an Seann duine, "so dhuit siosar, agus so bogha agus saighead. Anns a' mhadainn am màireach seasaidh tu air a' Chreig Mhòir a tha cùl a' Chaisteil, agus cuiridh tu 'n siosar' air barr do shaighde, agus leigidh tu as i dìreach anns an athar. An rathad a bhitheas an siosar a' coimhead an uair a thuiteas e sin an rathad a dh' fhéumas tusa d' aghaidh a chur. Is iad na trì Ealachan a chunnaic thu trì nigheannan Righ a' Churraichd Ruaidh a tha 'fuireachd fad' air falbh anns an Eilean so. Tha e 'g an gleidheadh fo gheasaibh gus an tig curaidh g' an iarraidh mar tha thusa. An sin togaidh e na geasan diù, agus bithidh iad 'n an trì òighean maiseach. Thàinig iomad curaidh romhads' air an son, ach bha na déuchainnean a leagadh orra cho cruaidh a 's nach do bhuanaich aon aca té de na h-igheannaibh. Ach o 'n fhuair thusa air d' aghaidh cho fada ri so cuidichidh mise leat 'an aon ni 'is urrainn mi 'dheanamh air do shon. Tha na trì ealachan a' snàmh an ceart uair so air Lochan Sèamh Gàraidh Mhòir Chraobh nan Ùbhlan Òir 's an Eilean Uaine 'n iomall an Domhain Toir. An uair a ruigeas tu 'n Lochan èulaidhidh tu orra le d' shaighead, cuiridh tu do shnàthad 'n a barr, agus cuimsichidh tu i air an té air am bheil do mhiann. Cho luath 's a bheanas an t-snàthad dhi itealaichidh an trì air falbh o 'n Loch, agus cha stad iad gus an ruig iad Caisteal Mòr Righ a' Churraichd Ruaidh, an athair."

Air an ath mhadainn chaidh e mach, agus ràinig e mullach na Creige Mòire 'bheir cùl a' Chaisteil. Chuir e 'n siosar air barr na saighde, agus leig e as dìreach anns an athar i, agus 'n uair a thuit i bha 'n siosar a' coimhead air a' mhuir fo 'n àite s an robh e 'n a sheasamh. An sin dh' fhalbh e 'n rathad a bha 'n siosar a' coimhead gus an d' ràinig e taobh na mara. Ach ni b' fhaide na sin cha b' urrainn e dol. Thubhairt e 'n so ris féin gu 'n tilleadh e, agus gu 'n tugadh e leis Gonach-ridh. Ach mu 'n d' fhalbh e thug e sùil agus chunnaic e a' Mhaighdean-mhara 'n oir na tuinne air thoiseach air.

"A Mhic Righ Eirionn," thubhairt i, "tha thu smaoint-eachadh air tilleadh agus Gonachridh a thabhairt leat do 'n Eilean Uaine, ach cha dean i 'n gnothuch dhuit. Oir cho luath 's a dh' fhalbhadh tu leatha dh' éireadh ceò drùidheachd bharr an Eilein, agus chuireadh e cho fad' air seachran sibh 'us nach ruigeadh sibh fearann gu bràth. Ach an là 'thug thu dhomh-sa mo chochull gheall mi 'bhi 'm bhan-charaid mhaith dhuit, agus cuideachadh leat 'an àm do chruaidh-chàis. Agus a nis ni mi fuasgladh ort as a' chàs anns am bheil thu. Thig agus suidh air an earball agamsa, agus cha chuir ceò druidheachd Eilein Mhòir Spiorad a cheò mis' air seachran gus an cuir mi thu air tìr gu sàbhailt' anns an Eilean Uaine 'n iomall an Domhain Toir. Ach ged chuireas mi 'n sin thu cha toir mi as thu. Theid an Seann duine leis an robh thu 'n raoir air bòrd Gonachridhe còmhla ri càch, agus ruigidh iad thu 'n àm d' fhéuma. Ach, a Mhic Righ Éirionn, seall nach caill thu do mhisneach gus an tig iad."

An sin shuidh e air earball na Maighdein-mhara. Chuir ise a h-aghaidh ris a chuan, agus shnàmh i air falbh le luathas mòr. Cha deachaidh iad ro fhad' air an aghaidh 'n uair a thug esan an aire do bhadan ceò ag éiridh bharr an Eilein. Bha 'n ceò 'tighinn 'n an déigh, agus a' buidhinn orra gu luath. An ùine ghoirid rug e orra, agus chòmhdaich e iad féin agus a' mhuir. Agus bha e cho dòmhail 'us nach faiceadh e bho h-earball ceann na Maighdein-mhara. An sin thubhairt i, "A Mhic Righ Éirionn, gu dé 'dheanadh tu féin agus do Ghonachridh a nis?" "Oh, gu dé ach gu 'n caillinn mo chùrsa, agus nach bitheadh fios agam ceana 'bhithinn a' dol," ars' esan. Dh' fhàs an ceò ro thiugh agus ro dhorcha 'nis, agus thubhairt a' Mhaighdean-mhara ris, "Ge b' e nì a chì no chluinneas tu féuch nach caraich thu do cheann a null no' nall, agus nach freagair thu facal a théid a ràdh riut gus am bruidhinn mise. Is coingeis leamsa falbh air uachdar na mara no fo 'n mhuir. Tha mi 'nis dol a chur mo chinn fodha, agus an sin cha chuir ceò Eilein a' Cheò as mo chùrsa mi."

Air dhi so a ràdh thug i a ceann fo 'n uisge, agus dh' fhalbh i le luathas mòr. Bha Mac Rìgh Éirionn 'g a fhaicinn féin 'n a ònar a nis, agus bhuail eagal gu 'm faodadh e tuiteam bharr earbaill na Maighdein-mhara e. Ach chuimhnich e air a comhairle, agus rinn e mar dh' iarr i air. Cha deachaidh iad ro fhad' air an aghaidh 'n uair a dh' fhairich e plub laimh ris. Thug e claon-shùil thar a ghualainn, agus bha leis gu 'm fac' e boirionnach anns an uisge. An sin chunnaic e làmh anns an uisge, agus chual e guth 'g ràdh, "A Mhic Rìgh Éirionn, thoir dhomh do làmh, oir tha mi 'g am bhàthadh." Dhì-chuimhnich e 's an àm a ghealladh, agus bha e dol a bhreith air laimh oirre 'n uair a chuir a' Mhaighdean-mhara a ceann an uachdar, agus a ghlaodh i ris, "A Mhic Rìgh Éirionn, thoir an an aire ort féin, agus cuimhnich cean' a tha thu 'dol. Tha thu féin 'an cunnart a 's mò gu mòr na tha 'n té sin. Is coingeis leatha muir no athar. Scall gu 'm bi thu air d' fhaicill nach tig i rathad eil' ort."

Air dhi so a ràdh thug i 'ceann fodha rìs, agus shiubhail i le luathas anabarrach gus an do ghlan an ceò air falbh. Thug i 'n sin a ceann an uachdar, agus dh' fhalbh i air aghaidh na mara gus an d' thàinig iad an scalladh fearainn. Cho luath 's a chunnaic Mac Rìgh Éirionn am fearann air thoiseach air dh' éirich inntinn cho mòr 'us gu 'n do chaill e cuimhn' air gach eagal agus àmhghar tromh 'n d' thàinig e. An uair a bha iad a' dlùthachadh ri tìr thàinig faoileann ag itealaich os a cheann, agus thubhairt i ris, "A Mhic Rìgh Éirionn, so dhuit sgrìobhadh : éirich agus beir air uam." Ach chuimhnich e 'ghealladh, agus cha do fhreagair e i. "A Mhic Rìgh Éirionn," ars' i rithist, "beir air an sgrìobhadh uam, agus innsidh e dhuit rud air nach 'eil fhios agad." Ach chuimhnich e 'n dara h-uair air a ghealladh, agus cha do fhreagair e i. An uair a bha iad fagus do thìr thug àilleachd an fhearainn air thoiseach orra, agus briadhad nan craobh fo 'm meas aire gu buileach o gach ni a dh' iarradh air agus a gheall e 'dheanamh. Anns an doille sin theirinn an fhaoileann an treas uair, agus thubhairt i, "A Mhic Righ Éirionn, beir air an sgrìobhadh so, oir is ann o d' mhuime 'tha e, 'g a d' chuireadh gu banais do bhràthar." Cho luath 'sa chual e ainm a bhràthar 'g a luaidh thug e éiridh air féin, agus shìn e 'làmh a bhreith air an sgrìobhadh. Dh' fhairich se e féin ag aomadh thairis, agus a' dol a thuiteam anns an uisge. Bha fhios aige na 'n tuiteadh e 's an uisge gu 'm bitheadh e caillte. Ach thug a' Mhaighdean-mhara 'n aire ciod a bha dol a thachairt, agus ghlaodh i ris a rìs, "A Mhic Righ Éirionn, nach cuimhnich thu do ghealladh?" Ach dh' aom esan cho fada thairis 'us gu 'm b' ann 's an uisge 'bhitheadh e mur bhi gu 'n robh e cho dlùth do thìr, agus gu 'n do thilg i le aon bhreab d' a h-earball air talamh tioram e.

"Nis," thubhairt i, "tha thu air tìr. Seall gu 'm bi thu dìleas, agus nach dìchuimhnich thu ni a thubhairt mise riut. Na caill do mhisneach, oir thig Gonachridh gu d' iarraidh. Théid thu air d' ais leatha gu Eilean Mòr Spiorad a' Cheò. 'Nuair a ruigeas tu 'n t-Eilean sin coinnichidh Righ a' Churraichd Ruaidh le thrì nigheannaibh thu air a' chladach, agus their e riut gu dé 'tha thu 'g iarraidh, no gu dé 'th' agad r' a thabhairt seachad. Their thu ris ma thig e féin agus a nigheannan air bòrd gu 'n leig thu fhaicinn doibh gu dé 'th' agad. Thig iad, agus sìnidh tu 'n t-snàthad do 'n Righ, agus innsidh an treas Seann duine dhuit gu dé 'ni thu 'n a dhéigh sin. Cuir do bhogha 's do shaighead 'an òrdugh, agus siubhail romhad gu Lochan Sèamh Gàraidh Mhòir nan Ùbhlan Òir, agus féuch gu 'm bi do chuimse math. Aon chomhairl' eile : Air muir no air tìr, 'an cruaidh-chàs no 'n éiginn air bith 's am bi thu seall nach dìchuimhnich thu do ghealladh 'am fad a's beò thu. Mo bheannachd leat. Cha-n eil féum tuillidh agad ormsa."

Dh' falbh e 'n sin a dh' ionnsaidh an Lochain. Mar bha e dol air aghaidh bha gach ni a' fàs ni 'bu bhriadha gus mu dheireadh an robh aillleachd nan craobh agus bòidhichead an fhearainn a' cur as aire 'n gnothuch a bha roimhe. Ach ghrad chuimhnich e comhairle na Maighdein-mhara 'bhi air 'fhaicill a' ruigsinn an Lochain. Sùil g' an tug e air thoiseach air chunnaic e 'n Lochan agus na trì Ealachan a' snàmh air 'uachdar. Ghrad leig e air a ghlùinibh e féin, agus dh' fhalbh e a' màgaran agus a' cumail gach craobh agus tolman a thachradh air eadar e agus iadsan gus an d' fhuair e 'an astar urchair saighde dhoibh. Chuir e 'n sin a shaighead 'an crois, tharrainn e 'n taifeid, agus le cuimse cho math 's a b' urrainn e 'ghabhail leig e air falbh i. Ruith an t-saighead troimh iteach dhroma Eala Bhàn a' Mhuineil Réidh, agus le sgriach ghointe léum i anns an athar, agus dh' itealaich i air falbh 's an dithis eile 'g a leantainn.

Chum e a shùil an taobh a ghabh iad gus an deachaidh iad cho fad' air falbh bhuaith 's gu 'n dɔ chaill e sealladh orra. Cha robh aige 'n sin ach falbh an taobh a ghabh iad, agus chum e air gus an d' ràinig e taobh na mara. N' a b' fhaide na sin cha b' urrainn e dol.

Bha e 'siubhal air ais agus air aghaidh, a' cumail a shùl anns gach oisinn, feuch am faiceadh e a' Mhaighdean-mhara, ach gus an do chuimhnich e gu 'n d' thubhairt i ris nach faiceadh e ise tuillidh. An sin thug e togail air a shùil ris a' mhuir, agus chunnaic e Gonachridh a' tighinn. Dh' éirich a mhisneach, ghabh e dìreach 'n a coinneamh, agus b' iad na céud fheadhainn a chunnaic e air bòrd oirre na trì Seann bhràithrean.

Cho luath 's a ràinig Gonachridh an cladach chaidh e air bòrd, agus dh' iarr e air an Sgioba 'cur mu 'n cuairt. Rinn iad sin. Shuidh e féin an sin aig an stiùir, agus leag e cùrsa na luinge cho dìreach 's a b' urrainn e 'n taobh a ghabh na h-ealachan. Chum e oirre gus am fac' e fearann fad' as a' tighinn 's an fhradharc', ach ma b' fhada bhuaith' e cha b' fhada 'ga ruigheachd.

An uair a bha iad dlùth do thìr thubhairt an treas Seann duine, "A Mhic Righ Éirionn, cho luath 's a ruigeas sinn an cladach chi sinn Righ a' Churraichd Ruaidh agus a thrì nigheannan a' feitheamh oirnn. Is e a' cheud ni a dh' fheòraicheas e dhìot 'gu dé 'tha thu 'g iarraidh no gu dé 'th' agad r' a thabhairt seachad?' Bheir thu 'n aire nach téid thu air tìr, ach their thu ris ma thig e féin agus a nigheannan air bòrd gu 'n leig thu fhaicinn doibh cuid de na nithibh a th' agad ri thabhairt seachad. Thig iad air bòrd, agus sìnidh tu

N

'n sin do 'n Rìgh an t-snàthad an toiseach, am mèuran a rìs, agus an Siosar mu dheireadh. An sin sìnidh esan iad aon an déigh aon do thé mu seach d' a nigheanaibh o 'n té a 's sine gus an té 's òige. Agus ma ghleidheas do roghainn-s' iad bitheadh misneach mhath agad."

Ràinig iad tìr, agus fhuair iad Rìgh a' Churraichd Ruaidh agus a thrì nigheannan a' feitheamh orra mar dh' innis an Seann duine. Thug Mac Rìgh Éirionn sùil orra, agus an uair a chunnaic e Nighean Òg Rìgh a' Churraichd Ruaidh thubhairt e, "Sin mo roghainn-sa, oir tha i cho briadha 'm shealladh ri Eala Bhàn a' Mhuineil Réidh."

An sin ghlaodh Rìgh a' Churraichd Ruaidh, "A Mhic Rìgh Éirionn, gu dé 'tha thu 'g iarraidh an so, no gu dé 'th' agad r' a thabhairt seachad?" Fhreagair Mac Rìgh Éirionn, "Tha mi 'g iarraidh agus bheir mi seachad. Ma thig thu féin agus do nigheannan air bòrd chi sibh cuid de na nithibh a th' agam ri thabhairt seachad."

Thànaig iad air bòrd. Shìn Mac Rìgh Éirionn a shnàthad do Rìgh a' Churraichd Ruaidh. Dh' amhairc an Rìgh oirre, agus shìn e i d' a Nighinn Mhòir. Cha do ghabh an Nighean Mhòr ach beag suim dhi, agus shìn i do 'n Nighinn Mheadhonaich i. Cha do ghabh an Nighean Mheadhonach tuillidh suim dhi na ghabh an té mhòr, agus shìn i do 'n Nighinn Òig i. Ghabh an té so tlachd mòr dhi, agus cha d' fhàg i crò no barr air nach do choimhead i. An uair a thàinig an t-àm dhi a sìneadh air a h-ais bha i mar gu 'm bitheadh i duilich dealachadh rithe. Thug Mac Rìgh Éirionn so fainear, agus thubhairt e rithe ma bha tlachd 's am bith aice do 'n t-snàthaid gu 'm faodadh i a gleidheadh. Shìn e 'n so am mèuran do 'n Rìgh, shìn an Rìgh e d' a Nighinn Mhòir, agus shìn na h-igheannan e d' a cheile gus an d' fhàgadh e aig an Nighinn Òig mar dh' fhàgadh an t-snàthad. An sin shìn e 'n Siosar do 'n Rìgh, agus dh' fhuirich e còmhla ris na rudan eile aig an Nighinn Òig.

"Nis," arsa Rìgh a' Churraichd Ruaidh, "a Mhic Rìgh Éirionn, ghabh thusa gaol air Eala Bhàn a' Mhuineil Réidh, agus thug thu bòid 'an Eirinn nach stadadh tu agus nach gabhadh tu tàmh gus am faiceadh tu boirionnach cho briadh'

ann ad shealladh ris an Eala. Chunnaic thu nis i, agus is i
sin Deàrsadh-gréine, mo Nighean Òg-sa, agus roghnaich ise thu
le d' shnàthaid, le d' mhèuran, agus le d' shiosar. Ach mu 'n
d' thàinig thusa thàinig iomad aon 'g a h-iarraidh nach do thill
agus nach d' fhuair i ; agus cha-n fhaigh thus' i gus an coisinn
thu i le déuchainnean a 's cruaidhe na so fathast. Thig air
tìr, agus falbh leamsa 'dh' ionnsaidh mo Chaisteil, agus ma
bhuidhneas tu i anns gach déuchainn a chuireas mis' ort
gheibh thu i."

Thionndaidh Mac Righ Éirionn r' a sgioba, agus thubhairt e
riù, "Cha-n 'eil fhios agamsa c' uin' a thilleas mi, ach bitheadh
Gonachridh agaibhsa deas a dh' fhalbh a là agus a dh' oidhche.
Cha till mise gun Deàrsadh-gréine maille rium."

Léum e 'n sin air tìr, agus an treas Seann duine còmhla ris.
Chum iad air an aghaidh gus an d' ràinig iad Caisteal Righ a'
Churraichd Ruaidh. Thug an Righ a 's tigh iad do sheòmar
briadha, tharrainn e 'mach bòrd air meadhon an ùrlair, agus fhuair
e a dhìsnean. "Nis," ars' e, "a' Mhic Righ Éirionn, theid thu
chluich còmhla riumsa, agus ma choisneas tu Deàrsadh gréine
ormsa bithidh do chéud déuchainn seachad, ach ma chailleas
tu caillidh tu do bheatha." Thòisich a' chluich, agus bhuidhinn Mac Righ Éirionn tri uairean an déigh a cheile air Righ a'
Churraichd Ruaidh. "Mata," arsa Righ a' Churraichd Ruaidh,
"choisinn thu i le cluich nan dìsne, ach cha-n fhaigh thu i le
sin fathast. Féumaidh tu déuchainn eile a sheasamh, agus mur
buidhinn thu tri uairean an déigh a cheile caillidh tu do bheatha
ris."

Tharrainn e 'n sin brat-sgàil eadar dà thaobh an t-seòmair,
agus chuir e a thriùir nigheannan air dara taobh a' bhrait agus dh'
fhuirich e féin le Mac Righ Éirionn air an taobh eile. "Nis,"
thubhairt e ri Mac Righ Éirionn, "stobaidh mo nigheannan an
t-snàthad tromh 'n bhrata tri uairean, agus ma bheireas tus' oirre
ach 'n uair a bhitheas i aig mo Nighinn Òig caillidh tu do
bheatha." Ach bha fhios aig Deàrsadh-gréine romh laimh air
an déuchainn, agus chagair i romh laimh 'an cluais Mhic Righ
Éirionn gu 'm b' e crò na snàthaid a chumadh ise ris. Chaidh
Righ a' Churraichd Ruaidh a 's tigh fo 'n bhrat, agus thug e am
mèuran do thé d' a nigheanaibh. Thill e 'n sin a mach, agus

thubhairt e ri Mac Righ Éirionn, "Beir air an t-snàthaid."
Thubhairt Mac Righ Éirionn, "Cha bheir mi oirre uaipe sin
fathast." Chaidh an Righ a 's tigh an dara h-uair, agus thug e
'n siosar do thé eile. Thàinig e 'n sin a mach, agus thubhairt e
ri Mac Righ Éirionn, "Beir air an t-snàthaid." Fhreagair Mac
Righ Éirionn a rìs, "Cha bheir mi oirre uaipe sin fathast."
Chaidh an Righ a 's tigh an treas uair, agus thug e 'n t-snàthad
d' a Nighinn Òig. Thàinig e mach, agus dh' iarr e air Mac
Righ Éirionn breith oirre. Chaidh Mac Righ Éirionn a null,
agus an uair a chunnaic e crò na snàthaid tromh 'n bhrat rug e
oirre.

"Rinn thu 'n gnothuch," arsa Righ a' Churraichd Ruaidh,
"agus gheibh thu i." Chaidh am pòsadh a dheanamh gun dàil,
agus an déigh dha 'bhi seachad thubhairt Righ a Churraichd
Ruaidh ri Mac Righ Éirionn, "Ma theannas tu ri teicheadh
air falbh as an Eilein bithidh do bheatha féin agus beatha do
mhnatha ris."

Thug Mac Righ Éirionn ùine mhath 's an Eilean, ach bha 'n
Sgioba daonnan a' gleidheadh Gonachridh deas airson falbh.
Air oidhch' àraidh an déigh do Righ a' Churraichd Ruaidh
tuiteam 'n a chadal thubhairt Deàrsadh-gréine r' a fear, "'S e
nis d' àm agus do chothrom, agus mur gabh thu iad cha-n
fhaigh thu iad gu bràth tuillidh." "Togaidh sinn oirnn, agus
falbhaidh sinn mata," ars' esan.

Dh' fhalbh iad, agus ràinig iad an cladach. Chaidh iad an
sin air bòrd Gonachridh. Ach cho luath 's a bhean cas Deàrsadh-gréine dhi ghlaodh Righ a' Churraichd Ruaidh 'n a leaba,
"Dh' fhalbh Gonachridh, agus theich Mac Righ Éirionn le m'
nighinn." Ach chaidh an Nighean Mhòr a' s tigh, agus thubhairt i ris, "Cha do theich; cha-n 'eil thu ach a' cluinntinn
fuaim na gaoithe 'dol tromh chraobhan a' ghàraidh." Cho
luath 's a chuir Gonachridh mar sgaoil ghlaodh e rithist, "Tha
Gonachridh air falbh, agus theich Mac Righ Éirionn le m'
Nighinn Òig. Ach bheir mis' air nach teid e fada gus am bi
sin daor da."

Léum e mach, agus dh' fhalbh e as an déigh. Dh' aithnich
Deàrsadh-gréine gu 'n robh e 'tighinn, agus thubhairt i r' a fear,
"Tha m' athair a' tighinn, agus mur bi thu cruaidh cuiridh e

fodha 'm bàta agus bàthaidh e sinn uile, a chionn cha-n 'eil a
bhàs air an t-saoghal ach 'an aon bhall-dóbhrain a th' air 'am
bonn-dubh[1] na coise."

Chunnaic iad e a' tighinn 'n an déigh air an t-snàmh, agus a'
cur na mara 'n a sradan teine air thoiseach air. Cha b' urrainn
Mac Righ Éirionn cuimse fhaotainn air bonn a choise cho fad
's a bha e 'n a dhéigh. Ach an uair a bha e tighinn a nìos ri
taobh a' bhàta léum Deàrsadh-gréine agus spìon i 'm bogha
agus an t-saighead a lamhan a fir. Chum i 'n sin an t-saighead
ri bonn coise a h-athar, agus an uair a bha e dol seachad oirre
chuir i anns a' bhall-dóbhrain i. Chuir esan car dh' e anns
a' mhuir, agus bha e marbh. Thionn Deàrsadh-gréine 'n sin
r' a fear, agus thubhairt i ris, " A Mhic Righ Éirionn, bi dileas
dhomh as a dhéigh so, oir mharbh mi m' athair air do shon."

Chum iad air an aghaidh gu Eilean Mòr Faileas nan Réul,
agus chuir iad air tìr an dara Seann Duine. Cho luath 's a
bhuail a chasan an cladach thionndaidh e agus thubhairt e, " A
Mhic Righ Éirionn, o 'n bha thu cho math 's do ghealladh
dhòmhsa fanaidh tu air aoidheachd còmhla riumsa 'nochd."
Dh' fhalbh Mac Righ Éirionn leis an t-Seann Duine, agus
ràinig iad a Chaisteal. B' e sin an Tigh Mòr àlainn nach fhac
e riamh a leithid. Bha pailteas do gach biadh agus deoch a b'
fhearr na chéile ri fhaotainn a 's tigh, agus bha faileas nan réul
ri fhaicinn ann a mach. Aig an t-suipeir thubhairt an Seann
Duine, " A Mhic Righ Éirionn, mur bhi mo bhràthair agus
buaidh a shiosair cha d' fhuair thu Deàrsadh-gréine."

Air an ath mhadainn dh' fhàg iad beannachd aig an t-Seann
Duine, agus dh' fhalbh iad le Gonachridh. Chum iad air an
aghaidh gus an d' ràinig iad Eilean Mòr nam Muca-mara.
Chuir iad a' chéud Sheann Duine air tir, agus cho luath 's a
bhuail a bhuinn an cladach thionndaidh e mu 'n cuairt, agus
thubhairt e, " A Mhic Righ Éirionn, fhuair thu leat Deàrsadh-
gréine, ach mur bhi mo dhara bràthair agus buaidh a mhéur-
ain cha d' fhuair thu i. Agus mur bhi mi féin agus mo
shnàthad cha d' amais thu riamh air an àite 's an robh i. Ach
so Eilean mo ghaoil agus Eilean mo ghràidh ! Cha d' fhuair mi

---

[1] Seang a' bhuinn, *i.e.*, the slender part of the sole.—J. M'D.

mo leòir o 'n dh' fhàg mi e." An sin shìn e a làmh, agus thug e
nuas a sgeilp creige slat mhòr iasgaich le driamlaich agus le
dubhan, agus le cliob air an dubhan. Thug e aon siabadh
mòr leatha mach air an loch, agus dh' iasgaich e muc-mhara,
agus dh' ith e i. Thug e 'n sin siabadh an déigh siabaidh, agus
mu 'n deachaidh Gonachridh a fradharc an Eilein dh' iasgaich agus dh' ith e seachd muca-mara !

Sheòl Mac Righ Éirionn air ais a dh' ionnsaidh a' cheart
chalaidh 'an Éirinn o 'n d' fhalbh e. An uair a bha e 'dol air
tìr thuirt Deàrsadh-gréine ris, " Tha thu 'nis a dol do thigh d'
athar fàr am bheil banais do bhràthar gu bhi air a gleidheadh
an nochd. Cho luath 's a chi a' ghalla mhial-choin thu tighinn
ruithidh i a' d' choinneamh, ach bheir thu 'n aire nach bean i do
mhìr a d' aodann no 'd' chraicionn, oir ma bheanas cha bhi
cuimhn' agad gu 'm fac thu mise riamh." "A Dheàrsadh-
gréine," thubhairt e, " cha-n 'eil nì air an t-saoghal a chuireas
tus' as mo chuimhne-sa." " Cuimhnich mata ciod a thubhairt
mi riut, agus soirbheachadh math dhuit."

Dh' fhalbh e, agus an uair a bha e 'dlùthachadh ri Caisteal
athar thàinig a' ghalla 'n a choinneamh, agus mu 'n d' fhuair e
a làmh a thogail léum i, agus bhuail i e le 'gnos anns a' bhéul.
Air ball dhìchuimhnich e gu 'm fac e Deàrsadh-gréine riamh.

Bhuail e 's tigh do 'n chuideachd, agus rinn athair othail
mhòr ris, agus nochd a mhuime tuillidh caoimhneis d 'a na
rinn i riamh roimhe.

Thubhairt Déarsadh-gréine ri Sgioba Gonachridh, " Dh'
fhalbh am fear ud, phòg a' ghalla mhial-choin e, agus dhìchuimhnich e gu 'm fac e mise riamh. Cha till e 'n so gus an
téid mis' as a dheigh, agus an toir mi air ais e. Ach fanaidh
sibhse air bòrd Gonachridh gus an tig mi."

Dh' fhalbh i 'n sin air tìr, agus ràinig i tigh Seann ghobhainn
a bh' aig an Righ. Dh' iarr i cead fuireachd 's an tigh, ach
dhiùlt e sin d'i an toiseach, a chionn nach robh àite freagar-
rach aige d' a leithid do bhean-uasail. Thubhairt i gu 'n
cuireadh i féin an tigh 'an uidheam na 'n leigeadh esan fuireachd
dh' i. Dh' iarr e oirre dol a 's tigh, agus thubhairt e na 'm
faigheadh i cead a mhnatha nach bitheadh esan 'n a h-aghaidh.
Chaidh i 's tigh, agus an uair a chunnaic bean a' ghobhainn

àilleachd a' bhoirionnaich thuirt i gu 'm b' e a beatha fuireachd na 'n deanadh i i féin toilichte 'n a leithid do dh' àite.

Chuir i tigh a' ghobhainn 'an uidheam anabarrach briadha le fùirneis agus leis gach ni a bha féumail ann an tigh.

Bha tobar mòr laimh ris an lùchairt, agus b' ann as a bha 'n t-uisg' air a tharrainn airson féum an Righ. Bha Deàrsadh-gréine gach feasgar a' gabhail sràid rathad an tobair 'an dòchas gu 'm faiceadh i a fear, ach cha d' fhuair i sealladh dh' e.

Air là àraid dh' iarr i air a' ghobhainn coileach òir agus cearc òir a dheanamh dhise. Thubhairt an gobhainn nach robh de dh' òr aigesan na dheanadh coileach agus cearc. Thubhairt i ris gu 'n tugadh i féin da na dh' fhoghnadh. Fhuair an gobhainn an t-òr, agus thòisich e air a' choileach, ach dh' fhairslich air a dheanamh. An sin dh' iarr i 'an t-òrd air, agus 'an ùine ghoirid bha 'n coileach aice deas, agus an sin rinn i a' chearc. Lìomh an gobhainn iad dhi, agus an deigh sin thug i leatha iad a 's tigh.

An ath oidhche chaidh i a dh' ionnsaidh an tobair. An déigh dhi a ruigsinn thàinig Àrd-bhuidealair an Righ a dh' iarraidh uisg' a ghlanadh casan an Righ. An uair a chróm e os ceann an tobair chunnaic e faileas Dheàrsadh-gréine 's an uisge. Air ball ghabh e gaol oirre, agus cha deanadh ni air bith an gnothuch ach gu 'm faigheadh e i r' a pòsadh. Dh' fheòraich i dh' e cò e? Fhreagair e gu 'm b' esan Àrd-bhuidealair an Righ. Thubhairt i ris gu 'm pòsadh i e air chùmhnantan. "Gu dé na cùmhnantan a dh' iarradh tu nach fhaigheadh tu?" thubhairt esan. "Mata, 's iad na cùmhnantan a bhitheas agam ort gu 'm faigh mi romh laimh céud bonn òir agus searrag de dh' fhìon an Righ, agus gu 'm fair thu taobh mo leapa gu madainn. Ma ni thu sin pòsaidh mi thu 'm màireach." Gheall e dhi gach ni a dh' iarr i air.

Thàinig e 'n oidhche sin a dh' fhaireadh, agus thug e dhi céud bonn òir agus searrag fhìona. Thubhairt i ris gu 'n robh e 'n a chleachdainn aicese greis cluiche 'bhi aice mu 'n rachadh i 'laidhe. Fhuair i 'n sin an coileach agus a' chearc, agus chuir i air a' bhòrd iad. Léum an coileach agus thug e pioc as a' chirc. "Oh," thubhairt a' chearc, "cha b' e

do chomain, agus gu d' chùm mi crò na snàthaid riut." Thug
an coileach pioc eil' as a' chirc. "Oh," thubhairt a' chearc,
"cha b' e do chomain, 'us gu d' chuir mi air d' earalas thu
romh 'n ghalla mhial-choin." Chòrd an sealladh ris a' bhuidealair gu mòr, oir cha-n fhac e riamh roimhe a leithid.

An déigh dhi dol a laidhe thubhairt i ris a' bhuidealair deoch
de 'n fhìon a thabhairt di. Chaidh e null a dh' ionnsaidh bùird
a bh' aig taobh eile 'n t-seòmair, agus rug e air an t-searraig.
Thug e ionnsaidh air a togail, ach cha tigeadh i leis. Lean a
làmh ris an t-searraig, an t-searrag ris a' bhòrd agus am bòrd
ris an ùrlar, 'us anns an t-suidheachadh sin bha e fad na h-
oidhche. Air an ath mhadainn thubhairt am boirionnach
ris, "Gu dé 'bha thu 'deanamh an sin fad na h-oidhche? An
ann mar sin a tha thu a' faireadh taobh mo leapa-sa? Bhrist
thu na cùmhnantan, agus chaill thu 'n t-òr agus mise."
"Oh," thubhairt am buidealair, "bha 'n oidhche cho reòta 'us
gu d' lean mo làmh ris an t-searraig, an t-searrag ris a' bhòrd
agus am bòrd ris an ùrlar, 'us as a so cha-n fhaighinn. Tha 'n
t-àm dhomh a bhi aig an tigh, oir ma dh' éireas an Righ mu 'n
ruig mi caillidh mi m' àite."

Ghlaodh am boirionnach air a ghobhainn agus thàinig e.
Rug e air a' bhuidealair agus thug e slaodadh fuathasach air,
ach cha tigeadh e leis. Fhuair bean a ghobhainn uisge teth,
agus dhòirt i mu chasan a' bhùird e, agus dh' fhuasgail iad o 'n
ùrlar. Dhòirt i 'n sin an t-uisg' air màs na searraige, agus
thàinig an t-searrag o 'n bhòrd, ach ged sgald i lamhan a
bhuidealair, cha tigeadh iad o 'n t-searraig. "Oh," ghlaodh
am buidealair, "tha 'n t-àm a suas, agus féumaidh mi falbh.
Dé ni mi?" "Oh, falbh mar th' agad," thubhairt am boirionnach. "Oh, ma chì 'n Righ an t-searrag caillidh mi m' àite
ris." "Féumaidh tu, mata, tighinn do 'n cheàrdaich." Dh'
fhalbh e leatha. Thug i air a' ghobhainn lamhan a' bhuidealair a chumail 's an teine, agus chaidh i féin a shéideadh a'
bhuilg. Cha b' fhada gus an do ghlaodh am buidealair a
leigeil as, a chionn nach b' urrainn e 'n cràdh a sheasadh ni
'b 'fhaide. An uair a bha 'n ùine fagus do bhi suas thubhairt
i, "Feuchaidh mi aon dòigh eil' ort fhathast." Rug i 'n sin air
màs na searraige, dhòirt i 'ni fion m' a lamhan, agus thàinig

iad o 'n t-searraig. "Mata, bho 'n fhuair mis' as, cha till mi tuillidh," ars' am buidealair, agus dh' fhalbh e.

Air an ath fheasgar choinnich i Àrd-chòcair' an Righ aig an tobar, agus gheall i esan a phòsadh na 'm faigheadh i céud bonn òir agus poit de bhrot an Righ, agus na 'm faireadh e taobh a leapa gu madainn. Dh' aontaich e ri so a dheanamh, agus thachair gach ni dhasan mar thachair do 'n bhuidealair ach gu d' lean a làmh ri brod na poite, am brod ris a phoit, agus a' phoit ris an ùrlar.

Air an treas feasgar choinnich i Àrd-ghille-carbaid an Righ, agus dh' aontaich i esan a phòsadh na 'n tugadh e dhi céud bonn òir, agus gu 'm faireadh e taobh a leapa gu madainn.

Thàinig e gu tigh a' ghobhainn 's an oidhche. Aig àm dol a laidhe chuir am boirionnach an coileach agus a' chearc air a' bhòrd. "Oh, nach bòidheach iad?" ars' esan. "Am bruidhinn iad?" "Bruidhnidh," ars' ise. An sin léum a' chearc 'us thug i pioc as a' choileach. "Oh," ars' an coileach, "thug thu àit' an t-seann ghobhainn fo 'n Righ do ghobhainn eile." "Am bheil sin ceart," arsa Deàrsadh-gréine ris a ghille-charbaid. "Tha," ars' esan. "Mata, bheir thu air ais dha e, mu 'm pòs mise thu." Cha d' thubhairt e dad ri so. An sin léum an coileach, agus phioc e 'chearc. "Oh, cha b' e do chomain, 'us gu d' chum mi crò na snàthaid riut," ars' a' chearc.

An déigh do 'n bhoirionnach dol a laidhe thubhairt i gu d' dhìchuimhnich i' n dorus a dhùnadh. "Druididh mis' e," thubhairt an gille-carbaid. Dh' éirich e, agus dhruid e 'n dorus, ach lean a làmh ris a' chrann, an crann ris an dorus, agus an dorus ris na lùdiain, agus as a sin cha d' fhuair e fad na h-oidhche. Air an ath mhadainn thuirt i ris mar thuirt i ri càch, agus fhreagair esan mar fhreagair càch.

Thàinig an gobhainn agus a bhean, agus dh' fheuch iad a tharrainn o 'n dorus, ach cha b' urrainn iad. Dh' fheuch iad an sin an dorus a tharrainn bharr nan lùdlan, ach dh' fhairslich sin orra. An uair a bha 'n ùine fagus agus do bhi mach, agus a fhuair e pailt uibhir cràidh ri càch, rub am boirionnach ìocshlaint r' a lamhan, agus leig i as e.

Air an ath oidhche bha a fear a' dol a phòsadh bean-uasal

àrd-inbheach.   Fhuair gach duine mu 'n Chaisteal cuireadh chum na bainnse.   An uair a bha iad uile cruinn bha ni-éiginn d' an dìth, agus b' e sin cuid-èiginn a bheireadh àbhachd dhoibh le cleasaibh.   Thubhairt am buidealair gu 'n robh boirionnach 'an tigh an t-Seann ghobhainn a dheanamh na cleasan a b' iongantaiche 'chunnaic esan riamh.   "Oh tha, oir chunnaic mis' i," ars' an t-Àrd-chòcaire.   "Oh, chunnaic agus mise," ars' an t-Àrd-ghille-carbaid.   "Tha coileach agus cearc aice, agus bruidhnidh iad.   Dh' innis iad dhomhsa gach ni a rinn mi riamh."   "Faigheadh an so i," ars' an Righ.

Thàinig Deàrsadh-gréine, ach cha d' aithnich a fear gu 'm fac e riamh i.   Chuir i 'n coileach agus a' chearc air a' bhòrd. Léum an coileach, agus phioc e a' chearc.   "Oh, cha b' e do chomain e, 'us gu d' chum mi crò na snàthaid riut," ars' a' chearc.   Léum a' chearc an sin, agus phioc i 'n coileach. "Oh, cha b' e do chomain, 'us gu d' bhuidhinn mi tri uairean thu le m' shnathaid, le m' mhèuran, agus le m' shiosar," ars' an coileach.   Léum an coileach a rìs, agus thug e pioc as a' chirc. "Oh, cha b' e do chomain, 'us gu d' mharbh mi m' athair air do shon," ars' a' chearc.   Thòisich Mac an Righ a nis air a' chluasan a bhiorachadh.   Léum an coileach agus phioc e a' chearc an treas uair.   "Na dean, oir chuir mi air d' earalas romh phòig na galla mhial-choin thu," ars' a' chearc.

"A Dheàrsadh-gréine! mo ghaol de mhnathan an t-saoghail!" arsa Mac Righ Éirionn, 'us e léum fàr an robh i, a' cur a làmh an m' a muineal, agus 'g a pògadh.   Dh' innis e' n sin do 'n chuideachd gu 'm b' i Deàrsadh-gréin' a bhean, agus Nighean Righ a' Churraichd Ruaidh.   Fhuair bean-na-bainnse cead a siubhail, agus chum iad a suas a' chuilm fad là 'us bliadhna; agus mur d' fhàg iad an Caisteal o sin tha iad ann fhathast.

# VIII.

## THE SON OF THE STRONG MAN OF THE WOOD,



WHO WAS TWENTY-ONE YEARS ON HIS MOTHER'S
BREAST.

THERE was before now a big man whom people called
the Strong Man of the Wood.  This man's employment
was always hunting deer and drawing home fuel for
fire.  On a certain day he went away to cut a large oak
tree which he had seen the day before in the wood.
When the tree was bending over, it fell on him, and
bruised him dreadfully ; but the man was strong, and
so succeeded in dragging himself out from under it.
When he rose up on his feet, he took hold of the tree
by its trunk and dragged it between root and top home
with him.  As soon as he threw it off his shoulder at
the door he fell.

His wife came out, and when she saw how he was, she
helped him in and placed him sitting on the bed-side.
He then drew a great sigh, and said that he got his
death-hurt.  His fist was closed, and when he opened
it, there was an acorn in his hand.  He looked at it,
and then handed it to his wife.  He said to her, " I
am going to die, but thou shalt plant this acorn in the
midden-stead before the door.  Thou art going to have
a son, and on the night when he comes into the world
the seedling of the acorn shall be coming in sight
through the ground.  Thou shalt nourish him on thy
knee, with the sap of thy breast and side, until he become
so strong that he can take the tree, which shall grow

from the acorn, out of its base and roots." After he had said this to his wife he lay down and rose no more.

When the time came, the woman had a son, and as soon as he was born she told the midwife to go out and look if there was a seedling from the acorn. The seedling of the acorn was after breaking well out of the ground. She took her son, and nourished him for seven years on her knee. Then she took him out to the tree, and said to him that he was to try whether he could take yon tree from its root. He attacked the tree, and gave it a terrible shaking and pulling, but it was so firmly rooted in the earth that he did not move it.

When his mother saw that it beat him, she carried him with her into the house, and gave him seven years more of the breast. Then she took him out to the tree, and told him that he was to try whether he or the tree was stronger that day (to-day). He took hold of the trunk of the tree and pulled it dreadfully, but it had taken hold so strongly in the earth that he did not manage it.

When his mother saw that it beat him the second time, she carried him in, and gave him other seven years of the breast. Then she took him out to the tree, and asked him to try which of them was stronger—himself or the tree. He gave terrible bounds over where it was, took hold of it with his two hands, shook it and made it shake, and with three or four pulls had it out of its foundation and roots. He then began at its top, broke and smashed it, until he made firewood of it, and left it in a heap at the door.

His mother said, " Thou art long enough sucking the sap of my breast and side, and art thoroughly able to earn a livelihood for thyself in future. Come in, and I will bake for thee a bannock, thou shalt get it with my blessing, and then thou shalt go away to win a fortune for thyself."

He got the bannock, and departed. He travelled onwards to see whether he should happen to come on a place where he might get employment. At last he arrived at a fine large steading with more corn-stacks about it than he ever saw together. He thought that he might get work in that place, and took his way straight to the house.

He knocked at the door, and wanted to see the master. The Master came, and asked of him what he wanted? The Big Lad answered that he wanted work. "Thy appearance will do," said the Master. "I have enough of work, and I do not know why thou shouldst not get it. Canst thou thrash?" "Yes," replied the Lad. "Thou art tired," said the Master. "Make thyself acquainted over the town to-night, and to-morrow early in the morning thou shalt begin thrashing." "Where shall I begin?" "In the barn, for there is as much corn there as will keep two men thrashing for six weeks, let them work ever so well. When that is done there is behind the barn a large yard full of corn-stacks, and every straw of them is to be thrashed."

The barn and the stack-yard were built on a *brae* above the house of the Landlord. When the Lad got his food he went up to the barn to see those who were thrashing there. He went in, and after having looked at them for a while, he took hold of the flail which one of them had, and said, " The flails you have are worthless. When I begin to-morrow you shall see the flail which I will have."

He then went away to the wood to cut a flail for himself, and when it was ready its handle resembled the mast of a ship.

At that time the rule was that the men-servants must work from star (setting) to star (rising). The Big Lad knew this ; he rose therefore early in the morning, and commenced thrashing before the (morning) star had left the sky. He began thrashing the mow which was in the barn, laid at it in one end, and as he was advancing he was sending the roof out of the building. He kept on at that rate until there was not a straw unthrashed on the floor before breakfast time arrived.

After he had got his breakfast he turned out again. He took his way to the stack-yard, carried with him a stack under each arm and one between his two hands, placed them in the barn, and thrashed them. He kept working away in that manner until there was not a stack in the yard unthrashed before dinner time had come. All the town was then white with straw, and the walls of the barn nearly full of grain.

He went then where the Landlord was. The Landlord met him on the way, wondering greatly what made the town full of straw. But he uttered not a syllable to the Big Lad. Then the Lad asked what would he go to do. " Thou shalt go thrash in the barn," said the Landlord. The Big Lad replied, " I have no thrashing which I can do." " What dost thou say ! There is as much thrashing in the barn as will keep two men at work for six weeks, let them work ever so well." " No. There is not a straw in the town—in barn or stack-yard—that is not already thrashed." The Landlord knew not what to say to this, but he told the Lad to go in and get his dinner, while he himself went to the barn to see whether the Lad told him the truth or not.

He reached the barn, and when he saw the appearance which everything before him had, the roof sent out of the barn, the straw scattered through the town, and every stack in the yard thrashed, he was seized with great fear, and what caused him the greatest terror was the flail which the Big Lad had.

He returned home trembling with fear, and took a

back road rather than meet the Big Lad when he came out from his meal. But the Big Lad noticed him, and took his way straight to meet him. He asked of him what would he go to do? The Landlord knew not very well what answer he should give, but what he said was, " Since thou hast worked so well before dinner time, thou hadst better take a rest for this evening." Then the Big Lad said, " Thou hast seen my work now, and thou knowest what I can do. I must get more food for my dinner than I am getting." " How much must thou get ? " " A quarter of a chalder of meal in brose one day, and a quarter of a chalder of meal in bannocks with the carcass of a two-year-old stot another day." " Thou shalt get that," said the Landlord, trembling with fear.

The Landlord went in, and told the people of the house what food they had to make ready for the Big Lad every day in future.

The Landlord and the wise men who were about him thought of the matter, and saw that the Big Lad would ruin the town in food unless they could find out a method of destroying him, or of sending him away. There was a truly old man in the town whom people called Big Angus of the Rocks (Echo), and one of the men said, "If Big Angus does not know what we should do with him, there is no other man in the place who can tell us."

The Landlord sent for Big Angus. Angus came, and the Landlord told him every particular about the big giant who came on them—how he thrashed the corn, and the sort of flail with which he worked. " Alas ! " said Angus, " did he come at last ! I heard my grand-father talking of him when I was a little boy. He was as old as I am at this day while he was telling how it was said that this place would be ruined yet by a big giant, and I have no doubt at all but that it is he who has come here." "Canst thou think of any method by which he can be destroyed?" "The only method I can imagine is this:—That thou shalt tell him to open a big well in the middle of the field over yonder, and go so deep that the water will meet him. It is a deep sandy bottom, and he must go a great depth before he can reach the spring. But when he will reach it, have every man who can handle a shovel about thee, and when he shall happen to stoop at the bottom of the hole, let every man be equal to two men driving the stuff in on the top of him. But if you see him stand up, let every man of you run away; for if he will get his head raised he will be out in spite of you and kill you." The Landlord consented to do this.

He sent for the Big Lad that same night. The Lad came, and the Landlord told him that the water was getting exceedingly scarce, and that he therefore wanted to open a well in the field over yonder. "Right enough," said the Lad. "Thou shalt begin it as thy first morning work to-morrow," said the Landlord.

When the daylight came the Big Lad began to open the well. The men also were early on the ground. They went away with the Landlord to watch the Big Lad, to see how he was getting on with the hole. When they got a sight of him, only the top of his head was above the ground, and a great heap of stuff was thrown out by him. They got afraid that they would be too late, but they were in good time at the hole. The Landlord stood at the mouth of the hole, and when the Lad stooped cried to the men to begin. They began to put the stuff in upon him as nimbly as they could ply a shovel. But they were not long at that work when the Big Lad stood up in the hole, shook his hand, and shouted, "Whish!" The Landlord cried to his men to run away, and every man of them went off as fast as his feet could carry him.

But the Big Lad finished the hole before he had stopped. He then went up to the Landlord's house. When he was approaching the house he was wondering much that no man was to be seen about the town. He reached the door, and put his hand on the bar, but the door was so strongly shut on the inside that it would not open for him. He then laid his palm against the bar, and pushed it stronger than he wished. The bar broke, and the door opened. He went in, and found the Landlord crouching under the table and trembling.

Then the Landlord came out on the floor, and asked of the Big Lad if he had got the hole finished? The Lad said that he had. "But why," said he, "didst thou not send a man to keep away the rooks? They nearly put out my eyes, scratching the sand for worms. But what shall I go to do now?" "Oh, go and get thy dinner," said the Landlord. The Big Lad went as he was told.

When the Landlord got out of his way he sent for the old man again, and said to him, "Yon plan will do no good. He made the hole more than thirty feet in depth, I had every man about the place round the hole, I watched the opportunity until he was stooping at the bottom, I called to the men to begin, every man began equal to two men pouring (spouting) stuff in on the top of him, but he stood up in the hole and shouted ' Whish ! ' Then we fled.

"In a short time he came home after us. He went to the door, and though it was shut and barred, he sent it in before him with one push of his hand. He came in then, and forsooth said to me, why did I not send a man to keep away the rooks, because they had nearly put out his eyes scratching the sand in on the top of him while he was cleaning the bottom of the hole." "Oh, then," said Big Angus, "we will try another plan with him." "What plan is that?" "Send him to plough the Crooked Ridge of the Field of the Dark Lake. Out of that never came man or beast that was ploughing there to the going down of the sun." "We will try that same plan with him," said the Landlord.

He sent for the Big Lad, and said to him that he was to go next morning to plough in the Crooked Ridge of the Field of the Dark Lake. "Very right," said the Lad. "I will do that."

Early in the morning he made ready for the ploughing. He carried the plough with him on his shoulder, he had the two horses by the reins after him, and reached the Field of the Dark Lake. He thrust the plough in the end of the Crooked Ridge, and yoked the horses. There was a large tree in the middle of the Ridge, and he said to himself, "I will open the ground straight on the tree" (or in a line with the tree). Then he began to plough.

He was getting on well during the day, but at the going down of the sun he heard a dreadful plunge in the Lake. He gave a look, and saw a big black uncouth object (*Ùsp*) moving in the water, but paid no attention to it, and kept ploughing away as he was doing before. As soon as the sun went out of sight the beast came to land, and went up the shore of the Lake to the farthest away end of the Crooked Ridge. He then put about, and walked towards the team of horses in the very furrow in which the Big Lad was ploughing with them. The Big Lad kept going forward with his horses, and they met the beast near the tree that was in the middle of the Ridge. The Big Lad cried to the beast that he was to keep back, otherwise he would see what would happen to him. But the beast gave no heed to him, but opened his mouth and swallowed one of the horses alive and whole. "That will do," said the Big Lad. "I will make thee put him out as quickly as thou didst swallow him." He then let go the plough, and closed with the beast. They had terrible bouts of wrestling, but the Big Lad was above the beast at last. "Put out the horse now," said the Lad. But the beast did not heed him. "I will make thee put him out," said he again. He then took hold of the beast by the tail, dragged him to the tree, pulled the tree out of its root, and belaboured him with it until he had only as much of the top as he held in his hand. Then he said, "Wilt thou put out the horse now?" The beast did not heed him yet. "Well," said the Lad, "I will make thee do the work of the one thou hast eaten, at any rate."

The other horse had broken the traces and ran home. When he reached the house, and the Landlord saw the scared appearance he had, he said, "Oh, there is no doubt that the Big Lad and the other horse are dead now! The Water-horse of the Dark Lake has put an end to him at last!"

But the Big Lad was about his own business. He tied the beast in the plough and began ploughing with it, and before he stopped there was not a furrow in the Crooked Ridge that he did not turn over. When he was done he went home, holding the Big Horse by the head.

He reached the Landlord's door, and cried to him to come out. But no man answered, for everybody in the town fled, and went into hiding as soon as they saw him and the Horse coming. He then gave deafening blows to the door, and at last the Landlord came out, trembling with fear.

The Big Lad asked him what would he do to-morrow? "Oh, thou shalt plough," said the Landlord, with a tremulous voice. "I have no ploughing I can do." "What dost thou say? There is as much land in the Crooked Ridge as would keep a pair of horses ploughing for six weeks." "There is not. I ploughed every furrow before I stopped." "And didst thou notice anything which troubled thee while thou wert at work?" "I noticed nothing but a nasty thing of an ugly beast that came out of the Lake, and ate one of my horses. I tried to make him put the horse out, but he would not heed me. I then put him in the plough, and ploughed every furrow of the Crooked Ridge with him, but he did not put the horse out yet." "And where is he?" "He is here at the door." "Oh, let him go! let him go! let him away!" "I will not until I get the horse from him."

He then turned to the beast, and laid him on his back. He drew his own big knife, split up the beast's belly with it, and took out the horse alive and whole. Then he said to the Landlord, "I do not know what to do with him unless I put him in the hole in the middle of the field, and if there was no water in it before there will be then." He dragged the beast over to the field, threw him head foremost in the hole, put the stuff in on the top of him, and left him there.

The Landlord sent again for Big Angus of the Rocks. Angus came, and said to the Landlord, "What news hast thou now?" "I have only poor news. Yon attempt did no good. I sent him to plough the Crooked Ridge; while he was ploughing, a fearful beast came out of the Lake, and ate one of the horses. He seized the beast, tied him to the plough, and before he stopped ploughed with him every furrow of the Ridge. He then took him home, holding him by the end of a halter, he threw him down at the door, and took the horse alive and whole out of his belly. Then he drew him by the tail after him, and threw him head foremost in the hole. And now I do not think that we need strive with him any longer. We may run away, and leave the place to himself." "We shall give him another trial yet." "What trial is that?" "Say to him that the meal has failed on thee, and that thou shalt not have a morsel of food for him until he himself returns from the Mill. Thou shalt send him away with a sled of corn to the Mill of Leckan (*Muileann Leacain*). Thou shalt cause him to make haste, in order that he may work in the Mill all night, and I warrant thee that the Big Brownie (*Ùruisg*) of the Mill of Leckan will not let him home more than any other man. But if he will, and you see the Lad coming, all of you between small and great, young and old, may run away, for he cannot be destroyed, and he will ruin the place at any rate."

The Landlord sent for the Big Lad, and said to him that the meal had failed, and that he would not have a morsel of food for him until he came with meal from the Mill. "Take with thee any one of the horses thou pleasest and the Big Sled, and fill it with sacks of corn, and thou shalt come home as soon as thou canst. Thou must work all night in the Mill in order that thou mayst be back early in the morning. "Very right," said the Big Lad; "I will do that."

He went away with the grain without any delay, and reached the Mill in the dusk. The Miller had ceased grinding, and the Mill was shut. He loosened the horse out of the sled, and let him go to pasture. He went then to the Miller's house, and cried to him at the door to get up, because he had come with a sled of grain, and must get it ground that night. "It matters not who thou art, or whence thou hast come, but there is not a man on the face of the earth for whom I would open the Mill any more this night." "Oh, thou must get up. I am in a hurry, and the grain must be ground to-night." "Hurry or no hurry, I never saw a man for whom I would go to the Mill to-night." "If thou do not go, give me the key, and I will go myself." "Well, if thou enter it, thou shalt not come out of it alive." "I have no fear at all; give me the key."

The Miller gave him the key, and he went away to the Mill. He carried the grain in, made a great fire of seeds and peats, placed a layer of corn on the kiln, hardened the corn, and put it in the hopper. He then set the Mill going, ground as much of the oats as he dried, riddled the meal, and at last began to knead bannocks, for he was very hungry. When they were kneaded he put them on the kiln to bake.

While he was baking and turning them, he noticed an uncouth object (*Ùsp*) coming in sight in a corner of the kiln. He called on the *Ùsp* to keep back, but he heeded him not. He stretched out his paw, and took with him one of the bannocks. "Do not that again," said the Big Lad. But the *Ùsp* did not heed him. In a short time he again stretched out his paw, and took with him another bannock. "Do that once more, and I will make the bannocks dear to thee," said the Big Lad. The fellow in the corner paid little attention to the threat, and took with him the third bannock. "Well," said the Big Lad, "if thou give no heed of thine own free will thou shalt give heed against thy will. I will make thee put back what thou hast taken with thee."

Then he gave a great heavy leap, ending in a fall, and was above the Brownie (?) (*Ùruisg*). They went in each other's grips, and wrestled dreadfully. With a turn or two they threw down the kiln, they shattered the Mill, and people far and near heard the terrible deafening noise which was in the Mill. The Miller heard it in his bed, and it put him in such fear that he wrapped the bed-clothes about him, and crept down at the foot of the bed. His wife, shrieking, leapt over on the floor, and went on all-fours in under the bed. At last the Big Lad subdued the Brownie (?). The Brownie asked to let him go, but the Big Lad said he would not let him go in that way. "Thou shalt not get away until thou repair the Mill and put up the kiln with the bannocks on it as thou didst find them." Then he gave him further terrible bruisings. The Brownie cried, "Let me go, and I will do everything that thou biddest me." " I will not let thee go, but thou must do it while I have a hold of thee."

Then the Brownie began to repair the Mill, and in a short enough time he put everything in its own place as it formerly was. "Let me go now, for everything is as I found it," said the Brownie. The Big Lad gave a look, and saw that the three bannocks were not on the kiln, and he said that everything was not as it was. "Where are the bannocks thou didst take with thee?" He now gave the Brownie further dreadful blows and bruisings. The Brownie cried, "Let me go, and thou shalt find the bannocks in the fireplace." " I will not let thee go, but go thou and find them for me." The Brownie went, the Big Lad having a hold of him, and found the bannocks. " Put them now on the kiln where thou didst find them," said the Big Lad. The Brownie did that, and the Big Lad gave him the next bruisings. The Brownie cried to let him go, and that he would leave the Mill and never trouble it after that night. " Well, since thou hast promised that, I will let thee go," said the Big Lad, and he gave him a shove out through the door. The Brownie gave three horrible screams, and drew away. The Miller heard the screams, and his wife uttered a piercing cry in under the bed.

When the Brownie went away the Big Lad began to eat the bannocks, and when he ate enough of them he dried and ground the remainder of the grain. He then riddled the meal, put it in the sacks, and put the sacks on the sled. He had now everything ready; and therefore he locked the door of the Mill, and went home with the key.

He reached the Miller's house, and shouted at the door, but no person answered him. He shouted again, and heard the Miller answering with a faint voice within. The Big Lad asked him to open the door, because he had come home with the key. "O!" said the Miller, "be off! be off! and take with thee the key along with the other things!" "It is I, let me in," said the Big Lad. But the Miller did not answer him at all, therefore he pushed the door before him, and went in. "Here," said he, "is the key for thee, for I have ground the grain, and I am going home." When the Miller heard that the grain was ground he took his head out of the clothes, and looked at the man. "Oh, how art thou alive after being in the Mill all night!" "Pooh! thou mayest go to the Mill, and stay in it all night now! I have made the thing that was in it run away, and it shall never more trouble thee or another man." "Oh, wife, art thou hearing yon?" said the Miller. But his wife answered not a word. The Big Lad asked where she was. The Miller said that she fled, and hid herself under the bed when she heard the noise that was in the Mill. The Big Lad gave a look under the bed, and drew her out on the floor. But she was dead, for her heart went out of its casing (*cochull*) with fear.

The Big Lad left the Miller's house, and turned home. There was a brae above the Mill, and because the horse began to stop in the ascent he gave him a blow in the shoulder with the back of his hand. The blow was so heavy that the shoulder broke, and that the horse fell on the road. He was very sorry for what happened, but there was no help for it. He loosed the horse out of the sled, threw him on the top of the sacks, and went to draw the sled. He set off cheerily with it until he reached the top of the brae.

The Landlord had a watch on every road by which the Big Lad could come. At last one of the watchers saw him afar off dragging the sled after him, and the horse on the top of the sacks. The man threw off his footgear, with every bit of clothing which would hinder his running, and stretched away as fast as he could until he reached the Landlord's house.

The Landlord asked him whether he saw a sight of the Big Lad. " Did I see a sight of him ? 'Tis I who saw a sight of him ! He would not wait for the horse, but threw him on the top of the sacks, and he himself is drawing the sled after him with great speed." " Oh, then we may go away, for he will kill us all and will ruin the place at any rate." They drew away then, and left the place to him.

In a short time the Big Lad came home. He took the horse down off the top of the sled, and put the sacks in. He looked round, but not a man was to be seen about the town. He searched every hole and corner in which he could think that a man might be hidden, but found none. At last he understood that every person who was in the town had fled, and that they left it to himself.

He then thought that he would go for his mother, and that he would take her to the fine place which he had. He went, and found her at the foot of the wood. He told her of the great good luck he had, and that he came for her to go and stay with him. She told him that she was old, and that the distance was too long for her to walk it. " Well, mother, it shall not be so. Thou didst take a long time carrying me, and I will carry thee thus far now." He lifted his mother on his back, and did not let her go until he reached the place which he got for himself. They lived there in plenty and ease, and if they are alive they are there still.

# MAC CEATHARNACH NA COILLE
## 'BHA BLIADHN' THAR FHICHEAD AR CÌCH A MHÀTHAR.

BHA ann roimhe so duine foghainteach ris an abradh iad Ceatharnach na Coille. B' e obair an duine so daonnan sealgach nam fiadh, agus tarrainn connaidh dhachaidh gu teine. Air là àraid dh' fhalbh e a ghearradh craobh mhòr dharaich a chunnaic e 's a choille 'n là roimhe sin. An uair a bha 'chraobh ag aomadh thairis thuit i air, agus bhrùth i e gu h-uamhasach. Ach bha 'n duine làidir, agus le sin fhuair se e féin a shlaodadh a mach uaipe. An uair a dh' éirich e 'n a sheasamh air a chasan rug e air bhun air a chraoibh, agus shlaod e i eadar bhun 'us bharr dhachaidh leis. Cho luath 's a thilg e i bharr a ghualainn aig an dorus thuit e.

Thàinig a bhean a mach agus dar chunnaic i mar bha e chuidich i 's tigh e, agus chuir i e 'n a shuidhe air taobh na leapa. Thug e osna mhòr as an sin, agus thubhairt e gu 'n d' fhuair esan acaid a bhàis. Bha 'dhòrn dùinte, agus dar dh' fhosgail se e bha té de dhuircibh an daraich 'n a laimh. Choimhead e oirre, agus an sin shìn e i d' a bhean. Thubhairt e rithe, "Tha mise 'dol a bhi marbh, ach cuiridh tu 'n duirc so 'an làraich an dùin mu choinneamh an doruis. Tha mac 'dol a bhi agad, agus an oidhch' a thig am mac chum an t-saoghail bithidh bachlag an duirc a' tighinn 'am fradharc tromh 'n talamh. Beathaichidh tu air do ghlùn e le sùgh do chléibh 'us do chliathaich gus am bi e cho làidir 's gu 'n toir e a' chraobh a chinneas as an duirc as a bun agus as a frèumhaichean." An déigh dha so a ràdh r' a bhean laidh e sìos 'us cha d' éirich e tuillidh.

Au uair a thàinig an t-àm bha mac aig a bhoirionnach, agus cho luath 's a rugadh e dh' iarr i air a' bhean-ghlùin dol a mach agus coimhead an robh bachlag air an duirc. Bha bachlag an duirc an déigh bristeadh am mach gu math as an talamh. Rug i air a mac, agus bheathaich i e fad sheachd bliadhn' air a glùn. An sin thug i mach e a dh' ionnsaidh na craoibhe, agus thubhairt i ris e 'dh 'fhèuchainn am b' urrainn e a' chraobh ud a thabhairt as a bun. Chaidh e 'n carabh na craoibhe, agus thug e crathadh agus spìonadh uamhasach oirre, ach bha i air frèumhachadh cho daingeann anns an talamh 's nach d' thug e glidneachadh oirre.

An uair a chunnaic a mhàthair gu 'n d' fhairslich i air, thog i 's tigh leatha e, agus thug i seachd bliadhn' eile cìche dha. An sin thug i mach e a dh' ionnsaidh na craoibhe, agus thubhairt i ris e 'dh 'fhèuchainn co dhiù 'bu treis' e féin na 'chraobh an diugh. Rug e air bun na craoibhe, agus thug e slaodadh fuathasach oirre, ach bha i air gramachadh cho làidir anns an talamh 's nach d' rinn e 'n gnothuch oirre.

An uair a chunnaic a mhàthair gu 'n d' fhairslich i air an dara h-uair, thog i 's tigh e, agus thug i dha seachd bliadhn' eile cìche. An sin thug i mach e dh' ionnsaidh na craoibhe, agus dh' iarr i air e dh' fhèuchainn co dhiù 'bu treis' e féin na chraobh. Thug e sùrdagan uamhasach a null fàr an robh i, rug e oirre le dhà laimh, chrith 'us chrath e i, agus le trì no ceithir a shlaodaidhnean bha i mach as a bun agus as a frèumhaichean aige. Thòisich e 'n sin oirre as a barr, 'us bhrist 'us phronn e i gus an d' rinn e connadh teine dhi, agus an d' fhàg e i 'n a dùn aig an dorus.

Thubhairt a mhàthair, " Tha thu fada gu leòir a' deoghal sùgh mo chléibh 'us mo chliathaich-sa, agus tha thu làn chomasach air cothachadh air do shon féin tuillidh. Thig a 's tigh agus deasaichidh mise bonnach dhuit, gheibh thu e le 'm bheannachadh, agus falbhaidh tu 'n sin a chothachadh fortain duit féin."

Fhuair e 'm bonnach, agus dh' fhalbh e. Shiubhail e air aghaidh dh' fhèuch an tigeadh e air àite fàr am faigheadh e cosnadh. Mu dheireadh ràinig e aitreabh mhòr bhriadha le tuillidh mhulan timchioll oirre na chunnaic e riamh roimhe còmhla. Smaointich e gu 'm faigheadh e obair 's an àite sin, agus ghabh e dìreach a dh' ionnsaidh an tighe.

Bhuail e aig an dorus, agus dh' iarr e am maighstir fhaicinn. Thàinig am maighstir, agus dh' fheòraich e dh' e gu dé 'bha e 'g iarraidh? Fhreagair an Gille Mòr gu 'n robh e 'g iarraidh obair. "Ni do choltas an gnothuch," ars' am Maighstir. "Tha obair gu leòir agamsa, agus cha-n 'eil fhios agam carson nach faigheadh tu i. An dean thu bualadh?" "Ni," fhreagair an Gille. "Tha thu sgìth," ars' am Maistir. "Bi 'g ad dheanamh féin eòlach air feagh a' bhaile 'nochd, agus tòisichidh tu air bualadh moch 's a mhadainn am màireach." "C' àite 'n tòisich mi?" "Anns an t-sabhal, oir tha de dh' arbhar an sin na chumas dithis dhaoine 'bualadh gu ceann shè seachdainnean air fheabhas 'g an oibrich iad. An uair a theirgeas sin tha iothlann mhòr cùl an t-sabhail làn mhulan, agus tha 'h-uile sràbh dhiù r' am bualadh."

Bha 'n sabhal 's an iothlann air an togail air bruthach os ceann tighe 'n Uachdrain. An uair a fhuair an Gille a bhiadh chaidh e suas do 'n t-sabhal a dh' fhaicinn nam feadhnach a bha 'bualadh an sin. Chaidh e 's tigh, agus an déigh dha coimhead orra tacan a' bualadh rug e air a' bhuailtein a bh' aig fear dhiù, agus thubhairt e, "Cha-n fhiach na buailteinn-ean a th' agaibh. An uair a théid mis' 'an greim am màireach chi sibh am buailtein a bhitheas agam."

Dh' fhalbh e 'n sin do 'n choille a ghearradh buailtein da fhéin, agus an uair a bha 'm buailtein deas bu choimeas a lorg-shùiste ri crann luinge.

'San àm sin bi 'n riaghailt gu 'm féumadh na gillean oibreach-adh o rionnaig gu rionnag. Bha fhios aig a' Ghille Mhòr air so; uime sin dh' éirich e tràth anns a' mhadainn, agus bha e 'n greim anns a' bhualadh mu 'n d' fhalbh an rionnag bharr nan spéur. Thòisich e air bualadh na daise 'bh' anns an t-sabhal, ghabh e dhi anns an dara ceann, agus mar bha e 'dol air aghaidh bha e 'cur a' mhullaich as an tigh. Aig an dol sin chum e air gus nach robh sop air ùrlar gun bhualadh mu n' d' thàinig àm braiceis.

An déigh dha 'bhraiceas fhaotainn thionn e 'mach a rithist. Ghabh e do 'n iothlainn, thog e leis mulan anns gach achlais agus fear eadar a dhà laimh, chuir e anns an t-sabhal iad agus bhuail e iad. Mar sin chum e air aghairt gus nach robh mulan anns an iothlainn gun bhualadh mu 'n d' thàinig àm dinnearach. Bha 'n sin am baile uile geal le fodar, agus ballachan an t-sabhail béul ri bhi làn sìl.

Dh' fhalbh e 'n sin far an robh an t-Uachdran. Choinnich an t-Uachdran e air an rathad, agus e fo ioghnadh mòr gu dé 'chuir am baile làn fodair, ach cha do ghabh e diog air ris a' Ghille. An sin dh' fheòraich an Gille dh' e gu dé 'rachadh e 'dheanamh. "Théid thu 'bhualadh 's an t-sabhal," ars' an t-Uachdran. Fhreagair an Gille Mòr, "Cha-n' eil bualadh agam a ni mi." "Gu dé 'tha thu 'g ràdh ! Tha de bhualadh anns an t-sabhal na chumas ri dithis dhaoine gu ceann shè seachdainnean air fheabhas 'g an oibrich iad." "Cha-n' eil. Cha-n' eil sop 's a bhaile 'an sabhal no 'n iothlainn nach 'eil buailte cheana." Cha robh fhios aig an Uachdran gu dé 'theireadh e ri so, ach dh' iarr e air a' Ghille doll a 's tigh agus a dhinneir fhaotainn, agus dh' fhalbh e féin do 'n t-sabhal fèuch am faiceadh e 'n d' innis an Gille 'n fhirinn da no nach d'innis.

Ràinig e 'n sabhal, agus dar chunnaic e 'n coltas a bh' air a' h-uile rud air thoiseach air—am mullach air a chur as an t-sabhal, am fodar air a sgapadh air feadh a' bhaile, agus gach mulan 's an iothlainn buailte ghabh e eagal mòr, agus b' e 'n ni 'bu mhò a chuir de dh' uamhas air am buailtein a bh' aig a' Ghille Mhòr.

Thill e dhachaidh air chrith leis an eagal, agus ghabh e rathad cùil seach an Gille Mòr a choinneachadh dar thigeadh e 'mach o bhiadh. Ach thug an Gille Mòr an aire dha, agus ghabh e dìreach 'n a choinneamh? Dh' fheòraich e dh' e gu dé 'rachadh e 'dheanamh? Cha robh fhios aig an Uachdran gu ro mhath gu dé 'n fhreagairt a bheireadh e seachad, ach is e thubhairt e, "O 'n dh' oibrich thu cho math romh àm dinnearach is fearr dhuit d' anail a leigeil air an fheasgar so." An sin thubhairt an Gille Mòr, "Chunnaic thu m' obair a nis, agus tha fhios agad gu dé 's urrainn mi 'dheanamh. Féumaidh mi tuillidh bithidh fhaotainn gu 'm dhinneir n' a tha mi 'faighinn." "Gu dé na dh' fhéumas tu fhaotainn ?" "Ceithreamh salldair mine 'am *bruais* an dara latha, agus ceithreamh salldair mine 'n a bhonnaich le carcais dà-bhliadnach daimh an là eile." "Gheibh thu sin," ars' an t-Uachdran 'us e air chrith leis an eagal.

Chaidh an t-Uachdran a 's tigh, agus dh' innis e do mhuinn-

tir an tighe am biadh a bh' aca ri 'dheasachadh airson a' Ghille
Mhòir gach là tuillidh.

Smaointich an t-Uachdran agus na daoine glice 'bha timchioll
air mu 'n chùis, agus chunnaic iad gu 'n sgriosadh an Gille
Mòr am baile ann am biadh mur faigheadh iad dòigh air cur
as da, no air a chur air falbh.   Bha fìor sheann duinne air a'
bhaile ris an abradh iad Aonghas Mòr nan Creag, agus thubhairt fear de na daoine, " Mur bheil fhios aig Aonghas Mòr gu
dé 'ni sinn ris cha-n 'eil duin' eile 's an àite 's urrainn innseadh
dhuinn."

Chuir an t-Uachdran fios air Aonghas Mòr.   Thàinig
Aonghas, agus dh' innis an t-Uachdran da a' h-uile car mu 'n
fhamhair mhòr a thàinig orra—mar bhuail e 'n t-arbhar, agus an
seòrsa buailtein leis an robh e 'g obair.   " Ochòin !" ars'
Aonghas, " an d' thàinig e mu dheireadh !   Chuala mise mo
sheanair a' bruidhinn air an uair a bha mi 'am ghiollan.   Bha e
cho sean 's a tha mise 'n diugh, 'us e 'g innseadh mar bha e air
a ràdh gu 'n rachadh an t-àite so a sgrios fathast le famhair
mòr, agus cha-n 'eil teagamh 's am bith agam nach e' tha 'n so
an déigh tighinn."   " An urrainn thu smaointeachadh air dòigh
's am bith air an gabhar cur as da ?"   " 'S e 'n aon dòigh a 's
urrainn mise smaointeachadh so—gu 'n iarr thu air tobar mòr
fhosgladh 'am meadhon na dalach ud thall, agus dol cho
domhain 'us gu 'n tachair an t-uisg' air.   Is e grunnd domhain
gainmheich a th' ann, agus féumaidh e dol doimhne mhòir mu
'n ruig e 'mhàthair-uisge.   Ach dar ruigeas e i bitheadh gach
duine 's urrainn breith air sluasaid agad mu d' thimchioll,
agus dar bhitheas esan cròm 'an grunnd an tuill bitheadh gach
duine 'n a dhithis a' sparradh a 's tigh an stuth air a mhuin.
Ach ma chì sibh e 'g éiridh 'n a sheasamh teicheadh a' h-uile
duin' agaibh, oir ma gheibh e 'cheann a thogail bithidh e
'mach ge b' oil leibh, 'us marbhaidh e sibh."   Dh' aontaich an
t-Uachdran ri so a dheanamh.

Chuir e fios air a' Ghille Mhòr an oidhche sin féin.   Thàinig
an Gille, agus dh' innis an t-Uachdran da gu 'n robh an t-uisge
fàs anabarrach gann air, agus uime sin gun robh dhìth air tobar
fhosgladh 's an dail ud thall.   "Glé cheart," ars' an Gille.   "Tòisichidh tu air mar do chéud obair mhadainn am màireach,"
thubhairt an t-Uachdran.

An uair a thàinig an là chaidh an Gille Mòr 'an gréim a dh'
fhosgladh an tobair.   Bha na daoine mar an céudna tràth air
a' ghrunnd.   Dh' fhalbh iad leis an Uachdran a dh' fhàireinn-
eachd air a' Ghille Mhòr féuch ciamar a bha e 'faotainn air
aghaidh leis an toll.   An uair a fhuair iad sealladh air cha robh
an uachdar dh' e ach mullach a chinn, agus bha tòrr mòr de
stuth air a thilgeil a mach aige.   Ghabh iad an t-eagal gu 'm
bitheadh iad air dheireadh, ach bha iad an deagh àm aig an
toll.   Sheas an t-Uachdran aig béul an tuill, agus dar chròm
an Gille ghlaodh e air na daoine 'bhi 'n greim.   Thòisich iad
air an stuth a chur a 's tigh air a mhuin cho dian 's a b' urrainn
iad sluasaid a chluich.   Ach cha robh iad fad' aig an obair sin
an uair a dh' éirich an Gille Mòr 'n a sheasamh 'san toll, a
chrath e 'làmh, agus a ghlaodh e, " Thuis !"   Ghlaodh an t-
Uachdran r' a dhaoine teicheadh, agus dh' fhalbh a 'h-uile
duine dhiù cho luath 's a b' urrainn an casan an tabhairt as.

Ach chrìochnaich an Gille Mòr an toll mu 'n do sguir e.
Ghabh e 'n sin a suas gu tigh an Uachdrain.   An uair a bha e
'tighinn dlùth do 'n tigh  bha e 'gabhail iongantais mhòir nach
robh duine ri fhaicinn timchioll a' bhaile.   Ràinig e 'n dorus
mòr, agus chuir e a làmh air a' chrann, ach bha 'n dorus dùinte
cho làidir air an taobh a 's tigh 'us nach fosgladh e dha.
Chuir e 'n sin a bhas ris a' chrann, agus dh' fhùc e n' a bu
treis' e na bha thoil aige.   Bhrist an crann, agus dh' fhosgail
an dorus.   Ghabh e 's tigh, agus fhuair e 'n t-Uachdran 'n a
chrùban fo 'n bhòrd 'us e air chrith.

An sin thàinig an t-Uachdran a mach air an ùrlar, agus dh'
fheòraich e de 'n Ghille Mhòr an d' fhuair e deas an toll ?
Thubhairt an Gille gu 'n d' fhuair.   " Ach carson," ars' e, "nach
do chuir thusa duine a chumail air falbh nan ròcais ?  Theab iad
na sùilean a chur asam, a' sgrìobadh na gainmhich airson nam
biathainne.   Ach gu dé 'théid mi 'dheanamh a nis ?"   " Oh,
falbh 'us faigh do dhinneir," ars' an t-Uachdran.   Dh' fhalbh
an Gille Mòr mar dh' iarradh air.

An uair a fhuair an t-Uachdran as a charabh e chuir e fios
air an t-Seann duine 'rithist.   Thàinig an Seann duine, agus
thubhairt an t-Uachdran ris, " Cha dean an dòigh ud math
air bith.   Rinn e 'n toll còr 'us deich troidhean fichead air

doimhneachd, bha 'h-uile duine timchioll an àite agam mu 'n cuairt air an toll, dh' fhair mi 'n cothrom gus an robh e cròm 'an grunnd an tuill, ghlaodh mi riù iad a bhi 'n an gréim, thòisich gach duine 'n a dhithis air spùtadh an stuth a' s tigh air a mhuin, ach dh' éirich e 'n a sheasamh anns an toll, agus ghlaodh e 'Thuis!' An sin theich sinne.

"An ùine ghoirid thàinig e dhachaidh 'n ar déigh. Ghabh e' dh' ionnsaidh an doruis, agus ged bha e dùinte agus crannta, chuir e roimh' e le aon phùcadh de 'laimh. Thàinig e 's tigh, agus 's ann thubhairt e rium, carson nach do chuir mi duine 'chumail air falbh nan ròcais, a chionn gu d' theab iad na sùilean a chur as a' sgrìobadh na gainmhich a 's tigh air a mhuin am fad 's a bha e 'glanadh grunnd an tuill." "Oh, mata," ars' Aonghas Mòr, "fèuchaidh sinn dòigh eile air." "Gu dé 'n dòigh tha sin?" "Cuir e a threabhadh Imire-cròm Dhail an Lochain Duibh. Cha d' thàinig duine no beathach riamh as a' sin a bha treabhadh ann gu dol fodha gréine." "Fèuchaidh sinn sin féin da," thubhairt an t-Uachdran.

Chuir e fios air a' Ghille Mhòr, agus thubhairt e ris gu 'n robh e ri dol a threabhadh an dara mhàireach do dh' Imire- cròm Dhail an Lochain Duibh. "Ro cheart," ars' an Gille. "Ni mise sin."

Moch 's a' mhadainn chuir e 'n òrdugh air son an treabhaidh. Thog e 'n crann leis air a ghualainn, bha 'n dà each air thaod aige as a dhéigh, agus ràinig e Dail an Lochain Duibh. Stob e 'n crann 'an ceann an Imire-chrùim, agus chuir e 'n greim na h-eich. Bha craobh mhòr ann am meadhon an Imire, agus thubhairt e ris féin, "Fosglaidh mi 'n talamh dìreach air a' chraoibh." An sin thòisich e air treabhadh.

Bha e faotainn air aghaidh gu math fad an latha, ach mu chromadh na greine chual e plub fuathasach anns an Lochan. Thug e sùil agus chunnaic e Ùsp mòr dubh a' gluasad anns an uisge, ach cha do ghabh e suim 's am bith dh' e, agus chum e air aghaidh a' treabhadh mar bha e roimhe. Cho luath 's a chaidh a' ghrian as an fhradharc thàinig am beathach air tìr, agus ghabh e suas cladach an Lochain a dh' ionnsaidh a' chinn a b' fhaid' air falbh de 'n Imire-chròm. Chuir e 'n sin mu 'n cuairt, agus choisich e 'n coinneamh na seisrich anns a' cheart sgrìob anns an robh an Gille Mòr a' treabhadh leò. Chum an Gille Mòr air aghaidh le chuid each, agus choinnich iad am beathach aig a' chraoibh a bha 'm meadhon an Imire. Ghlaodh an Gille Mòr ris a' bheathach e dh' fhuireachd air ais, air neò gu 'm faiceadh e gu dé 'dh' éireadh dha. Ach cha d' thug am beathach feairt air, ach dh' fhosgail e 'bhéul, agus shluig e fear de na h-eich beò slàn. "Ni sin an gnothuch," thubhairt an Gille Mòr ris a bheathach. "Bheir mis' ort gu 'n cuir thu mach e cho ealamh 's a shluig thu e." Leig e as an crann, agus chaidh e 'n carabh a' bheathaich. Bha cuir uamhasach eatarra, ach mu dheireadh bha 'n Gille Mòr air muin a' bheath-aich. "Cuir a mach an t-each a nis," ars' an Gille, Ach cha d' thug am beathach feairt air. "Bheir mis' ort gu 'n cuir thu mach e," thubhairt e rithist. Rug e 'n sin air a' bheathach air earball, shlaod e dh' ionnsaidh na craoibh' e, spìon e 'chraobh as a bun, agus dh' éirich e air leatha gus nach robh aige dhi ach na bha 'n a laimh d' a barr. An sin thubhairt e, "An cuir thu mach an t-each a nis?" Cha d' thug am beathach feairt air fathast. "Mata," ars' an Gille, "bheir mis' ort gu 'n dean thu obair an fhir a dh' ith thu co dhiù."

Bha 'n t-each eile 'n déigh na ceanglaichean a bhristeadh, agus teicheadh dhachaidh. An uair a ràinig e 'n tigh agus a chunnaic an t-Uachdran an coltas fiamhach a bh' air, thubhairt e, "Oh, cha-n 'eil teagamh nach 'eil an Gille Mòr agus an t-each eile marbh a nis! Chuir Each-uisg' an Lochain Duibh as da mu dheireadh!"

Ach bha 'n Gille Mòr mu thimchioll a ghnothuich. Cheangail e 'm beathach anns a' chrann, agus thòisich e air treabhadh leis, agus mu 'n do sguir e cha robh sgrìob anns an Imire chròm nach do thionndaidh e. An uair a bha e deas dh fhalbh e dhachaidh 'us an t-each mòr air cheann aige.

Ràinig e dorus an Uachdrain, agus ghlaodh e ris tighinn a mach. Ach cha do fhreagair duin' e, oir theich gach duine a bh' air a' bhaile, agus chaidh iad am falach cho luath 's a chunnaic iad e féin 'us an t-each a' tighinn. Thug e 'n sin bodhairneadh do 'n dorus, agus mu dheireadh thàinig an t-Uachdran a mach 'us e air chrith leis an eagal.

Dh' fhèoraich an Gille Mòr dh' e gu dé 'rachadh e 'dheanamh

am màireach ? " Oh, theid thu 'threabhadh," ars' an t-Uachdran 'us a ghuth air chrith. " Cha-n 'eil treabhadh agam a ni mi." " Gu dé tha thu 'g ràdh ? Tha de thalamh 's an Imire-chròm na chumadh treabhadh ri paidhir each gu ceann shè seachd-ainnean." " Cha-n' eil. Dhearg mise 'h-uile sgrìob mu 'n do sguir mi." " 'S an d' fhairich thu ni air bith a chuir dragh ort am fad 's a bha thu 'g obair ?" " Cha d' fhairich mise dad ach trusdar de bheathach grànd' a thàinig as an Lochan, agus a dh' ith fear de na h-eich orm. Dh' fhèuch mi 'thabhairt air an t-each a chur a mach, ach cha d' thugadh e feairt orm. Chuir mi 'n sin anns a' chrann e, agus threabh mi 'h-uile sgrìob de 'n Imire-chròm leis, ach cha do chuir e 'mach an t-each fathast." " 'Us c' àit am bheil e ?" " Tha 'n so aig an dorus." " O, leig as e ! leig as e ! leig air falbh e !" " Cha leig mi gus am faigh mi 'n t-each uaith."

Thionndaidh e 'n sin ris a' bheathach, agus leag e air a dhrùim e. Tharrainn e a chorc mhòr féin, sgoilt e leatha brù a' bheathaich, agus thug e 'n t-each beò, slan a mach as. An sin thubhairt e ris an Uachdran, " Cha-n 'eil fhios agam gu dé 'ni mi ris mur cuir mi anns an toll am meadhon na dalach e, agus mur robh uisg' ann roimhe bithidh e ann an sin." Shlaod e 'm beathach a null do 'n dail, thilg e 'n coinneamh a chinn anns an toll e, chuir e 'n stuth a 's tigh air a mhuin, agus dh' fhàg e 'n sin e.

Chuir an t-Uachdran fios a rìs air Aonghas Mòr nan Creag. Thàinig Aonghas, agus thubhairt e ris an Uachdran, " Gu dé an naigheachd a th' agad a nis ?" " Cha-n 'eil ach naigheachd bhochd. Cha d' rinn an ionnsaidh ud math 's am bith. Chuir mi e a threabhadh an Imire-chrùim. Am feadh a bha e treabhadh thàinig beathach uamhasach a mach as an Loch, agus dh' ith e fear de na h-eich air. Rug e air a' bheathach, cheangail e ris a' chrann e, agus dhearg e 'h-uile sgrìob de 'n Imire leis mu 'n do sguir e. Thug e 'n sin dachaidh e air cheann taoid, leag e aig an dorus e, agus thug e 'n t-each beò slàn as a bhroinn. An sin shlaod e as a dhéigh e air earball, agus thilg e 'n coinneamh a chinn anns an toll e. Agus a nis cha-n 'eil mise 'smaointeachadh gu 'n ruig sinn leas a bhi fèuchainn ris ni 's faide. Faodaidh sinn teicheadh agus an

t-àit' fhàgail aige féin." "Bheir sinn aon déuchainn eile dha
fhathast." "Gu dé i an déuchainn sin?" "Abair ris gu 'n do
theirig a' mhin ort, agus nach bi gearradh bithidh agad dha
gus an tig e féin as a' mhuileann. Cuiridh tu air falbh e le
càrn sìl do Mhuileann-Leacain. Cuiridh tu cabhag air a
chum 'us gu 'n oibrich e anns a' Mhuileann fad na h-oidhche,
agus theid mis' 'an urras duit nach leig Ùruisg Mòr Mhuileann-
Leacain esan dachaidh ni 's mò na fear air bith eile. Ach ma
leigeas agus ma chì sibh e 'tighinn, faodaidh sibh uile eadar
bheag 'us mhòr, shean 'us òg, teicheadh, oir cha ghabh e cur
as da', agus sgriosaidh e an t-àite co dhiù."

Chuir an t-Uachdran fios air a' Ghille Mhòr, agus thubhairt
e ris gu 'n do theirig a' mhin air, agus nach bitheadh gearradh
bithidh aige dha féin gus an tigeadh e as a' mhuileann le min.
"Thoir leat aon 's am bith a thogras tu de na h-eich agus an
Càrn Mòr, agus lìon e le pocaibh sìl, agus bithidh tu dhachaidh
cho luath 's is urrainn thu. Féumaidh tu oibreachadh fad na
h-oidhch' anns a' mhuileann chum gu 'm bi thu aig an tigh
tràth am màireach." "Ro cheart," thubhairt an Gille Mòr.
"Ni mise sin."

Dh' fhalbh e gun dàil leis an t-sìol, agus ràinig e am muileann
'am béul na h-oidhche. Bha am Muillear an déigh sgur a bhleith,
agus am muileann dùinte. Dh' fhuasgail e 'n t-each as a' chàrn,
agus leig e chum ionaltraidh e. Dh' fhalbh e 'n sin gu tigh a'
mhuilleir, agus ghlaodh e ris aig an dorus e dh' éiridh, a chionn
gu 'n robh esan air tighinn le càrn sìl, agus gu 'm féumadh
e 'n sìol fhaotainn air a bhleith an oidhche sin. "Cha dean e
mùthadh cò thu, no cia as a thàinig thu, ach cha-n 'eil duin'
air uachdar na talmhainn d' am fosglainn-s' am muilleann tuillidh
an nochd." "Ù, féumaidh tu éiridh! Tha cabhag ormsa, agus
is éiginn an sìol a bhi bleithte 'n nochd." "Cabhag no gun
chabhaig cha-n fhaca mise duine riamh airson an rachainn do
'n mhuileann an nochd." "Mur teid thus' ann, thoir dhomh
fhéin an iuchair, 'us théid mi ann." "Mata, ma théid thu ann
cha tig thu as." "Cha-n 'eil eagal 's am bith orm; thoir thusa
dhomh an iuchair."

Thug am Muillear dha an iuchair, agus dh' fhalbh e 'n mhuileann. Thog e 's tigh an sìol, chuir e air teine mòr de chàth

agus de mhòine, chuir e barr air an àth, chruadhaich e 'm barr, agus chuir e 's an treabhailt e. Leig e 'n sin am muileann air shiubhal, bhleith e na chruadhaich e de 'n choirce, chriathair e 'mhin, agus an sin thòisich e air deasachadh bhonnach, oir bha 'n t-acras mòr air. An uair a bha iad deasaichte chuir e air an àth iad 'g am bruich.

Am feadh' bha e 'g am bruich 'us 'g an tionndadh thug e 'n aire do dh' Ùsp a' tighinn am fradharc 'an oisinn na h-àtha. Ghlaodh e ris an Ùsp fuireachd air ais, ach cha d' thug e feairt air. Shìn e 'spòg, agus thug e leis aon de na bonnaich. "Na dean sin tuillidh," ars' an Gille Mòr. Ach cha d' thug an t-Ùsp feairt air. An ùine ghoirid shìn e rithist a spòg, agus thug e leis bonnach eile. "Dean thusa sin aon uair eile, agus bheir mis' ort gu 'm bi na bonnaich daor dhuit," thubhairt an Gille Mòr. Cha do ghabh am fear a bha 's an oisinn mòran suim de sud, agus thug e leis an treas bonnach. "Mata," ars' an Gille Mòr, "mur toir thu feairt 'ad dheòin bheir thu feairt ad aindeòin. Bheir mis' ort gu 'n cuir thu air an ais na thug thu leat."

An sin thug e aon dudarléum mòr, agus bha e air muin an Ùruisg. Chaidh iad 'an greimibh a chéile, agus ghleac iad gu h-uamhasach. Le car no 'dhà leag iad an àth, chuir iad am muileann as a chéile, agus chual iad am fad agus am fagus am bodhairneadh uamhasach a bha 's a' mhuileann. Chual am Muillear e 'n a leaba, agus chuir e a leithid de dh' eagal air 'us gu 'n do shuain e 'n t-aodach uime 's gu 'n do chrùbain e 'n casaibh na leapa. Léum a bhean 's a ghlaodhaich a null air an ùrlar, agus chaidh i air a màgan a 's tigh fo 'n leaba. Mu dheireadh chìosnaich an Gille Mòr an t-Ùruisg. Dh' iarr an t-Ùruisg air a leigeil as, ach fhreagair e nach leigeadh mar sin. "Gus an càirich thu am Muileann, agus an cuir thu suas an àth 's na bonnaich oirre mar fhuair thu iad cha-n fhaigh thu as." An sin thug e brùilleadhnan uamhasach eile air. Ghlaodh an t-Ùruisg, "Leig as mi, agus nì mi 'h-uile ni a tha thu 'g iarraidh orm." "Cha leig mi as thu, ach féumaidh tu 'dhean-amh agus greim agam ort."

An sin thòisich an t-Ùruisg air càradh a' Mhuilinn, agus an ùine glé ghoirid chuir e gach ni 'na àite féin mar bha e roimhe.

"Leig as a nis mi, oir tha 'h-uile ni mar fhuair mis' iad," ars' an t-Ùruisg. Thug an Gille Mòr sùil, agus chunnaic e nach robh na trì bonnaich air an àth, agus thubhairt e nach robh a h-uile ni mar bha iad. "C' àit' am bheil na bonnaich a thug thu leat?" Thug e 'n so builean, agus brùillidhnean fuathasach eil' air an Ùruisg. Ghlaodh an t-Ùruisg, "Leig as mi, agus gheibh thu na bonnaich 'an lag an teine." "Cha leig mi as thu, ach falbh thusa, agus faigh dhomh iad." Dh' fhalbh an t-Ùruisg 'us greim aig a' Ghille Mhòr air, agus fhuair e na bonnaich. "Cuir a nis iad air an àth fàr an d' fhuair thu iad," ars' an Gille Mòr. Rinn an t-Ùruisg sin, 'us thug an Gille Mòr na h-ath bhrùillidh- nean air. Ghlaodh an t-Ùruisg, a leigeadh as 'us gu 'm fàgadh e am Muileann, 'us nach cuireadh e dragh air gu bràth tuillidh an déigh na h-oidhche sin. "Mata, o 'n gheall thu sin leigidh mi as thu," ars' an Gille Mòr, agus thug e urchair da 'mach an dorus. Thug an t-Ùruisg trì sgrèuchan fuathasach as, agus tharainn e. Chual am Muillear na sgrèuchan, agus thug a bhean glaodh goint' aiste 's tigh fo 'n leaba.

Dar dh' fhalbh an t-Ùruisg thòisich an Gille Mòr air itheadh nam bonnach, agus dar dh' ith e' leòir dhiù chruadhaich agus bhleith e 'n còr de 'n t-sìol. Chriathair e 'n sin a' mhin, chuir e anns na pocaibh i, agus na pocanna anns a' chàrn. Bha gach ni deas age nis; uime sin ghlais e dorus a' mhuilinn, agus dh' fhalbh e dhachaidh leis an iuchair.

Ràinig e tigh a' Mhuilleir, agus ghlaodh e aig an dorus, ach cha do fhreagair duin' e. Ghlaodh e 'rithist, agus chual e am Muillear a' freagairt a 's tigh le guth fann. Dh' iarr an Gille Mòr air an dorus fhosgladh, a chionn gu 'n robh esan air tighinn dachaidh leis an iuchair. "O!" thubhairt am Muillear, "bi falbh, bi falbh, 'us thoir leat an iuchair còmhla ris a chòr." "Is mi féin a th' ann, leig a 's tigh mi," ars' an Gille Mòr. Ach cha do fhreagair am Muillear idir e; uime sin phùc e 'n dorus roimhe, agus chaidh e 's tigh. "So," ars' esan, "an iuchair, oir bhleith mi 'n sìol agus tha mi falbh dhachaidh." An uair a chual am Muillear gu 'n robh 'n sìol air a bhleith, thug e 'mach a cheann as an aodach, agus choimhead e air an duine. "Oh, ciamar tha thu beò an déigh dhuit a bhi 's a' mhuileann fad na h-oidhche!" "Fùth! faodaidh tusa dol do 'n mhuileann 'us fuireachd ann fad na h-oidhche nis. An rud a bh' ann chuir mis' air theicheadh, 'us cha chuir e dragh ortsa no air duin' eile gu bràth tuillidh." "Oh, 'bhean, am bheil thu 'cluinntinn sud?" ars' am Muillear. Ach cha d' fhreagair a' bhean facal. Dh' fheòraich an Gille Mòr c' àit' an robh i? Thubhairt am Muillear gu 'n do theich i agus gu 'n d' fholaich i fo 'n leaba, 'n uair a chual i 'n straighlich a bh' anns a' mhuileann. Thug an Gille Mòr sùil fo 'n leaba, 'us shlaod e mach i air an ùrlar. Ach bha i marbh, oir chaidh a cridhe as a' chochull leis an eagal.

Dh' fhàg an Gille Mòr tigh a' Mhuilleir, agus thionn e dhachaidh. Bha bruthach os ceann a' mhuilinn, agus a chionn gu 'n do thòisich an t-each air stad 's an uchdaich thug e buille dha le cùl a laimh anns an t-slineig. Bha 'm buille cho tròm 's gu 'n do bhrist e 'n t-slineig, agus gu 'n do thuit an t-each air an rathad. Bha e ro dhuilich mar thachair, ach cha robh comas air. Dh' fhuasgail e 'n t-each as a' chàrn, thilg e air mullach nam pocannan e, agus chaidh e féin a shlaodadh a' chùirn. Dh' fhalbh e 'n sin leis gu h-uallach gus an d' ràinig e mullach a' bhruthaich.

Bha freiceadan aig an Uachdran air a 'h-uile rathad air am b' urrainn an Gille Mòr tighinn. Mu dheireadh chunnaic fear de 'n luchd-fair' e fad as a' slaodadh a' chùirn na dhéigh, agus an t-each aig' air uachdar nam pocanna. Thilg an duine dheth a chais'eart maille ris gach ball a chuireadh moille air a ruith, agus shìn e as cho luath 's a b' urrainn e gus an d' ràinig e tigh an Uachdrain.

Dh' fheòraich an t-Uachdran d' e am fac e sealladh air a' Ghille Mhòr? "Am faca mi sealladh air? Is mi a chunnaic an sealladh air! Cha bhitheadh e 'feitheamh ris an each, ach thilg e air muin nam pocannan e, agus tha e féin a' slaodadh a' chùirn 'n a dhéigh le luathas mòr." "Oh mata faodaidh sinne falbh, oir marbhaidh e sinn uile, agus sgriosaidh e 'n t-àite co dhiù." Tharruinn iad an sin, agus dh' fhàg iad an t-àit' aige féin.

An ùine ghoirid thàinig an Gille Mòr dhachaidh. Thug e 'n t-each a nuas bharr mullach a' chùirn, 'us chuir e stigh na pocanna. Sheall e mu 'n cuairt, ach cha robh duine ri fhaicinn timchioll a' bhaile. Dh' fhèuch e gach cùil 'us toll anns an saoileadh e gu 'm b' urrainn duine 'bhi 'm falach, ach cha d' fhuair e aon. Mu dheireadh thuig e gu 'n do theich a' h-uile duine a bh' air a' bhaile, agus gu 'n d' fhàg iad e dha fhéin.

Smaointich e 'n sin gu 'n rachadh e airson a mhàthar, 'us gu 'n d' thugadh e i do 'n àite bhriadha a bh' aige. Dh' fhalbh e, agus fhuair e i fàr an d' fhàg e i 'am bun na coille. Dh' innis e dhi am fortan mòr a bh' air, agus gu 'n d' thàinig e air a son a dhol a dh' fhuireachd leis. Thubhairt i ris gu 'n robh ise sean, agus gu 'n robh an t-astar tuillidh 's fada dhi r' a choiseachd. " Mata, a mhàthair, cha-n ann mar sin a bhitheas. Thug thusa ùine mhòr 'g am ghiùlan-sa, agus giùlainidh mise thusa 'm fad so a nis." Thog e a mhàthair leis air a mhuin, 'us cha do leig e as i gus an d' ràinig e 'n t-àit' a fhuair e dha fhéin. Bha iad an sin gu sòghail, soisneach, agus ma tha iad beò tha iad ann fathast.

## IX.

# THE FARMER OF LIDDESDALE.

THERE was in Liddesdale (in Morven) a Farmer who suffered great loss within the space of one year. In the first place, his wife and children died, and shortly after their death the Ploughman left him. The hiring-markets were then over, and there was no way of getting another ploughman in place of the one that left. When Spring came his neighbours began ploughing ; but he had not a man to hold the plough, and he knew not what he should do. The time was passing, and he was therefore losing patience. At last he said to himself, in a fit of passion, that he would engage the first man that came his way, whoever he should be,

Shortly after that a man came to the house. The Farmer met him at the door, and asked him whither was he going, or what was he seeking? He answered that he was a Ploughman, and that he wanted an engagement. "I want a ploughman, and if we agree about the wages, I will engage thee. What dost thou ask from this day to the day when the crop will be gathered in ?" "Only as much of the corn when it shall be dry as I can carry with me in one burden-withe." "Thou shalt get that," said the Farmer, and they agreed.

Next morning the Farmer went out with the Plough-man, and showed him the fields which he had to plough. Before they returned, the Ploughman went to the wood, and having cut three stakes, came back with them, and placed one of them at the head of each one of the fields. After he had done that he said to the Farmer, " I will do the work now alone, and the ploughing need no longer give thee anxiety."

Having said this, he went home and remained idle all that day. The next day came, but he remained idle as on the day before. After he had spent a good while in that manner, the Farmer said to him that it was time for him to begin work now, because the spring was passing away, and the neighbours had half their work finished. He replied, " Oh, our land is not ready yet." " How dost thou think that ?" " Oh, I know it by the stakes."

If the delay of the Ploughman made the Farmer wonder, this answer made him wonder more. He resolved that he would keep his eye on him, and see what he was doing.

The Farmer rose early next morning, and saw the Ploughman going to the first field. When he reached the field, he pulled the stake at its end out of the ground, and put it to his nose. He shook his head and put the stake back in the ground. He then left the first field and went to the rest. He tried the stakes, shook his head, and returned home. In the dusk he went out the second time to the fields, tried the stakes, shook his head, and after putting them again in the ground, went home. Next morning he went out to the fields the third time. When he reached the first stake he pulled it out of the ground and put it to his nose as he did on the foregoing days. But no sooner had he done that than he threw the stake from him, and stretched away for the houses with all his might.

He got the horses, the withes, and the plough, and when he reached the end of the first field with them, he thrust the plough into the ground, and cried :

" My horses and my leather-traces, and mettlesome lads,
　The earth is coming up !"

He then began ploughing, kept at it all day at a terrible rate, and before the sun went down that night there was not a palm-breadth of the three fields which he had not ploughed, sowed, and harrowed. When the Farmer saw this he was exceedingly well pleased, for he had his work finished as soon as his neighbours.

The Ploughman was quick and ready to do everything that he was told, and so he and the Farmer agreed well until the harvest came. But on a certain day when the reaping was over, the Farmer said to him that he thought the corn was dry enough for putting in. The Ploughman tried a sheaf or two, and answered that it was not dry yet. But shortly after that day he said that it was now ready. "If it is," said the Farmer, "we better begin putting it in." "We will not until I get my share out of it first," said the Ploughman. He then went off to the wood, and in a short time returned, having in his hand a withe scraped and twisted. He stretched the withe on the field, and began to put the corn in it. He continued putting sheaf after sheaf in the withe until he had taken almost all the sheaves that were on the field. The Farmer asked of him what he meant ? " Thou didst promise me as wages as much corn as I could carry with me in one burden-withe, and here I have it now," said the Ploughman, as he was shutting the withe.

The Farmer saw that he would be ruined by the Ploughman, and therefore said :

> " 'Twas in the Màrt I sowed,
> 'Twas in the Màrt I baked,
> 'Twas in the Màrt I harrowed.
> Thou who hast ordained the three Màrts,
> Let not my share go in one burden-withe."

Instantly the withe broke, and it made a loud report,

which echo (*mac-talla*) answered from every rock far
and near. Then the corn spread over the field, and the
Ploughman went away in a white mist in the skies, and
was seen no more.

## TUATHANACH LÌODASDAIL.

BHA Tuathanach 'an Lìodasdail a dh' fhuluing call mòr 'an
taobh a 's tigh de 'n aon bhliadhna. Anns a' chéud àite
chaochail a bhean 'us a chlann, agus goirid an déigh am bàis-
san dh' fhàg an Sgalag e. Bha na faidhrichean an sin air dol
seachad, agus cha robh dòigh air Sgalag eil' fhaotainn an àit'
an fhir a dh' fhalbh. An uair a thàinig an t-earrach chaidh na
coimhearsnaich 'an greim anns an treabhadh, ach cha robh
duin' aige san a ghleidheadh crann, agus cha robh fios aige gu
dé 'dheanadh e. Bha 'n ùine 'dol seachad, agus le sin bha e
'call' fhoighidinn. Mu dheireadh thubhairt e ris féin ann an
corruich gu 'n gabhadh e a' chéud duin' a thigeadh an rathad
cò air bith e.

Goirid an déigh sin thàinig duin' a dh' ionnsaidh an tighe.
Choinnich an Tuathanach e aig an dorus, agus dh' fheòraich
e dh' e cean' a bha e dol, no gu dé 'bha e 'g iarraidh? Fhreagair e gu' m bu Sgalag e, agus gu 'n robh e 'g iarraidh muinnt-
iris. "Tha Sgalag a dhìth ormsa, agus ma chòrdas sinn mu
'n tuarasdal cuiridh mi muinntireas ort. Gu dé 'bhitheas tu 'g
iarraidh o 'n àm so gus an là 's am bi 'm bàrr cruinn?" "Cha
bhi ach na bheir mi leam 'an aon ghad-cuail de 'n choirce 'n
uair a bhitheas e tioram." "Gheibh thu sin," thubhairt an
Tuathanach, agus chòrd iad.

Air an ath mhadainn chaidh an Tuathanach a mach leis an
Sgalag, agus leig e fhaicinn da na dailtean a bh' aige ri
'threabhadh. Mu 'n do thill iad chaidh an Sgalag do 'n choille,
agus air dha trì stuib a ghearradh thàinig e air ais leò, agus
chuir e aon diù an ceann gach aon de na dailtean. An déigh
dha sin a dheanamh thubhairt e ris an Tuathanach, " Ni mi

féin an gnothuch a nis, agus cha ruig an treabhadh leas cùram a chur ortsa tuillidh."

Air dha so a ràdh chaidh e dhachaidh, agus dh' fhan e 'n a thàmh fad an là sin. Thàinig an ath là ach dh' fhuirich e dìomhanach mar air an là roimhe. An déigh dha ùine mhath a chaitheadh mar sin thubhairt an Tuathanach ris gu 'n robh an t-àm aige tòiseachadh air an obair a nis a chionn gu 'n robh an t-earrach a' dol seachad, agus gu 'n robh leth na h-obair dèant' aig na coimhearsnaich. Fhreagair e, "Oh, cha-n 'eil an talamh againne deas fathast." "Cia mar tha thu smaointeachadh sin ?" "Oh, tha mi 'g a aithneachadh air na stuib."

Ma chuir dàil an Sgalag ioghnadh air an Tuathanach chuir an fhreagairt so tuillidh air. Chuir e roimhe gu 'n cumadh e sùil air, agus gu 'm faiceadh e gu dé 'bha e deanamh.

Dh' éirich an Tuathanach moch air an ath mhadainn, agus chunnaic e 'n Sgalag a' falbh a dh' ionnsaidh na céud dalach. Dar ràinig e 'n dail, shlaod e 'n stob aig a ceann as an talamh, agus chuir e r' a shròin e. Chrath e a cheann, agus chuir e 'n stob air ais anns an talamh. Dh' fhàg e 'n sin a chéud dail, agus chaidh e 'dh' ionnsaidh chàich. Dh' fhéuch e na stuib, chrath e 'cheann, agus phill e dhachaidh. Am béul na h-oidhche chaidh e mach an dara h-uair a dh' ionnsaidh nan dailtean, dh' fhéuch e na stuib, chrath e 'cheann, agus an deigh dha an cur a rìs anns an talamh chaidh e dhachaidh. Air an ath mhadainn chaidh e mach an treas uair chum nan dailtean. Dar ràinig e 'chéud stob shlaod e as an talamh e agus chuir e r' a shròin e mar rinn e air na làithean roimhe. Ach cha bu luaith' a rinn e sin na thilg e air falbh an stob, agus a shìn e as le uile neart chum nan tighean. Fhuair e na h-eich, na goid, agus an crann, agus dar ràinig e ceann na céud dalach leò shàth e 'n crann anns an talamh, agus ghlaodh e :

> " M' eich 'us m' éill, 'us mear-ghillean,
> Tha 'n talamh a' tighinn an àird."

Thòisich e 'n sin ri treabhadh, chum e air fad an là le sgrìob uamhasaich, agus mu 'n deachaidh a' ghrian fodha 'n oidhche sin cha robh lèud boise de na trì dailtean nach robh treabhta, cuirte, cliatht' aige. An uair a chunnaic an Tuathanach so bha e anabarrach toilichte, oir bha 'n obair aige deas cho luath r' a choimhearsnaich.

Bha 'n Sgalag ullamh, ealamh a dheanamh gach ni 'bha air iarraidh air, agus le sin chòrd e féin agus an Tuathanach gu math gus an d' thàinig am fogharadh.

Ach an uair a bha 'bhuain seachad, air là àraidh thuirt an Tuathanach ris gu 'n robh e smaointeachadh gu 'n robh 'n t-arbhar tioram gu leòir airson a chur a 's tigh. Dh' fhéuch an Sgalag sguab no dhà, agus fhreagair e nach robh fathast. Ach goirid an déigh an là sin thuirt e gu 'n robh e deas a nis. "Ma tha," ars' an Tuathanach, "is fearr dhuinn tòiseachadh air a chur a 's tigh." "Cha thòisich ach gus am faigh mise mo chuid féin as an toiseach," ars' an Sgalag. Dh' fhalbh e 'n sin do 'n choille, agus an ùine ghoirid thill e le gad sgrìbte, sniamht' aige 'na laimh. Shìn e 'n gad air an achadh, agus thòisich e air an arbhar a chur ann. Chum e air aghaidh a' cur sguaib an déigh sguaib anns a' ghad gus nach mòr nach robh na bh' air an achadh aige leis. Dh' fheòraich an Tuathanach dh' e gu dé 'bha e 'ciallachadh? "Gheall thu dhomh mar mo thuarasdal na bheirinn leam de 'n arbhar ann an aon ghad-cuail, agus so e agam a nis," ars' an Sgalag, agus e 'dùnadh a' ghoid.

Chunnaic an Tuathanach gu 'n bitheadh e air a sgrios leis an Sgalag, agus uime sin thubhairt e :

> " Is ann 'am Màrt a chuir mi,
> Is ann 'am Màrt a dh' fhuin mi,
> Is ann 'am Màrt a chliath mi.
> Fhir a dh' òrduich na trì Màirt,
> Na leig mo chuid-sa 'n aon ghad-cuaill."

Air ball bhrist an gad, agus rinn e braigheadh mòr a fhreagair mac-talla bho gach creag am fad agus am fagus. An sin sgaoil an t-arbhar air an achadh, agus dh' fhalbh an Sgalag 'n a cheò bàn anns na spéuran, agus cha-n fhacas tuillidh e.

X.

## A TALE ABOUT THE SON OF THE KNIGHT OF THE GREEN VESTURE,

### PERFORMING HEROIC DEEDS WHICH WERE FAMED ON EARTH SEVEN YEARS BEFORE HE WAS BORN.

——————

BEFORE now there lived a Landlord who had a fine place, and an abundance of cattle and poultry. In his time, landlords like him valued poultry so highly that they were in the habit of keeping about them a shrewd woman whom people called the Hen-wife. This Landlord also had a Hen-wife who was very shrewd, and who had a pretty young boy whom she called her son, and who called her his mother.

The boy was growing up a fine lad, and gave promise of becoming a brave man. But far and near he got no other name than the Son of the Hen-wife; yet that gave him not the least annoyance.

The Hen-wife was well off under the Landlord, having a house, three cows, and everything else she needed. When the boy grew up a young lad he was accustomed to go away with the cows, and herd them all day. On a certain day he drove them further away than he was wont to do, to a place where the pasture was exceedingly good. As soon as the cattle took to the grass, he reached a pretty knoll where he would be in sight of them, and sat down. He passed a great part of the day there, taking delight in everything he saw. At last he beheld, ascending from the hollow under him to the place where he was sitting, a young maiden with the red of the rose on her cheek, and her golden hair hanging down in pretty ringlets over her two shoulders.

She reached the place where he was sitting, and having given him the salutation of the day, said that he was lonely herding the three cows. He answered her readily, and said that he was not lonely now since she had come with him. Then she asked of him, would he sell her one of the cows? He told her that he must not, because his mother would scold him. "Oh no, if thou get her value for the cow." "And what wilt thou give me for her?" "I will give thee a stone of virtues (charm-stone)." "What are the virtues that the stone possesses?" "There is not a virtue that thou needest for thy system or for thy body which thou shalt not find as long as thou keep it, and there is not a place where thou biddest thyself and as many as thou likest be in which thou shalt not be in an instant." "Let me have a look of the stone." The maiden handed him the stone, and it was beautiful to look at. He took hold of it, and thought that he would test it before he gave the cow for it. He was thirsty at the time, and thought that he would like a drink from the spring of the Red-stone behind his mother's house. No sooner had the thought come into his mind than he was sitting beside the well. He took a drink, and returned in the same way in which he came. He then gave the cow for the stone, and was perfectly well satisfied with the exchange which he had made.

Then the maiden of the rose-red cheeks went away with the cow that she bought, and he returned home with the other two cows in the dusk. When his mother saw that he had only two, she asked of him where the third was? He told her that he sold her. She said to him, what did he get for her? He answered that he got a stone for her. When his mother saw the stone, and she could not understand its use, she flew into a rage, and scolded him dreadfully. He listened calmly to every word she said, and spake not a syllable against her. When her wrath had abated, she told him to put in the two cows in order that they should be milked. He did so, and that night the two had as much milk as the three had before then.

In the morning, after he had got his breakfast and the cows had been milked, his mother told him to drive them to the place in which they were on the day before. He went away with them, and left them in the very same spot. As soon as they arrived the cattle took to the pasture, and he sat down on the same knoll on which he was on the past day.

About the time when he first saw the Maiden he saw her this day again ascending the hollow beneath him. She reached the place where he was sitting, and asked of him, would he sell another of his cows? He said that he would not, because on the past night he got a frightful scolding from his mother on account of the one he had already sold. " Oh, if thou get her value for her, she will not scold thee." " What, then, wilt thou give me for her?" I will give thee a healing jewel for her." " What sores will the jewel heal?" " Any sores on thy flesh or on thy skin, any disease of the body or of the mind it will heal when thou dost rub it against thee." There was a wound on the lad's toe, and he asked the Maiden to show him the jewel. He got it, and as soon as he rubbed it against his toe it was healed. Then he gave her the cow, and was perfectly pleased with the exchange he had made.

When the evening came, he went home with the remaining cow. His mother met him coming, and asked of him what he got for the cow he had sold? He said that he got a jewel for her. When she heard this, if she flew into a rage the day before, she flew into a sevenfold worse rage this day. She calmed down at last, and told him to put in the remaining cow in order that she might be milked. He did that, and she had as much milk as the three had formerly.

In the morning, after the cow had been milked, his mother told the Lad to drive her to the place in which she was on the preceding day. He went away with her, and when he reached the place he sat down, as he was wont to do, on the knoll. The Maiden came where he was, and asked of him whether he would sell the only cow he had? "Oh, I dare not, for I got a terrible scolding on account of the last one I sold." "Oh, thou shalt not get a scolding if thou get her value for the cow." "And what then wilt thou give me for her?" "I will give thee a little bird-net." "What sort of birds will the net catch, or how is it to be set?" "Thou hast nothing to do but to spread it on the tops of the bushes, and leave it there all night; and in the morning it shall be full of all kinds of birds thou hast ever seen or heard, and there shall be in it twelve birds the like of which thou hast never seen or heard." He gave the cow for the net. She went away with the cow, and he returned home with the net.

When his mother saw that he came home without any cow at all with him, she could not utter a word, but she cast a woful look at him. He was very sorry that he displeased her so much, but he was sure that she would be satisfied when she saw the number of birds he would have in the net on the morrow.

As soon as he got up next day he went to see the net, which he had set on the night before, and such a sight of birds he never saw till that moment. He went home with them, and when his mother saw what a number he had, she asked of him where he found them? He said that he caught them in the net. "And wilt thou get more with it?"   " I will get this number every time that I set it."   She was now better pleased, and they had never been so well off with the milk of the cows as they were with the flesh of the birds.

The Lad grew up a comely man in appearance, and wise in his conduct.   The Landlord took a liking to him, and made him a footman in his house.   He did well in his situation, and every person about the house respected him.

Now the Landlord had a daughter whom people called Berry-eye.   She was exceedingly beautiful, and the Lad fell deeply in love with her.   She also fell in love with him, but she would never acknowledge that she did, because he was only the Hen-wife's son.   She would go out of his way, and hide herself in every bush lest he should see her.   But he had the charm-stone, and with the help of the stone he would be found standing at her side wherever she happened to be.   But she would then call on her father, and he had to go away lest he should be seen.   This often happened, but on a certain day he bad that he should be with her in the house, and in an instant he was there.   As soon as she saw him, she tried to call on her father, but before she had time to utter a word he sprang and embraced her in his arms, and said, "Would that thou and I were in the Green Isle at the Extremity of the Uttermost World, where thy father would not hear thy voice, and my mother would not say that I was her son!" Without knowing how, they were, in the twinkling of an eye, standing in each other's embraces in the Green Isle.

They were there a good time living on the fruit of the trees.   But on a certain day, while they were sitting together on a hillside and looking at the ocean before them, he laid down his head on her lap and slept. While he was sleeping she began to consider how they

could have come to that place, and in the end she supposed that he must have had magic or something
possessing wonderful properties by which he had drawn
them where they were. As soon as this occurred to
her she searched his clothes to see if she could find
anything in them to correspond with her suspicion ;
and having opened his breast, there she found the
stone and the jewel carefully hidden. She looked at
them (and they were beautiful to behold) ; and she
said to herself that it must have been with those things
he drew them yonder. She then took her scissors and
cut away the front of her clothes with them, and left it
under his head. As soon as she got up, she said
" Would that I were once more at my father's house," and
before the words went out of her mouth she was in her
father's house.

When he awoke he looked round to see if he could
behold her, but he beheld her not. He then looked on the
ground and saw the front of her dress where she had left
it under his head. He quickly put his hand on his breast
and found it open, and the stones taken away. He now
knew how the matter stood, and became sorrowful and
downcast, and he would rather that he had never come
to the place, for he had neither means nor plan of getting
out of it.

On a certain day he was wandering beside the shore,
when he noticed a clump of trees near a wood which
was before him. He reached the clump, and saw in it
trees bearing fruit such as he had not seen since he came
to the Island. On some of the trees were as beautiful
apples as he ever saw, and on others were the ugliest.
He was downcast and sick with grief and weariness,
and he thought that he would eat one of the beautiful
apples to see if he would be the better of it. But as
soon as he ate it, his feet began to shake, and his flesh
to melt off his bones. He thought that as death was

inevitably before him, and as he was in great pain, he would eat one of the ugly apples to see if it would hasten the approach of death. But as soon as he ate the ugly apple his flesh ceased to melt away, and his bones to shake, and before he had eaten another of them he was as whole and sound as he ever was. He now saw that if he lost a *jewel* he found a *leech*. He at once began to make creels, and when they were ready he filled them with the apples. Then he put them in a safe place, in the hope that they might yet be of use to him.

On a certain day he saw far out on the ocean a ship making straight for the Island. He put up signals to see if he could draw the attention of the crew towards him, and when she came within hearing distance he began to shout to them. They noticed him, and sent a boat ashore where he was. The boat's crew asked of him what sent him there, or how did he come thither? He answered that the vessel in which he sailed was lost, and that he alone got ashore on the Island. They then asked of him what was he doing on the vessel. He said that he was a physician. "Oh, how pleased we are!" said they. "Our Captain is sick, and given up by the physician. Perhaps thou canst do something for him." He replied, "We shall see what can be done when we reach him."

He put the creels in the boat, and when he reached the ship he left them in a safe place on board of her. He then took one or two of the apples with him in his pocket, and went into the place where the Captain was. He looked at him, and said if he would take what he gave him he would be healed. The Captain answered that he would take anything that would do him good. Then the Physician gave him a bit of one of the beautiful apples, and as soon as he ate it his flesh and skin began to melt away off him. When the crew saw this, they were going to tie the Physician to the mast and scourge him to death with the end of a rope. But he begged them to give him another hour, and said that if he did not heal the Captain in that time they might then bind him and scourge him to death if they pleased. They told him that he should get the time he asked, and even till night. They went away then, and left him alone.

He shut the door on them, and began to cure the Captain with the ugly apples, and ere the end of the hour was come he had him as strong and healthy as he was before he grew ill. When the crew saw this, they were very obedient to the Physician, and knew not what they could do to please him. The Captain asked of him what did he wish them to do for him? He answered that he wanted nothing but that they should land him in the haven which he had first left. They at once put the ship about and made straight for the haven he named. And when they reached it, he took the baskets with him and went ashore.

He left farewell with the Captain and his men, and made straight for the place whence he departed.

He set up as a physician, and began to heal sick people. None of his old acquaintances knew him, but his name went far and near as a good physician who was healing people of every sickness and all sores which afflicted them.

On a certain day word came to him from the Landlord that he was to come in haste to visit his daughter, who was at that time very ill. He went away without delay, and reached the Landlord's house. He entered the room where the daughter was, and having examined her, said that she was suffering under a strange malady. "Thou hast committed theft," said he to her, "and until thou confess it thou canst not be healed." She answered that she was not aware of having ever committed theft.

He said that she must have taken from somebody something that was very valuable to him.  Then she remembered the stones which she took from the Hen-wife's son in the Green Isle, and she told the Physician everything that happened between them.  He asked of her where were the stones which she took from his breast?  She said that they were on the window-ledge.  Instantly he got the stones and put them in his pocket, saying, "Since thou hast told the truth thou canst be healed."  Then he gave her some of the ugly apples, and before next night came she was well and healthy.

The Physician pleased the Landlord so well that nothing in existence would satisfy him but that the former would marry Berry-eye, his daughter.  The Physician agreed to take her, and the marriage-day was appointed.

The Lad did not reveal himself to his mother yet, but on that night he went to her house, and told her that he was going to marry Berry-eye, with the full consent of her father.  "But, mother," said he, "do not let on that I am your son until the marriage is over."  She promised him that, and rejoiced greatly at his arrival.

The wedding-day came at length, and among those preparing the feast none was busier than the Hen-wife.  During the day Berry-eye came in, accompanied by her father and the Physician, and when she noticed that the old woman was first in everything, she went over where she was, and said to her pretty sharply, "Woman, I know not what business you have here.  You had better go out for the present."  The Hen-wife turned on her and said fiercely, "What dost thou say?  I know not where I should have business unless I have it here preparing for my son's wedding."  Berry-eye gave a painful shriek, she sprang to her father and laid hold of his hand.  When she recovered her breath, she said to the Hen-wife, "Is he your son, woman?" "Yes," said the Hen-wife. "Well, if he is, I will not marry him." Sadness now fell on all present, and especially on the Lad. But ere another got an opportunity of speaking, the Hen-wife said, "He is not my son, but the Son of the Knight of the Green Vesture, performing heroic deeds which were famed on earth seven years before he was born, and who fell fighting in the play of swords against the Fierce Earl of the Wood-of-Masts (*Coille-nan-Crann*) by a stroke in the back from the Eldest Son of the Fierce Earl, and I was Nurse with him at that time, and when he was slain, I fled with this Lad and I nursed him and brought him up, and now he is able to avenge his father's death, and to select his chosen sweetheart for wife." When the Lad heard what the Hen-wife said, he took courage and said to her, "Woman, if I am that, I will not marry her." "But may my thousand malisons rest on the women for their loquacity!" said the Landlord.

The Son of the Knight of the Green Vesture had now his jewel and stone of virtues in his bosom, and he gave his word and oath that he would neither return nor stop for the sake of man or thing until he saw a fairer maiden than Berry-eye, and out of that standing he departed. He kept going forward, ascending bens and hills and hillocks, and going through holes and glens and hollows, until he reached an exceedingly fine place. He did not go to the Castle which was there, because he knew not what or who might be before him. But the night was coming, and therefore he went for shelter among the bushes which were behind the Castle. As soon as he reached them, he saw the fairest maiden he ever beheld coming towards him. Her eyes were like the heath-berry, and her bosom whiter than the snow of one night. She passed without noticing him, but he got a sight of her which drove Berry-eye completely out of his memory.

After she had gone out of sight he left the bushes and went away to see if he could meet any one who would tell him who she was. He did not go far when he beheld a very beautiful young damsel having a gold comb in the back of her head, driving cows into a byre. He approached her, and inquired of her who the maiden was whom he saw walking through the bushes behind the castle? She answered that she was Smooth-brow (?), daughter of the King of Tòrr Uaine (the Green Mound), and that she was under great anxiety for the last six weeks. "What is the cause of her anxiety?" "Come into the byre, and I will tell thee that." He went in, and she gave him a drink of milk. Then she said that the cause of Smooth-brow's anxiety was a dream which she had seen almost a year before. "She thought that she was walking through the bushes behind the castle, when she beheld a brave hero coming towards her, his countenance as the sun, and his appearance like that of a lion. His curly hair was (black) as the raven, and whiter than milk was his bosom. Many are seeking the Maiden in marriage, and her father wishes her to marry a certain one of them. But she vowed that she would never marry until she beheld the countenance of the Hero she saw in her sleep. This did not please her father; wherefore he gave her a day and year to select her choice of a sweetheart, and said to her that if she let that time pass without making any choice for herself, she must thereafter take his choice. The time has now run out except four days from to-morrow, and this is causing her so great anxiety that she takes a walk every evening through the bushes to see if she can meet the brave Hero whom she saw in her dream. To-day, in the morning, she almost yielded to her father, but before she actually yielded she thought that she would go for advice to the Sorceress (*Iorasglach-ùrlair*).  She told the Sorceress her dream, and everything else from beginning to end.  The Sorceress said to her, 'Do not lose courage, but run thy race to its end, for the Brave Hero's time has not yet come.'"

Then the Stranger said to the Damsel, "Where can I get an opportunity of speaking to her?"  "To-morrow night watch well the place in which thou sawest her to-night."  He stayed that night in a place which the Damsel provided for him, and next day kept out of everybody's way until evening, the time when he first saw the Maiden.

He then went to the back of the Castle, and was there but a short time when he saw her coming.  As soon as he got a sight of her he went towards her, and stretched out his arms to embrace her.  She looked in his face, and, as if she had always known him, said, "Hast thou come at last?"  She put her arms about his neck, and nestled her head in his bosom.  Then she made known to him all her misery, and told him to go with her, and that she would find him a place in which he might stay that night.  He went with her, and she put him in a secret chamber, where he was to stay until her time had run out.

Next morning she was more cheerful than she was wont to be.  The Sorceress noticed this, and asked her whether she was among the bushes last night?  She replied that she was, and that she found the Brave Hero of her dream.  "Run thy race to its end, that he may take thee with victory," said the Sorceress.

Then the Maiden went to the room where the Young Hero was, and while they were conversing, he heard a loud noise through the house which made him wonder greatly.  He asked her what the noise meant, and said that he must go and see what its cause was.  She answered that word of the approach of a band of pursuers had come to her father, and that a Red-haired, Squint-eyed Cook, who took in hand to turn them back, was making ready to go. "What does the band of pursuers seek?" "They are from the Big Son of the Fierce Earl of the Wood of Masts (*Coille-nan-crann*), and if my father has no man to repel them, I and half the kingdom are his." When the Young Hero heard the name of the Eldest Son of the Fierce Earl mentioned, he trembled on his feet, his eyes kindled in his head, he clenched his fists, and said that he must go and see how the arms became the Cook. "Thou shalt stay here, and show not thyself to thy father until I return." And having said that, he turned out, and took a back road after the Cook.

The Cook had not gone far from the Castle when the Young Hero overtook him. He asked of him where was he going? The Cook answered with great vigour that he was going to drive back a band of pursuers who were coming to the King of the Green Mound (*Tòrr Uaine*) from the Eldest Son of the Fierce Earl of the Wood of Masts (*Coille-nan-crann*), and that when he would drive the pursuers back, Smooth-brow and half the kingdom would be his. "Right enough," said the Young Hero; "but wilt thou lend me thine arms to see how they suit me?" "I will indeed; it is I who will," replied the Cook. He put the arms off, and the Young Hero put them on, and it was he who had a right to them! Then the Cook said, "How didst thou know that I was going away?" "I heard the noise which the point of thy sword made against one of the pots when thou wast going out." "Oh, how pleased I am!" said the Cook.

When they were nearing the place where the meeting was to be held, they saw the pursuers coming. Then the Young Hero said to the Cook, "Thou hadst better put these arms on before they come nearer." The Cook gave a look, and when he saw the Eldest Son of the Fierce Earl and his men approaching, he said, " No, no. Leave them on thee, for they become thee better. Hide me in some place or other." There was a precipice near them, and a large cleft in the face of the rock, and the Young Hero thrust the Cook into the cleft, and said, " Stay thou there until I return."

Then the Son of the Knight of the Green Vesture advanced to meet the Eldest Son of the Fierce Earl. They attacked each other, but with the third stroke of his sword the Son of the Knight of the Green Vesture swept the head off the Eldest Son of the Fierce Earl. He then assailed the men, and having killed them all, he lifted the head of the Earl's Son on the point of his sword, and returned carrying it over his shoulder.

He reached the Cook, and told him to come out of the cleft. The Cook came as he was bidden. He looked first at the Young Hero, and then at the head, and said, " Thou hast a head !" " Yes," replied the Hero. " His eyes are open ! Will he meddle with me ?" " I do not think he will at present." Then they went away together, and when they came near the Castle, the Brave Hero said to the Cook, " Thou hadst better put on these arms now, and take the head in to the King." The Cook put on the arms, and the Hero handed him the head in parting. " We are not going to part in that manner," said the Cook. " Thou shalt go with me to the cooking-place, that thou mayst get something I will give thee. When I am King, thou shalt be my Cook." The Brave Hero went with him, and when they entered the cooking-place the Cook gave him a large bunch of white tow, and said, " Thou shalt keep this to wipe the perspiration off thy face. When I *was* a Cook, the man who gave me a bunch of tow I esteemed a friend." " I also esteem him a friend," said the Brave Hero, and they parted. The Cook took his way with the head to the

King, and the Son of the Knight of the Green Vesture went to Smooth-brow. He found her where he had left her, but he told her nothing further than that the Cook drove back the pursuit.

When the King saw the Cook having the head with him he was very well pleased, and said that he would be as good as his promise to him. But the Cook was in a great hurry to have the marriage completed without delay. The King told him to have patience until they had dined, and said that he would then do everything as he had promised. The table was covered, and they all sat down to dinner. But before it was past, word came from the Second (Middle) Son of the Fierce Earl to drive back the pursuit, otherwise that Smooth-brow (*Caoin-shlios*) and half the kingdom were his.

The King now sent for his men, and asked who would go and drive back the pursuit? The Cook cried out, "Who should drive it back if not I? I drove it back already, and I will drive it back again." "Right enough," said the King. "Do that, and I will be as good as my promise to thee."

Next morning the Cook was making ready to depart, and when he was under full armour he gave a great stroke to the pot and went away. The Brave Hero heard the sound, and said to Smooth-brow that he must go and see what was yonder. "Thou need'st not," said she; "it is only the Cook going to repel another band of pursuers to-day." "I will go and see how the arms become him, but do thou not show thy face to thy father until I return." He then turned out after the Cook.

This day he suffered him to advance a good distance before he overtook him. The Cook's step was getting slower, and his look was oftener behind him the longer the Hero was in coming. At length he saw him afar off, and stood until he overtook him. "Didst thou hear the stroke I gave the pot to-day ?" said the Cook. "Yes, it was that which took me away," replied the Hero. When they were approaching the trysting-place the Cook said, "Thou wouldst do well to put on these arms, for they become thee better." The Hero put on the arms, and when they saw the men coming, the Cook cried, "There they are! there they are! hide me." There was a soft marsh a short distance off, and when they reached it, the Hero thrust the Cook feet foremost in the ground beneath a dripping bank overgrown with heather (*beul-fhothragh-adh*), and told him to stay there until he should return.

Then the Hero met the Second (Middle) Son of the Fierce Earl, and with the second stroke of his sword threw his head off from the shoulders. He next attacked the men, and before he stopped left not a man of them alive. He then seized the head of the Fierce Earl's Second Son by the hair, and carried it with him on his shoulder. He reached the Cook, and called on him to come out from the bank under which he was. The Cook came, and said, "Thou hast a head to-day again! Oh, it grins! Will it meddle with me?" "It will not at present," said the Hero, and they returned the way they came. When they were coming near the Castle, the Brave Hero told the Cook to put on the arms and take the head in to the King. He put on the arms, and when the Hero was going to part with him, he said, "We are not going to part in that manner. Thou shalt go with me to the cooking-place, that thou mayst get something that I will give thee." When they entered, the Cook gave him a dumpy spoon, and said, "Keep that until thou art Cook with me. When I *was* a Cook, I reckoned the man who gave me a dumpy spoon as a friend." "I also reckon him a friend," said the Hero, and they parted.

The Cook took his way in where the King was, and the Son of the Knight of the Green Vesture went where Smooth-brow was.

The King rejoiced greatly when he saw that the Cook drove back the pursuit the second time.  He said that he would be as good as his promise to him.  But nothing would satisfy the Cook but that the marriage should be consummated without any further delay.

The King said to him, " Thou art tired after the hard fight thou hast fought, and we are hungry.  We shall take dinner first, and after that I will be as good as my promise to thee."   But before the dinner was over, word came from the Young Son of the Fierce Earl to go and drive back the pursuers, otherwise that Smooth-brow and half the kingdom would be his.

The King was now seized with great alarm, and he sent once more for his men.  He told them that notice of a pursuit came from the Young Son of the Fierce Earl, and said that he would be as good as his promise to the man who should turn it back.  The Cook sprang up, and having stood before the King's face, said, " Who should turn it back if I would not?  I turned it back twice already, and I will turn it back again."  " Very right," said the King ; " I will do as I promised."

When the Cook got his armour and his arms on, if he gave a stroke to the pots on the two preceding days, he gave them a seven times louder stroke this day.  He then turned away, but the Hero was in no haste to follow him.  He went off at last, but if he did go he was hiding himself until they were nearing the place of meeting.  He then saw the Cook sitting down.  He went forward with a lively step where he was.  " Hast thou come at last?" said the Cook?   " Yes," said the Hero. " It is I who was afraid that thou wouldst not come at all. Put on these arms, for verily they become thee better." " I daresay they will to-day," replied the Brave Hero. The arms were scarcely on him when they beheld the pursuers coming, and a very fierce looking Hero at their head.  The Cook said, " Oh, hide me !  Put me out of their sight!" Near them was a stagnant pond, and he thrust the Cook down to the neck in the pond, and said, "If thou art anyway hard pressed take thy head under water, but if not, stay as thou art."

The Heroes encountered each other, and with one stroke of his sword the Son of the Knight of the Green Vesture threw the sword out of the hand of the Fierce Earl's Young Son. He then took hold of him, and tied his three smalls in one withy band. He left him bound, and faced the men. He made a fierce attack on them, over and under them, and left not a man of them alive to tell the tale of woe. He then lifted the Earl's Son on his shoulder, and reached the Cook with him.

The Cook came ashore, wet and dirty, and covered with the white moss of the marsh. He then went home after the Hero. As soon as they came in sight of the Castle, the Hero said to him, "Thou hadst better put on the arms now, and take this man in to the King." When he put the arms on he looked at the man, and when he saw him moving, he cried, "Oh, he is alive! he will meddle with me!" "He is alive," said the Hero, "but he can do thee no harm at present. Take him, as he is, to the King." The Cook said, "The pursuit is all over now. Thou mayst be getting ready. When I get the King's daughter I will have thee as my Head-Cook." Then they parted.

The Cook went in with the man to the King, and when the King saw the appearance of the man he praised the Cook for his heroism, and said to him, "I will fulfil my promise to thee. But loose the man, that he may be with us at dinner."

The Cook went where the man was, and tried to unbind him. But for every knot he would untie, seven knots would go on the withe. At length he said that he could not unbind the man. "Dear me!" (*Oov, oov!*) said the King, "who could not unbind the man he has

bound ?"   " It was not he who bound me," said the man.
" He could not bind me, and he cannot unbind me.   But
he who bound me can unbind me."   "Who is that ?"
said the King.   " The Son of the Knight of the Green
Vesture, performing heroic deeds which were famed on
earth seven years before he was born, and who has fought
against our men for the last three days, and who was
sleeping in thy Castle at night—it is he who bound me,
and it is he who can unbind me."

Word was sent for the Hero, and he came in.   The
King looked at him, and when he saw his heroic appearance he went on his knees before him.   When he had
stood up, he told him to unbind the man who was bound.
The Hero caught the knot of the withe with one hand,
and with it lifted the man from the earth.   He then let
go his hold, and instantly the withe-band sprang off the
man.   As soon as the man got on his feet he turned to
the King, and said, " Were it not for the loquacity of the
Hen-wife, and the advice of the Sorceress to Smooth-
brow, there were not in the kingdom of Green Mound
as many men as should turn back the pursuit of the
Young Son of the Fierce Earl, or keep Smooth-brow
from him.   But *he* is worthier of her than I am."

Then Smooth-brow came in, and said to her father,
" To-day is the last day of the time thou gavest me to
select my choice of a sweetheart.   Here is my choice
now, and fulfil to me thy promise."   "With all my
heart," said the King, "and all that I have thou shalt
have with him."

The Cook went back to his cooking, the marriage was
consummated, and no one in the kingdom saw so comely
a pair as Smooth-brow and the Son of the Knight of the
Green Vesture.   They made a feast and rejoicing, and if
they have not ceased eating and drinking they are at it
still.

## SGÉUL AIR MAC FEAR AN EARRAIDH UAINE RI GAISGE,

### A BHA AINMEIL AIR THALAMH SEACHD BLIADHNA MU 'N D' RUGADH E.

BHA ann roimhe so Uachdaran fearainn aig an robh àite briadha, agus pailteas spréidh agus èunlaith. 'Na àm bha meas cho mòr aig uachdarain cosmhail ris air an èunlaith 'us gu 'n robh iad a' gleidheadh mu 'n timchioll boirionnach tùrail ris an abradh daoine Cailleach-chearc. Bha aig an Uachdaran so mar an ceudna Cailleach-chearc a bha ro thùrail agus aig an robh balachan òg bòidheach ris an abradh i a mac agus a theireadh rithe 'mhàthair.

Bha 'm balachan a' fàs a suas 'n a ghille briadha 'us coltas air gu 'm bitheadh e 'n a dhuine foghainteach. Ach cha-n fhaigheadh e guth 'am fad agus 'am fagus ach Mac Cailleach-nan-cearc. Gidheadh cha robh sin a' cur smuairein 's am bith air.

Bha 'Chailleach gu math dheth fo 'n Uachdaran le tigh agus trì mairt, agus gach ni eile a dh' fhéumadh i. An uair a dh' fhàs am balachan suas 'n a ghille bhitheadh e falbh leis na mairt agus 'g am buachaileachd fad an là. Air là àraidh shaodaich e iad ni 'b fhaid' air falbh na b' àbhaist da gu àite fàr an robh ionaltradh anabarrach math. Cho luath 's a thug an crodh a dh' ionnsaidh an fheòir ràinig e tolman bòidheach fàr am bitheadh e 'n am fradharc, agus shuidh e sìos air. Thug e roinn mhòr de 'n là 'n sin, a' gabhail toileachadh as a' h-uile ni a bha e 'faicinn. Mu dheireadh chunnaic e 'dìreadh na glaice 'bha fodha 'dh' ionnsaidh an àite 's an robh e 'n a shuidhe gruagach òg agus deirgead an ròis 'n a gruaidh, 's a falt òr-bhuidhe 'n a chamagan bòidheach a sìos thar a dà ghualainn.

Ràinig i 'n t-àite fàr an robh e 'n a shuidhe, agus air dhi fàilt an là a chur air thubhairt i ris gu 'n robh e aonarach a' buachaileachd nan trì mairt. Fhreagair e gu h-ealamh i, 'us thubhairt e nach robh e aonarach a nis 'us i féin air tighinn còmhla ris. An sin dh' fheòraich i dhe an reiceadh e té de 'n chrodh? Thubhairt e rithe nach faodadh e, a chionn gu 'm bitheadh a mhàthair a' trod ris. " Ù, cha bhi, ma gheibh thu a fiach air son a mhairt." " Agus gu dé 'bheir thu dhomh oirre?" " Bheir clach bhuadhach." " Gu dé na buadhan a th' air a' chloich?" " Cha-n 'eil buadh a dh' fhéumas tu airson do chuirp no airson do choluinn nach faigh thu cho fad 's a ghleidheas tu i, agus cha-n 'eil àit' anns an òrduich thu thu féin agus na 's math leat a bhi, anns nach bi sibh air ball." " Leig faicinn domh de 'n chloich." Shìn a' ghruagach dha a' chlach, agus bha i bòidheach ri amharc oirre. Rug e oirre, agus smaointich e gu 'n cuireadh e déuchainn oirre mu 'n tugadh e 'm mart air a son. Bha 'm pathadh air aig an àm, agus smaointich e gu 'm bu mhath deoch a Fuaran-na-cloiche-deirge aig cùl tigh' a mhàthar. Cha bu luaith' a thàinig an smaoint 'n a inntinn na bha e 'n a shuidhe taobh an tobair. Dh' òl e deoch, agus thill e air ais air a' cheart dòigh air an d' thàinig e. Thug e 'n sin am mart airson na cloiche, agus bha e làn thoilichte leis a' mhalairt a rinn e.

An sin dh' fhalbh Gruagach nan gruaidhean ròs-dhearg leis a' mhart a cheannaich i, agus thill esan dachaidh leis an dà mhart eile 'm béul na h-oidhche. An uair a chunnaic a mhàthair nach robh aige ach an dithis dh' fheòraich i dhe, C' àit' an robh an treas té? Dh' innis e dhi gu 'n do reic e i. Thubhairt i ris gu dé 'fhuair e air a son? Thubhairt e gu 'n d' fhuair e clach oirre. Dar chunnaic a mhàthair a' chlach, 'us nach b' urrainn i 'm féum a bh' innt' a thuigsinn chaidh i air boile, agus throd i ris gu fuathasach. Dh' éisd e ris gach facal a thubhairt i gu ciùin, 'us cha d' thug e guth na h-aghaidh. An uair a thraoigh a feirg dh' iarr i air an dà mhart a chur a 's tigh, 'us gu 'n rachadh am bleoghainn. Rinn e sin, agus bha uibhir bainne aig an dithis an oidhche sin 'us a bh' aig an triuir roimhe sin.

Anns a' mhadainn an déigh dha 'bhraiceas fhaotainn agus an crodh a bhi air am bleoghainn, dh' iarr a mhàthair air an saodachadh do 'n àite 's an robh iad an là roimhe. Dh' fhalbh

e leò, agus dh' fhàg e iad anns a cheart ionad. Cho luath 's a
ràinig iad thug an crodh a dh' ionnsaidh an ionaltraidh, agus
shuidh esan air a' cheart tolman air an robh e 'n là a chaidh
seachad.

Mu 'n àm a chunnaic e 'Ghruagach an toiseach chunnaic
è i an là so 'rìs a' dìreadh na glaice 'bha fodha. Ràinig i 'n
t-àite fàr an robh e 'n a shuidhe, agus dh' fheòraich i dh' e an
reiceadh e té eile de 'n chrodh? Thubhairt e nach reiceadh,
a chionn gu 'n d' fhuair e trod uamhasach o 'mhàthair air an
oidhche 'chaidh seachad airson na té a reic e cheana. "Ù,
ma gheibh thu a fiach air a son cha bhi i trod riut." "Gu dé,
mata, 'bheir thu dhomh oirre?" "Bheir mi dhuit léug slàn-
uchaidh oirre." "Gu dé na créuchdan a ni i slàn?" "Créuchd
air bith air d' fheòil no air do chraicionn, tinneas colainn no
inntinn, leighisidh i 'n uair a shuathas tu riut i." Bha créuchd
air òrdaig cois' a' ghille, agus dh' iarr e air a' Ghruagach an
léug a leigeil fhaicinn da. Fhuair e 'n léug, agus cho luath 's
a shuaith e i r' a òrdaig bha i leighiste. An sin thug e dhi am
mart, agus bha e làn thoilichte leis a' mhalairt a rinn e.

An uair a thàinig am feasgar chaidh e dhachaidh leis an aon
mhart. Choinnich a mhàthair e 'tighinn, agus dh' fheòraich
i dh' e gu dé 'fhuair e air a' mhart a reic e? Thubhairt e gu
'n d' fhuair e léug oirre. An uair a chual i so, ma ghabh i
'n cuthach air an là roimhe ghabh i seachd cuthaich an là so.
Shìobhaltaich i mu dheireadh, agus dh' iarr i air an t-aon mhart
a bh' ann a chur a 's tigh, 'us gu 'n rachadh a bleoghainn. Rinn
e sin, agus bha uibhir aice de bhainne 's a bh' aig an trì
roimhe.

Anns a' mhaduinn, an déigh do 'n bhò 'bhi air a bleoghainn,
dh' iarr a mhàthair air a' ghille a saodachadh do 'n àite 's an
robh i 'n dé. Dh' fhalbh e leatha, agus an uair a ràinig e 'n
t-àite shuidh e sìos mar b' àbhaist da air an tolman. Thàinig
a' Ghruagach fàr an robh e, agus dh' fheòraich i dh' e an
reiceadh e an t-aon mhart a bh' aige? "Oh, cha-n fhaod mi,
oir fhuair mi trod uamhasach airson na té mu dheireadh a
reic mi." "Ù! cha-n fhaigh thu trod, ma gheibh thu 'fiach
air a' mhart." "'Us dé, mata, a bheir thu dhomh oirre?"
"Bheir mi dhuit lìonan èunaich oirre." "Gu dé na h-eòin

air am beir an lìonan, no ciamar 'tha è ri 'chur?"    "Cha-n
eil agad ach a sgaoileadh air bharraibh nam preas 'us fhàgail
an sin fad na h-oidhche, agus dar thig a' mhaduinn bithidh
e làn de gach seòrs' èun a chunnaic no 'chual thu riamh,
agus bithidh dà èun déug ann nach fac agus nach cual thu
riamh an leithid."    Thug e 'm mart airson an lìn.    Dh' fhalbh
ise leis a' mhart, agus thill esan dachaidh leis an lìon.

An uair a chunnaic a mhàthair gu 'n d' thàinig e dhachaidh
gun mhart idir aige, cha b' urrainn i facal a ràdh, ach bha
gruaim na dunaidh oirre ris.    Bha esan ro dhuilich gu 'n do
chuir e a leithid de mhì-thlachd oirre, ach bha misneach aige
gu 'm bitheadh i toilichte 'n uair a chitheadh i na bhitheadh
aige de eòin anns an lìon air an ath mhaduinn.

Cho luath 's a dh' éirich e 'n ath-latha chaidh e a dh' fhaicinn
an lìn a chuir e air an oidhche roimhe, agus a leithid de
shealladh air eòin cha-n fhac e gu sin.    Dh' fhalbh e dhachaidh
leò, agus an uair a chunnaic a mhàthair na bh' aige dhiù dh'
fheòraich i dh' e, C' àit' an d' fhuair e iad?    Thubhairt e gu 'n
do ghlac e iad anns an lìon.    " 'Us am faigh thu tuillidh leis?"
"Gheibh mi an uibhir so a' h-uil' uair a chuireas mi e."    Bha
i 'n so ni 'bu toilichte, 'us cha robh iad riamh cho mhath dheth
air bainne nam mart 's a bha iad air sithinn nan èun.

Dh' fhàs an Gille suas 'n a dhuine dreachail 'n a choltas agus
glic 'n a ghiùlan.    Ghabh an t-Uachdaran spéis de, agus rinn
e gille-bùird dh' e 'n a thigh féin.    Rinn e gu math 'n a àite,
agus bha meas aig a' h-uile duine mu thimchioll an tighe air.

'Nis bha nighean aig an Uachdaran ris an abradh iad Dearc-
shùil.    Bha i anabarrach bòidheach, agus ghabh an Gille gaol
mòr oirre.    Ghabh ise mar an ceudna gaol airsan, ach cha-n
aidicheadh i gu bràth gu 'n do ghabh a chionn nach robh ann
ach mac Cailleach-nan-cearc.    Dh' fhalbhadh i as an rathad
air, agus rachadh i 'm falach anns gach preas air eagal gu 'm
faiceadh e i.    Ach bha 'chlach-bhuadhach aige-san, agus le
cuideachadh na cloiche bhitheadh e na sheasamh r' a taobh
c' àit' air bith 's am bitheadh i.    Ach ghlaodhadh ise 'n sin air
a h-athair, agus dh' fhéumadh esan falbh air eagal gu 'n
rachadh 'fhaicinn.    Thachair so gu minic, ach air là àraidh
dh' òrduich e gu 'm bitheadh e leatha anns an tigh, agus air

ball bha e ann. Cho luath 's a chunnaic i è thug i ionnsaidh air glaodhaich r' a h-athair, ach mu 'n d' fhuair i facal a ràdh léum e, agus rug e oirre eadar a dhà laimh, agus thubhairt e rithe, "O, nach robh mi féin agus thu féin anns an Eilean Uaine an Iomail an Domhain-Toir fàr nach cluinneadh d' athair do ghuth, agus nach abradh mo mhàthair gu 'm bu mhise a mac!" Gun fhios cia mar, bha iad 'am priobadh na sùla 'n an seasadh 'an glacaibh a chéile 's an Eilean Uaine.

Bha iad ùine mhath an sin a' tighinn beò air meas nan craobh. Ach air là àraidh 'us iad 'n an suidhe còmhla air taobh cnuic, agus ag amharc air a' chuan m' an coinneamh leig esan a cheann sìos 'n a h-uchd agus chaidil e. Am feadh a bha e 'na chadal thòisich i air smaointeachadh cia mar a b' urrainn iad teachd do 'n àit' ud, agus bhreithnich i mu dheireadh gu 'm féumadh gu 'n robh aige drùidheachd no ni-eiginn air an robh buaidhean iongantach leis an do thairainn e iad fàr an robh iad. Cho luath 's a thàinig so fainear dhi, rannsaich i 'aodach, feuch am faigheadh i ni 's am bith annt' a fhreagradh d' a h-amharus; agus air dhi a bhroilleach fhos-gladh fhuair i a chlach agus an léug air am falach ann gu cùramach. Choimhead i orra, agus bha iad ro bhòidheach r' am faicinn, agus thubhairt i rithe féin gu 'm féumadh gu 'm b' ann leis na nithe sin a tharrainn e 'n sud iad. Ghabh i 'n sin a siosar, agus ghearr i béul a h-aodaich air falbh leis, agus dh' fhàg i fo 'cheann e. Cho luath 's a fhuair i 'n a seasamh thubhairt i, "O, nach robh mis' aig tigh m' athar aon uair eile;" agus mu 'n deachaidh na briathran as a béul bha i 'n tigh a h-athar.

An uair a dhùisg esan choimhead e mu 'n cuairt feuch am faiceadh e i, ach cha-n fhac. Sheall e 'n sin air an làr, agus chunnaic e béul a h-aodaich fàr an d' fhag i fo 'cheann e. Ghrad chuir è a làmh air a bhroilleach, agus fhuair e fosgailt e agus na clachan air an toirt air falbh. Dh' aithnich e 'n so mar bha 'chùis, agus dh' fhàs e gu dubhach, tròm-inntinneach, agus b' fhearr leis nach d' thàinig e riamh do 'n àite, oir cha robh dòigh no seòl aig air faotainn as.

Air là àraidh bha e siubhal ri taobh a' chladaich an uair a thug e 'n aire do dhoire 'm fagus do choille a bh' air thoiseach air.  Ràinig e 'n doire, agus chunnaic e ann craobhan air an robh measan nach fac e 'n leithid o 'n thàinig e do 'n Eilean.  Air cuid de na craobhan bha ùbhlan cho briadha 's a chunnaic e riamh, agus air cuid eile dhiù na h-ùbhlan 'bu ghràind' a chunnaic e riamh.  Bha e féin gu tròm-inntinneach, tinn, le mulad 'us le sgìos, agus smaointich e gu 'n itheadh e aon de na h-ùbhlan briadha feuch am b' fheàird se e.  Ach cho luath 's a dh' ith e 'n t-ubhal chaidh e air chrith air a chasaibh, agus thòisich fheòil air sruthadh bharr a chnàmh.  Smaointich e, a chionn gu 'n robh 'm bàs roimhe cò dhiù agus gu 'n robh e 'n cràdh mòr, gu 'n itheadh e aon de na h-ùbhlaibh gràuda feuch an greasadh i 'm bàs g' a ionnsaidh.  Ach cho luath 's a dh' ith e 'n t-ubhal gràuda, stad fheòil a shruthadh, 'us a chnàmhan a chrith, agus mu 'n robh aon eile dhiù itht' aige bha e cho slan fhallain 's a bha e riamh.  Chunnaic è 'n so ma chaill e léug gu 'n d' fhuair è léigh.  Thòisich è air ball air deanamh chliabh, agus an uair a bha iad réidh lìon è iad leis na h-ùbhlan.  Chuir è 'n sin iad 'an àite tèarainte 'an dòchas gu 'm bitheadh iad chum féum dha uair eiginn fathast.

Air là àraidh chunnaic e fada mach air a chuan lòng a' deanamh dìreach air an Eilean.  Chuir e suas comharan feuch an tàirneadh e aire 'n Sgioba g' a ionnsaidh, agus an uair a thàinig i 'n astar cluinntinn thòisich e air glaodhaich riù.  Thug iad an aire dha, agus chuir iad bàta air tir fàr an robh e.  Dh' fheòraich Sgiob' a' bhàta dhe gu dé 'chuir a' sud è, no cia mar thàinig e ann?  Fhreagair e gu 'n deachaidh an Soitheach air an robh e a chall, agus gu 'n d' fhuair esan 'n a aonar gu tìr air an Eilean.  Dh' fheòraich iad an sin d' e gu dé 'bha e a' deanamh air an t-Soitheach?  Thubhairt e gu 'n robh e 'n a Léigh oirre.  "Oh nach sinn a tha toilichte," ars' iadsan.  "Tha 'n Sgiobair againn gu tinn, agus air a thabhairt a suas leis an Leigh.  Theagamh gu 'n urrainn thusa ni-eiginn a dheanamh air a shon?"  Fhreagair e, "Chì sinn gu dé 'ghabhas deanamh an uair a ruigeas sinn e."

Chuir e na cléibh anns a' bhàta, agus an uair a ràinig e 'n long dh' fhàg e iad an àite sàbhailt air bòrd oirre.  Thug e 'n sin aon no dha de na h-ùbhlan leis 'n a phòca, agus chaidh e 's tigh do 'n àite fàr an robh an Sgiobair.  Choimhead

e air, agus thubhairt e ris na 'n gabhadh e 'n rud a bheireadh
esan da gu 'm bitheadh e air a leigheas. Fhreagair an Sgiobair
gu 'n gabhadh e ni 's am bith a dheanadh féum dha. An sin
thug an Léigh dha pìos de aon de na h-ùbhlan briadha, agus
cho luath 's a dh' ith se e thòisich 'fheòil agus a chraicionn air
sruthadh dheth. An uair a chunnaic an Sgioba so, bha iad a'
dol a cheangal an Léigh ris a chrann, agus g' a sgiùrsadh gu
bàs le ceann buill. Ach ghuidh e orra uair eil' a thabhairt
da, agus thubhairt e mur leighiseadh e 'n Sgiobair anns an tìm
sin gu 'm faodadh iad a cheangal agus a sgiùrsadh gu bàs an
sin na 'n toilicheadh iad. Thubhairt iad ris gu 'm faigheadh
e 'n ùin' a dh' iarr e, agus eadhon gu h-oidhche. Dh' fhalbh
iad an sin, agus dh' fhàg iad leis féin e.

Dhùin esan an dorus orra, agus thòisich e air an Sgiobair a
leigheas leis na h-ùbhlan grànda, agus mu 'n d' thàinig ceann
na h-uaire bha e cho làidir fhallain aige 's a bha e mu 'n d' fhàs
e gu tinn. An uair a chunnaic an Sgioba so bha iad ro ùmhal
do 'n Léigh agus cha robh fhios aca gu dé 'b' urrainn iad a
dheanamh g' a thoileachadh. Dh' fheòraich an Sgiobair dh'
e ciod a b' àill leis gu 'n deanamh iad air a shon? Fhreagair
e nach robh e 'g iarraidh ni orra, ach gu 'n cuireadh iad air
tìr e anns a' chaladh a dh' fhàg e 'n toiseach. Air ball chuir
iad niu 'n cuairt an lòng, agus rinn iad dìreach air a chaladh
a dh' ainmich e. Agus dar ràinig iad e thug esan leis na cleibh
agus chaidh e air tìr.

Dh' fhàg e beannachd aig an Sgiobair agus a dhaoine, agus
rinn e direach air an ait' o 'n d' fhalbh e.

Chuir e suas mar Léigh, agus thòisich e air daoine tinn a
leigheas. Cha d' aithnich gin d' a sheann luchd-eolais e, ach
chaidh ainm am fad agus am fagus mar Lighiche math a
bha slanuchadh dhaoine bho gach tinneas agus créuchd a bha
cur orra.

Air là àraidh thàinig fios g' a ionnsaidh o Uachdaran an
fhearainn gu 'n robh e ri tighinn le cabhaig a dh' fhaicinn a
nighinn 'us i bhi ro thinn aig an àm sin. Dh' fhalbh e gun dàil,
agus ràinig e tigh an Uachdarain. Chaidh e 's tigh do 'n
t-seòmar fàr an robh an nighean, agus air dha a ceasnachadh
thubhairt e gu 'm b' e tinneas ionganntach a bh' oirre.

"Rinn thu mèirle," ars' è rithe, "agus gus an aidich thu i cha ghabh thu leigheas." Fhreagair i nach b' fhiosrach i gu 'n d' rinn i mèirle riamh. Thubhairt esan gu 'm b' éiginn gu 'n d' thug i o chuid-eiginn ni-eiginn a bha ro luachmhor dha. An sin chuimhnich i air na clachan a thug i o Mhac Cailleach-nan-cearc anns an Eilean Uaine, agus dh' innis i do 'n Lighiche gach ni a thachair eatarra. Dh' fheòraich e dhi c' àit' an robh na clachan a thug i a 'bhroilleach? Thubhairt i gu 'n robh iad air bac na h-uinneig. Ghrad fhuair e na clachan, agus chuir e iad 'n a phòc ag radh. "O 'n dh' innis thu 'n fhìrinn gabhaidh tu leigheas." An sin thug e dhi cuid de na h-ùbhlan grànda, agus mu 'n d' thàinig an ath oidhche bha i slàn fallain.

Chòrd an Lighiche cho math ris an Uachdaran 'us nach dèanadh nì air bith an gnothuch leis ach gu 'm pòsadh è Dearc-shùil, a nighean. Dh' aontaich an Lighich' a gabhail, agus chaidh latha na bainnse chuir a mach.

Cha do leig an Gille e féin ris d' a mhàthair fathast, ach air an oidhche sin chaidh e 'dh' ionnsaidh an tighe aice, agus dh' innis e dhi gu 'n robh e 'dol a phòsadh Dearc-shùil le làn-thoil a h-athar. "Ach, a bhean," ars' e, "na gabhaibh-s' oirbh gur mi bhur mac gus am bì am pòsadh seachad." Gheall i sin da, agus rinn i gàirdeachas mòr r' a theachd.

Thàinig là na bainnse mu dheireadh, agus 'am measg luchd-ullachaidh na cuirme cha robh aon a bu trainge na Cailleach-nan-cearc. Air feadh an là thàinig Dearc-shùil a' s tigh le h-athair, agus leis an Leigh, agus an uair a thug i 'n aire gu 'm be 'Chailleach a bha 'n toiseach gach gnothuich, chaidh i null far an robh i, agus thubhairt i rithe gu math sgaiteach, "A Bhean, cha-n 'eil fhios agam gu dé 'n gnothuch a th' agaibh-s' an so." "Is fearr dhuibh-se dol a mach an dràst." Thionndaidh a' Chailleach rithe, agus thubhairt i gu fiadhaich, "Gu dé 'tha thu 'g ràdh? Cha-n 'eil fhios agam c' àit' am bitheadh gnothuch agam, mur bitheadh e agam an so a' deasachadh airson banais mo mhic!" Thug Dearc-shùil glaodh goint' aiste, léum i 'dh' ionnsaidh a h-athar, agus rug i air laimh air. Cho luath 's a fhuair i a h-anail thubhairt i ri Cailleach-nan-cearc, "An e bhur mac-s' a th' ann, a bhean?" "Is e," thubhairt a'

Chailleach. "Mata, ma 's e cha phòs mis' e." An so thuit sprochd air gach duine 'bha làthair, agus gu sonraicht' air a' ghille. Ach mu 'n d' fhuair aon eile cothrom bruidhne thubhairt a' Chailleach, "Cha-n e mo mhac-se 'th' ann, ach Mac Fear an Earraidh Uaine ri gaisge a bha ainmeil air thalamh seachd bliadhna mu 'n d' rugadh e, agus a thuit a' cath le iomairt lann ri Iarla Borb Choille-nan-crann le buile-cùil fo mhac mòr an Iarla Bhuirb, agus is mis' a bu bhan-altrum dha 's an uair sin, agus an déigh dha bhi air a mharbhadh theich mi leis a' ghille so, agus dh' altrum agus dh' àraich mi e, agus a nis tha e comasach air bàs athar a dhioladh agus a roghainn leannain a thaghadh mar mhnaoi !" An uair a chual an Gille ciod a thubhairt a' Chailleach-chearc, ghabh e misneach agus thubhairt e rithe, "Ma 's e sin a th' annam, a bhean, cha phòs mise ise." "Ach mo mhìle mallachd air na mnathan le 'n luathaire-theanga !" ars' an t-Uachdaran.

Bha nis a léug agus a chlach-bhuadhach féin aig Mac Fear an Earraidh Uaine 'n a bhroilleach, agus thug e bòid agus briathar nach tilleadh e 'us nach stadadh e airson ni no neach ach gus am faiceadh e òigh 'bu mhaisiche na Dearc-shùil. Agus as an t-seasamh sin shiubhail e. Chum e air aghaidh a' dìreadh bheann 'us mheall 'us thulaichean, agus a dol troimh thuill, 'us ghlinn, 'us ghlacaibh, gus an d' ràinig è àit' anab-arrach briadha. Cha deachaidh e 'dh' ionnsaidh a' Chaisteil a bha 'n sin, a chionn nach robh fhios aige ciod no cò a dh' fhaodadh a bhi air thoiseach air. Ach bha 'n oidhch' a' tighinn, agus uime sin chaidh e 'ghabhail fasgaidh anns na pris a bha cùl a' Chaisteil. Cho luath 's a ràinig e iad chun-naic e 'n aon òigh 'bu mhaisich' a chunnaic e riamh a' tighinn 'n a choinneamh. Bha 'dà shùil mar dhearcag-an-fhraoich, 'us a cneas ni 'bu ghile na sneachd na h-aon oidhche. Chaidh i seachad gun aire a thabhairt da, ach fhuair esan sealladh oirre-s' a chuir Dearc-shùil gu h-iomlan as a chuimhne.

An déigh dhi dol as an t-sealladh dh' fhàg e na pris agus dh' fhalbh e feuch an coinnicheadh e duine 's am bith a dh' innseadh dha cò i. Cha deachaidh' e fada dar chunnaic e Gruagach àluinn òg agus cìr òir 'an cùl a cinn a' cur cruidh a 's tigh do bhàthaich. Ràinig è i, agus dh' fheòraich e dhi cò i an òigh a chunnaic e dol tromh na pris cùl a' Chaisteil? Fhreagair i gu 'm bi sin Caoin-shlios, Nighean Righ an Tòirr Uaine, agus gu 'n robh i 'an iomagain mhòir o cheann shé seachdainnean. "Ciod è fàth a h-iomagain?" "Thig a 's tigh do 'n bhàthaich, agus innsidh mi sin duit." Chaidh e 's tigh, agus thug i dha deoch bhainne. An sin thubhairt i ris gu 'm b' e fàth iomagain Chaoin-shlios aisling a chunnaic i o cheann béul ri bliadhna. Air leatha gu 'n robh i 'coiseachd tromh na pris cùl a' Chaisteil an uair a chunnaic i tréun-laoch òg a' tighinn 'n a coinneamh, a ghnùis mar a' ghrian, agus a choltas mar choltas leòmhain. Bha 'fhalt bachlach mar ·am fitheach, 'us bu ghile na 'n gruth a chneas. Tha mòran ag iarraidh na h-òigh r' a pòsadh, agus tha 'h-athair toileach gu 'm pòs i aon àraidh dhiù. Ach thug i bòid nach pòsadh i 'm feasd gus am faiceadh i gnùis a' ghaisgich a chunnaic i 'n a cadal. Cha do chòrd so r' a h-athair; uime sin thug e dhi là 's bliadhn' a thaghadh a roghainn leannain, agus thubhairt e rithe na 'n leigeadh i 'n ùine sin seachad gun roghainn a dheanamh air a son féin gu 'm féumadh i a roghainn-san a ghabhail 'n a dhéigh sin. Tha 'n ùine nis air ruith a mach gu inbhe cheithir làithean o 'm màireach, agus tha so a' cur iomagain cho mòr oirre 'us gu 'm bheil i gach oidhch' a' gabhail sràid tromh na pris feuch an coinnich i 'n tréun-laoch a chunnaic i 'n a h-aisling. An diugh 's a mhaduinn cha mhòr nach do ghéill i d' a h-athair, ach mu 'n do ghéill i smaointich i gu 'n rachadh i fàr an robh an Iorasglach-ùrlair airson combairle. Dh' innis i do 'n Iorasglaich an aisling, agus gach ni eile o thoiseach gu deireadh. Thubhairt an Iorasglach rithe, "Na caill do mhisneach, ach ruith do réis g' a ceann, oir cha d' thàinig àm an tréun-laoich fathast."

An sin thubhairt an Coigreach ris a Ghruagaich, "C'àit' am faigh mise bruidhinn rithe?" "Thoir an aire mhath air an ath oidhche do 'n àit' anns am fac thu i 'nochd." Dh' fhuirich e an oidhche sin 'an àit' a fhuair a' Ghruagach dha, agus air an ath latha ghleidh è a rathad gach duine gus an d' thàinig dorchadh nan tràth, an t-àm air am fac e 'n Òigh air tùs.

Chaidh e 'n sin gu cùl a' Chaisteil, 'us cha robh e ach goirid gus am fac e i 'tighinn. An uair a fhuair e sealladh dhi chaidh

e 'n a coinneamh, agus sgaoil e mach a dhà laimh g' an cur
mu 'n cuairt oirre. Thug ise sùil 'n a aodann, agus mar gu 'm
b' aithne dhi riamh e ghlaodh i, "An d' thàinig thu mu
dheireadh?" Chuir i a dà laimh mu 'n cuairt air 'amhaich
agus neadaich i 'ceann 'n a bhroilleach. An sin dh' innis i dha
a truaighe uile, agus thubhairt i ris falbh leatha-se 's gu 'm
faigheadh i dha àit' anns am fuireachadh e 'n oidhche sin.
Chaidh e leatha, 's chuir i è ann an seòmar uaigneach fàr an
robh è ri fuireachd gus am bitheadh a h-ùine-se mach.

Air an ath mhaduinn bha ise ni 'bu shunndaiche na b'
àbhaist di. Thug an Iorasglach an aire dha so, agus dh'
fheòraich i dhi an robh i 's na pris an raoir? Fhreagair i gu
'n robh, 'us gu 'n d' fhuair i tréun-laoch a h-aislinge. "Ruith do
réis g' a ceann, 'us gu' m faigh e do ghlacadh le buaidh," ars'
an Iorasglach.

An sin dh' fhalbh an òigh do 'n t-seòmar fàr an robh 'n laoch
òg, agus am feadh 'bha iad a' còmhradh chual esan air feadh
an tighe straighlich a chuir mòran iongantais air. Dh'
fheòraich è dhi gu dé 'bu chiall do 'n straighlich ud, agus
thubhairt e gu 'm féumadh e dol a dh' fhaicinn ciod a b'
aobhar di. Fhreagair ise gu 'n d' thàinig fios Tòir g' a h-athair,
agus gu 'n robh Còcaire Claon Ruadh a ghabh fo 's laimh
an Tòir a thilleadh a' deanamh deas airson falbh. "Gu
dé tha 'n Tòir ag iarraidh?" ars' esan. "Tha 'n Tòir
o Mhac Mòr Iarla Bhuirb Choille-nan-Crann, 'us mur bi
duin' aig m' athair a thilleas an Tòir is leis mise 's leth na
righeachd." An uair a chual an laoch òg ainm Mhic Mhòir an
Iarla Bhuirb air ainmeachadh chrith e air a chasan, las a dhà
shùil 'n a cheann, dhaingeinnich e 'dhùirn, agus thubhairt e gu
'm féumadh e dol a dh' fhaicinn cia mar 'bha na h-airm a'
freagairt do 'n Chòcaire. "Fanaidh tusa 'n so, agus cha nochd
thu d' aghaidh do d' athair gus an till mise." Agus air dha sin
a ràdh thionn e mach, agus ghabh e rathad cùil an déigh a'
Chòcaire.

Cha deachaidh an Còcaire fad air falbh o 'n Chaisteal an
uair a rug an Laoch Òg air. Dh' fhaighnich e dh' e, C' àit' an
robh e dol? Fhreagair an Còcaire le spraic mhòir gu 'n robh
e dol a thilleadh Tòir a bha 'tighinn gu Righ an Tòirr Uaine

o Mhac Mòr Iarla Bhuirb Choille-nan-Crann, 'us dar thilleadh è 'n Tòir gu 'm bu leis Caoin-shlios agus leth na righeachd. "Gle cheart," ars' an Laoch Òg, "ach an toir thu dhomhsa na h-airm feuch cia mar thig iad domh?" "Bheir gu dearbh; is mi a bheir," fhreagair an Còcaire. Chuir e dheth na h-airm, agus chuir an Laoch Òg iad air, agus b' ann àige féin a bha 'n gnothuch riù. An sin thubhairt an Còcaire, "Cia mar bha fhios agad gu 'n robh mise 'falbh?" "Dh' fhairich mi 'n straighlich a rinn barr a' chlaidheimh agad air fear de na coireachan an uair a bha thu 'dol a mach." "Oh, nach mi tha toilicht," ars' an Còcaire.

An uair a bha iad a' dlùthachadh ris an àite fàr an robh a' choinneamh ri bhi chunnaic iad an Tòir a' tighinn. An sin thuirt an Laoch Òg ris a' Chòcaire, "Is fearr dhuit na h-airm so a chur ort mu 'n tig iad ni 's faigse." Thug an Còcaire sùil, agus dar chunnaic e Mac Mòr an Iarla Bhuirb 's a dhaoine 'dlùthachadh ris thubhairt e, "Cha chuir, cha chuir. Fàg ort iad, oir is ann duit féin 'is fearr a thig iad. Cuir mis 'am falach an àit' air chor-eiginn." Bha stac creige dlùth dhoibh, agus còs mòr an aodann na creige, agus sparr an Laoch Òg an Còcaire 's tigh 's a chòs, agus thubhairt e ris, "Fan an sin gus an till mise."

An sin chaidh Mac Fear an Earraidh Uain' an coinneamh Mac Mòr an Iarla Bhuirb. 'Bhuail iad air a chéile, ach leis an treas buile d' a chlaidheamh sgath Mac Fear an Earraidh Uain' an ceann deth Mhac Mòr an Iarla Bhuirb. An sin thug e 'n aghaidh air na daoine, agus air dha cur as doibh uile thog e ceann Mac an Iarla air barr a chlaidheamh, agus thill e air ais agus e aige thar a ghualainn.

Ràinig e 'n Còcaire, agus ghlaodh e ris tighinn a mach as a' chòs. Thàinig an Còcaire mar dh' iarradh air. Sheall e 'n toiseach air an Laoch Òg, agus an sin air a' cheann, agus thubhairt e, "Tha ceann agad." "Tha," fhreagair an Laoch. "Tha 'shùilean fosgailte: am bi e rium?" "Cha chreid mi gu 'm bi an dràst." Dh' fhalbh iad an sin còmhla, agus an uair a thàinig iad am fagus do 'n Chaisteal thubhairt an Tréun Laoch ris a' Chòcaire, "Is fearr dhuit féin na h-airm so a chur ort a nis, agus an ceann a thabhairt a 's tigh a dh' ionnsaidh

an Righ." Chuir an Còcair' air na h-airm, agus shìn an Laoch
an ceann da 's an dealachadh. "Cha-n 'eil sinn dol a
dhealachadh mar sin," ars' an Còcaire. "Theid thu leamsa
gu àite na còcaireachd, 'us gu 'm faigh thu ni-eiginn a bheir
mise dhuit. An uair a bhitheas mise 'm Righ is tus' a bhitheas
'ad Chòcair' agam." Dh' fhalbh an Tréun Laoch leis, agus
dar chaidh iad a 's tigh do dh' àite na Còcaireachd shìn an
Còcaire dha bad mòr de dh' ascairt ghil, agus thubhairt e,
"Gleidhidh tu sin airson an fhalluis a shuadhadh bharr d'
aodainn. An uair a *bha* mis' am Chòcaire bu charaid leam
am fear a bheireadh dhomh bad ascairt." "Is caraid leams'
e cuideachd," ars' an Tréun Laoch, agus dhealaich iad. Ghabh
an Còcaire 'dh' ionnsaidh an Righ leis a' cheann, agus chaidh
Mac Fear an Earraidh Uaine gu Caoin-shlios. Fhuair e i fàr
an d' fhàg e i, ach cha d' innis e dhi ni 's am bith ni 'b' fhaide
na gu 'n do thill an Còcaire 'n Tòir.

An uair a chunnaic an Righ an Còcaire agus an ceann aige,
bha e ro thoilichte, agus thubhairt e ris gu 'm bitheadh esan
cho math r' a ghealladh dha. Ach bha 'n Còcair' ann an
cabhaig mhòir airson gu 'm bitheadh am pòsadh air a dheanamh
gun dàil. Dh' iarr an Righ air foighidinn a bhi aige gus am
faigheadh iad an dinneir, agus thubhairt e gu 'm bitheadh gach
ni air a dheanamh an sin mar gheall esan. Chaidh am bòrd
a chur 'an uidhim, agus shuidh iad uile sìos aig an dinneir.
Ach mu 'n robh i seachad thàinig fios o Mhac Meadhonach an
Iarla Bhuirb an Tòir a thilleadh air neò gu 'm bu leisan
Caoin-shlios agus leth na righeachd.

Chuir an Righ fios an so air a dhaoine, agus dh' fheòraich
e dhiù, Cò rachadh a thilleadh na Tòire? Ghlaodh an Còcaire,
"Cò thilleadh i mur tillinn·s' i? Thill mi chean' i, 'us tillidh
mi rithist i." "Glé cheart," ars' an Righ. "Dean sin, agus
bithidh mise cho math 's mo ghealladh dhuit."

Air an ath mhaduinn bha 'n Còcaire 'deanamh deas airson
falbh, agus dar bha e fo làn armachd thug e stràilleadh mòr
do 'n choire agus thionn e mach. Dh' fhairich an Tréun Laoch
an fhuaim, agus thubhairt e ri Caoin-shlios gu 'm féumadh e
dol a dh' fhaicinn gu dé bha 'n sud. "Cha ruig thu leas,"
ars' ise ; "cha-n 'eil ann ach an Còcaire 'dol a thilleadh Tòir

eile 'n diugh." "Theid mi 'choimhead cia mar tha na h-airm a' tighinn da, ach na seall thusa do ghnùis do d' athair gus an till mise." Thionn e 'n sin a mach an déigh a' Chòcaire.

An là so leig e leis dol astar math air aghaidh mu 'n d' rug e air. Bha céum a' Chòcair' a fàs ni 'bu mhoille, agus bha 'shùil ni 'bu trice 'n a dhéigh mar a b' fhaide 'bha 'n Laoch gun tighinn. Mu dheireadh chunnaic e 'm fad as e, agus sheas e gus an d' rug e air. "An cual thu 'm buille 'thug mi air a' choire 'n diugh?" ars' an Còcaire. "Chuala; b' e sin a thug air falbh mi," fhreagair an Laoch. An uair a bha iad a' dlùthachadh ri àit' a' choinnimh thubhairt an Còcaire, "Is fearr dhuit féin na h-airm so a chur ort; oir is ann duit 'is fearr a thig iad." Chuir an Laoch air na h-airm, agus an uair a chunnaic iad na daoine 'tighinn ghlaodh an Còcaire ris, "Sin iad, Sin iad! Cuir mise 'm falach." Bha lòn bog goirid as, agus an uair a ràinig iad e stob an Laoch an Còcaire 'n còmhail a chas fo bhéul-fhothraghadh, agus thubhairt e ris fuireachd an sin gus an tilleadh esan.

An sin chaidh an Laoch an coinneamh Mac Meadhonach an Iarla Bhuirb, agus leis an dara buille d' a chlaidheamh thilg e 'n ceann deth o 'n ghualainn. Thug e rithist aghaidh air na daoine, agus cha d' fhàg e aon beò dhiù mu 'n do sguir e. Rug e 'n sin air fhalt air ceann Mac Meadhonach an Iarla Bhuirb, agus thug e leis e air a ghualainn. Ràinig e 'n Còcaire, agus ghlaodh e ris tighinn a mach o 'n bhruaich fo 'n robh e. Thàinig an Còcaire, agus thubhairt e, "Tha ceann agad an diugh a rithist! Oh tha draoin air! am bi e rium?" "Cha bhi 'n drast," ars' an Laoch, agus thill iad air an ais an rathad a thàinig iad. An uair a bha iad a' tighinn am fagus do 'n Chaisteal thubhairt an Tréun-Laoch ris a' Chòcaire na h-airm a chur air, agus an ceann a thabhairt a 's tigh a dh' ionnsaidh an Righ. Chuir e air na h-airm, agus an uair a bha 'n Laoch a' dol a dhealachadh ris thubhairt e, "Cha-n 'eil sinn 'dol a dhealachadh mar sin. Theid thu leamsa gu àite na còcaireachd 'us gu 'm faigh thu ni-eiginn a bheir mise dhuit." An uair a chaidh iad a 's tigh, thug an Còcaire dha cutag spàine, agus thubhairt e, "Gleidh sin gus am bi thu 'ad Chòcair' agamsa. An uair a *bha* mise 'm Chòcaire bu charaid

leam am fear a bheireadh cutag spàine dhomh." " Is caraid,
leams' e cuideachd," ars' an Laoch, agus dhealaich iad.

Ghabh an Còcaire 's tigh leis a' cheann fàr an robh 'n Righ,
agus chaidh Mac Fear an Earraidh Uaine fàr an robh Caoin-
shlios.

Rinn an Righ gàirdeachas mòr an uair a chunnaic e gu 'n
do thill an Còcaire 'n Tòir an dara h-uair. Thubhairt e ris gu
'm bitheadh esan cho math 's a ghealladh dha. Ach cha 'n
fhoghnadh ni air bith leis a' Chòcaire ach gu 'm bitheadh am
pòsadh air a dheanamh gun tuilidh dàlach. Thubhairt an Righ
ris, " Tha thu féin sgìth an déigh a chath chruaidh a chuir thu,
agus tha sinne acrach. Gabhaidh sinn an dinneir an toiseach,
agus an déigh sin bithidh mise cho math 's mo ghealladh dhuit."
Ach mu 'n robh 'n dinneir seachad thàinig fios o Mhac Òg an
Iarla Bhuirb 'dol a thilleadh na Tòire, air neò gu 'm bu leisan
Caoin-shlios agus leth na righeachd.

Chaidh an Righ an so 'am fiamh mhòir, agus chuir e fios aon
uair eil' air a dhaoine. Dh' innis e dhoibh gu 'n d' thàinig
fios Tòir o Mhac Òg an Iarla Bhuirb, 'us thubhairt e gu 'm
bitheadh esan cho math 's a ghealladh do 'n duin' a thilleadh
i. Léum an Còcaire, agus sheas e suas ri broilleach an Righ,
agus thubhairt e, " Cò' thilleadh i mur tillinn-s' i ? Thill mi
chean' i dà uair, agus tillidh mi rithist i." " Ro cheart," ars' an
Righ. " Ni mise mar gheall mi."

An uair a fhuair an Còcaire 'n a airm 's na éideadh air an
treas maduinn, ma thug e stràilleadh air na coireachan an dà là
roimhe thug e stràilleadh seachd uairean ni 'bu mhò orra 'n là
so. Thionn e 'n sin air falbh, ach cha robh cabhag 's am bith
air an Laoch airson a leantainn. Dh' fhalbh e mu dheireadh,
ach ma dh' fhalbh bha e 'g a fhalach féin gus an robh iad a'
dlùthachadh ri àite na coinnimh. Chunnaic e 'n sin an Còcair'
a' suidhe sìos. Chaidh è air aghaidh le céum sgairteil fàr an
robh e. " An d' thàinig thu mu dheireadh ?" ars' an Còcaire.
"Thàinig," ars' an Laoch. " 'S ann orms' a 'bha 'n t-eagal nach
tigeadh tu idir. Cuir ort na h-airm so, oir gu dearbh is ann
duit 'is fearr a thig iad." " Tha mi creidsinn gur h-ann an
diugh," fhreagair an Tréun Laoch. Cha robh na h-airm ach
gann air an uair a chunnaic iad an Tòir a' tighinn agus Laoch

ro bhorb air an ceann. Ghlaodh an Còcaire, "O! cuir mis, am falach! Cuir as am fradharc mi!" Bha bréun-lochan laimh riù, agus stob e 'n Còcaire gu ruig an amhaich anns an lochan, agus thubhairt e ris, "Ma thig éiginn 's am bith ort thoir do cheann fodha, 'us mur tig fan mar th' agad."

Chaidh na Laoich an coinneamh a cheile, 'us le aon bhuile d' a chlaidheamh thilg Mac Fear an Earraidh Uaine 'n lann a laimh Mhic Òig an Iarla Bhuirb. Rug e 'n sin air féin, 'us cheangail e 'thrì caoil ann an aon ghad. Dh' fhàg e ceangailt e, 'us thug e aghaidh air na daoine. Thug e ruathar fòpa 's tharta, 'us cha d' fhàg e beò dhiù fear a dh' innseadh sgéul na truaighe. Thog e 'n sin Mac an Iarla air a ghualainn, agus ràinig e 'n Còcaire leis.

Thàinig an Còcair' air tìr, fliuch, salach, agus còmhdaichte le fionn-chòinnich na dìge. Dh' fhalbh e 'n sin dachaidh an déigh an Laoich. Cho luath sa thàinig iad 'am fradharc a' Chaisteil thubhairt an Laoch ris, "Is fearr dhuit na h-airm a chur ort a nis, agus an duine so a thabhairt a 's tigh a dh' ionnsaidh an Righ." An uair a chuir e air na h-airm thug e sùil air an duine, agus dar chunnaic se e 'carachadh ghlaodh e, "O tha e beò! Bithidh e rium!" "Tha e beò," ars' an Laoch, "ach cha-n urrainn e dad a dheanamh ort an dràst. Thoir thus' e mar tha e 'dh' ionnsaidh an Righ." Thubhairt an Còcaire, "Tha 'n Tòir uile seachad a nis. Faodaidh tusa 'bhi deanamh deas. An uair a gheibh mise nighean an Righ bithidh tus' a' d' Ard-chòcair' agamsa." An sin dhealaich iad.

Chaidh an Còcaire 's tigh leis an duine 'dh' ionnsaidh an Righ, agus an uair a chunnaic an Righ coltas an duine mhol e 'n Còcair' airson a ghaisge agus thubhairt e ris, "Coimhlionaidh mise mo ghealladh dhuit. Ach fuasgail an duine chum gu 'm bi e maille ruinn aig an dinneir."

Chaidh an Còcaire fàr an robh 'n duine, agus dh' fhéuch e r' a fhuasgladh. Ach an àite gach snaim a dh' fhuasgladh e rachadh seachd snaimeannan eil' air a' ghad. Mu dheireadh thubhairt e nach b' urrainn e 'n duine fhuasgladh. "Ùbh, Ùbh!" ars' an Righ. "Cò nach fuasgladh an duin' a cheangail e?" "Cha-n esan," ars' an duin', "a cheangail mi.

Cha b' urrainn e mo cheangal, agus cha-n urrainn e m' fhuasgladh. Ach am fear a cheangail mise fuasglaidh e mi." "Cò e sin?" ars' an Righ. "Tha Mac Fear an Earraidh Uain' ri gaisge a bha ainmeil air thalamh seachd bliadhna mu 'n d' rugadh e, agus a bha cogadh ris na daoin' againne bho cheann thrì laithean agus a bha cadal anns a' Chaisteal agadsa 's an oidhche. Is esan a cheangail mise, agus 's è 'is urrainn m' fhuasgladh."

Chaidh fios air an Laoch, agus thàinig e 's tigh. Sheall an Righ air, agus an uair a chunnaic e a thréun-choltas chaidh e air a dhà ghlùn da. An uair a dh' éirich e, dh' iarr e air an duine 'bha ceangailte fhuasgladh. Rug an Laoch air snaim a' ghoid le aon laimh, agus thog e 'n duine leis o 'n talamh. Leig e as d'a ghreim an sin, agus air ball léum an gad bharr an duine. Cho luath 's a fhuair an duin' air a chasan thionn-daidh e ris an Righ, agus thubhairt e, "Mur bhi luathaire theanga na Caillich-chearc, agus comhairle na h-Iorasglaich-ùrlair do Chaoin-shlios cha robh 'an Righeachd an Tòirr Uaine na thilleadh air a h-ais Tòir Mhic Óig an Iarla Bhuirb, no chumadh Caoin-shlios uaithe. Ach is e féin a's airidh oirre na mise."

An sin thàinig Caoin-shlios a 's tigh, 'us thubhairt i r' a h-athair, "Is è 'n diugh an là mu dheireadh do 'n ùine 'thug thu dhomh a thaghadh mo roghainn leannain. So a nis mo roghainn, agus coimhlion do ghealladh dhomh." "Le m' uile chrithe," ars' an Righ, "agus gach ni a th' agamsa bithidh agadsa còmhla ris."

Thill an Còcaire 'dh' ionnsaidh a chòcaireachd, chaidh am pòsadh a dheanamh, agus cha-n fhaca neach a bha 's an Righeachd càraid a b' eireachdala na Caoin-shlios agus Mac Fear an Earraidh Uaine. Rinn iad cuirm agus greadhnachas, agus mur do sguir iad a dh' itheadh agus a dh' òl tha iad ris fathast.

# NOTES.

*(All the references to MacInnes are to the second volume of this series : " Folk and Hero Tales," collected, edited, and translated by the Rev. D. MacInnes, with Notes by the Editor and Alfred Nutt. 1890.)*

## TALE I.

PAGE I. This tale, like all the other tales in the volume, was taken from Alexander Cameron, whose name has been already mentioned.   But it is known also to John Rankin, a man of eighty years of age, residing in Duror, and to Archibald McArthur, a Braes man living at Fort Augustus. It is one of three tales which are linked together by some incidents in the history of the Grey Dog.   It tells how the Grey Dog was found by Finn in the Castle, and given to the Big Young Hero of the Ship.   The second tale of the group Cameron has forgotten, and I have not met with any other person who knows it.   Cameron just remembers that the tale told how the Big Young Hero, when alone at the seaside, was surprised by a Lochlan chief and his crew, and compelled to ransom his own life by giving the dog to his assailants.   The Chief, on his return home to his own country, presented the dog to the King.   But the animal having afterwards gone mad through grief for the loss of his first master, was allowed to run wild in the Great Glen of Lochlan.   The third tale of the group, the second in this collection, tells how Finn went to Lochlan, and, with the help of Bran's chain, recovered the Grey Dog in the Great Glen already mentioned.—J. McD.

P. I. "At the back of the wind."   This is said to be the position of Finn sitting on the sheltered side of the knoll. He is there quite unconscious of the wind while it blows behind the knoll or sweeps over his head, but no sooner does it begin to shake the branches of the trees or agitate the surface of the water *in front* of him, than he becomes aware of its presence.   The place where it commences to produce these effects, he regards as the point whence it starts on its course.　And as he is behind that point, he is also at the back of the wind which enters there on its race, and which afterwards speeds away from him.—J. McD.

P. 1. *Macan*, the diminutive of *Mac*, is literally a little son. Here, however, it is, according to the reciter of the tale, the eldest son, while in his minority, of a person of consequence. Such a youth as this would be the very first to mock the Big Young Hero had he failed in his efforts to pull his boat beyond the reach of the tide, and had he left it to be tossed about by the surf.—J. McD.

P. 1. *Broilleach* (breast) is the part of the gunwale of a boat between the stem and the shoulders.—J. McD.

P. 1. *Fair' oidhche* is sometimes a night-watch, and at other times night-watching in the sense of remaining awake at night. As the object of the Young Hero is to impress on Finn, not how long he took in coming, but the trials through which he passed on the way, the word must be here translated night-watching.—J. McD.

P. 2. *Sìthide* or *sìthde*, is the genitive of *sìthid*, a female fairy, *sìochair* being the male.　In other bespelling runs similar to that in the text, we have, instead of *sìthide*, *mnatha sìthe*, *i.e.*, of a fairy woman.　See Campbell's *West Highland Tales*, vol. ii, pp. 410 and 420; MacInnes's *Tales*, p. 347, etc. But as both terms convey the same meaning, and either one of them preserves the alliteration and rhythm of the run well enough, it is hard to choose between them.—J. McD.

P. 2. *Tràth* signifies a season of the day, as in *tràth-maidne* (morning-tide), *tràth-mheadhon-là* (noontide), *tràth-feasgair* (eventide).　The word denotes also the season of the flow or ebb of the tide.　It is taken here in the former sense; and *naoi tràth* is translated nine days because the phrase, as I take it, denotes nine recurrences of the same season of the day.　It is true, however, that it might, with equal justice, have been translated nine tides, *i.e.*, flowings and ebbings of the sea.　In the MacInnes similar tale (No. II) we have, instead of *tràth*, *seòlmara*, a word free of all ambiguity, and whose sole meaning is tide.—J. McD.

P. 3. Here the marvellous acuteness of the listener's sense of hearing is demonstrated by his being able to perceive the most distant sound.　The same thing is done in other tales by proving that the hero can detect near but inconceivably faint sounds. Heimdall, the porter of Asgard, for example, "had an ear so fine that he could hear the very grass grow in the meadows, and the wool on the back of the sheep." See Bohn's edition of Mallet's *Northern Antiquities*, p. 95.— J. McD.

P. 3. *Domhan Tor.*—*Domhan* is now the universe, but in folk-tales it is simply the world. In this collection, however, mention is made of two distinct worlds,[1] *Domhan* and *Domhan Tor*. See House of *Blàr-buidhe*, where it is said that Finn's Wooden-crower (*Gura-fiodha*) could be heard not only in the seven divisions of the World (*Domhan*), but also at the extremity of the *Domhan Tor*. The former is simply the natural world, or rather as much of it as was known to the composers of these tales, and therefore only a part of the western seaboard of the Old World. The latter (*Domhan Tor*) is the world of enchantment and of all sorts of wonders, a world the story-tellers place far away beyond the western ocean.

In some versions of Highland tales *Domhan Tor* becomes *Domhan Tòir*, or the world of pursuit. It is so called, we are told, because it is the world men are still in pursuit of, *i.e.*, the Undiscovered World. One step more and America is reached ; and the step has been taken by some. But the change of the word to *Domhan Tòir* may have been made through ignorance by the successors of the old professional story-tellers. *Tor* having become obsolete, and its meaning having been forgotten, the former may have substituted for it the more familiar form, *tòir*, and given the latter whatever currency it possesses. Whether this explanation be accepted or not, it must be admitted that *tor* is the form still generally used in this connection.

Assuming *tor* to be the proper form of the word, what does it mean ? It is difficult to answer this question categorically. But as *o* and *u* are interchangeable before *r*, as in *corr* which becomes *curr* in this very tale, *tor* may now be represented by *tur*, a word generally used as an adverb, but sometimes also, though rarely, as an adjective. As an

---

[1] In Northern mythology, also, a plurality of worlds appears. For example, Hela, the goddess of the Underworld, is said to have "the government of nine distinct worlds into which she distributes those who are sent to her", and Heimdall's trumpet "could be heard through all the worlds". (Mallet, pp. 96 and 95).— J. McD.

adjective it has a privative meaning, and denotes that the object indicated by the word it qualifies is accompanied by no other object. Taken in this sense, Domhan Tor is the world which has with it no other world in the far distant west, or, in other words, the sole world there. Hence it is commonly translated the Uttermost World.

Beyond the remotest bounds of this mythical world is a still more wonderful mythical island, which is called "An t-Eilean Uaine an iomall an *Domhain Toir*", or the Green Island at the extremity of the Uttermost World. This, *in popular opinion*, is a floating, shifting island which lies beneath the waves of the sea, and which is therefore sometimes identified with Land Underwaves. Occasionally it rises to the surface, and has been seen (at least we are told so) in almost every latitude of the west coast, from Cape Wrath in Scotland to Cape Clear in Ireland. The 12th century Giraldus Cambrensis mentions an island which suddenly appeared off the west coast of Ireland, and Martin in his *Description of the Western Isles*, about 1665, mentions an island which was discovered thirty leagues south-west of Islay, and which was, according to his authorities, visited by an English captain. But the former was too substantial to be the airy isle of pure imagination, and the latter, though called the Green Isle by Martin, could scarcely have been the Green Isle of legendary lore. Had it been the latter, and had anything at all, even a bit of stone or handful of earth, been taken from the natural world and thrown upon it, the enchantment should have been instantly dissolved, and the island itself, like another Delos, should have been fastened down, then and there, to the bottom of the sea !

Somewhat different from the foregoing description of the Green Isle is what may be gathered concerning it from the folk and hero tales. True, that even in the latter it enjoys a perpetual summer, that its fields are ever green, and that its trees are always laden with fruit. But then its surface is diversified by mountain and valley, lake and stream ; and its coast is at least partly surrounded by a wall of rocks in whose lofty face the griffin (*grìbhinneach*) builds her nest and rears her offspring. Indeed, to the eye it bears the closest resemblance to the real world. Its surface presents the same outward appearance, and so also do its products and even its inhabitants. But this resemblance is in appearance only. A closer examination proves that there is an essential difference between the two worlds, and that this difference is constituted by magic. All the products of the Green Isle possess magical properties, and its inhabitants are all adepts in the art of magic. For example, the water taken from its "mystic spring" restores to life and health ; and its apples either cure, or kill, or transform those who eat them. See " Brown Bear" in vol. i, and " Conall Gulbain" in vol. iii of Campbell's *West Highland Tales*, " The Son of the Knight of the Green Vesture" in this collection, and the third version of the " Three Soldiers" in vol. i of *W. H. Tales.*

The Green Isle is generally regarded as the Paradise of the early Gael, just as Avalon is that of the ancient Briton. It may be so, and no doubt it can be proved to be so from other Celtic tales. But in all Highland folk and hero tales known to me, it is the living, and not the dead, who visit it. They go to it and return from it under the influence of magic[1] (*druidh- eachd*), or spells[1] (*geisean*), or by means of charm-stones[1] (*clachan buadha*), or by the assistance of some real creature like the eagle[2] (*iolair*), or fabulous creature like the griffin[3] (*grìbh- inneach*). But when Finn and the Feinn, the principal actors in these tales, finally depart, they go, not to the Green Isle, but to some vast cavern in a rock, such as the Smith's Rock in Skye, or into a mound such as Tomnahurich near Inverness. There they rest in a profound enchanted sleep, until some one having the necessary strength and courage shall enter the cavern and sound Finn's whistle three times. See "The Smith's Rock" in this collection, and "The Man in the Tuft of Wool", by the late Rev. Dr. Maclachlan, in vol. ii of the *History of the Highlands*, edited by John S. Keltie. See also *Leabhar na Fèinne*, p. 198, where Ossian is represented as having gone, not to *Tìr na h-Oige*, but into a rock where he stayed with his mother many centuries before he returned to the world.—J. McD.

P. 4. In the similar MacInnes tale (No. II) the land is Lochlan, and the man in the boat is a king of that country. But here the land is distinct from Lochlan, and the Big Young Hero has Finn for his friend, and the Lochlan people for his foes. See the first of the foregoing notes.—J. McD.

P. 8. Here Bran's dam is the bitch found in the giant's castle. But in Campbell's *W. H. Tales*, vol. iii, p. 350, he is the son of *Buidheag* (Booyag), whose owner was Black Arcan, the

---

[1] Cf. "Son of the Knight of the Green Vesture".
[2] " Brown Bear", in Campbell's *W. H. Tales*, and perhaps in the " Kingdom of the Green Mountains", No. V of the MacInnes *Tales.*
[3] In a tale known as *Mac an Tuathanaich a thàinig a Raineach* (The Farmer's Son who came from Ranoch).

slayer of Cumhal.   And in some Irish tales he is Finn's own
cousin, being the son of Tuireann, the aunt of Finn.—J. McD.

## TALE II.

P. 17.   This tale was told to me by Alexander Cameron, who,
more than forty years ago, got it and Tales I, IV, VI, VII
from Donald McPhie, who, at the time of relating the tales,
was upwards of ninety years old.   This tale is still pretty
widely known.   Among those who have frequently heard it
recited may be mentioned Archibald and James Cameron,
Duror.—J. McD.

Kennedy knew a tale somewhat similar to this.   He gives an
epitome of it in his "argument", quoted by J. F. Campbell,
p. 153 of *Leabhar na Fèinne.*

Finn there appears to have been bespelled, as in Tale II of
this collection, to go alone to Lochlan on a visit to the King.
On arriving there, he found that the King's object in sending
for him was, not to entertain him hospitably, but "to torment
him a few days, and then kill him".   When the Norsemen
were going to lay hands on him, he drew his sword and killed
eighty of them.   His sword then broke, and he was made
prisoner, and bound hand and foot by his enemies.   After
being subjected to great extremes of heat and cold, under the
roast-drippings inside the house by day, and under the rain
drops from the eaves outside the house by night, he was left
to choose between death by the sword, and the risk of passing
through a Glen in the kingdom, which was haunted by "evil
spirits and wild beasts".   He chose the latter, and went away,
armed with nothing but his broken sword.   He entered the
Glen at one end, and after passing through "great dangers",
arrived at the other.   Here he saw a "wild dog" coming, with
open mouth, towards him.   At first he knew not what to do,
but he remembered at last that his stepmother gave him a
magic "belt" called *Con-taod* (Dog-bridle), telling him to take
good care of it, and assuring him that he would find it useful
some day.   He took the belt out of his pocket and shook it
before the Dog.   The Dog immediately became tame, and
approached him in a fawning manner.   He then put the belt
on the animal and led him away with him.   This Dog,
according to Kennedy's next "argument", was "Sceòlainn", and
Sceòlainn was not, as in other tales, the sister, but the dam of
Bran.   Be that as it may, Finn travelled with the beast through
the Glen until he arrived at the house of a Smith who lived

there, and who mended the hero's broken sword. Here, also, he fell in with Gràine, a beautiful maiden who was kidnapped by the Smith. The latter he killed, and he and Gràine returned to Ireland.—J. McD.

P. 17. Finn must not take with him to Lochlan "a dog or a man, a calf or a child, a weapon or an adversary but himself." A person who goes on a journey quite alone is said to go "without a dog or a man" (*gun chù, gun duine*). One who has neither means nor family to depend on for future support is said to have "neither calf nor child in the world" (*gun laogh, gun leanabh anns an t-saoghal*). One who is "without weapon or adversary but himself" is one who can do his foe little harm. Finn, then, is to have no friendly companion with him on the journey to Lochlan, to make no provision for his support in that country, and to take with him no instrument or follower to hurt its king or its people. See also "Fair Gruagach" in Campbell's *W. H. Tales*, vol. ii, p. 411.—J. McD.

P. 18. Finn "could not touch the Big Lad with a stick." In other words, Finn, though a fast traveller, could not get near enough to touch with a stick in his outstretched hand the Big Lad who went before him.—J. McD.

P. 21. The "squint-eyed, red-haired man", according to the narrator of the tale, was Oscar, son of Ossian, and grandson of Finn. Among the Clanna Baoisgne he stood next to Finn in point of heroism, and his only match in the Fein was Goll, the head of the Clanna Mòirne.—J. McD.

## TALE III.

P. 27. Cameron got this tale from his grandfather, an old soldier who died in Ardnamurchan about forty-four years ago, and from Donald McPhie, whose name has already been mentioned. The tale is well known; I heard it told in my boyhood. Several versions of it were collected by Campbell, though none of them was ever published by him. See *W. H. Tales*, vol. iii, p. 147, footnote. A fragment of it appears in the "Bent Grey Lad" in the MacInnes *Tales* (No. II). And I have no doubt there are some old men still in Argyleshire who can recite the tale, or who, in their earlier years, heard it told by others. For Irish similars, see Nutt's note on the "Bent Grey Lad" in the MacInnes *Tales*, p. 443.—J. McD.

P. 27. *Gille nan Cochla-craicinn* is put down as I heard it pronounced, but it should be *Gille nan Cochulla-craicinn.* A still better form would be *Gille nan Cochuill-chraicinn.* The Gaelic title is here translated "The Lad of the Skin-coverings", but in Campbell's *W. H. Tales*, "The Lad of the Skinny Husks". Skinny Husks, however, now signify skins which transform the persons encased in them into the same kind of animals as those to which they properly belong. But as the skins mentioned here were used simply as clothing, and as they seem to have had no transforming effect on the wearer, it is better to translate it, as in the text, "The Lad of the Skin-coverings."—J. McD.

P. 27. Green Insh. *Innis* (Insh or Inch) has a variety of meanings, but of these one of the most common is island. If this be the signification of the word here, it follows that *Innis Uaine* is the same as *Eilean Uaine*, and, therefore, also as the Green Isle at the Extremity of the Uttermost World, or the Celtic Hesperides. But if Finn could travel over "bens and glens and heights" from the time he left his own dwelling until he arrived at Green Insh, the latter can scarcely be regarded as an island. Insh, then, may signify a field in a hollow near water.—J. McD.

P. 28. The Big Lad's reward is virtually the same as that of the "Bent Grey Lad" at p. 35 of the MacInnes *Tales*, and as that of the "Goodherd" in the "Slim Swarthy Lad" at p. 299 of vol. i of the *W. H. Tales.*—J. McD.

P. 28. Conan was a brother of Goll and of Garry, and therefore belonged to the Clann Mòirne tribe. For his character, or rather one phase of it, see the MacInnes *Tales*, p. 443.—J. McD.

P. 29. He "put a balk on his foot". A person going to lift a heavy burden places it first on some rest, such as a bank of earth, in order that he may afterwards raise it with greater ease on to his back. But the Big Lad made a rest of his bent left knee, to which he first drew his burden, and from which he then threw or swung it by a joint effort of hands and left shoulder over the latter.—J. McD.

P. 29. Here Conan is the Big Lad's guide, but in the MacInnes *Tales* Finn himself is that of the "Bent Grey Lad". —J. McD.

P. 30. The Cup, in this tale, is four-sided (*ceathrarach*), and in the "Bent Grey Lad" quadrangular (*ceithir-chearnach*). It has, therefore, the same shape in both tales. Here it is a wishing-cup, for no sooner does the Big Lad think of a certain drink than the magical vessel is full to the brim. It is called a cup of virtues ; and it is no doubt the same as Finn's cup of healing. The Norsemen coveted it, and made frequent attempts to get it into their possession. One of these attempts is the subject of the poems on pages 59 and 60 of *Leabhar na Féinne.* A frightful-looking Hag, sent from Lochlan, forced her way into the sanctuary or place of safety (*tèarmunn*) where it was kept, and, in spite of the strong guard over it, snatched it from its place and escaped. Finn, with two of his swiftest followers, pursued her from Bear (Béura) in the S.W. of Ireland to Eassaroy (Easruadh), near Ballyshannon, in the north. Here he overtook her, transfixed her with his spear, and recovered his lost cup.

Another attempt, or another version of the foregoing one, forms the subject of a tale called the "Muileartach", contributed by the Rev. J. G. Campbell to the *Scottish Celtic Review*, to be reprinted in vol. iv of this series. There, Finn's cup, which is of clay, and not of gold, as in the generality of Gaelic tales, is called the "Cup of Victory" (*Còrn-Buadhach*), because it made the Féinn who drank from it always victorious. The Muileartach, a Hag who was nurse of Manus, King of Lochlan, came to Finn's dwelling and drove in the well-secured door with a kick of her foot. She then entered the house, went to the chest of jewels (*ciste nan sèud*), and having snatched the Cup from it, departed. Oscar pursued and overtook her at the Hill of Howth. He seized her first by the foot and next by the grey hair which streamed out behind her. But she turned upon him, and with a touch of her left hand crushed as many of his bones as lay under her palm, adding as she did so, " If you have strength to go home, tell Finn that I have the Cup of Victory." She then resumed her journey, and when she arrived in Lochlan she handed the cup to Manus, her foster-son. Manus mustered his men immediately, and went to fight Finn. Both met at Dun Kincorry, where all the followers of Manus were slain, and the Cup of Victory was recovered.

This latter stealing of Finn's Cup may be that which is presupposed in the Cup incident in the "Lad of the Skin Coverings". But if so, the two tales differ widely in their account of the manner in which it was afterwards recovered See further, Nutt's note at p. 444 of the MacInnes *Tales.*
—J. McD.

P. 30. The travelling run. The first part of this run, which makes the hero outstrip the Swift March Wind, occurs frequently in Gaelic tales. See "Young King of Easaidh Ruadh", at p. 4 of vol. i, "Fair Gruagach", p. 415 of vol. ii, and "Conall Gulban", p. 207 of vol. iii of *W. H. Tales ;* see also the Rev. D. Campbell's tale in vol. i of this series.—J. McD.

P. 31. The palace of the King of Lochlan was defended by seven guards. The palace was surrounded by seven walls, one within the other; and a body of men were stationed as guards at the gate of every wall. Through each of these the Big Lad had passed before he arrived at the palace.—J. McD.

P. 32. Green Lakelet (*Lochan Uaine*). A small pond overgrown with grass is so called. It may also be added that a castle moat, either with stagnant water, or with water covered with grass, is called a Green Ditch (*Dìg Uaine*). The leafy marsh (*boga duilich*) is the soft-bottomed margin of the lake with the leaves of water-plants floating on the surface.— J. McD.

P. 33. Ben Aidan is the Hill of Howth.—J. McD.

P. 33. Leathern garter (*èill ioscaide*) is, literally, the leather thong of his hough. In other words, it is the long narrow strip of undressed leather which formed one of the Big Lad's garters. —J. McD.

P. 34. The Smith of the White Glen. *Geal,* translated here white, signifies also bright. For example, *Geal-ach,* the Gaelic for moon, is the bright or shining one. Hence Gobhainn a' Ghlinne Ghil may be rendered The Smith of the White Glen. Smiths, mythical or mythological, often appear in West Highland tales. There are, for instance, Lonn Mac Liomhain, the ugly, one-eyed Smith who forged the weapons of the leaders of the Féinn, and his brother, the Ocean Smith (Gobhainn nan Cuan), the husband of the Muileartach. (See the "Song of the Smithy", p. 65, and "A Mhuileartach", p. 67 of *Leabhar na Féinne.*) These two were undoubtedly Norse. But the Smith of this tale, which is so highly mythological, was, in my opinion, the Celtic Vulcan. His smithy was in the glen, and the light from the flaming forge may be the imaginary cause of its being called the White Glen.—J. McD.

P. 34. The Great Hunt of the White Glen. Great as this hunt or drive was, it was surpassed by that of Caoilte. Finn was the prisoner of Cormac Mac Art, the King of Ireland, and Caoilte went to deliver him. But Cormac refused to give him his liberty until Caoilte had accomplished the task of gathering together a pair of every animal in Ireland, and driving them before him to Tara. "Caoilte's Rabble" consisted not only, as here, of four-footed beasts, but also of birds and fishes, and even "two whales"! See *Dean of Lismore's Book*, lxii, 42, 43.—J. McD.

P. 36. Finn saw the Lady or Mistress of Green Insh cutting rushes down in a hollow beneath him, and a turn of her right breast over her left shoulder. The Son of the King of Lochlan saw, in a far-away island, "a big, big woman," who is similiarly described, and who was similarly employed (MacInnes' *Tales*, p. 239). And Diarmaid beheld, in "Realm Underwaves", "a woman, as though she were crazed," engaged in the very same work. He asked her "what use she had for rushes?" She answered that the Daughter of King Underwaves was ill, and that a bed of rushes was what she found wholesomest (*W. H. Tales*, vol. iii, p. 413). I believe that the Lady of Green Insh down in the valley or Underwaves is Night, which brings sleep and rest, symbolised by the bed of rushes, to the sick and wearied.—J. McD.

P. 36. Finn's object, in taking hold of the Lady of Green Insh by the breast, was to bring himself into the relation of foster-son to her. After that she was bound, by one of the strongest ties, to grant him his boon.—J. McD.

P. 37. The golden doors, or silver doors, are, in my opinion, the openings of the western sky at sunset.—J. McD.

P. 38. Finn is the Sun, and the Yellow-haired Lad of the Skin Coverings is the golden Dawn or Twilight, overcast with fleecy clouds (*breac-a-mhuiltein*).—J. McD.

P. 38. Avasks is, in Gaelic, Amhaisg or Amhais. For a description of Avasks, see the footnote at 220 of vol. iii of the *W. H. Tales*. Campbell thinks that the Avasks may be the same as the Northern Baresarks. Here they represent the clouds of darkness, which threaten to extinguish both sun and twilight.—J. McD.

P. 39. *Carraig an uchd*, translated breastbone, is, literally, the rock of the chest. Here there is a hidden metaphor, the breastbone, under the thin layer of skin and flesh, being compared to a rock almost cropping out through the light soil.— J. McD.

This tale is mythological from one end to the other, but the last part, the journey of Finn to the place of the Queen of Roy (Red), is clearly so. I believe that the Lady of Green Insh is Night, that her yellow-haired son, the Lad of the Skin Coverings, is the golden Dawn with its fleecy clouds (or *breac-a-mhuiltein*), and that his brother, the Son of the King of Light, is Day or Daylight. Finn is the Sun, and as such the King of Light. His journey to the place of the Queen of Roy (Red) is the Sun's daily course from east to west. The latter is accompanied on its way by the Dawn, which remains invisible until it comes forth in the evening as Twilight. Both then enter the golden or silver portals of the west. The struggle between the Dawn as Twilight and the clouds of darkness—represented by the Avasks—now begins, and terminates afterwards in favour of the former—a result supposed to be rendered evident enough by "the heaps" or masses of clouds piled outside the portals of night, or just above the western horizon. Next morning the Sun wakens the Dawn. The latter goes forth, encounters the clouds of darkness at the threshold, and again comes off victorious. There it enters on a more prolonged struggle with the advancing Day. This struggle begins before sunrise, and ends after sunset. From one point of view they part then for the night, but from another they both fall dead in each other's embraces, and are carried back by the setting Sun to their mother, Night. She restores them to life, but only to enter again on the same course, and to pass through the same experiences as they had on the preceding day. —J. McD.

## TALE IV.

P 56. Alexander Cameron got this version of a well-known tale from Donald McPhie, to whom he is indebted for the most of his lore. Another Alexander Cameron, who also belongs to Ardnamurchan, but who now resides in Lochaber, heard it recited by the same McPhie, to whom he was nearly related.— J. McD.

There are several versions of the tale still extant, the majority of them under different titles. In the Lay of Diarmad, the dying hero, in recalling his many rescues of Finn from extreme danger, places that from the Rowan-tree Dwelling (*Bruighin Chaoruinn*) first. Two prose versions of the tale, under this very title, are preserved in the Advocates' Library. One of them is in a MS. which was written in 1600, and which belonged to the McVurichs, the once famous bards of

Clanranald. The other is in the Dunstaffnage MS., which bears the date of 1603, and which was written by a local scribe named Ewen McPhail. See *Leabhar na Féinne*, pp. 86-8. A third version, entitled "Maghach Colgar", is in vol. ii of the *W. H. Tales*. A fourth, headed "Fionn le Feachd na Féinne air cùl Bheinn Éidin a' sealg", was found by the late Mr. Donald McPherson of the Advocates' Library. And "'Tigh a' Bhlàir Bhuidhe" (The House of Yellow Field) in this collection may be reckoned the fifth. There is an English version in Dr. Joyce's old Celtic romances (p. 177 *et seq.*) made from three Irish MSS. of 1733, 1766, and 1841.—J. McD.

P. 57. Some incidents which are omitted in this version, but which are preserved in the fragment in *Leabhar na Féinne*, and summarised in a note appended to "Maghach Colgar", may be briefly told here.

A King of Lochlan invaded Ireland with the intention of conquering the whole island. But he was met, and, with two of his sons, was slain in battle by Finn and the Féinne. His third son, Miodhach MacColgain, fell into the hands of Finn; but his life was spared, and he then became King of Lochlan. He pretended to be so grateful and attached to his preserver that nothing would satisfy him but to live near the latter, and spend his revenue from the Kingdom of Lochlan in that of Ireland. His wishes were for a time gratified, but he was always distrusted by some of the Féinn. At length, on the advice of Conan and Ossian, he was removed from Finn's neighbourhood, and sent to live on a distant island in the Shannon. Here he seems to have cherished a purpose of being revenged on Finn for the death of his father and brothers, and to have waited for an opportunity of accomplishing it. What appeared a good opportunity presented itself to him at last. Finn and his men went on a hunting expedition to Munster. During their stay there, and while they were seated on a knoll, they saw a tall young hero approaching. He was well armed, and wore on his head a helmet set all round with precious stones. When he arrived he said that he was a poet, and that he came to bind Finn by oath to accompany him to a certain dwelling in Ireland should Finn fail in solving a string of riddles which he propounded. Finn, however, solved the riddles; and Conan recognising in the stranger Miodhach MacColgain, reproached him for his want of hospitality to his benefactor. Thereupon Miodhach invited all present to a feast prepared by him in a dwelling "on sea", *i.e.*, on the island in the Shannon, but which was to be consumed in a dwelling "on land", *i.e.*, on the opposite bank of the river. And to make sure of their presence at the feast, he bespelled, or bound by oath, Finn straightway to accompany him to the latter. This was the Enchanted Dwelling of the Rowan-tree, or of Blàr Buidhe.—J. McD.


P. 57. The Big Lad in the version in this collection is simply Miodhach, the son of Colgan. But neither here nor in "Maghach Colgar" of the *W. H. Tales* is a reason given as in the foregoing fragment for the King of Lochlan's hatred to Finn.—J. McD.


P. 57. The conference to determine the order of travelling to the House of Yellow Field is held in a "House of Conference", or "Tigh-Comhagail". The latter should be Tigh Comhagalamh. Agalamh, a discourse, is found in "Agallamh-na-Senorach", the "Discourse of the Ancients".—J. McD.


P. 57. Caoilte (Slender), first called Daorghlas and Luathas, was the son of Ronan, and a relative of Finn. He was the swiftest of foot in the Féinn. When at full speed his shoulders rose so high that he looked as if he had three heads, and then he would outstrip the swift March wind. See "Gruagach Bàn" in vol. ii, and "Duan na Ceardaich" in vol. iii of *W. H. Tales*. An instance of his speed has been already given from the *Dean of Lismore's Book*. Another will be found in the "Song of the Smithy" in vol. iii of the *W. H. Tales, Leabhar na Fèinne*, p. 65, etc. From his fairy sweetheart (*leannan sìth*) he received a strengthening belt which greatly increased his power of endurance, and a ring which made him always victorious (*Leabhar na Fèinne*, p. 54). He was almost as heroic as he was swift-footed. Instances of his heroism are (1) his slaying of the enchanted boar, and (2) of the five-headed giant (*Leabhar na Fèinne*, pp. 52-7). He was also one of the chief bards of the Féinn."—J. McD.


P. 57. Cuchulin, the third in the race to Lochlan, or rather to the banks of the Shannon, was the Hero of Ulster, as Finn was that of Leinster. He is supposed to have lived in the first century of the Christian era, and to have been contemporary with Conaire Mac Eidersgeoil, King of Ireland, and Conchobar Mac Nessa, King of Ulster. Yet he is here alive in the third century, in the time of Finn and Cormac Mac Art. For further information about Cuchulin see the poems under his name from p. 1 to p. 19 of *Leabhar na Fèinne*.—J. McD.

P. 57. The House of Blar-buie, or Yellow-field. This house was called after the field on the banks of the Shannon on which it was, or was supposed to be erected. In the Fragment in *Leabhar na Féinne* Yellow-field is not the site of the house of that name, but the scene of the battle in which Miodhach's father and brothers fell. The house is there called the Rowan-tree Dwelling, because its walls consist of rows of wooden posts driven into the ground and interwoven with wattles of the rowan-tree. It was constructed by the three Kings of Insh Tilly, wicked magicians or Druids who were in alliance with Miodhach. It was enchanted, and formed to serve as a trap in which Finn and his men should be taken.—J. McD.

P. 57. Here Finn is the first to enter the enchanted dwelling, but in the Fragment Conan takes the lead. The description of the interior in the latter, reminds one of the interior of a house in the *Arabian Nights*. The walls are lined with boards of a great variety of colours, white, black, blue, green, and red. The seats and the floor are covered with gold-embroidered cloth of every hue. There are rich silk garments for the use of the guests. And finally the house is filled with a delicious perfume which cheers and invigorates all who inhale it. But no sooner do the Féinn take their seats than all this rude grandeur vanishes. Finn speaks first. He thinks it a wonder that the feast is not coming. Goll considers it a greater wonder that the sweet perfume has become a disgusting odour. Glas reckons it a greater wonder than that, that the many-coloured boards have disappeared, and left nothing but bare walls of wattle. Faolan holds it a still greater wonder that the Dwelling which had seven doors when they entered, has now only one. And Conan maintains that it is the greatest wonder of all that not a thread of the silk garments and embroidered cloth is left, and that he feels as if he were plastered with clay, and the clay as cold as the snow of one night.

Finn now suspects that they are caught in a snare, and at the request of Goll puts his finger under his knowledge-set-of-teeth, and discovers the whole truth. Miodhach, who for fourteen years had been plotting evil against the Féinn, got the dwelling constructed; and now he has with him in the island a strong hero of the Greeks called the King of the Great World, sixteen Kings of the "Fairadh", each of them surrounded by seven bands of men, and the three Kings of Insh Tilly who are over the sixteen Kings of the "Fairadh". This revelation disheartens the Féinn. But

Finn tells them to face death with full courage, because they had got their allotted time in the world ; and he added that the "*Òrd Fian*" would play, and serve them in place of music at the time of death.—J. McD.

P. 58. Finn's "knowledge-set-of-teeth". See how he acquired "the Knowledge of the two Worlds" in *Leabhar na Fèinne*, p. 38, and *W. H. Tales*, vol. ii, p. 362.—J. McD.

P. 58. "The blood of the three sons of the King of Insh Tilly filtered through rings of silver into cups of gold" is the only thing that will release Finn and his men. In the Fragment it is the blood of the *three Kings* of Insh Tilly mixed together. But in "Maghach Colgar" it is the blood of the three Daughters of King Gil. In neither of the two last versions is there any mention of the rings and cups.—J. McD.

P. 58. Here the absent heroes are only two in number, and of these Oscar is the leader. But in "Maghach Colgar" three are absent, with Diarmad as their head, and in the Fragment of the "Rowan-tree Dwelling" five are left under Ossian, Finn's oldest son.—J. McD.

P. 58. The Wooden-crier, or *Gurra-fiodha*. What was it? Here it is of wood, and is sounded by blowing into it. In the next short tale (p. 73) it is like a hollow baton or pole for carrying in the hand, and is sounded by blowing into one end of it. The inference from all this is that it must have been either a wooden whistle or trumpet. But that it was the former and not the latter is evident from its being called *fìdeag, i.e.*, whistle, in the tale of "Fear a' Gheadain Chlòimhe" (The Man in the Tuft of Wool). See p. 58 of vol. ii of *A History of the Scottish Highlands*, edited by J. S. Keltie. Its use was to sound the alarm when Finn's life was in extreme danger.—J. McD.

In "Maghach Colgar" the signal of danger is made by striking a blow with the hammer of Finn (Òrd Fhinn) ; and the sound of the blow instantly travels all the way from Lochlan to Ireland. In the Fragment so often quoted already, an "Òrd Fian" (Fian Hammer?) is also mentioned. But though this instrument did alarm the absent friends of Finn, yet it does not appear that it was set agoing for that purpose. On the contrary, its musical sounds seem to have been substituted for the dirge. Is this the Celtic hand-bell, such as that of Kilmichael Glassary, or of St. Fillan, tolling the death of the seemingly doomed heroes?—J. McD.

P. 59. "The ford-mouth of the river." Taking the Fragment as our guide, "the river" is the Shannon, and the "ford-mouth" is on the branch of the Shannon which separates the site of the Enchanted Dwelling from the island in which Miodhach (pronounced Miach) and his allies are waiting.—J. McD.

P. 59. The Gaper, or *Craosnach*, is a dart or javelin. *Craosnach* is from *craos*, a wide mouth, and the dart is so called from the gaping wounds it makes.—J. McD.

P. 59. The "Big House" is on the island. The heroes reach it by crossing the ford.—J. McD.

P. 59. The "fierce hero" lifting the haunch of venison from the caldron is one of the three sons of the King of Insh Tilly. He and his two brothers, being Druids or Magicians, are easily identified by the transformations they undergo.—J. McD.

P. 60. The "great host" are no doubt a part of the "bands" following the sixteen Kings of the "Fairadh".—J. McD.

P. 61. On his second visit to the Big House, Oscar brings with him his three-edged blade (*lann trì fhaobharach*). The blade must have resembled a bayonet, for the point can scarcely be called an edge.—J. McD.

P. 61. Wherever "she" appears for eagle, read "he".—J. McD.

P. 62. Here Lohary, the Son of the King of the Hunts (*Laoghaire Mac Righ nan Sealg*), takes the place held in the Fragment by "Innsi Mac Suibhne t-Sealge", and in "Maghach Colgar" by "Innsridh Mac Righ nan Sealg".—J. McD.

P. 64. Here Conan acquired the nickname of *Conan Maol*, or Bald Conan, because he, in his effort to tear himself away from the enchanted hearth-stone, left behind him the skin and hair of the back of his head. But in the MacInnes *Tales* he was surnamed *Maol*, because he was "crop-eared".—J. McD.

## TALE V.

P. 73. This legend Alexander Cameron got from his father, John Cameron, who died in Ardnamurchan upwards of forty years ago. It is identified with several places in the Highlands, and especially with Tom na h-Iùbhraich, near Inverness. See "The Man in the Tuft of Wool", by Dr. McLauchlan, in vol. ii of *A History of the Highlands.*—J. McD.

P. 74. "Wooden graips" are long-pronged graips or forks made of wood, and used in lifting sea-ware, bracken, etc. —J. McD.

P. 74. "Sailean dharagaibh daraich" are beams made of trunks of bog oak.—J. McD.

## TALE VI.

P. 76. Alexander Cameron told me this tale, Donald McPhie told it to him, and the other Alexander Cameron, mentioned in the Notes to Tale IV, heard it recited by McPhie. I heard, long ago, another version of the tale under the somewhat different title of "Crochadair na Tàirgne" (The Hangman of the Nail), but I forget it now.

The Hangman of the Nail earned his distinction by hanging his prisoners on *nails* from the highest turret of his castle, and the Bare-Stripping Hangman earned his by stripping his victims naked before he suspended them on *hooks* in the same position. —J. McD.

This, I believe, is the first version of Tale VI, as a whole, that has yet appeared in print. It consists of two parts, the first ending and the second beginning at the marriage of Cormac with the Daughter of the King of Riddles. The former might be called the Tale of the King of Riddles, and the latter the Tale of the Bare-Stripping Hangman. The King of Riddles would then correspond in part with the "Knight of Riddles" of the *W. H. Tales*, and similar riddle tales in other languages; and the Bare-Stripping Hangman would have its semi-similars in the "Herding of Cruachan" in the MacInnes *Tales*, "The Young King of Easaidh Ruadh" in the *W. H. Tales*, and "Cathal o Chruachan agus Buachaille na Greigh" (Cathal from Cruachan and the Herd of the Stud), another version of the "Herding of Cruachan" in my possession. As similars in other languages, "Koschei the Deathless" in Ralston's *Russian Folk-tales*, and "The Giant who had no Heart in his Body" in Dasent's *Norse Tales*, may be mentioned. See, further, Mr. Nutt's notes to the "Herding of Cruachan" in the MacInnes *Tales* (p. 455-57). But let it not be supposed that the tale really consists of two other tales, and that these can be actually separated from one another without doing violence to either of them. Had this been attempted, the second tale would be left without a beginning, allusions in the course of the narrative would become unintelligible, and the incidents at the close, so characteristic of Highland tales, must be struck out altogether, thus leaving the tale without any proper ending. True, "The Riddle" in Grimm's *Tales* ends with the marriage of the prince and princess. But the "Knight of Riddles" does not end at the marriage of the elder brother with the daughter of the Knight of Riddles. The younger brother then returns home, and his elder brother becomes hero. As hero, the latter finds enough to do before he rids the borders of his kingdom of giants, and earns the honour of knighthood from his grim father-in-law. Nor are his trials then at an end. As Knight of the White Shield he meets his younger brother in single combat, and is overcome. The latter once more returns home, but is met on the way by his twelve sons, and forced to yield to the weakest of them. Here then, as in the "Bare-Stripping Hangman", several incidents follow the marriage, and "The Riddle" of other languages forms but one of the many incidents of the tale.—J. McD.

P. 76. The Henwife is here presented in her usual character of mischief-maker, and the stepmother is simply her tool. She does not appear in "The Knight of Riddles", and consequently the part she acts in this tale is omitted there. Her request is so put that it looks moderate enough. She wants only the full of the little black jar of meal and butter, etc. Her terms should then be accepted by the Queen, and not, as in the tale, after the extent of her demands are made known. These terms form a series of riddles, but their solution is omitted. A similar incident, however, occurs in "Conn Eda" in *Folk and Fairy Tales of the Irish Peasantry* (Camelot series), and the solution of the request made there may be virtually that of the first part of the request made here. The Henwife in "Conn Eda" requested that the cavity of her arms should be filled with wool, and that the hole she would bore with her distaff should be filled with red wheat. Her request was granted. She "thereupon stood in the door of her hut, and bending her arm into a circle with her side, directed the royal attendants to thrust the wool into her house through her arm, until all the available space within was filled with wool. She then got on the roof of her brother's house, and having made a hole through it with her distaff, caused red wheat to be spilled through it until that was filled up to the roof with red wheat." —J. McD.

P. 76. A chalder is equal to 16 bolls.—J. McD.

P. 79. Here only four ravens are poisoned, but in "The Knight of Riddles" there are twelve.—J. McD.

P. 79. Alastir (or Art, as I believe he should be called) "had virtues (*buaidhean*) about him by which he knew what was to meet them". In other words, he had the second sight. But, according to my Sheanachy, although the mysterious power he possessed enabled him to foresee the danger before him, it did not show him how he was to get out of it. For this he must depend on his wits alone.—J. McD.

P. 80. The adventure with the robbers being over, the brothers resolve that Cormac shall travel as the Son of the King of Ireland, and Alastir as his page. But notwithstanding this arrangement, Alastir never ceases to be the real hero of the tale from its beginning to its close.—J. McD.

P. 81. For comments on Head-crowned Stakes, see Nutt's note at p. 403 of the MacInnes *Tales.*—J. McD.

P. 83. The incidents at the Castle of the King of Riddles are substantially the same as at that of the Knight of Riddles. —J. McD.

P. 83. Alastir, seeing his brother Cormac married, and out of danger, does not return home like the younger brother in "The Knight of Riddles", but enters alone on a new series of adventures, in which heroism is of more help than wit. —J. McD.

P. 84. The Dog-Otter befriends Alastir for his faithfulness to his brother. His first act of friendship to the latter is to snatch him away over the sea to Lochlan, the country to which his own thoughts are turning, and the scene of his future triumphs. Similar services rendered by other creatures to man are mentioned in other tales. For example, the Mermaid carries the hero of the next story on her tail all the way to the

Green Isle, and the Fox, transformed into a ship, conveys Mac Iain Dìrich to the several countries to which his quests lead him. The Otter's next act of friendship to Alastir is to fetch him the salmon, a bite of which imparts such wonderful strength.—J. McD.

P. 84. The White Red-eared Hound next befriends Alastir. The Otter brought him to the country where he is to receive the reward of his faithfulness, and now the hound brings him into contact with the man in whose service he is to earn his reward. This he does, as I think, in the following manner : The King of Lochlan and his twelve Champions are out hunting with the White Red-eared Hound. The Great White-buttocked Deer starts up before them. The Hound pursues, and purposely drives the deer to the hut, where he kills it, and leaves it at Alastir's feet. His object in this is two-fold : (1) to provide more of strengthening food for Alastir, and (2) to bring him, as already stated, in contact with the King. The White Red-eared Hound turns up pretty often in Highland tales. See, for instance, " The Lay of the Big Fool," at p. 160 of vol. iii of the *W. H. Tales*. It also appears in a tale in my possession, called " The Knight of the Bens, of the Glens, and of the Mountain Passes".—J. McD.

P. 86. Three of the King's daughters are stolen by the Great Giant of the Black Corrie of Ben Breck. Other instances of stolen children are common enough. See the first tale in this collection, " The King of Lochlin's Three Daughters" in vol. i of the *W. H. Tales*, "Coise Céin" at p. 265 of the MacInnes *Tales*, etc.—J. McD.

P. 87. The Golden Eagle attacks the Champions in the Giant's Den, and compels them to flee. The soul seems to have fled for safety out of the Giant's body when the latter was attacked, and to have hidden itself first in the eagle. This, then, is not an instance of transformation, but of the passing of the soul from one body to another. Instances of both kinds are common enough in Highland tales.—J. McD.

P. 88. Black Brood-mare, or *Àlaire Dhubh*. *Àlaire* derived from *àl*, brood, signifies brood-mare. Another word allied to it is Fàlaire, which MacLeod and Dewar derive from *fàl*, sod. If their translation be correct, then *Fàlaire* means a horse *at grass*, as opposed to one at work. And as only brood-mares and saddle-horses answer that description, the word is applied only to them. See the dictionaries, where it is translated either by ambler or mare.  *Fàlaire* is of frequent occurrence in Gaelic tales.  For example, there is a *Fàlaire Bhuidhe* (Yellow Ambler) in " MacIain Dìreach", *Fàlaire Dhonn* (Brown Ambler) in " The Fair Gruagach", and *Fàlaire Dhubh* (Black Ambler) in " The Knight of the Red Shield", all in vol. ii of the *W. H. Tales.*—J. McD.

P. 88.  The catching of the Black Brood-mare.  This is one of three tasks imposed on Alastir in Lochlan.  The first is the fight for his life against the twelve Champions of the King. The second is the catching of the Brood-mare for winning the King's Fourth Daughter.  And the third is the quest for the soul of the Bare-stripping Hangman, with the object of preserving the latter after she is won.—J. McD.

P. 88.  In catching the Brood-mare three trials are allowed— one on each of three successive days.  On the first and second day, she flees so fast up the side of Ben Buie (Yellow Mountain) that she "sends water out of the stones, and fire out of the streams".  However impossible these assertions may be, they help to heighten our idea of the Mare's speed.—J. McD.

P. 89.  The Sorceress, or *Iorasgach-ùrlair*, is described as an old haggard-looking woman, who is careless of her person and of her dress.  Her hair is dishevelled, and the skirt of her garment hangs down unequally.  Hence an untidy person is still called in contempt " Iorasglach".  Her favourite posture is sitting on the floor.  Hence another name she bears, *Clàrsach-ùrlair*. According to the version I first heard, she struck, before she gave forth her responses, the ground three times, as if she would thus summon to her help the Underworld power or powers from whom she received her inspiration.  In " Tuairisgeul Mòr", a tale contributed by the Rev. J. G. Campbell to the *Scottish Celtic Review*, the *Eachrais-ùrlair*, translated there " Trouble-the-house", appears.  She is a great enchantress who, by a stroke of her magic beetle, transforms the King's three sons by his first wife into three wolves.  But whether she is the same character as the Sorceress of this tale I cannot tell.—J. McD.

P. 89.  The "friends", to whom the Sorceress alludes, are the Otter and the " White Red-eared Hound".—J. McD.

P. 90.  With the old bridle Alastir catches the Black Mare. The Mare evidently possesses a wonderful degree of affection, and marvellous powers of recognition.  She recognises the bridle

worn by her dam, and it may be by her grandam, and hastens
to put her head where their heads once were. A like thing
happens in Tale II. There the Grey Dog first identifies
Bran's golden chain, then he approaches Finn with evident
signs of affection, and at length suffers the latter to put the
chain about his neck, and lead him away where he pleases.
In *Leabhar na Fëinne*, however, the Wild Dog of the Glen is
tamed and caught, not by Bran's golden chain, but by a Dog-
bridle (*con-taod*) possessing magical properties. For similars
see Rusty Bridle in "Widow's Son", "The Tether" in
version 3, "The Rusty Bridle" in versions 6 and 7 of ditto,
and The Bridle in "Daughter of the King of the Skies", all in
vol. i, *W. H. Tales.* For "Bridle of Transformation" see
Nutt's note at p. 462 of the MacInnes *Tales.*—J. McD.

P. 93. The Rocky Path of Ben Buie. This is a narrow path
running right over the top of the Yellow Mountain to its foot
on the opposite side. Throughout its whole length it is hemmed
in by lofty precipices, over which only a bird on the wing can
pass. Its first or ascending half is the most difficult to travel.
At its beginning this half is simply rocky, but higher up it is
honey-combed with deep, transverse fissures; and still higher
up it comes to an abrupt termination, and leaves nothing
before the traveller but a deep, yawning chasm. On one side,
however, it leaves a remnant of itself, which forms a broken
ledge of unequal breadth along the face of one of the enclos-
ing precipices. Alastir crosses the fissures one after another
in the same manner. His method is first to throw his body
across the near side of a fissure, then to stretch his arms
over the intervening gap to the farther side, and, when he gets a
firm hold of the latter, to drag himself gradually on to it. His
method of crossing the ledge is of course different. When
the ledge is broad enough he walks on it, and when its gaps
are narrow enough he springs over them; but when it becomes
too narrow or the gaps too wide, he must cross like any crags-
man, by clinging with hands and feet to every projection in the
face of the precipice. I think a similar path appears in the
*W. H. Tales,* but I forget where.—J. McD.

P. 93. The buzzard is simply the Sorceress transformed. It
is also the form assumed in Tale IV by the first of the three
Druid Kings of Insh Tilly.—J. McD.

P. 94. The Red Lake. The space between the precipices
seems to widen out in the descent, but the Path continues
narrow, and passes like a causeway through the Red Lake.

This Path Alastir always keeps, and by so doing crosses the Lake in safety.—J. McD.

P. 94. The Yellow Mountain with its Rocky Path is part of an old myth. It is the vault of heaven, which is yellow or golden in the morning, and of the same colour again in the evening. The Rocky Path is that which the Sun takes in its daily course, and which is difficult to climb but easy to descend. And the Red Lake through which Alastir passes is the red evening sky.—J. McD.

P. 95. *Ùdabac*, translated porch, is really a semi-circular stone wall built before the outer door to shelter it from the wind and rain. A more primitive *ùdabac* was formed by a cairn of stones placed on the more exposed side of the door.—J. McD.

P. 95. The Giant comes with a fairy motion—*i.e.*, with great speed, but without any perceptible effort. He moves his hands and feet so rapidly that they become invisible, and that he seems to glide through the air without touching the ground.—J. McD.

P. 96. The King of Ben Buie is the King of Lochlan.—J. McD.

P. 99. The Dragon, according to Cameron, was the cause of all the obstructions and difficulties in the Path over the Yellow Mountain. It was she who made the fissures, the chasm, and the Red Lake. It was she who placed the Giants in the first two Castles. And further on it will be seen that it was she also who kidnapped the King's younger brother and transformed him by her spells into the Bare-stripping Hangman.—J. McD.

P. 99. The Balsam, or Healing-ointment, is generally used externally for healing, but here it is used also internally for strengthening.—J. McD.

P. 101. The couples referred to here were different from those of the present day. A modern couple consists of two rafters having their upper ends joined together, and their lower ends drawn out like the legs of a compass and placed one opposite the other on the side-walls. But the lower ends of the rafters of a Great Barn Couple rested on upright *posts* which were built into the side-walls and whose bases stood on the floor. The rafters and posts were so joined together at their points of meeting as to form *curves*, and not angles. The posts were the Stoops or *Crùb*, and the Curves, the Bends or *Lùb* of the Couple. I should add that the upper ends of the rafters of this kind of couple stood about six inches apart, and that the rafters themselves were tied together in that position by a balk crossing them a few inches lower down. The space left between the ends of the rafters was for the admission of the ridge-pole, and the ridge-pole when admitted rested on the balk, which was called the hat ("*Ad*").

There was a still more primitive couple, which consisted of two "cabers" of equal length and with equal bends at the point, corresponding with that in which the Stoops and Rafters of the foregoing couple met.

The Barn is said to have had only as many Bends and Stoops as it had couples. How is this to be explained? I can only guess. Perhaps the Barn was a "lean-to," with its roof supported by single "cabers" of the sort described above.—J. McD.

P. 102. The incident of the Old Men occurs in "The Man in the Tuft of Wool". See *Scottish Highlands*, vol. ii, p. 98. The incident, in one form or other, is often met with in Highland tales. See, further, Nutt's "Old, Older, and Oldest", at p. 460 of the MacInnes *Tales.*—J. McD.

P. 102. The Hero is recognised by the sword he wears from the time he arrives with the King's sword at the first castle until he meets the first Old Man.—J. McD.

P. 103. The Crooked Stick, or *Maide Cròm*. No old man in the surrounding district could tell me what this meant, but a Lewis man explained it to me a few weeks ago. Assuming the hearth to be on the middle of the floor, the crooked stick has its ends resting on the corresponding spars of the two couples which are nearest the hearth. Its use there is to support the crook. The old man in the bunch of moss was placed behind the crooked stick—that is, resting on the same spars with it, but on the side of it furthest away from the door. Here the old man is wrapped in a bunch of moss, but in "The Man in the Tuft of Wool", as the title indicates, in a tuft of wool. In both these tales he rests behind the crooked stick ; but in "The Kingdom of the Green Mountains" of the MacInnes *Tales*, he is rocked in a cradle.—J. McD.

P. 104. King Cormac was Cormac the Son of Art, the third century Ulster chief, and a contemporary of Finn and the Féinne.—J. McD.

P. 105. The pulp, or *cothan*, meant here is such as is produced by the friction of the oars against the rowlocks of a boat.—J. McD.

P. 105. The jar of ointment. If this ointment be the same as the balsam or healing-ointment of other tales, here is a third use to which it is applied, viz., to render the body invulnerable.—J. McD.

P. 106. This "wayfaring run" occurs in a variety of forms in other tales. See "Conall" at p. 152, "Widow's Son" at p. 198, and "Fair Gruagach" at p. 412 of vol. ii of *W. H. Tales.* See also "Herding of Cruachan" at p. 105, and Nutt's note on the same at p. 457 of the MacInnes *Tales.*—J. McD.

P. 107. The helping animals here are three in number—the dog, otter, and falcon. In "Cathal o Chruachan", another tale in my possession, the number is, as in "The Herding of Cruachan", four. But the "Brown Wren of the Stream of Guidance" of the former takes the place of the Duck of the latter. Helping animals are of frequent occurrence in Highland tales. See Nutt's note at p. 457 of the MacInnes *Tales.* —J. McD.

P. 107. *Creachan*, or rocky region of a mountain. The mountain-side is divided into three regions. The lowest is the acclivity (*brudhach*). This region was, not so long ago, wooded. The next is the grassy region (*fireach*) ; and the last, or highest, is the rocky region (*creachan*).—J. McD.

P. 110. The first version of the tale I heard differed from this in several particulars. The Giant of the Nail of the former not only carried off the King's Youngest Daughter, but had her living with him in his Den in the Black Corrie of Ben Breck. Every morning he left his Den driving his flock of goats before him, while he spun flax on a distaff with one pair of hands, and played on an instrument called the *Òruinn-Òruinn*, supposed to be the shepherd's pipe, with another. He returned home in the evening, not only driving, spinning, and playing as in the morning, but also carrying a dead old woman for his own supper and a fresh-water salmon for that of the King's Daughter. His soul was hid, like that of the Bare-stripping Hangman, in an egg in a falcon in the Hind. The Hind, however, took refuge, not as here in a Wood, but in the Great Castle of threescore and ten doors in the Black Corrie of Ben Breck. The Giant was killed, not by crushing the egg wherein his soul was hid, but by hitting him with it on a mole in his forehead.—J. McD.

P. 112. The coracle, or *curach*, requires not to be described. It turns up now and again in Gaelic tales. See "The Knight of the Red Shield" at p. 465 of .vol. ii, *W. H. Tales*, "Conal" at p. 208 of vol. iii of ditto, and "The Kingdom of Big Men" at p. 185 of *Scottish Celtic Review.*—J. McD.

P. 112. This "tag", or "nonsense-ending", is only another version of that with which "The Swarthy Champion" concludes. See p. 300 of vol. i of the *W. H. Tales*. Dr. Douglas Hyde, at p. 176 of his *Irish Folk-Tales*, published by Nutt, says: "It is remarkable that there seems little trace of them (nonsense-endings) in Campbell. The only story in his volumes which ends with a piece of nonsense is 'The Slender Grey Champion'" (not "Kerne", as Dr. Douglas Hyde makes it). This is scarcely correct. The fact is that there are five in vol. i alone of the *W. H. Tales*. "The Battle of the Birds", version 3, ends in these words: "If they have not died since then, they are alive, merry, and rich." "The Sea Maiden" ends almost in the same words. "The Girl and the Dead Man" has for its conclusion, "They returned home; they left me sitting here, and if they were well, it is well; and if they were not, let them be." "The King of Lochlin's Three Daughters" closes thus: "I left them dancing, and I know not but that they are cutting capers on the floor till the day of to-day." But the most extraordinary assertion of Dr. Hyde is at the close of the note: "Why the Highland tales have lost this distinctive feature I cannot even conjecture, but certain it is that this is so." Certain it is that it is not so. There are four in this collection alone, and I could add many others to the number.—J. McD.

## TALE VII.

P. 145. Cameron heard this tale in Ardnamurchan in his boyhood, but forgot it afterwards. He recovered it last year from James Campbell, a native of Gairloch, in Ross-shire, but now a shepherd in the Strath of Appin. John McFarlane, constable, Port-Appin, heard it from a Colonsay man in Jura nearly fifty years ago. The tale, therefore, is, or within living memory was, widely known along the coast of the West Highlands. And I am convinced that it can be traced back to the end of the last century at least.—J. McD.

P. 145. The only other version of this tale known to me is "Black White Red" of vol. i of the *W. H. Tales.*—J. McD.

The subject of this tale is the Queen's jealousy of her stepson, with all its consequences. Her jealousy gives rise to a long train of incidents, of which the greater number are so linked together as to form an episode out of all proportion with the rest of the tale. The subject of the episode is the quest by the hero of the tale of the Swan-Maiden, who was the Young Daughter of the King of the Red Cap. Some incidents in this quest remind one of classical mythology, and especially of the Odyssey. I believe the resemblance between them is purely accidental. But whether this is so or not, the reader may rest assured that he has the tale as I got it, and that I am convinced it can be traced back to the end of the last century at least.—J. McD.

P. 146. The Mermaid divested of her husk or fish-skin becomes a handsome woman. Stories founded on similar incidents to this have been handed down by tradition. Perhaps the Mermaid marries her captor, is kindly treated by him, and bears him a family, but after all she is not happy. Some day, in her husband's absence, she searches the house, and finds her husk where he has hidden it. She at once betakes herself with it to the sea-side, puts it on, and returns to her native element. She may afterwards visit the bay beneath her old home to meet her children and to comb their hair, but never to stay even with them until her husk is once more seized, and finally destroyed.—J. McD.

The Mermaid occurs in the "Sea-Maiden" and its many versions in vol. i of the *W. H. Tales.*—J. McD.

P. 147. The Three Swan-Maidens. Similar Swan-Maidens appear in the third version of "The Three Soldiers", at p. 189 of vol. i of the *W. H. Tales*. See also Nutt's note at p. 436 of the MacInnes *Tales.*—J. McD.

Another version of the Swan-Maiden quest occurs in a tale which I heard long ago, and which was called "Mac an Tuathanaich a Thàinig a Raineach" (The Farmer's Son who came from Rannoch). The Farmer's Son was an only child, of whom his father and mother were very fond. They wished him to stay with them on the farm, and to succeed them after their death. But he found life too dull at home, and nothing would satisfy him but to go forth and seek his fortune in the world. Finding their efforts to dissuade him vain, they allowed him to have his own way at last. With the smaller half of a bannock and his mother's blessing, he set out on his journey, and met on the way with several adventures, which I forget. At last, however, he arrived at an inn, where he resolved to stay for a time.

He rose early next morning, and went to a lake in the neighbourhood to have a shot. When he was approaching the lake, he saw three white swans swimming on its calm surface. He crept towards them, and with some trouble got within proper range. But when he lifted his gun to his shoulder and was going to take aim, they became the three most beautiful maidens he had ever seen. He dropped his gun at once, and no sooner had he done so than they returned to their swan-form. He repeated the same actions again and again, but always with the same results. Wondering at what he had seen, he returned for breakfast to the inn, and resolved to visit the lake at the same hour next morning.

When morning came he returned to the lake, and found the swans, as he had left them, swimming on its surface. He prepared to fire, but as often as he lifted his gun they were maidens, and as often as he laid it down they became swans. He returned for breakfast to the inn, wondering more than ever at the sight he had seen. When breakfast was past, he thought over the matter, and made up his mind to go back to the lake in the evening.

When evening came he went a third time to the lake. He approached it as cautiously as he could ; but, when he came in sight of it, the swans were nowhere to be seen. He thought they had flown ; but, on advancing nearer the lake and looking round its border, he saw three maidens bathing in the water, and their swan-skins lying on the beach. He crept towards the skins, and having got hold of them, refused to restore them unless the youngest of the three sisters—for sisters they were—agreed to marry him. She agreed at last, and then she and her sisters got back their swan-skins. Thereafter she ascended a green knoll above the lake, touched it with a white wand she held in her hand, and up sprang a fine castle, richly furnished, and stored with everything necessary for their comfort and happiness.

Here, for a time, he remained contented. At last, however, a longing came over him to visit his parents, and back therefore to Rannoch he would go. When he was leaving, his wife told him that if he would mention her name or the castle in which they lived he would have neither wife nor castle before him when he returned. He promised that he would remember her warning, and departed. In due time he arrived at his father's house, and was not long there when he broke his promise to his wife. No sooner had he done so than he remembered her warning, and got so anxious to know the worst that he set off that moment for home. But when he arrived at the lake there was neither wife nor castle to be seen, and the green knoll was as bare as it was the first day he beheld it.

Then he gave word and oath that he would not give rest to his foot nor let a pool of water out of his shoes until he reached the place where his wife was. He went away, and travelled far long and full long until night was coming. Then he looked before him, and saw a light a long way off, but he took not long in reaching it. It came from a small bothy. He went in to the bothy, and found an old woman before him. She addressed him by his name, and told him that she was his wife's aunt, that his wife slept in her house last night and left it in the morning, and that she was then far away in the house of her second aunt. He took his supper and went to bed. Early in the morning he awoke, and found breakfast ready. After it was over the old woman gave him a pair of shoes that would bring him to the house of her second sister, and that would, when pointed in the right direction, travel back of their own accord. He went away, and reached the second sister's house in the evening. She also recognised him, and told him that his wife left in the morning, and was then at her third aunt's house. Next morning she gave him something (I forget what) which he rode to the third sister's house. She, like the other two sisters, knew him, and told him that his wife, who was in her house last night, was now far away over the ocean in the Green Isle at the Extremity of the Uttermost World. Next morning she told him to kill her dun polled cow, place the carcase on a knoll before the house, and allow her to sew him up in the hide. She told him further that the Griffin (*Gribh-inneach*) would come, and after devouring the carcase, carry him over the sea to the Green Isle. He did as he was told, and the Griffin carried him to a crevice in the face of a fearful pre cipice overhanging the sea in that island. She left him there as food for her young, and flew away. He then cut his way out of the hide, and threw the young griffins over the rock into the sea. When the old griffin returned and found her nest harried, she drove her talons into his body and bore him away until she dropped him into the sea near the mouth of a stream. He swam with difficulty to the shore, and was found there by some women, who took pity on him and gave him food and shelter. They told him that they were washing for the King's Young Daughter, who was going to be married a second time, unless her first husband appeared before a certain day. The

day came, but not her husband. She then ordered all the
men in the kingdom to pass the door of the palace, and at last
recognised him in the wounded sailor who was staying with the
washerwomen.—J. McD.

P. 147. The hero's vow neither to stop nor rest till he should
see as handsome a woman as the White Swan of the Smooth
Neck has many parallels in Gaelic tales. See " Black White
Red" at p. 58, and " Baillie Lunnain" at p. 281 of vol. i, and
" Conall Gulban" at p. 200 of vol. iii of the *W. H. Tales.* See
also " Deirdre" at p. 19 of *Leabhar na Féinne.* See further the
"blood-drops incident" in "The Son of the King of Eirin" at
p. 3, with Nutt's note at p. 431 of the MacInnes *Tales.*—J. McD.

P. 147. Gonachry is no doubt of the same class of mythical
ships as that of the Phaeacians in the *Odyssey,* and as Skidbladnir, Frey's ship, in *The Prose Edda.* But it is not necessary to go so far away for similars; a good number are to be
found in Gaelic tales. See the Ship of Alder in Tale I, and
the Coracles of the Sorceress in Tale VI of this Collection.
See also the " Birlinn" (Galley) at p. 58, and the ship built by
the Ùruisg at p. 237 of vol. i, " The Speckled Barge" at p. 437,
and the Coracle at p. 469 of vol. ii, and the Steed to whom sea
or land was all one at p. 13 of vol. iii of the *W. H. Tales.* See
further the Ships at pp. 59 and 349 of the MacInnes *Tales,*
with Nutt's notes on the same, and the Ships at p. 189 of the
Scottish *Celtic Review.*—J. McD.

P. 148. The hero in his quest passing from island to island
may remind the reader of Ulysses ; but the three old brothers
who inhabit these islands can scarcely be compared to the
savage man-eating Laestrygones and Cyclopes of the *Odyssey.*
They are rather a combination of the old men of Tale VI and
the skilful companions of other tales. Men and women of
enormous strength and stature, but less irascible and savage
than the genuine race of giants, are occasionally met in Gaelic
tales.—J. McD.

P. 148. Old man. See the old man in " Black White Red",
p. 58 of vol. i of *W. H. Tales.*—J. McD.

P. 149. The ship's course is set in the direction in which the
fallen arrow points. This mode of fixing the ship's course
reminds one of the method of fixing sides in a game of shinty
by throwing up a shinty in the air, and marking the hand on
which it falls, or the side of the field to which its club end

points after it has fallen.   But the former may carry us back to
a time when divination by means of arrow-throwing was prac-
tised by the Celts, as it certainly was by the Teutons, and by
many Eastern nations of antiquity. —J. McD.

P. 149. The Beautiful Isle of the Shadow of the Stars.
The idea of this island may have been caught from ob-
serving a calm spot in the sea, or from a sheet of winter
ice reflecting the stars as they shone in a cloudless sky
by night.   Or it may have been taken from actually wit-
nessing icebergs, or from the description of others who had
witnessed them in the Northern Sea.   At any rate, monks of
the early Celtic Church had traversed the Northern Sea and
found the solitude they wanted in Iceland at a very early
period.   And it is most unlikely that others did not follow on
their track and bring back accounts of what they had witnessed
on sea and on land since they had left.—J. McD.

P. 153. The hero is carried to the Green Isle on the tail of
the Mermaid.   This incident resembles the story of Arion,
who, on his return from Sicily, threw himself, to escape being
murdered by the sailors, into the sea, and was then carried on
the dolphin's back all the way to Tænarus.—J. McD.

P. 154. The woman here acts the part of the Sirens in the
*Odyssey*.
The Great Garden of the Golden Apples resembles the Garden of the Hesperides.   But similar gardens are common
enongh in Gaelic tales.—J. McD.

P. 157. This is the first trial of the Son of the King of Ireland.   The second is winning at dice-playing with the King of
the Red Cap.   And the third is the identifying of the Giant's
Young Daughter by means of the needle which she holds in her
hand while she stands with her sisters behind the curtains.   All
the trials in "Black White Red" resemble the last.   See p. 59
of vol. i, *W. H. Tales*.—J. McD.

P. 160. The hero is forbidden by the Giant to attempt to
leave the island, but disobeys.   He escapes with his wife to
the seaside, and finds Gonachry drawn up on the beach.   The
crew launch her; and the sound made by her keel in passing
over the gravel alarms the Giant in his bed.   His Eldest
Daughter makes him believe that it is only the sound of the
wind passing through the trees of the garden.   But when the
ship sets sail he is so alarmed that he pursues her, and swims—

not wades, like the Giant of Tale I—after her, and overtakes her. As he is swimming past the stern he exposes the mole in the sole of his foot, under the instep (*bonn*[1] *dubh na coise*, or *seang na coise*), and is killed by his Youngest Daughter, who shoots him in the vulnerable spot. The corresponding incident in "Black-White Red" differs from this in several particulars. First the ship is a *Bìrlinn* (Galley), which, like the boat in "Shortshanks", can go on land as well as on sea. The sound of her keel moving over the gravel is compared, not to the wind, but to a peal of thunder. The pursuing Giant, instead of swimming after the ship, throws a black clue into her, and then seating himself on the ground, begins to pull her back. But while he is thus engaged he exposes the mole to his daughter's view, and is shot. The escaping hero pursued by the Giant reminds us of Ulysses and the Cyclops.— J. McD.

See other instances of Giants being deceived by their daughters in "Battle of the Birds" at p. 32, "Widow's Son", p. 47, version 3 of "The Battle of the Birds", p. 50 of vol. i of the *W. H. Tales.*—J. McD.

P. 162. The first Old Man fishing has a parallel in the "Angling Giant" at p. 263 of the MacInnes *Tales.*

The hero warned against allowing the hound to kiss him. For other instances of the "kiss taboo", see "The Battle of the Birds" and its versions in vol. i of the *W. H. Tales.* See also p. 25 of the MacInnes *Tales*, with Nutt's note at p. 438. —J. McD.

For similars of the remaining incidents of this tale, see "The Son of the King of Eirin" in the MacInnes *Tales*; "The Battle of the Birds" and its various versions, "The Hoodie", and "The Daughter of the King of the Skies", in vol. i of the *W. H. Tales.*—J. McD.

## TALE VIII.

P. 187. Cameron says that he got this tale from Donald McPhie, a native of Sunart, about thirty-two years ago. But he heard it since that time from William McPhie, a crofter in Lochaber, who is still living.—J. McD.

The nearest parallel to this tale is Grimm's tale of "The

---

[1] *Bonn dubh na coise* is the very middle of the sole of the foot. *Seang na coise* is the slender part of the foot, and therefore the same as the foregoing.—J. McD.

Young Giant". The resemblance between them is only in their general outlines. In every other respect they differ widely.—J. McD.

P. 187. *Ceatharnach* is one fit to bear arms, a soldier, a kern. Such a man as this, when outlawed, and leading the life of a freebooter in the woods (*coille*), is a *Ceatharnach-coille*, or "cateran". This, however, is not the same as *Ceatharnach-na-coille*. *Ceatharnach*, in the latter combination, is used in a non-military sense to denote a manly person or a person distinguished from his neighbours by his superior strength and courage. *Ceatharnach-na-coille* is, therefore, the Strong Man or Champion of the Wood.—J. McD.

P. 187. The Big Lad, in his birth, growth, and trials, is just the oak-tree personified. His father falls with the oak he has felled, and he himself is born as the seedling from the acorn is breaking through the ground. He is nursed for seven years, and is then taken out by his mother to try if he can pull the young oak from its roots. This is also about the time when the oak-wood undergoes its first thinning. He is nursed another seven years, and has then his second trial of strength against the oak-tree. This is again about the time when the oak-wood undergoes its second thinning. At the end of a third period of seven years—the time when he arrives at maturity, and when the oak-wood undergoes the last thinning— he goes to the tree, pulls it out of its roots, and thus proves that of the two he is the stronger. Grimm's "Young Giant", at first a mere "thumbling", was fed six years by the Giant who stole him. Every second year his strength was similarly tested, and was not considered perfect until he "tore out of the ground the thickest oak-tree there was, as if it were merely a joke". Volsung was six years old before he was born. And the horse "Dapplegrim", of the Norse tales, was three years sucking twelve mares. On the other hand, the nursing of "Manus" lasted only a certain number of days, but in that time he killed all his nurses except the last, the fairy maiden with the green kirtle.—J. McD.

P. 187. The acorn is planted in the middenstead. See also the "Sea-Maiden" and its versions in vol i of the *W. H. Tales*. —J. McD.

P. 188. The Big Lad is launched on the world with nothing but a bannock and his mother's blessing. He receives not even a weapon to defend him such as the Young Giant wanted, and Lod, the Farmer's Son, got. On his way out he serves not with any person as the Young Giant served with the Smith. But when he reaches the farm with the large stack-yard he calls and engages with the owner. Here he accomplishes three tasks, namely, the thrashing of the corn, the digging of the well, and the ploughing of the Crooked Rig with the Water-Horse. On the farm where he served the Yount Giant performed only one task, the fetching of the wood, but it bears no resemblance to any of the foregoing tasks. His ploughing feat which he accomplished before he left home may, however, be regarded as a sort of parallel to the third.—J. McD.

P. 189. The Big Lad's flail. "Johnny's Flail", though apparently little, was almost equally effective. See p. 62 of vol. ii of the *W. H. Tales.*—J. McD.

The Big Lad's daily fare is a quarter of a chalder—that is four bolls—of oatmeal made into brose, or the same quantity of meal baked into bannocks and taken with the carcase of a two-year-old ox. The supernatural beings of these tales are often enormous gluttons. Mac-Vic-Allan's fairy wife consumed daily a whole cow to dinner. (See "MacPhie's Black Dog" in *S. C. Review.*) Lod, the Farmer's Son's weekly allowance of meal, though moderate compared with that of the Big Lad, was four times that of an ordinary herd. (See the MacInnes *Tales*, No. VII.) And Grimm's Young Giant ate as much victuals as would have satisfied his father and mother for eight days at the least, and then he devoured the contents of a large fish-kettle, which he reckoned only "a good bit".—J. McD.

P. 191. Angus Mòr, or Big Angus of the Rocks, is a familiar name for echo. Its proper name is *Mactalla*, the Son of the Rock. Angus advises the Landlord to send the Big Lad to open a deep well in the field, and when he stoops at the bottom, bury him alive with the earth shovelled over him. And the Bailiff in Grimm's tale, after consulting with his secretaries, decides to send the Young Giant to wash himself in the pond, and then "roll upon his head one of the mill-stones, so as to bury him for ever from the light of day." But the two plots are equally unsuccessful.—J. McD.

P. 193. The ploughing of the Crooked Rig. The thrashing of the corn being a voluntary act, this is really the second task laid by his Master on the Big Lad. He carries, on his shoulder, the old Highland wooden plough—which, roughly speaking, was

shaped like a shinty with the end of the club shod with iron—
and reaches the field.   He strikes the share into one end of the
Rig, yokes his horses, and ploughs away unmolested by any
creature until evening comes.   Then, when the sun's disc
touches the horizon (*mu chromadh na gréine*), he hears a plunge
in the Dark Lake, and on looking in the direction of the sound,
sees a great black *Ùsp*, or shapeless object, moving in the
water.   When the sun disappears beneath the horizon, the
beast lands, walks up to the team, and swallows one of the
horses alive and whole.   An incident partly similar to this was
known to the late Mr. Campbell of Islay.   For at p. lxxxvi of
his Introduction to the *W. H. Tales*, he says, in his description
of the Water-Horse, " He is harnessed to a plough, and drags
the team and the plough into the loch, and tears the horses to
bits."   In the MacInnes *Tales* there appears an "uncommon
beast that would swallow a team of six horses, the plough, and
the ploughman", but it is very doubtful whether this monster
was a water-horse.   The Big Lad, after vainly trying to force
the Water-Horse, for such it was, to disgorge the horse he
swallowed, harnesses him to the plough, and makes him turn
over every furrow in the field before it is quite dark.   This is
no doubt a good day's work, but it is equalled, if not surpassed,
in the next tale by the mysterious servant who ploughs, sows,
and harrows all the fields on the farm in one day.   Once his
work is finished, the Big Lad leads the Water-Horse home,
kills him, and buries him in the well he opened in the field,
adding, as he does so : "If there was no water in it before,
there will be now."   This belief appears also in the Introduction to the *W. H. Tales*, where it is said that if the Water-
Horse "is killed, nothing remains but a pool of water."—J.
McD.

What is the Water-Horse?   And how is the foregoing belief
to be explained?   The Water-Horse is a mythical creature
which is said to live in the freshwater lakes and pools of the
winding glens and desert moors of the Highlands.   He resembles a real horse in everything except his wild-looking eyes,
his slimy skin, and his feet, which are sometimes webbed like
those of an amphibian.   Its colour, in the *W. H. Tales*, is grey
or bay, but here it is dusky or black.   He possesses a wonderful power of self-transformation.   At one time he assumes a
human form, at another that of a bird or beast.   He preys on
men, and hence he takes the shape that best suits his purpose
of getting them into his power.   Sometimes he appears as a
stray horse, saddled and bridled, at the road-side, tempting
the unwary traveller to mount him and ride him to the nearest
stage.   But no sooner does he get his dupe on his back,

and stuck fast to his slimy coat, than off he dashes with a "fiend-like yell" to his favourite pool or lake, where he devours his captive, and leaves no trace of him except the broken bones which the waves afterwards cast up on the strand. At other times he grazes, or pretends to graze, near the margin of the water it frequents; and, by his seeming tameness, coaxes children who wander into his haunt to mount him, one after another, while he lengthens his back to receive them all. Then when he gets them into his power he gallops away with them into the water, disappears beneath its surface, and disposes of them as he is said to dispose of the unhappy wayfarer. Often the passer-by traces his course beneath the wave by the wake he leaves behind him, and sees his mane and back raised a few inches above the surface as he is about to plunge back to the bottom whence he came. And we have seen that when he is killed or buried, he vanishes, and leaves behind him nothing but a pool of water. See for further information the pages referred to in the Index to the *W. H. Tales*, and Grant Stewart's Water-Kelpies in his *Highland Superstitions and Amusements.*—J. McD.

The Water-Horse, I believe, is nothing else than the personification of the sudden blast of wind or of whirlwind which sweeps over the surface of the lakes and pools of the winding glens and desert moors of the Highlands. The latter strikes the water suddenly, leaves behind it a ripple like the wake of a living creature swimming beneath the surface, and then, halting for a moment, raises, a few inches above the surface, a dark crest of little waves which bear a remote resemblance to the back and mane of such a creature. But here the Water-Horse is the whirlwind charged with the spindrift, which it raises and whirls into its folds as it sweeps over sea-loch and freshwater lake. When the whirlwind thus charged collapses in its after career over the land, and discharges the water it holds in suspense, it leaves behind it no trace of its former existence except, it may be, a pool of water in the place where it vanishes. The collapsed Whirlwind or Waterspout is the dead Water-Horse, and the pool left by the one is the same as that left by the other. The Water-Horse of Highland tales thus resembles Vikhor, the Whirlwind of the Russian folk-tales. "Vikhor, after soaring on high, struck the ground, and fell to pieces, becoming a fine yellow sand." See p. 227 of Ralston's *Russian Folk-Tales.* See also the Brown Filly in Grimm's "Two Travellers", and the myth of Pegasus and Hippocrene.—J. McD.

P. 197. The third and heaviest task laid on the Big Lad is to grind a sled-load of corn in the haunted Mill of Lecan after nightfall.   There is, or was, a mill of this name, *Muileann Leacainn*, on the north side of Loch Fyne, but of course neither it nor any other mill of the same name is to be identified with that of this tale.   The Miller, refusing to enter the mill after dark, the Big Lad goes alone, and does the work of the miller.   As soon as he has a sufficient quantity of meal ground and sifted, he kneads it into bannocks, and places them on the kiln to bake. While he is waiting until they are hard enough, an *Ùruisg*, from a dark corner of the kiln, stretches out his paw-like hand (*spòg*) three times, and each time carries off a bannock in spite of the Big Lad's threats.   The Big Lad, unable to stand this any longer, takes, without rising first from his crouching posture (*gurraban*) before the kiln fire, a heavy spring ending in a fall (*dudairlèum*) on the Ùruisg, and both get into grips.   Then follow the wrestling, deafening blows (*bodhairneachadh*), wrecking of the buildings, and other incidents, which end in the expulsion of the Ùruisg from the mill, and his final departure from the place, yelling with mingled feelings of grief and anger.—J. McD.

A similar task to the foregoing was laid by the Bailiff on Grimm's Young Giant, but the two differ widely in their details.—J. McD.

P. 198.   The *Ùruisg* was a supernatural being, having the appearance of a man with long shaggy hair and beard.   But Sir Walter Scott says that he had a figure between a goat and a man, or that of a Greek Satyr.   The latter part of his name, *Ur-uisg*, connects him with water, and tradition always places him in the neighbourhood of some stream or other.   He lived, we are told, in gloomy caves in the rocky sides of deep ravines, high waterfalls, or wild mountain corries.   Hence the word Ùruisg enters so frequently into such place-names as *Allt-nan-Ùruisg-ean*, *Eas-nan-Uruisgean*, and *Coire-nan-Ùruisgean*.   His haunts were dreaded, and shunned after nightfall.   Sometimes he left his rocky den in the distant mountain-side or in the lonely glen, and followed the course of the stream, in whose sides he found shelter, until he reached the nearest mill, which he afterwards made either his permanent abode or the scene of his nightly visits.   He was a useful friend, but a much dreaded enemy.   Occasionally he attached himself to an individual or family who showed him kindness, and rendered them whatever service he could give.   An instance of such attachment may be seen in the tale about a *bòcan* or bogle, who was really an *Ùruisg*, at p. 91 of vol. ii of the *W. H. Tales*.   Dr. Graham describes him as "a lubberly supernatural who could be gained over by kind attention"; and, he adds, "it was believed that many Highland families had some of the order so tamed as to become attached to them." Here the *Ùruisg* is identified with the undoubted Browny, who haunted old castles, and followed certain old families. The latter, however, is described as having been either a *Fleasgach* (Bachelor), or *Gruagach* (Long-haired Maiden), and sometimes also as having been handsome and beautiful. The genuine *Ùruisg* was a being of super-natural strength, and hence it was thought that this one would vanquish and kill the Big Lad. Other instances of his strength may be seen in Tale VI, p. 91 of vol. ii, *W. H. Tales.* In later traditional stories he is simple and easily cheated, but in the older tales he possesses supernatural know-ledge and ingenuity. See in "The King of Lochlan's Three Daughters" the Ùruisg who knew beforehand the quest of the Widow's Son, and who constructed a ship that would sail on sea and on land. He becomes attached to his place of abode, but still more to his friends. See his expulsion from the Mill as proof of the former assertion, and his voluntary exile from his haunts in the neighbourhood of Loch Traig to America, rather than part with his friend, Callum Mòr MacIntosh, as evidence of the latter.—J. McD.

## TALE IX.

P. 216. Cameron heard this legend told, in his boyhood, by his grandfather, an old soldier, who died in Ardnamurchan many years ago. The legend is well known, and can be easily picked up anywhere in Upper Argyllshire. Among those who heard it may be mentioned Alexander McColl and John Livingston, Duror.—J. McD.

A somewhat similar tale is "Master and Man", in vol. iii, *W. H. Tales.*—J. McD.

This legend is put down here simply because it presents another instance of extraordinary ploughing. The Big Lad ploughed the Crooked Rig with the Water Horse in one evening; and the mysterious ploughman in this story ploughed, and also sowed and harrowed, every field on his master's farm in one day. The farm is that of Liddlesdale, in Morven.—J. McD.

P. 216. The farmer, in an unguarded moment, invited even malevolent beings from the other world to offer him their services. Hence the visit he had from the Big Lad. It seems that evil-disposed supernaturals of all kinds could do men no harm until the latter, by word or deed, put themselves in their power.—J. McD.

P. 216. The wages asked by the Big Lad was as much of the corn, when ripe, cut, and ready to be gathered in, as he could carry in one withy-band. The wages of the Young Lad, in "Master and Man", was, for the first year, as many grains of corn as he could catch in his mouth, while thrashing in the barn, and as much of the best land on the farm as would sow the grains thus caught; for the second year the produce of the first year's sowing added to the grains caught in the barn, and as much of the best land as would sow the whole; and so on, the wages increasing in the same ratio each succeeding year to the end of the seventh. See also the reward of the Hen-wife in the "Bare-stripping Hangman." The withy-band is similar to the Bent Grey Lad's cord and the heather rope of the Lad of the Skin Coverings.—J. McD.

P. 217. The Big Lad, by smelling the stakes, knew that the ground was now ready for the reception of the grain. And as it would not continue long in that condition, he hurried away to the farm-steading for his master's horses, plough, and withy-bands with which the horses were to be fastened to the plough. Perhaps the horses and the withy-bands should have been left at home, and the plough alone taken to the field. At any rate, no sooner had the Big Lad arrived there, and thrust the plough in the ground, than he called for his super-natural horses, traces of leather, and Mettlesome Lads, adding, as a reason for his haste, that the ground was coming up, or swelling. The call was obeyed, and the work done proved that the horses and the lads were of no ordinary sort!—J. McD.

P. 218. When the harvest came, and the corn was cut and ready for gathering into the yard, the Big Lad would not suffer a sheaf to be lifted from the fields until he had his reward. But when the Farmer saw almost all the sheaves on the fields in the Big Lad's withy-band, he uttered the following prayer or counter charm:

> " 'Twas in the Màrt I sowed,
> 'Twas in the Màrt I baked,
> 'Twas in the Màrt I reaped,
> Thou who hast ordained the three Màrts,
> Let not my share into one burden-withy-band."

Màrt here means the fit time for doing any particular part of agricultural work. For example, the "*Màrt-cuir*" is the fit time of sowing. This began on the twelfth day of April and ended at *Bealltainn*, or Mayday (O. S.). No sowing should take place before the former day, or after the latter. The following old rule was strictly observed. "Olc no math mar thig an sìon, cuir an sìol 'san fhìor Mhàrt" ("Let the weather come bad or good, sow the seed in the right Màrt"). "*Màrt-fuine*", or the fit time of baking, began on the twelfth day of August. It was so called because no part of the growing corn was cut, and the meal made from it baked into bread before that day arrived. "*Màrt-buana*", or the fit time of reaping, began on the twelfth day of September. The Farmer having done everything in the appointed season, now appeals to Providence for help. The withy-band then bursts with a loud report, and the mysterious Lad from fairyland goes off in a white mist! The "Fuath" (Bogle) of Ben Alnac, in Grant Stewart's *Highland Superstitions and Amusements*, is no sooner hit in the large mole in his breast by the unerring arrow of James Grey than he vanishes "like the smoke of a shot". And the "Gentleman" whom the Black Smith of the Socks ("*Gobhainn Dubh nan Soc*") persuades to enter a purse, and strikes thrice with his heavy sledge-hammer, escapes, making so loud a report as he goes away that the Smith's wife thought the roof was blown off the smithy.—J. McD.

## TALE X.

P. **222**. Cameron heard this tale first from his grandfather, and then from Donald McPhie and others in Ardnamurchan. The tale was also heard, though it is not now remembered, by John McFarlane, Constable, Post-Appin.—J. McD.

P. **222**. The title of the tale is, literally, "The Son of the Owner of the Green Vesture, who was renowned on Earth for his Heroism seven years before he was Born." The name of the hero in the "Knight of the Red Shield" should, in my opinion, be the same as that of the hero of this tale. In the former, "*Mac an Earraich Uaine ri Gaisge*" ("Son of Green Spring by Valour"), *Earraich* should be *Earraidh*, and *Fear* should be restored after *Mac*. The renown of the Son of the Knight of the Green Vesture preceded his appearance in the world by seven years. The coming of the Knight of the Red Shield to the fire-girt island was also "in the prophecies". And "the name of a hero was on Conall Gulban a hundred years before he was born". See "Knight of the Red Shield" at p. 444 of vol. ii, and "Conall Galban" at p. **222** of vol. iii, *W. H. Tales*.—J. McD.

P. 222. The tale consists of two parts, the first embracing the time when the hero passed for the son of the Hen-wife, and the second when he appeared in his true character as the Son of the Knight of the Green Vesture. The former is mythological throughout, but the latter is a romantic story made up of ordinary, though greatly exaggerated, incidents. Similars of the first part are "The Three Soldiers" and its three variants in vol. i of the *W. H. Tales*. Similars of the second part are the rescue by the hero of the King's daughter from the three-headed sea-monster in the "Sea Maiden", and other like rescues in the variants of that tale in vol. i, *W. H. Tales*, and also the rescue of the King's daughter by Lod, the Farmer's Son, in the MacInnes *Tales*.—J. McD.

P. 222. The Hen-wife's son leading the cows into good pasture, reminds of the hero in the "Sea Maiden", and "Lod, the Farmer's Son", in the tale of the same name, trespassing on the parks of the giants. He, however, meets with a very different reception from that which awaited either of the two latter. On arriving at the pasture he sat down on a green knoll or fairy hillock, and soon afterwards saw the Maiden of the golden ringlets (*Gruagach*) approaching him. She was a female fairy, but instead of taking forcible possession of the trespassing cattle as the giants had done, she bought them with valuable things which possessed magic properties. The first day she gave him a charm-stone (*clach-bhuadach*) by means of which he could instantly transport himself to any place he pleased. The charm-stone thus resembled the "whistle" in the "Three Soldiers", which its owner would no sooner play than he was in the midst of his regiment ; the "gifts" in "Yellow Kenneth", which would make anyone who had them get anything he wanted, and the Scotchman's "Knife", which he would no sooner open than he would be wherever he wished. The second day, the Maiden of the golden ringlets gave the lad a healing jewel (*lèug shlànaighearachd*) which could heal all the wounds of the body and all the sorrows of the mind. This jewel has no parallel in any of the "gifts" which were received by the Three Soldiers in the tale of that name and in its variants. The third day she gave him the little net, which, if set on the bushes in the evening, would next morning be full of every kind of known and of twelve kinds of unknown birds. With this corresponds the towel in the "Three Soldiers", the table-cover in "Yellow Kenneth", and even the Englishman's purse in the second variant. See also the table cloth in Manus, vol. iii, p. 355 of the *W. H. Tales*, and the same in "The Ship that went to America" at p. 167 of the MacInnes *Tales*.—J. McD.

P. 226. The incident of the Hen-wife's son spiriting away Berry-eye to the Green Isle by means of the charm-stone is similar to that of John the Soldier transporting himself and the daughter of the King of Ireland on the towel to the "uttermost isle of the deep", and to that of the Irishman who, by the help of the Scotchman's knife, carried himself and another King's daughter to an "island which could hardly be seen in the far-off ocean". See the tale of the "Three Soldiers" and its variants, vol. ii, *W. H. Tales.*—J. McD.

P. 227. Berry-eye escapes from the Green Isle and returns home by means of the wishing charm-stones. The daughter of the King of Ireland does the same by the help of the wishing-towel, and the other King's daughter by that of the Scotchman's knife ("Three Soldiers" and its variants). There is a similar of the foregoing incident in Grimm's "Kingdom of the Golden Mountains". Like the female characters in the latter, the Queen in the former finds her opportunity when her husband is sleeping with his head on her lap. "Then she drew the ring off his finger, and carefully laid his head on the ground. Thereupon she took her child in her arms, and wished herself back in her kingdom. When, then, the King awoke, he found himself all alone, his wife and child all gone, and the ring from his finger too."—J. McD.

P. 227. The hero falls in with two kinds of apples in the Green Isle. One kind has a beautiful appearance, but as soon as he eats of it, causes the flesh to melt off his bones. The other is ugly, but possesses marvellous healing properties. Very different from all this were the effects of the apples in the tale of the "Three Soldiers". When John, the Soldier, ate one sort of them, he had on him a deer's head, and when he ate the other the deer's head fell off him. Similar to this were the effects of the apples in variant 3 of the latter tale. No sooner had the Irishman eaten of the red apples than his head was down and his heels up, from the weight of the deer's horns that grew on his head. "Then he bethought him that one of the grey apples would heal him, and he stretched himself out with his head downwards, and kicked down one of the apples with his feet, and ate it, and the horns fell off him." But when Yellow Kenneth, in another variant of the same tale, "ate *abhlan* (apples) of one kind, a wood like thatch grew on his head, and there remained until he ate *abhlan* of another kind, when the wood vanished."—J. McD.

P. 228. The Apple incident on board of the vessel. The hero, now a physician, after making the sick captain worse with the beautiful apples, cures him with the ugly ones, and is, out of gratitude, landed near the place which he had left. The corresponding incident in the similar tale of the "Three Soldiers" differs considerably from this. There the sailors opened the pack of apples of John, the Soldier, and "ate the sort that would put deer's horns on them, and they began fighting until they were like to break the vessel." The Captain came on board, and blamed John for the change which had come over the men. "What wilt thou give me," said John, "if I leave them as they were before?" The Captain, having taken him for a magician, or something worse, said "that he would give him the vessel and cargo at the first port they reached. John then gave the men the other sort, and the horns fell off them." This apple incident is omitted in variants 1 and 3 of the latter tale.—J. McD.

P. 230. The healing of Berry-eye. The Physician, after persuading her to confess her theft and to restore the charm-stones, cures her with the ugly apples. He is rejected by her when she hears that he is the Hen-wife's son, but she is rejected by him when he finds out that he is the Son of the Knight of the Green Vesture. John, the Soldier, disguised as a poor ragged costermonger, sold to the King's daughter some apples, with which he "put a deer's head and horns on her". The King having offered a reward of a peck of gold and a peck of silver, with his daughter in marriage to anyone who would heal her, John went to the palace to cure her, and after some opposition was admitted. He took a book (no doubt a *leabhar dearg na fiosachd*, or red book of supernatural knowledge), and pretended to read there the private history of his patient. She believed him, and gave him the three magic articles which she had "wheedled from a poor soldier". On his first visit she gave him the whistle, which, when it was played, took him into the middle of his regiment; and he gave her a bit of apple, and then one horn fell off her. On his second visit she gave him the purse which was always full, and he gave her another bit of apple, and the second horn fell off her. On his last visit she gave him the "towel of plenty", and he gave her a whole apple, and "when she ate it she was as she was before". Then she said to him, " Art thou going to marry me to-day?" " No, nor to-morrow," he answered, and departed.

In the third variant, the Irishman sailed in the ship "straight to the King's house. The lady looked out of a window. He sold her a red apple for a guinea. She ate it, the horns grew, and there were not alive those who could take her from that. They thought of saws, and sent for doctors; and he came."

The rest of the incident seems to have been the same as the
last, only that the magic articles were different.   There was a
purse which was always full ; a knife which, once it was opened,
would transport its owner wherever he wished ; and a horn,
which its possessor no sooner blew in the small end than a
thousand soldiers stood before him, and in the big end than
they vanished.   The corresponding incident in the first variant,
" Yellow Kenneth", agrees with the foregoing, only that wood,
and not horns, grew on the head of the King's daughter, and
that the gifts which she wheedled from the hero were a cup
always full, and a lamp of light, a " table-cover of plenty", and
a rest-giving bed.—J. McD.


P. 231. The hero, now Son of the Knight of the Green
Vesture, sets out on his quest of a fairer maiden than Berry-
eye.   He arrives at " Torr Uaine", Green Mound, or Green
Castle.   He is going to take shelter for the night in the
shrubbery behind the castle, when he gets a glimpse of a fairer
maiden than Berry-eye, passing through the bushes.   Curiosity
to know who she is leads him in the direction of the byre,
where he sees the dairy-maid, a comely, young, long-haired
damsel (*gruagach*) with "a gold comb in the back of her
head".   "Gruagach" indicates that the person, male or female,
real or mythical, to whom the name is applied, is long-haired.
For " comb", see under that word in the Index of the *W. H.
Tales.*—J. McD.


P. 233. Sorceress (*Iorasglach-ùrlair*), see notes on Tale VII.
—J. McD.


P. 234. The next three incidents have parallels in the Sea
Maiden and its variants.   The Son of the Knight of the Green
Vesture corresponds to the herds, the Fierce Earl's three sons
to the three-headed Sea-monster, giant, and dragon, and the
Squint-eyed Red-haired Cook to the General, Red-haired Lad,
and Red-haired Cook.   (" Sea Maiden" and variants in vol. i
of the *W. H. Tales.*)   See also the similar incident In Lod,
the Farmer's Son, in the MacInnes *Tales*, and the note by Nutt
on the Red-headed Cook at p. 474 of that volume.—J. McD.


P. 234. See also Knight of the Cairn, in the " Knight of the
Red Shield", vol. ii, *W. H. Tales*.   " The Knight of the
Cairn put off his arms and array, and the Son of the Green
Spring by Valour (?) went into his arms and array" before he
landed on the fire-girt isle.—J. McD.

P. 237. *Béul-fhothraghadh* is the grass or heath-covered edge of a peat-hag or bank over which the surface-water trickles. —J. McD.

P. 239. *Bréun-lochan* is from *bréun*, stagnant or fetid, and *lochan*, a lakelet. *Fionn-chòinneach* is the white, withered-looking moss which grows in marshy places on high moorlands.—J. McD.

P. 239. Like Conan, the Young Son of the Fierce Earl has his three smalls bound in one withy-band. The three smalls were the ankles, knees, and wrists, and the four smalls were the ankles, knees, wrists, and neck. Instances of binding the latter were rare, but of binding the former, common enough. The Cook could no more undo the knot on the withy-band with which the Earl's son was bound, than the Red-headed Lad in the third variant of the "Sea Maiden" could untie the knots with which the giants' heads were bound together on a withy by the herd. In both tales this failure led to the discovery of the true hero.—J. McD.

# INDEX.


Acorn, 187, *n.* 292

Alastir (Art), 76, *n.* 278; overhears the plot against his brother's life, 77; accompanies him in his flight, 78; incident of the ravens, 79; poisons the robbers, 80; adventures at the Castle of the King of Riddles, 81-83; is carried off by an Otter to Lochlan, 84; receives strengthening food from the Otter and the Hound, 84; overcomes the King of Lochlan's Champions, 85-86; accompanies the King to his palace, 87; catches the Black Brood-mare by following the advice of the Sorceress, 90; sets out in quest of the B. S. Hangman's soul, 92; crosses the Rocky Path of Ben Buie, 92-93; Red Lake, 93; reaches the Castle at the end of the Path, 94; hands the Sorceress's letter to the Woman, 94; strengthened with a draught of balsam, 94; kills the two-headed Giant, 95; next day, armed with the Giant's sword, reaches the Castle of the Eight Turrets, 96; kills the second Giant, 97; on the third day arrives at the Gloomy Castle and kills the Fiery Dragon, 100; sets off for the Big Barn of the Seven Couples, 101; meeting with the Old Men, 102-104; receives from the Man in the Bunch of Moss a jar of ointment to make him invulnerable, 105; meets the Dog, 106; the Otter, 107; Falcon, 108; hunts the Hind, 109; helped by the Dog, Otter, and Falcon, 108; kills the Giant by crushing the egg, 110; returns with the three daughters of the King to the Black Corrie, 110; takes with him the head and feet of the giant, 111; restores him to life, 111; marries the Youngest Daughter, 112

Apples, ugly, heal, and beautiful, kill, 228, 229; *n.* 301

Arion, *n.* 290

Arrow, its direction is that of the ship's course, 148, *n.* 289

Avasks, 38, *n.* 269

" Balk on his foot", 29, *n* 266

Balsam, vessel of, restores the lads to life, 41; strengthens Alastir, 94, 97, 98, *n.* 282; heals his wounds, 99; makes him invulnerable, 109, *n.* 284

Bare-stripping Hangman, 76, *n.* 276; steals the King's three daughters, 86; lives in the Black Corrie of Ben Breck, 74; transformed into an eagle, 87; puts on his head, 87; his life hid in the duck, etc., 110; is restored to life, 111

Barn of the Seven Couples, 101, *n.* 282-283

Ben Aidan, 32, *n.* 268

Ben Breck, 86-87

Berry-eye, 226-230, *n.* 301

Bespelling of Finn by the Big Young Hero, 2, *n.* 260; by a Messenger from the Queen of Roy, 35, *n.* 272

*Béul fhothraghadh, n.* 304

*Bréun-lochan, n.* 304

Big Angus of the Rocks is Echo, 191, *n.* 203; first plan to get rid of Big Lad, 192; second, ploughing of Crooked Rig, 194; grinding in the Mill of Lecan, 197

Big Lad's daily fare, 189, *n.* 293

Binding of the three smalls, 239, *n.* 304

Blade, three-edged, 60, *n.* 275

Blar-buie House, 57, *n.* 273-274

Blood of three sons of K. of Insh Tilly, the only thing to free the Féinn from their enchantment, 58, *n.* 274

Bran found in the Castle, 7-8, *n.* 263 ; his chain, 18-20, *n.* 264

Brood-mare, Black, is caught with the old bridle by Alastir, 90, *n.* 280

Brownie of the Mill of Lecan, 198, 199, *n.* 296-7

Butler incident, 163

Buzzard, the first son of the K. of Insh Tilly transformed, 59; the Sorceress transformed, 93

Caoilte (Slender), 57, *n.* 272

Carpenter, with three strokes of his axe, makes a ship of an alder stock, 2-3

*Carraig-an-uchd, n.* 269

Castle thatched with eel-skins, 6; of the King of Riddles, 81; of the Rocky Path, 94; of the Eight Turrets, 96; Gloomy Castle of the Fiery Dragon, 98

*Ceatharnach, n.* 292

Charms, 217-218

Charmstone, 223, *n.* 300

Climber can climb a silken thread to the stars, 3; climbs the Castle thatched with eel-skins, 6

Coachman incident, 165-166

Cock and hen of gold, speaking, 163-167, *n.* 291

Conan, 28, *n.* 266; goes before the Big Lad, 29; his back skinned by the Big Lad's toe-nails, 29; insists on the latter being dismissed, 29; challenges him to leap, 32; run, 33; and wrestle with him, 33; is bound by the B. L. with his garter, 33, *n.* 268; and unloosed by the Smith of the White Glen, 34; he dissuades Finn from engaging the Lad from Blar-buie, 57; lays himself down on the hearth, 58; loses his hair in the effort to tear himself from it, 64, *n.* 275

Cook incident, 165

Coracle, 112, *n.* 285

Cormac, 76; saved by his bro-

ther's help, 78; marries the daughter of the K. of Riddles, 83; goes to his brother's wedding in the coracle of the Sorceress, 112

Cows of Hen-wife, 222, *n.* 300

Crooked Ridge, 194, 195, 196, *n.* 293

Crooked Stick, 103, *n.* 283

Cuchullin, 57, *n.* 272

Cups of gold with rings of silver for filtering blood, 58, *n.*274

Cup, Four-sided, of Finn, 30, *n.* 267

Deer-hound, bitch, black, 6; deer-hound, bitch, companion of the K. of Ireland's son, 146

Deer-hunting, 1, 27, 56

Dice, or chess-playing, 158

Dinner, Big Lad's, 191, *n.* 293

Dog entertains Alastir, 107; catches the Hind, 109; *n.* on helping animals, 284

Dragon, Winged, of Shiel, third Son of the K. of Insh Tilly transformed, 63

Duck of the Smooth Feathers, 109

Eagle, Second Son of the K. of Insh Tilly transformed, 61; attacks the Champion in the Giant's Den, 87, *n.* 275

Egg in which Giant's Soul is hid, 105

Enchantment of Finn and the Féinn in the House of Blar-buie, 58

Fairy buys the Hen-wife's three cows, 223-5, *n.* 300

Farmer of Liddesdale, 216; losses of, 216; wants a ploughman and gets one, 217; engagement with the latter, 216; recovers his corn from the Mysterious Ploughman by means of a charm, 218

Fairy motion, 95, *n.* 282

Falcon of the Rock entertains Alastir, 108; helps him to catch the duck, 109

Index.      307

Fierce Earl, 231 ; his Eldest Son, 234 ; Second Son, 236; Youngest Son, 238-9

Finn bespelled to visit the Young Hero's place, 2 ; engages skilful companions, 2-3; steers the ship, 4 ; keeps awake by thrusting an iron bar through his palm, 5 ; goes in quest of stolen children, 6 ; recovers them in the Castle, 7 ; and finds Bran and the Grey Dog, 8. He binds himself to go alone with the Lad from Lochlan to that country, 17 ; takes his Fool's advice, 18 ; is sentenced to travel through the Great Glen haunted by the mad Grey Dog, 19 ; tames the Dog with Bran's chain, 20 ; and leads him back with him, 20. He is bespelled by a Lad to go alone to the Queen of Roy's place, takes the Lad of the Skin Coverings with him, promises the mother to bring her son, and whoever falls with him, back to her, 37 ; enters the house with the doors and posts of gold, 38 ; adventures there, 38-40; carries the two dead lads to Green Insh, 40 ; returns home, 41. He goes with his men to Blar-buie, 57 ; adventures there, 57-64. He sleeps with his Féinn in the Smith's Rock, 73 ; or Tomnahurich, *n.* 276

Fionn-chòinneach, *n.* 304

Flail, Big Lad's, 189, *n.* 293

Flight of the K. of Ireland's Son with his Wife in Gonachry, 160, *n.* 290

Ford, scene of the encounter with the Son of the K. of Insh Tilly, 60, *n.* 275

Four-sided cup, 30 ; quest of, 30-2, *n.* 267

Gaper (dart), 59, *n.* 275

Garden, Great, of the Trees of the Golden Apples, 152, *n.* 290

Giant of the Castle of the Rock, 6 ; Two-headed Giant, 95 ; Giant of the Three Heads, 97 ; Big Giant of the Black Corrie, 87

Goll, 34, *n.* 266

Gonachry, 147, *n.* 289

Green Insh, 28, *n.* 266, 361

Green Lakelet, 32, *n.* 268

Green Mound, 232-240

Grey Dog found in Castle, 7 ; given to a chief from Lochlan, 259 ; goes mad, 259 ; haunts the Great Glen, 19 ; scorches everything with his breath, 20 ; is tamed with Bran's chain, 20 ; his meeting with Bran, 21

Gripper, 2-3 ; pulls giant's hand out of the shoulder, 5

Gull, 154

Hand, Child-stealing, 4-5 ; pulls against Gripper, 5 ; is torn from the shoulder, 5 ; is the stolen infant's cradle, 6 ; has a fatal mole, 8

Hangman, Bare-stripping, 76, *n.* 276 ; other versions of tale, 276-277

Heads set on stakes, 81, *n.* 278

Hen-wife, 76, *n.* 277 ; her reward for poisoning Cormac, 77 ; is burnt, 104. Landlord's Hen-wife, 222

Hound, White, Red-eared, hunts the White-buttocked Hind for Alastir, 14

Houses with golden doors, and silver doors, 37, *n.* 269

Hunt of the White Glen, 34, *n.* 268

Husk of Mermaid, 146

Insh, Green, 27, *n.* 266

Island, Green, 3, *n.* 261, 153, 155 226, 228

Island, Beautiful, of the Shadow of the Stars, 149, *n.* 290

Island, Big, of the Spirit of the Mist, 153

Island, Big, of the Whales, 148, *n.* 226-7

Jewel, 224, *n.* 300

King of Insh Tilly's three sons,

58 ; their blood the only thing to release Finn and the Féinn, 58, *n*. 274

King Red Cap, 157-160, *n*. 290

Kiss-taboo, 162, *n*. 291

Knoll, shining like gold in the sun, 102

Knowledge-set-of-teeth of Finn, 8, 58, *n*. 274

Lad of the Skin Coverings, 27, *n*. 266 ; his engagement with Finn and reward, 28 ; his burden, 29 ; his quest after Finn's stolen cup, 30 ; his journey to and from Lochlan between one sunrise and the next, 31 ; recovers the cup, 30 ; races, 32 ; leaps, 33 ; wrestles with Conan, and comes off victor, 34 ; leaves the latter bound on Ben Aidan, and returns home to Green Insh, 34 ; accompanies Finn to the Queen of Roy's place, 36 ; enters the house with the doors of gold, 37 ; brains Avasks, 38 ; how he is awakened, 39 ; kills a thousand, 39 ; falls with the son of the K. of L., 40 ; restored to life by his mother, 41 ; accompanies Finn home, 41

Lady of Green Insh, 36, *n*. 269 ; cutting rushes, 36, *n*. 269 ; grants his request to Finn, 37 ; restores the two lads to life with the balsam, 41

Lakelet, tranquil, 155

Light-of-shade, 110

Listener, his acute hearing, 3, 7, *n*. 260

Lohary, 58, *n*. 275

Macan I, *n*. 260

Magic Mist, 151, 153

Maiden with the gold comb, 232

Man in the bunch of Moss, 104, *n*. 283

Marksman, 3 ; hits the giant in the mole in his hand, 8

Màrt, or fit season for doing a thing, 218, *n*. 298

Mermaid bathing, 146, *n*. 286 ;

gets back her husk, 146 ; promises to help the King's Son, 147 ; sends him to his father for a boat, 147 ; carries him on her tail to the Green Isle, 153, *n*. 290

Mill of Lecan, 197, *n*. 295-6

Mole, fatal, in the hand of the Giant of the Castle, 8 ; in the forehead of the Hangman of the Nail, *n*. 284 ; on the sole of King Red Cap's foot, 160, *n*. 291

Needle, thimble, and scissors, incidents of, 148, 150, 151, 158, 159, *n*. 290

Net for catching birds, 225, *n*. 300

Nonsense-ending, 112, *n*. 285

Oak-tree, two attempts to pull it out of the ground, vain, 188 ; third, successful, 188; personified, *n*. 292

Odyssey, *n*. 289

Old Brothers, 148-161, *n*. 289

Old Men, 102-106, *n*. 283

Oscar, squint-eyed and red-haired, 21, *n*. 265 ; attempts in vain to release Conan, 34 ; releases Finn and the Féinn from the enchantment of the House of Blar-buie, 58

Otter carries Alastir to Lochlan, 84, *n*. 278 ; entertains him, 107 ; catches the salmon for him, 109

Phaeacians, 289

Physician, 230, 231

Ploughman of Liddesdale, 216 ; engagement, 216, *n*. 298; method of ascertaining when the land is ready for ploughing, 217; charm, 217 ; ploughs all the arable land on the farm in a day, 218, *n*. 297; makes a withe and puts almost all the corn in it, 218, *n*. 298; deprived of his power by the Farmer's charm, 218, *n*. 298

Porch, or *Ùdabac*, 95, *n*. 282

Queen of Roy, 35

Ravens poisoned, 79, *n.* 278; kill robbers, 80; riddles founded on, 81

Reward of the Lad from Lochlan, 17; of the Lad of the Skin-coverings, 28; of the Lad from Blar-buie, 57

Red-haired Cook, 234-240

Red Lake, 94, *n.* 281

Riddles, 81-83

Robbers, adventures with, 79

Rocky Path of the Yellow Mountain, 92-94, *n.* 281

Salmon fetched by the Otter for Alastir, 84, *n.* 278

Salmon in the Hind's stomach, 105

Shepherd's pipe, *n.* 284

Shinties of gold and ball of silver, 6, 146

Shortshanks in Dasent's *Norse Tales*, *n.* 291

Skidbladnir, *n.* 289

Skilled companions, seven, 2-3; carpenter, tracker, gripper, climber, thief, listener, marksman

Skin-covering, 82, *n.* 266

Smith, Old, of the King of Ireland, 162

Smith of the White Glen releases Conan, 34, *n.* 268

Smooth-Brow, her dream, 232; meets the Knight's Son, 233; marries him, 240

Son of the King of Ireland persecuted by Stepmother, 145, *n.* 286; meets the Mermaid, 146, *n.* 286; vows to rest not till he sees as fair a woman as the Swan of the Smooth Neck, 147, *n.* 289; receives from his father the boat, Gonachry, 148; goes in quest of the Swan-Maiden; arrives at the Big Island of the Whales, 148, *n.* 289; gets a needle from Old Man, 148, *n.* 289; who accompanies him on Gonachry, 149; arrives next at the Beautiful Island of the Shadow of the Stars, 149, *n.* 290; gets a Thimble from second Old Brother, 150; is accompanied by the latter, 150; arrives at the Big Island of the Spirit of the Mist, 151; receives from the third Old Brother a pair of scissors, 152; leaves Gonachry and Old Brothers behind and is carried on the Mermaid's tail to the Green Isle, 153, *n.* 290; adventures on the voyage, 153-155, *n.* 290; is thrown by the Mermaid on the Green Island, 155; arrives at the Tranquil Lakelet of the Garden of the Golden Apples, 155, *n.* 290; sees the three daughters of King Red Cap in Swan-form on the Lake, 156; scares them with his arrow, 156; returns to the shore, where he finds Gonachry waiting him, 157; sails with her back to King Red Cap's place on the Island of the Spirit of the Mist, 157; meets him and his three daughters in their natural form on the beach, 157; wins the King's Youngest Daughter in three trials—(1) she keeps his gifts, 158, *n.* 290; (2) he wins at dice or chess playing, 158; and (3) identifies the Youngest Daughter by means of the needle, 159; escapes with his wife, 160, *n.* 290-1; is pursued by King Red Cap, who is killed by his daughter, 161, *n.* 291; leaves the Big Brothers in their respective islands, 161; arrives in Ireland, 162; is kissed by the bitch and forgets his wife, Sunshine, 163; is going to marry another woman, 166; recognises his first wife in the woman at the Smith's house, etc., 167

Son of the King of Light, 39-41, *n.* 270

Son of the Knight of the Green Vesture as the Hen-wife's Son, 222; herds her three cows, 222; sells the first to a Fairy for a charm-stone, 223; the second for a jewel, 224; the third for a net, 225; is taken into the land-lord's service, 226; by means of the charm-stone wishes himself and Berry-eye in the Green Isle, 226, *n.* 301 ; is deserted by his wife, 227, *n.* 301 ; discovers the apples, 227, *n.* 301; is taken on board a passing vessel, 228 ; cures the Captain by means of the ugly apples, 229, *n.* 301-2 ; is landed in the place he left, 229; gives out that he is a physician, ·229 ; cures Berry-eye, 230, *n.* 302; recovers the charm-stones, 230 ; is going to marry Berry-eye, 230 ; is betrayed by his stepmother, 230 ; rejected by Berry-eye, 231, *n.* 302; his true origin revealed, 231 ; goes in quest of a fairer maiden than Berry-eye, 231, *n.* 303 ; sees Smooth-brow behind the Castle, 231; meets the dairy-maid, 232, *n.* 303; meets Smooth-brow, 232; follows the Red-haired Cook, who is going to repel the invasion of the Fierce Earl's Eldest Son, 234, *n.* 303; slays the latter, 235; follows the Cook the next day, and slays the Earl's Second Son, 236-237; follows the Cook the third day and binds the Earl's Youngest Son, 238-239; unbinds the latter, 240; marries Smooth-brow, 240

Son of the Strong Man of the Wood, born when oak-seedling appears above ground, 187, *n.* 292 ; nursed seven years, and then tries to pull the young oak out of its roots, 188, *n.* 292 ; second trial of strength after fourteen years of nursing, 188 ; third trial after twenty-one years of ditto, 188 ; gets a ban-nock and is then sent to win his fortune, 189, *n.* 292 ; engages as a farm-servant with a Land-lord, 189 ; accomplishes three tasks—first, thrashing all the corn on the farm in a day, 190, *n.* 293 ; second, digging a well, 192, *n.* 293; ploughing the

Crooked Rig with the Water-horse, 195 ; grinding in the Mill of Lecan, 198 ; encounter with Brownie, 199 ; draws the sled with the horse and meal-sacks on it home to the Land-lord's house, 200 ; finds the farm deserted, 201 ; takes pos-session of it, 201 ; goes for his mother and brings her to the place he has got, 201

Sorceress meets Alastir, 91, *n.* 280; her advice to him, 92 ; in the form of a buzzard en-courages him to proceed on his journey, 93; brings Cormac and his Queen in a coracle to Lochlan, 112-233, *n.* 285

Stolen children, 214

Sunbeam, 110

Swan-Maidens, 147, *n.* 286

Swift-footed Hind, 105

Sword of the King, 85; of the two-headed Giant, 94; of the three-headed Giant, 97

Thick-foliaged Grove of the Trees, 105

Thief can steal the egg on which the heron is sitting, 3; steals the children, pups, coverings, shinties, and balls from the sleeping Giant's Castle

Thrashing of all the corn in the barn and stackyard by Big Lad, 190, *n.* 293

Tòm-na-h-Iùbhraich, *n.* 276

Tracker, 2; piloting the ship, 4

Trials of the Son of the K. of Ireland, 157-9, *n.* 290

Ùruisg, 296-7

Uttermost World, 3, *n.* 261-263, 58

Water-horse, 194, 195, 196, *n.* 294-295

Wakening. Finn keeps awake by thrusting a red-hot iron bar through his palm, 5 ; the Big Lad is awakened by striking him with a rock on the chest, or by cutting the breadth of his thumb from the top of his head, 39

Whale-fishing extraordinary, 161, *n.* 291

White Glen, 27

White Swan of the Smooth Neck, 147 ; Young Daughter of King Red Cap, 148 ; her name is Sunshine, 151; is transformed by her father into a Swan, 153; swimming on the Tranquil Lakelet in the Green Isle, 153; the spell broken by the arrow, 156; chooses the hero by accepting his gifts, 157; tells him how to identify her, 159; escapes with her husband, 160; kills her father, 161 ; accompanies her husband to Ireland, 162; stays at the Smith's house, 163 ; makes a speaking cock and hen, 163; the butler, 163; cook, 165; coachman, 166; recognised by her husband, 167

Wooden crier or whistle, 58 ; far sounding, 58, *n.* 274; enormous size, 73; three blasts of it will awaken the Féinn, 57, *n.* 274

Withe of Mysterious Ploughman, 218

Wooden-graips or forks, 74, *n.* 276

Woman, syren-like, pretends she is drowning, 154, *n.* 190; appears as a gull with a message from the Queen, 155

"Writing" (letter) from Sorceress to first sister, 93; from latter to second, 96; from second to third, 98

Young Giant in Grimm's Tales, *n.* 291


## RUNS.


Bespelling run, 2, *n.* 260, 35

Boat-beaching run, 1, *n.* 260

Resting run, 1, *n.* 259

Rejoicing run, 9, 22

Saluting run, 1, 17, 27

Travelling run, 29, 30, 31 ; another, 106, *n.* 284


LONDON : WHITING AND CO., 30 AND 32, SARDINIA STREET, W C.